John Steele was born and raise
1995, at the age of twenty-two he t
has since lived and worked on th
teen-year spell in Japan which ins
he has been a drummer in a rock b
and a teacher of English. He now lives in England with his wife and
daughter. He began writing short stories, selling them to North
American magazines and fiction digests. *Dry River* is his third
novel and the third Jackie Shaw book. The first two, *Ravenhill* and
Seven Skins, are published by Silvertail Books.

DRY RIVER

John Steele

SILVERTAIL BOOKS • London

Sapporo,
Japan

札幌
日本

Part One

Part One

Chapter 1

Another night, another man out there in the dark, watching her. She knows where he is, on the voyeur's perch in the black beyond the window, and that he will expect her to squirm as she sits.

She wonders where his eyes linger: on her face as she studies the tabloid magazine, staring at the lurid pages without seeing? Or her long, slim fingers as she flicks through the glossy paper, feigning interest? Perhaps they pause on her legs as she folds them under her body, her skirt riding up her thighs.

It doesn't matter. Fujiko Maki will never know because she will never meet the man who watches her from beyond the window. She will never ask him why he watches, or what he wants.

The studio apartment is well lit, neat and spotless, an imitation of a living space rather than a home. The room capacity is generous for a Japanese apartment, adding to the cold, overly-ordered plasticity of the space. The sofa sits in the centre of a hard wood floor, facing the wall-length sliding windows, on display. A writing desk hugs the wall to the left of the sofa with a fitted kitchen unit in the far corner. A single bed clings to the wall on the right and a cramped shower cubicle and toilet are set behind the sofa in the rear wall. A comfortable cell.

Fujiko shifts position on the sofa, unfurling one leg from under her body. Does the watcher move with her, she wonders, fidgeting in the dark as he sees her pivot her slender hips, sees her long, smooth limb extend? She stares harder at the page, wanting all the more to look up and face the window, the black void that swallows the wall in front of her. But Reizo would be furious if he heard.

That would be worst of all. If Reizo should get angry.

Fujiko tilts her body again, fighting a sudden urge to urinate. She

3

daren't use the toilet. She daren't expose herself, even to sit and pee. No exposure of her genitals and no bodily functions on show for the clientele. The merchandise didn't fart or piss or shit for the fifteen or thirty or however-many-minutes for which the voyeur-patron had paid. Reizo would not be happy, and she's more scared of Reizo than any of the faceless men who have sat and watched out there in the dark. This one is probably another cop.

She's lost count of the seconds and glances at her watch, catches herself in the middle of the action, and inwardly curses. To disguise her intention, she picks at imaginary lint on her sleeve, hoping the watcher hasn't caught her checking the time. She is on the seventh floor of the building and wonders for a moment what the other occupants are doing. Then she decides that, perhaps, she'd rather not know.

Fujiko puts down the magazine, stands, smooths the skirt down to mid-thigh, and walks on stockinged feet to the writing table.

An old lover, Tōru Ishihara, a diminutive post-graduate student from her years at university, had once said she was the soul of Japan, and she'd laughed. He had claimed she was the embodiment of the motherland: beautiful, refined, cultured. Even at that callow age, Fujiko Maki had known that the gift of good genes, privileged sponsors and an education at an imperial university meant little more than she was a good-looking young woman with a healthy trust fund and an impressive-sounding alma mater of which to boast.

Nevertheless, now she sits at the table, crosses her legs again, and begins drawing on a notepad: a rough image of how the 'Mother of Japan' might look. She sketches sweeping lines and rough hatching, a manga comic image. Long hair with a simple fringe; huge, glistening eyes set in a flawless face tapering to a pointed chin; a nub of a nose and petite, almost prim, mouth. The Mother wears a shapeless, knee-length dress with frilled hem and collar, the legs set slightly apart, hands shyly fumbling in front of her body. Cute, *kawaii*. Virginal, feminine, elegant, to be protected and sheltered and romanced.

Fujiko has the slim, sensuous contours of the Mother on the page, but she doesn't hide them beneath little-girl dresses. Her face is more defined than that of the sketch, the sharp bone below her ear lending a smooth sweep along the jawline to a delicate chin. Her mouth is a rosebud, her nose slender, her eyes almost doll-like with a fold in her upper eyelids – the 'double lid', much-prised among her countrywomen – saving them from a beady aspect. She is considered beautiful.

With a first-class honours degree from Hokkaido University, she is intelligent, resilient, cunning when necessary with a large capacity for empathy. She posseses a physical strength belied by her slender frame, and an, often frustrated, avaricious sexual appetite. What she does not possess, however, is a penis. Hence the resolute refusal from Reizo to permit Fujiko to pursue her own career and the indifference of society at large to the wastage of her considerable gifts.

The black vacuum behind the glass of the window lurks in her peripheral vision and she tortures herself with the thought of how the voyeur, secure in the darkness beyond, sees her. Not, she thinks, as the innocent woman-child of so many manga. Perhaps not as a living, breathing woman at all but more a sexual ideal too terrifying to actually approach. Better to observe, to leer from the cloak of anonymity and touch her, fuck her, possess her in his mind. In his fevered imagination there would be no challenge to his dominance. He couldn't disappoint her with his technique, his inadequacy, his childish fumbling. She hears the first, muffled impact as she shades a shadow on the page under the sketch of her idealised Mother.

The violence of the sound is dulled by the glass so that it seems to come from far away and she barely registers it. Then there is another, louder blow and the sole of a boot batters on the glass. She yelps and flinches, knocking the pad to the floor.

The boot flashes out of the void again, the glass vibrating with the impact. Fujiko stands, knocking the chair over.

Another kick, the boot dropping to the ground behind the glass

– a glimpse of blue jeans – before retreating into the darkness. Fujiko tries to scream but cannot believe what is happening. No one has ever tried to break the partition before. There has never been any violence.

She wants Reizo.

Fierce Reizo. Dangerous, unpredictable Reizo.

She backs toward the rear of the room. The darkness beyond the window opposite is

undisturbed. Her feet whisper on the wooden floor and the hum of the air-conditioner almost smothers her ragged breathing. Her skirt is twisted in rough folds, crumpled halfway up her thighs and the urge to piss, forgotten for a moment, is returning. She feels the first hot burn of tears.

Has someone discovered her secret? Is this sudden violence, unthinkable in this place, because someone knows the truth?

Her hand goes to her stomach and she swallows hard five or six times, fighting back the urge to retch. She stumbles, almost falls, when the slash of blood spatters the glass. It splays across the window in a ragged sprawl, like the poisonous spit of an unseen snake. Fujiko doubles over and part brays, part shrieks, part bawls. The tears come hot and fast, blurring her vision, frightening her more. A fierce smile parts the darkness beyond the window and she screams.

A large, square face with a long obscene nose, phallus-like, its tip tapping the glass, looms from the blackness. The mouth is part snarl, part rictus grin. The eyes are dark pinpricks set in huge white saucers, thick black eyebrows wrenched in fury, the features brutal and immovable. All hellish red, a demon's face floating in the black. The head tilts to the left. Fujiko groans. Her bladder goes.

A gloved hand raps the glass window with something small and metallic. Then the demon is gone, swallowed by the darkness.

Fujiko Maki collapses to the floor, sobbing, gulping air. She is curled under the desk when the men who heard her shrieking on the hidden microphones run into the room.

The girl curls her lip in an effort at playful scolding but to Goro Inaba she just looks like a drunk. Her cheeks are scarlet with booze, her eyes dark, thin slots, almost hidden by her fake eyelashes and heavy eyeliner, and her elbow teeters on the edge of the noodle bar counter as she clutches a cigarette lighter in her manicured fingers. She drawls her words, stretching the vowels like the steaming noodles dished out behind the counter.

'Aaawww, but you just got heeeeere. It's been two weeeeeeeks.'

Yeah, thinks Inaba, and four other women in my bed since I last gave you a turn around my apartment. He takes a gold clip from his hip pocket, fat with bills, and peels a couple off, tossing them on the counter of the noodle bar. The girl perks up when she sees the money.

'Reaaaaally? You are sooo kind, Inaba San.'

'Call me in a couple of days,' he says. He enjoys a glance at her legs, exposed to the tip of her crotch in her mini-skirt, and grabs her smokes from the counter. 'That should cover a new pack,' he says, nodding at the yen next to her teacup.

He clicks his tongue, grins and snatches a bill back, then ducks through the exit of the ramen noodle bar, a hole-in-the-wall stand-up joint sandwiched between two huge glass and steel buildings, and under the shoulder height curtain across the sliding wooden door. The street, nestled between South 4 and 5, is buzzing. What passes for a backstreet in the Susukino district, it has a scattering of drinking holes, restaurants, hostess bars and hidden-away sex emporiums, some behind an eating house or in the warren of businesses towering over the narrow thoroughfare. Many of those strolling along the sidewalk are on their way between the wide avenues of West 3 and 4, ablaze with LED and neon.

Goro Inaba has lived all of his twenty-nine years in Sapporo and knows every nook and cranny of Susukino's square kilometre. He has worked, brawled, drunk and fucked among the shot bars, izakayas, soap lands, health clubs, noodle bars and drinking dens as a yakuza ganagster of the Kanto Daichi-kai gang. For the last three months he has been confined to a single block, keeping the bastard Ishikawa sweet in his office in their largest premises, Big-Touch building.

He just wanted to grab a bowl of noodles and a little action with the new hostess they took on last month. Then he got a text on his phone from the syndicate requesting he get in touch immediately. As he strolls around the corner onto the boulevard of West 3, he calls the club. He yells into the mobile phone over a recorded jingle blaring from a mirrored building entrance on a loop.

'What the fuck is the problem? This better be fucking good!'

A panicked soldier jabbers down the line: a murder, the *oyabun's* woman threatened and their turf invaded. Their very home. The body, still in the fetish club, is of a man Inaba knows all too well.

He kills the call and passes a girl with a peroxide dye-job chatting to another in a French maid outfit outside a convenience store. He scowls, fishes a cigarette from his cancelled date's pack and sparks a zippo. Drugs were pretty low-risk and a dependable income; corporate and personal blackmail a great racket if you could dig up the right dirt. But women: women always brought problems.

As he turns at a right angle onto South 4 a gaggle of Westerners walk by, loud and brash, with an arrogant swagger. Inaba's face flushes and he bites down on the cigarette, ruining the smoke, then mentally chastises himself. Now he'll have to keep the spoiled cigarette until he finds a trash can and he doesn't want to get ash in the pocket of his one Armani jacket.

He calls the club again and says, 'I'm two minutes away. Has anyone heard from the oyabun yet?'

The soldier's panic is tempered by deference. 'No sir, not yet. Nakata San is speaking with him on the phone now.'

Nakata. Capable but unimaginative. He will do nothing until Inaba arrives.

Relieved, he says, 'What about Ishikawa? Does he know?'

'Yes, sir.'

'Where is he?'

'The basement office, sir.'

'If he comes up to get a look at the body, keep him occupied. I'm almost there.'

Goro Inaba offers a quick bow to the cops milling around the small Susukino neighbourhood police station, nestled under the towering cliff of neon and LED signs fronting this stretch of South 4 Street. The cops return the bow with nervous mutters. He reaches the glass double doors leading to a small entrance hall and a couple of elevators, and drops the spoiled cigarette in a standing ashtray. A group of revellers stand chatting. Inaba unlocks a door set in the corner of the entrance hall and walks through to the service elevator. A floor-length mirror is set in the wall and he punches the call button then studies himself as he waits for the elevator to arrive.

He looks tired. Older than his twenty-nine years.

He looks scared. Shit-scared.

Time to get his game face on. Time to cloak the fear in measured bravado, enough to maintain pride yet not belittle Ishikawa: the man is older and higher in rank in a much larger syndicate but, until a partnership is agreed and finalised, not Inaba's superior. In any case, it isn't Ishikawa he's most sacred of. He is fearful of how his boss – the oyabun – will react, yes. But his great, gut-wrenching terror is something much deeper. Something none of the yakuza he knows, friends and enemies alike, or the cops he courts with pay-offs and blackmail, would ever suspect.

Something that, after tonight, will haunt him for the rest of his days.

#

'Shit. He'll want blood tonight.'

Shintaro Ishikawa runs his hand through a thick crop of trimmed salt and pepper hair and looks up to the heating pipes snaking across the low ceiling.

'Shit!'

He remembers he is in company and gives himself a sharp mental rebuke for displaying such emotion in front of the footsoldiers in the room. He must lead his personal bodyguards by example.

The men standing on his left, hands placed in front of their waists, keep their heads lowered, avoiding eye contact.

In Tokyo he'd deal with the situation and everything would simply slip away, unnoticed: cops paid off and politically played, family intimidated into silence, media coerced to maintain the precious status quo. In Tokyo he wouldn't be standing in a fucking basement, sweating under the heating pipes. But here, among the hayseeds and potato farmers of Hokkaido, he has to defer to the head of the local family. And that boss, Reizo Himura, is at one of his slut's apartments, one hundred and forty kilometres away, in the city of Asahikawa. Meanwhile, Reizo's future wife – some say – Fujiko Maki, is being treated for shock in hospital and the fetish operation has ground to a halt.

Fucking hicks, thinks Ishikawa.

At least they had loose tongues. One of Ishikawa's men had wandered upstairs for a drink and a Kanto Daichi-kai yakuza blurted out the sordid story. A man just murdered in one of the fetish clubs, the working girl traumatised. Worst of all, when they checked the body, they found a cop ID.

Ishikawa is sweating, his shirt collar chaffing against his thick neck. The basement is overheated, the air heavy and stale, and he wants to unbutton the starched collar, loosen the knit tie, remove the suit jacket. But the three foot-soldiers awaiting orders are his own men, not Himura's, and he won't show weakness. There are standards to maintain, discipline and Japanese traditional values, and his men should show an example to the peasants up here.

He scratches his bollocks for a moment then turns to the nearest of the three bodyguards, a slim, delicate looking knife-man, and says, 'Let's have a look at this gay-bitch dead cop.'

The man bobs his head in a frantic series of bows. 'Yes, sir.' The deference is exaggerated, the fear less so.

Ishikawa strides past him, through the maze of corridors that form the basement level of Big-Touch building. Outside, the cool night is drenched in light and noise; in here, everything is shades of grey. They arrive at the service elevator. The footsoldiers hurry after him and crowd in, taking care not to touch him. The slim knife-man bobs his head before punching the button for the seventh floor.

A minute later, the men exit the lift and Ishikawa walks through a metal door into the stark, antiseptic light of an open, bare room. Three walls are naked concrete. The door to a small entrance lobby is set in the wall to the right. The flooring is grey linoleum, plain so that bodily fluids can be seen easily and wiped clean. Blood-spattered large glass windows partition the space from a mock-up of an apartment with simple furnishings, like a film set. Men in casual jeans and t-shirts, the absent boss Himura's men, stand around the apartment mock-up, smoking and chatting. One of them makes for a small glass door set in the far left of the partition.

Ishikawa tuts. His bodyguards flinch.

The smeared diagonal slash of blood on the glass is around shoulder height. Ishikawa walks around more blood on the floor. He approaches the body sitting in a chair in the centre of the bare concrete space. A table with a bottle of cheap whiskey, a dirty glass and a box of tissues stand on the right of the chair.

Sat in the chair, his trousers around his ankles, his dick in his hand, is the dead cop. The fingers of the corpse's right hand cannot close around the cock: A couple of fingers have been broken. The other hand lies on top of a pot belly. A vest and torn shirt, both stained with blood, has ridden up just above the navel. Ishikawa has to stand directly over the body to see the man's face as it hangs over the back of the chair, staring blindly at the ceiling. The cop's face has an indignant expression and a thread of blood has run from the lips toward the right ear. Ishikawa supposes the shithead bit his tongue. The man's hair is matted and stiffened with more blood. The neck is a ragged red mess. The body is almost at a ninety-degree angle from the skull. The cop's head has almost been severed from the body.

As he walks around the body, Ishikawa raises his eyebrows. He drops to his haunches, keeping his four hundred dollar shoes clear of the blood on the floor. Then the ghost of a smile flits across his stern features.

Chapter 2

Jackie Shaw would kill for a drink but he won't touch the hard stuff.

Won't touch it sure as the drink killed his da.

Ten hard hours through a twelve-hour flight to Hong Kong and his head feels as though someone shoved it in an airport storage locker and threw away the key. The recycled air in the cabin is stifling; the grinding monotony of the seconds crawling by sucks at his soul, even as the Boeing 777 devours the miles at 562 mph and he puts ever more distance between himself and London.

And yet the further he travels from the city, and the closer he gets to Hong Kong and his final destination of Japan, the stronger the dark echoes of the recent past he hopes to drown with the sound and sensory overload of East Asia.

Years ago, he sat on another plane bound for Kai Tak airport, ready to start over in the Royal Hong Kong Police; he'd been a peeler in Belfast, had been compromised, loyalists and republicans alike having a shot at adding him to the growing murder statistics in the bad old days of home. He'd served on Hong Kong Island and Kowloon until '97 and the Handover. East Asia had been good to him and he'd enjoyed the work: at times it was similar to home, jumping out of choppers with a rifle in his hands, chasing down Triads smuggling heroin instead of terrorists targeting victims. He'd seen other countries through the job: secondments to Thailand, Singapore and Malaysia, even the US and Japan, a country he has spent more time in in the region than any other bar The Territory.

Back in the day, he had told himself that he wasn't running away from home: he was striking out for new ground.

He shoulders into the rear toilet cubicle and stares at the man in the mirror. His skin is sallow thanks to the long-haul flight, like he's back on twenty fags a day. There is something in the face he doesn't recognise, as though someone has smudged the image. His eyes look tired in the harsh fluorescent lighting. Christ, he thinks, I've seen too much in my days. His eyes have seen men breathe their last. There are days he catches his reflection and his eyes don't seem to see much at all.

No fooling himself that he isn't running now.

Finished in the lavatory, he eases into his aisle seat next to his friend, Ian Sparrow. Sparrow sleeps with his mouth open. He'd told Jackie to get some sleep a while back. If only he knew. Sleep didn't come easy, not these days.

Sparrow has a daughter studying in the city of Sapporo on the northernmost of Japan's five big islands, Hokkaido. He was going to visit her and asked Jackie to come along. Jackie knew Ian was worried about him. Sparrow could see that something was eating away at his insides and told him a break would do him good. A holiday.

A break. An escape.

Jackie also knew his friend, a decent man, older and kinder than Jackie, was faintly terrified of the prospect of a trip to the Far East. Jackie, with his history in the region, would be welcome support. A mate, a companion, a guide and a comforting link with home. It was the least Jackie could do for the man who had become his one, true friend.

Two hours out from Hong Kong. A three-hour stopover, then a 747 direct to Sapporo.

He glimpses movement on a screen across the aisle. A kid playing a video game on the aircraft's entertainment system. Old school, pixels gliding around a maze, a frantic chase, three ghosts closing in on the player's avatar.

Jackie Shaw screws his eyes shut for a moment, then picks up a paperback.

#

A decade since he's been in Japan and yet, in one sense, everything is so familiar. The same red-raw eyes after the flight. The same drab greys and torpid eggshell white of the airport terminal. The same disconnect that Japan brings, the sense of a place where everything is a fraction off-kilter, a modern society with something older, something relentless, churning deep underneath.

He joins the queue for passport control.

His fellow travellers look haggard and drawn. Jackie is parched, his tongue swollen, his scars itching in the filtered air of the terminal. The Japanese, segregated in their own longer, busier immigration lines speak in hushed, conspiratorial groups.

Jackie and Ian are beckoned to an immigration official's station where their electronic fingerprints and photographs are taken. Jackie smiles when the immigration officer says, 'Business or pleasure?'

'My daughter is studying in Sapporo,' says Ian.

The officer looks at Jackie. 'And you?'

'Getting away from it.'

'You get away from what?'

'It's just an expression,' says Jackie.

The officer stares for a second, then begins fussing with their passports. He attempts a smile and says, 'Welcome to Japan.'

In the baggage hall, a gaggle of Thais squawk with laughter a couple of carousels over, fidgeting as though attached to tiny electrodes. Guarding the doors to the nation beyond, stand a detachment of solemn customs officers.

'I used to visit here with my missus, back when I was still married,' says a rumpled Australian on their right. 'She was from Saitama, just north of Tokyo. Never once got searched by those clowns. One New Year she flew in a week before me. I went through customs on my own and, well...' He laughs, hard and flat. 'You'll see.'

A young girl clings to her mother's legs a couple of yards from Jackie, staring up at him. What do you see? he thinks. A man in his forties, trim. Cropped hair, strong cheekbones in an open face; a country face, his mother used to say. But the features are drawn tighter these days. The nose a tad off-kilter and the left eyebrow sheared by a slim white arrow of bald skin. And then there is the patchwork of scars beneath his clothes and the unseen wounds running deepest of all under his spoiled skin.

He smiles at the girl. She slinks further behind the protection of her mother. He turns back to the carousel and grabs a case as it drifts by, wincing as he takes its weight at an awkward angle.

Ian shoots him a concerned look and says. 'Old war wounds?'

'Old age.' Jackie winks.

The Australian, walking behind them, says, 'Here we go.'

The first customs officer bows and makes to study their passports but is brushed aside by an older, haggard superior with bulging eyes. He glances at the foreign passports and barks a command. Other officers rush over so they outnumber the enemy three-to-one before opening every case and rifling through the contents. Shoes and socks are removed, bodies patted down, wash bags opened. Jackie and Ian stand back, watching the officers search for contraband. The superior snorts when nothing is found and he walks off, ordering his men to follow. A couple offer regretful glances to Jackie and Ian before hurrying away, leaving the original young officer and a debris-strewn table.

The young man bows and says, 'Sumimasen,' before carefully placing items back in the suitcases. Ian bobs his head and flashes a reassuring smile at the junior official, then joins him in repacking. Jackie mucks in.

As they walk to the information desk to inquire about train connections to Sapporo city, Jackie raises an eyebrow and mimics Ian's bow to the young customs man, smiling.

The train is delayed, a calamity for the Swiss-watch precision of Japan's national transport networks, but the news is met with a measured, stoic silence by the Japanese milling around the ticket gates for the JR train to Sapporo. Jackie and Ian wander back to the concourse and sit in a pristine café. Ian manages to attract the attention of a server then begins frantically pointing at the photos of beer on the small menu card lying on the counter. Jackie orders a coffee.

The server hurries off and returns with a bottle of Kirin beer and Jackie's coffee. She leaves the small beer glasses provided on the counter with a bow before sprinting to the next customer.

Ian pours the bottle of lager and passes Jackie the coffee.

Jackie turns Ian's bottle with his fingers, as though searching for an entrance. He rubs a small nub of hardened skin nestled between the thumb and forefinger of his right hand and stares at the bottle for a moment. Then he sets it back in front of Ian with reverence and turns it on the spot until the label faces his friend.

A voice says, 'I lived here years before I realised that wasn't a giraffe.'

The Australian, sitting nearby, walks over and points to the bizarre image of a cantering beast on the bottle, half goat, half dragon.

'How the hell could that be a giraffe?' says Ian.

'Kirin is the Japanese for giraffe. I thought this was their image of one back when they were an isolated island nation, you know, and just heard travellers' tales. Before they'd ever seen a giraffe for real.'

'So what is it, really?'

'Some kind of mythical creature. The kirin are generally lucky, you know? But they can be fearsome, punish the wicked and all that bullshit.'

Ian begins chatting with the Australian, a businessman on a three-day trip to the huge paper mills in the town of Tomakomai, 70 kilometres from Sapporo. Jackie takes a sip of coffee and looks around the concourse. The women are immaculate. The men are polished. This is Japan as he remembers it: presenting its best face at all times. The cities are urban ugliness on a monstrous scale, the architecture hideous. Apartment and office buildings are like giant children's blocks, cheek to jowl on the crowded streets like commuters packed on the commuter trains; but the roads and pavements are spotless. The neon shines pristine in the sweat-soaked summer nights. The cities are draped in fairytale lights in the Christmas season for no other reason than it looks enchanting, the illuminations ruthlessly stripped overnight on the twenty-fifth. The people scuttle through the great metropolitan hubs of Tokyo, Osaka, Fukuoka and Sapporo, hundreds of thousands of them: no one jostles, no tempers flare.

He'd thought of Hong Kong – Wan Chai and, in particular, Kowloon – as a city turned inside-out. Humanity teemed out of doors, its people seemingly incapable of swallowing inner thoughts and emotions. The urban sprawls of Japan, rather, are buttoned-up. At night, the legions of drunk students and office workers stumble dutifully to a taxi or stand swaying on the last trains home. No fights, no friction, little fuss. But the cities are no prudes. The alleys, avenues and precincts of Shin-Ōkubo and Kabukichō in Tokyo – or Susukino in Sapporo – after sundown are alive with connoisseurs of the twisted, the depraved, the debauched. And yet even in these districts, Japan never lets its seamier side spill onto the crowded streets. The real action takes place behind plain closed doors. The underworld, an innerworld.

The Australian and Ian shake hands, the careworn man nodding at Jackie before taking his leave.

'Better watch your girl isn't swept off her feet over here,' says Jackie, tipping his cup toward Ian. 'Plenty of delicate young pretty boys from the looks of the specimens draped around this terminal.'

Sparrow says, 'Not our Megan's style. She grew up scraping her knees on brambles and tumbling off horses. She came off a mare when she was a kid, less than ten years old, and dislocated her shoulder. We took her to casualty, they popped it back in and she asked to go back and finish her ride there and then.' He looks

18

around the young men on display at the gate. 'She'd scare the living daylights out of this crowd.' His voice is warm and mellow, the rich, rhotic West Country accent strengthened with pride.

'Another year to go on a Postgraduate in Agricultural Science. She loves it. Hokkaido University has a working farm on campus. Cow sheds and arable fields in the middle of two million people.'

'Here's to Megan,' says Jackie, lifting his coffee cup. They drink a quick toast before he says, 'Back in a minute,' and walks off in search of the toilets.

Ian Sparrow thinks of his daughter, twenty-three and living – thriving – on the other side of the world. At that age, he couldn't even drag her mother to Scotland for a holiday. He was stationed for a time in Germany, a NATO military base: Rose stayed with her mother in Stroud. When the offer of a move to the States came up she scuppered the opportunity, threatening divorce if he forced the issue. They were already growing apart but Sparrow, in love with the woman for all their problems, left the army and settled in Gloucestershire. Then Megan arrived, a beautiful, rambunctious little bolt from the blue, and the marriage had a stay of execution. It lasted fifteen more years before they admitted defeat and Rose took Megan to live in Yorkshire. Rose reverted to her maiden name of Cunningham, sent Christmas cards and put up a brave front on his regular visits to see his daughter. He was proud and pleased Megan had kept his surname.

He is pleased, too, that Jackie has come with him. The man needs a change, to put some space between himself and his demons.

He looks at the huge posters of various aeroplanes hung around the concourse. The sky had been darkening when they landed, as though God spilled his tea and the stain was seeping across the heavens. Judging by the windsock on the tower a way off, the breeze was picking up, too. He takes a pull on his beer and thinks any passengers milling around him could be in for a turbulent time.

Chapter 3

Reizo Himura tries to blink away the dull ache developing behind his right eye and expels a long stream of tobacco-and-booze riddled air through his nose, stifling a yawn. He hasn't been to bed – no, slept in a bed – for well over twenty-four hours and his murderous rage has burned down to a simmering anger. They all sit in this airless room while they should be out on the streets hunting for the bastard who defiled their territory and threatened Fujiko. He has been clenching his jaw with impatience since Ishikawa arrived.

Himura sits farthest from the door under a large painting of Lake Toya, the volcano Mount Usu brooding over the small hot-spring resort town by the water. He is cross-legged on the tatami floor matting, his knees tucked under a low wooden table. By the wall on his left sits Shintaro Ishikawa and his trio of bodyguards. By the opposite wall sits Eiji Nakata, the shateigashira – Reizo Himura's second lieutenant. Facing Himura over the low table in the centre of the small room are his wakagashira, first lieutenant Goro Inaba, and a foot soldier whose name he can't remember. Inaba kneels, keeping his head lowered, everything about his stance supplicant and remorseful. As he fucking well should be, thinks Himura. Technically, Inaba should bear responsibility for the outrage last night. He was in charge when some psychopath in a demon mask snuck in and slaughtered a patron on-site in full view of the one woman Reizo Himura loves. But the foot-soldier stepped up, insisting he took responsibility to spare his superior, Inaba, the low ranker bowing and scraping like a fucking mongrel.

Now the foot soldier's head is held at a lower angle than Inaba's. His body is still but his hands tremble on his lap.

The furoshiki cloth is too big for its purpose, but the motif is sombre enough to meet the needs of the ritual. The wrapping cloth has a simple pattern of overlapping Japanese fans in blues and greys: sober colours which will darken when soaked with the blood to come. It has been folded to a third of its true size. Next to the cloth, the tanto dagger lies, slim and elegant, gleaming in the room's stark lighting. It is pre-World War II era, the best they could dig up at short notice, and has none of the elegant decoration and calligraphy found on Muromachi or Edo era blades. Himura grinds his teeth at the thought that Ishikawa will see the makeshift nature of the tools of ritual as further proof of how coarse and uncultured Himura's people are: the dumb hicks of Hokkaido.

The foot soldier lifts his haunches in a slow, deliberate movement and stretches his arm across the polished table, placing his left hand palm down on the folded cloth. His right hand reaches for the tanto, the wooden shaft and clean blade so pure in purpose that the dagger seems a natural object rather than handmade. The man's fingers tremble so he seems about to fumble the knife – but the foot-soldier grasps the shaft and drops his wrist softly on the table, regaining control. He spreads the fingers of his left hand on the cloth and nods, almost imperceptibly. Then he brings the razor-sharp blade to bear on the top joint of the little finger of his left hand.

#

Weak, thinks Shintaro Ishikawa. Fucking weak like the rest.

In Tokyo it would have been done by now. The offending man would have folded the fingertip with care in silk, not cloth, and presented it with great ceremony to his superior. The yubitsume finger cutting ritual would see honour satisfied, obligation fulfilled.

Obligation and loyalty, the cornerstones of the yakuza and of the nation of Japan.

He remembers Inaba tumbling through the door last night, his face like a guilty schoolchild, all control gone until he had stopped a couple of yards from the body, bowed as though in prayer and taken a moment. When he had raised his head, the anger in the young man's gaze was as unbridled as his shock of thick black hair. He bowed again, the angle just shallow enough to send the message – *you are superior in rank but not my master* – and said, 'Ishikawa San, I apologise for this intolerable incident, and the inconvenience caused.'

Ishikawa had returned the bow with a fleeting nod and saw the young man's eyes flicker with tempered hatred. He had rebuked Inaba for his absence at such a crucial time. Unpardonably, the Sapporo yakuza had spoken back, insisting that Ishikawa should leave the matter to the Kanto Daichi-kai and take his leave of the scene. Shintaro Ishikawa, unable to contain his fury, had raged at the impertinent little shit – 'Call your fucking boss! Get your head out of your ass! Show me some fucking respect!'

The young punk Inaba had stood motionless for seconds that stretched for an age.

Ishikawa had counted four seconds before the impasse was broken. Then Inaba had performed a slow bow, the angle just the right side of forty-five degrees.

Ishikawa had barked a hurried, 'Carry on!' and turned for the elevator, his men in tow.

Now he watches Himura. The twitch in his jaw, the slim cord of pulsing vein in the oyabun's neck betray his anger and impatience. He is ill disciplined like his second-in-command.

Still, thinks Ishikawa as he glances at the Sapporo foot-soldier, his hand still clutching the dagger, the blade poised on the skin of the little finger, at least this one will learn something of what it means to be a true yakuza.

#

Reizo Himura wills his man to force the tanto dagger through flesh, gristle and bone and get it done. The longer this drags on, the harder he finds it to hold his temper.

He has no regrets. He had joined the gang as a teenager and worked his way through the ranks, becoming boss at thirty-three with a unanimous vote when his predecessor died of a drug overdose. They had been a small outfit – still were in comparison to the syndicates down south – but he'd been canny in forging alliances with other disorganised bands of scrappers, then consuming them, steadily growing the Kanto Daichi-kai until they could begin dealing with the Russians. Unlike many yakuza, he despised the oblique Japanese concept of tatemae: the construction of a public façade to conceal true desires and emotions. His expression, his eyes, the tension in his features, the flush of his skin, betrayed his true feelings. The Russians could see it, saw him as a straight-shooter, and favoured him above other Hokkaido outfits as a result.

Success brought reward and resentment. The money rolled in but the competition grew aggressive. Outsourced contraband like illegal imports of seafood and liquor for their clubs became scarce as previous associates cut ties and he was forced to turn to the Russians for many illicit goods. The Ruskies drove up the prices.

He reached out to the Yamaguchi gumi with reluctance but the huge southern syndicate brought stability, wealth, security. Even a path to a level of respectability.

He first met Shintaro Ishikawa in a bathhouse in the Ueno district of Tokyo, on Yamaguchi turf, and the man had said, 'You have tattoos only on your back and pectorals.'

'In Sapporo,' said Himura, 'tattooists carve colouring book doodles on trust fund kids and foreigner-wannabes. They use machines rather than the traditional method, inking by hand. There is no true yakuza artist, and I would be ashamed to defile our traditions with that garbage covering the entirety of my body. I visit a traditional master when I am south. It is a work in progress.'

In truth, he had grown bored of lying there while someone treated him as a pin-cushion, all for some anachronistic tradition that none of the younger men in his syndicate cared for. His excuse was weak and he could see in Ishikawa's pause that it didn't convince, but the charade had begun: he had shown respect and self-effacement. The basis had been established for a working relationship.

Now he catches Ishikawa studying the foot soldier as the man grips the dagger. For fuck's sake, thinks Himura, do it and be done.

Reizo Himura had been thinking the same last night as he laboured on top of the girl, a third-tier hostess in a Hakodate club with first rate tits. He had smoked some dope beforehand, was struggling to cum, and the bottle of whiskey he'd downed earlier was beginning to tell. Then his cell phone had rung and he'd snatched the excuse to roll off the bed in the love hotel room and take the call.

There had been babbling: 'Fujiko...customer...murdered...cut... in shock...hospital...'

Himura had said, 'Shut the fuck up and put Inaba on.'

'He isn't here: stopped out on some personal business. On his way now.'

'Then stop jabbering, calm down and tell me what's happening. You're my second lieutenant, for fuck's sake.'

Eiji Nakata had told him. Fujiko had seen a patron butchered at the Invisible Man Club. Only she hadn't seen it, just blood on the glass and a Tengu demon mask looming from the darkness beyond. She had been taken to a hospital near West 14 Street. Ishikawa was inspecting the body and Inaba was expected to turn up any moment.

And the dead patron was a cop.

The Hakodate hostess had screamed when he pulled the knife. She crawled into the corner while he slashed the bed, the pillows, the Disney character pictures on the wall. He'd wrenched the TV from its fixture and smashed it on the stripper-pole on the small stage in the corner, then punched the life-sized love-doll until he'd sat hard on his ass on the floor, drunk and exhausted, and burst into tears.

Where the fuck had Inaba been?

Himura looked at the girl, fetal in the corner, shaking. He stood, weary now, grabbed his wallet from the bedside table and fished a clutch of ten thousand yen notes from inside. He tossed them on the floor in front of her bruised knees and said, 'Take this. You earned it.'

He kept his counsel on the drive back to Sapporo, the two men up front in the BMW silent, the radio off. He had gone to Fujiko at the hospital, then back to his apartment for an hour of disturbed sleep before gathering the men who were at the fetish club last night together. The foot soldier had spoken up, taken the blame while Inaba had stood with his head bowed, silent. Himura had yet to speak in depth with Ishikawa.

Reizo Himura had called for a finger cutting. He'd never have subjected Goro Inaba to the ordeal, for all his faults, but a faceless nobody was an easy sacrifice. A gesture to Ishikawa and his Tokyo syndicate.

Himura can see Ishikawa in his peripheral vision, sneering with disgust. The light catches theTokyo men's metal syndicate pin-badges. Symbols and flags, thinks Himura, like a children's secret club, useless in a fight. Himura feels humiliated. The low-life mongrel clutching the dagger has frozen. It's as good as a 'fuck you' to the Tokyo boys, and Reizo Himura has had enough. He takes his hands from his knees and slowly places them on the table, fingers spread. His head immobile, his gaze benevolent, he addresses the foot soldier as his rank, shatei: he still can't remember the asshole's name.

'Little brother, perhaps I ask too much of you. Your superior is truly responsible for the failures of last night, not you.' Himura glances at Goro Inaba. His first lieutenant's head drops another couple of inches lower. 'But I appointed Inaba San as wakagashira. Am I, then, ultimately at fault?'

He reaches for the dagger and takes the handle from his man, gentle, his face impassive. The footsoldier, spellbound, stares at his oyabun. Reizo Himura lays his left hand palm up on the tabletop, close in to his body and makes to draw the razor-sharp tanto blade across the soft mound of flesh at the base of his thumb. He tilts his chin upward and peers down at his palm, imagining a torn seam of crimson blood following the arc of the blade. The footsoldier squawks, leans forward over the table, his hands reaching out but not daring to touch his oyabun, imploring – *stop! Please, stop!*

Himura snatches one of those grasping hands by the wrist and slams it hard on the table then brings the dagger down in one sweeping thrust. He feels tendons snap as he stabs through skin, flesh and gristle, and nails the man's left hand to the polished wood. The man's mouth wrenches in a silent scream. Reizo Himura leans in close.

'Suck it up! Suck it up or I'll gut you here and now!'

The man's eyes go wide in panic and fear, a child in terror of his furious father, but he nods and lowers his gaze.

Himura places his unblemished palms on the tabletop again.

Shintaro Ishikawa stands, buttons his jacket and leaves the room, his men following behind at a discreet distance.

Chapter 4

Jackie Shaw purses his lips and spits on the thin dirt at his feet, raises his face to the pale blue dome of the autumn sky and closes his eyes.

'What the hell are you doing?' says Ian Sparrow.

Jackie opens his eyes and looks at the small patch of dark earth where his spit landed. He rubs at the ground with his heel and, satisfied, says, 'Superstition. If you see a white horse, spit and close your eyes to bring good luck, but always rub it out after.'

'A bit random.'

'Over there,' says Jackie, pointing to a horse and trap outside the gates of the small park where they sit, the modest grounds of the red brick Old Hokkaido Government Building. There is a small hop-on, hop-off point on the horse and trap's tourist circuit around the city centre.

'Feeling homesick?' says Sparrow. 'Horses wandering around the city centre?'

'That'd be years ago in Dublin, not Belfast.' Jackie leans back on the wooden bench, taking in the lily pads on the pond at their feet, the neo-baroque American-style building beyond, like a more welcoming Addams Family mansion. Behind the landmark, a huge glass office block looms, brutal and monstrous. 'I could do with a bit of good fortune. My nose is itchy, means I'm going to have a fight with someone.'

'God help them,' says Sparrow. His expression darkens for a beat.

Jackie smiles. 'I wouldn't worry. I spent a bit of time in Japan, on and off. I never saw a hint of barney. Seen youngsters carried out of bars drunk, probably had to get their stomachs pumped; girls walking home through public parks at midnight, safe. I even saw some of the local thugs strutting about, all punch perms and cartoon snarls. But never a punch thrown.'

Sparrow nods and checks his watch, anxious. Jackie's friend hasn't seen his daughter in over a year and meeting her so far from home has him antsy. The two friends wait for Megan Sparrow in the small park, in the fresh autumn sun. Jackie and Ian haven't slept since the flight and they are beginning to feel the quicksand of jetlag suck at their reserves of energy. A woman passes in a business suit, immaculate, and smiles with a brief bow. A couple of businessmen hurry by, laughing. Jackie feels at ease for the first time in an age. He has been screwed tight with bad memories and a guilty conscience for so long he almost felt uneasy at the realisation that he was unwinding.

Christ, he thinks, I am actually on holiday. He smiles again.

Sparrow says, 'Enjoying yourself?'

A female voice says, 'Loving it.'

Megan Sparrow skips the last few steps to her father and throws her arms around his neck before he has time to react. Her dark hair is cut in a bob just below her jawline. Her jeans are tucked into boots and a small backpack is slung over her shoulders. Ian Sparrow discovered the joys of fatherhood in his late thirties. Megan is twenty-three and possessed of a scrubbed prettiness. Jackie can see her father in the wide mouth and cleft in her chin. She has his warmth in her eyes, too, but they have a feline aspect that must come from her mother.

Ian holds her, telling her how great she looks, how proud he is. Then he steps back and introduces Jackie. Megan Sparrow offers a broad grin, a mirror image of her father's, and extends a hand. Jackie takes it and makes the right noises – *great to finally meet, heard so much from your dad* – and can see in the steady gaze and cocked hip of the young woman's stance that he is being appraised. The verdict seems good: the smile takes on a lop-sided, flirtatious aspect. He's flattered but embarrassed. Megan Sparrow is the model of a bright young thing. Jackie Shaw is damaged goods.

He reminds himself that he is on holiday.

'Sorry I'm late,' says Megan, 'I was waiting for a call from my beau but it looks like I've been stood up.'

Ian says, 'A couple of minutes is hardly late.'

'That's just it, Dad. In this country, a couple of minutes is a capital offence. My boyfriend was meant to call me two hours ago and I'm still waiting. I wanted you to meet him but he must be tied up with work.'

'This is Yuri?'

'Yuji, Dad. Yuri is a girl's name.'

Jackie stands a couple of paces away.

Sparrow, more than anyone, knows the darker corners of Jackie's dreams and when Ian decided to fly to Japan to see his only daughter, he asked his friend to come along.

Ian says, 'Anyway, Jackie and myself are parched.'

'Come on then,' says Megan. 'Let's get you a proper brew.' She moves between them, linking an arm through one each of theirs and they set off on the spotless tiled path leading to the smooth, relentless flow of humanity in the city streets beyond the gates. Dorothy and her consorts, off to see the wizard.

#

A large blue monkey and what looks like a giant orange testicle hop from foot to foot on the pavement of the pedestrian plaza as a pretty girl in a pink uniform screeches into a microphone by their side. Mothers and kids crowd around, joined by a couple of single adult males taking photographs and waving comic books.

'Only in Japan,' says Megan.

They sit outside, a hint of the rich, earthy musk of autumn in the breeze, despite the urban surroundings. A massive office block towers over the plaza and the busy four-lane avenue – West 4 Street – that runs in a straight-shot from central station to the entertainment district of Susukino slices across the view to their right.

'You weren't kidding about the coffee', says Jackie. It is dark and strong with an aroma to give you a real kick up the arse. That's Japan, he thinks. If these people decide to do something, they do it right.

'We aim to please,' says Megan.

Her father says, 'Not so sure about the tea.'

'You mean it isn't brewed with a cheap teabag and so much suga you could stand your teaspoon up in it.'

'It tastes like grass, love.'

'Green tea, Dad. Loads of good stuff, clean out all that real ale and red meat in your belly.'

Megan scratches her left shoulder with manicured nails, stretching the wide neck of her t-shirt and revealing a glimpse of tribal strokes in black and grey, and a hint of something in a pastel shade.

Jackie says, 'What's the tattoo?'

'It's an abomination, is what it is,' says Ian.

'A dog,' says Megan.

Jackie says, 'I thought it was something Celtic.'

'Nope, just a dog. It represents me.'

'Bit harsh, you'd be alright with a swipe of lipstick.'

Ian shakes his head.

Megan pulls her t-shirt further over her shoulder to reveal a stylised illustration of a dog in black, grey and pale pink. 'I was born in the Year of the Dog. I am independent, brave, loyal and bring good luck.'

'And modest with it,' says Ian. He looks at Jackie. 'Dragon's more like it.'

Megan looks hard into Jackie's eyes. 'What are you?'

'No idea,' he says. 'Your dad would probably say I was a donkey.'

'Stubborn as one anyway,' says Ian.

'I peg you,' says Megan, boring into him with a hard stare, 'as a rat.'

Sparrow laughs and Jackie studies his coffee cup with a timid smirk.

Megan says, 'Like my dad said, you're smart but obstinate. I don't see you on a rocking chair in forty years' time with a gaggle of grandkids. I reckon you live for the moment.' Her tongue traces a line across her upper lip as she thinks up the rest of her improvised profile, having fun now. 'And you're fiercely, ferociously protective of those you love. You've fought hard in the past and you're a closed book: only you know where the bodies are buried.'

The silence throws her and, confused by Jackie's awkward quiet, she turns to her father for reassurance.

'You can tell all that just by looking at his ugly mug?' says Ian. He leans over to Jackie. 'Her mother and I don't agree on much, but we were of the same mind about that monstrosity on her shoulder.'

'Don't you have a tattoo, dad? Something from your army days?'

'Not the same, love. I was too young to know any better, drunk and influenced by a shower of other naïve young tossers. I regret it now and you will, too.'

'You won't be going to any of the hot springs, anyway. Tattoos are no-go in public over here thanks to the yakuza. You have any ink, you must be a gangster even if you're an English post-gradu- ate.' Megan shakes her head in mock despair.

Jackie says, 'What's Yuji think of it?'

'Loves it. Thinks it gives me an edge, makes me wilder, more ... dangerous than your average Japanese woman.' Megan laughs, a high-pitched fusillade of giggles. She points at Jackie's forearm, just visible below his sleeve. 'You should have followed Jackie's example, dear father, and had yours removed. What was it, Jackie? My dad told me you grew up in Belfast. Let me guess: a leprechaun. In a balaclava.' She erupts again. It is infectious and Jackie snorts.

He rolls back the sleeve to reveal the knotted, bruised scar where he'd had a tattoo removed years ago. 'You know,' he says, still laughing, 'you're not far wrong.' Ian splutters and they crack up again. A couple of men in dark green courier uniforms stare as they pass. Jackie says, 'I was going to get another one, you know. On my finger, of all places: the ring finger of my right hand. A Claddagh ring.'

Megan's eyebrows scrunch. 'A what, when?'

'Claddagh ring. A tattoo of an Irish Claddagh ring. I had one, wore it on that finger. It was a gift from my ma. When my da passed, I buried it with him. It seemed the right thing to do.' He raises a hand to stave off the usual platitudes as Megan shifts in her seat. It was a while ago and a lot has passed since then. 'I couldn't just buy another ring: they really have to be a gift from a loved one so I had the notion of a tattoo. But here's the thing. The centre of a Claddagh is a heart, for love. You have to wear it with the tip of the heart facing outwards if you're single because your heart is open. It has to point in toward your body if you're in love as your heart is taken.'

'And which way did you wear yours?'

'Out. But I'm ever the optimist, so I thought it was best not to risk it with a tattoo. Too permanent.'

'I get the feeling there isn't too much that's permanent in your life.'

'Megan,' says Ian.

'Sorry,' she replies. 'Too much time in-country. The Japanese are a polite, shy people but they can floor you with some pretty blunt opinions. I've been told I look strong, I've put on weight, I look old, have a scary face, and a small face.'

Jackie says, 'Lost in translation.'

The howl of a police siren surges through the blocks of high-rises in waves.

A violent clash of limbs and heads erupts next to them. A clutch of pigeons taking off in panic at a booming voice, swollen with theatrical rage. The thunderous roar barrels up the urban canyon of West 4 Street, the echoes caroming off the tall city centre buildings. People on the street go about their business, seemingly oblivious. Resolute in their ambivalence.

Ian says, 'What the bloody hell is that?'

Megan's face darkens, then she stirs her coffee with an insouciant flourish. 'It's up at the station by the sounds of it.'

'What is, the Nuremberg Rally?'

'They're ultranationalists. Banging on about a return to Imperial Japan, standing up to the Chinese, lying Koreans, insidious American culture. You name it.'

Jackie remembers. He had attended a law enforcement conference in Tokyo back in the nineties, one of a delegation representing the Royal Hong Kong Police. He had sat outside a hole-in-the-wall drinking joint one evening, supping beer with ice trickling down the chilled glasses. The noise had begun as a low rumble, gathering momentum as the crowd neared, swelling to a huge growl, cannoning off the buildings. Then they saw the mob emerge into the square next to Shimbashi Station.

There had been a small van top-heavy with speakers blasting militaristic marching tunes, a squat figure bawling into a microphone. Rising Sun flags, the war flag of the Imperial Japanese army, fluttered from wooden poles jutting out of windows like rifles from an armoured vehicle. A small group of men marched behind the van. Jackie grabbed his beer and wandered up to the mouth of the sidestreet to get a better look. And the good people of Tokyo had hurried, strolled or cycled by, studiously ignoring the unsightly commotion.

The bawling isn't getting any closer. Megan must be right; the local fascists are pitched somewhere near the station.

Jackie realises Megan and Ian have been chatting, oblivious to his trip through memory lane. They sit close, laughing. His friend is different here. Fatherhood suits him. Ian has told him a few snippets in quiet conversations about his ex-wife, Paula Cunningham, Megan's mother. Parting of the ways when the girl was still relatively young. Ian and his ex chat on the phone on occasion but his bond with Megan remains strong. She is, by all accounts, her father's daughter.

Jackie hopes Yuji is a decent fella, deserving of his friend's daughter. He stands and Ian and Megan turn to him. Jackie points to the café and Megan says, 'Second door, just past the counter on the right.' He nods and makes for the glass door.

A man stands about sixty yards away, hidden from view by a tree but revealed in the angled reflection of the glass café door. Jackie stops and rifles through his pockets, checking the figure out. Slim, narrow shoulders, loitering in front of a Godiva chocolatier, fiddling with a mobile phone. The phone is vertical, parallel to his body but angled around the tree trunk. Jackie would take six-to-four the joker is taking snapshots.

But here? Now? Jackie and Ian are on holiday in Japan's fourth largest city. They don't know anyone. Megan is a student. No one in Sapporo could possibly have any cause to surveille them.

Catch yourself on, Jackie Shaw. A foolish notion. He's tired, needs to get back to the hotel, sleep off the jetlag for an hour or so.

And yet.

If experience has taught Jackie anything, it's always better to be safe than sorry.

He sweeps the plaza. Everyone else is in transit, sitting at a table or head-down engrossed in a book or mobile phone. Perhaps the man is some kind of voyeur. Jackie shakes his head as though he's forgotten something and walks along the row of shopfronts on the south side of the plaza, heading for the large avenue of West 4. If he can skirt the pedestrian space and approach the man as he watches Megan and Ian, he can scare him off. Better still, he can mortify him by having a go in public, a great shame to the Japanese.

He has taken a few steps when Ian and Megan call out to him, asking where he's going.

'Back in a minute,' he says. He walks another ten yards before common sense prevails. He is paranoid. The price for a life of violence: thousands of miles from home, he's seeing shadows that aren't there.

I'm on holiday.

He glances across the plaza at the Godiva shopfront. The windows blaze white in the reflected afternoon sun, obscuring the interior. The man has gone.

I am changed. Changed utterly.

Before, I was a man, with all the impurity and guilt of man. Guzzling alcohol, coveting the finer things in life, sniffing girl's armpits and saving for my very own sex doll.

Bear witness to my revelation, my transformation.

I was born in Japan but I was not of Japan. My life was blighted by avarice, the new Japanese religion of consumption. I worked my corporate-owned balls off for the right clothes, to eat the food fetishized on our lobotomised television shows, to impress the right giggling woman-child and grab a quick fuck in a love hotel. I was a salaryman.

Then I slit the craven bastard's throat in that dark little box of concrete and glass and everything changed.

The Christians have a story of a man who walked to a city and a light shone revealing the truth of their God. A revelation. The man was converted. Fairy tale nonsense, so typical of the big-nosed barbarians with their body-stink and their shitty food and their Justin-fucking-Bieber and Kim-fucking-Kardashian. An English teacher told me a joke once, 'What's the difference between a yoghurt and America? Leave a yoghurt for a couple of hundred years and it will develop a culture.' He was Australian. Sometimes even the Westerners' boorish manner can be amusing.

I stood in that black hovel last night with my victim and saw the blinding light of our Mother, the Sun Goddess, through a glass wall. The Shinto religion tells us the Mother, Amaterasu, painted the void with her light and the power of her brothers' great gifts, the God of the sea and the God of the moon, and the fruits of their incestuous conception is this divine land, Japan and the imperial family, the Chrysanthemum Throne. But I saw the truth of the Mother. She is Mother of wanton grace, a slut, a peerless whore.

Hot-as-fucking-hell.

She spoke to me and I was transformed from man to spirit. A goblin. Demon.

Tengu.

The Mother bade me slaughter the apostate before me and I took the mask of the Tengu – her terrible champions, her dogs of war – and cut the fucker from ear to ear, butchered him like the pig he was. I felt the hot life gush out of him over my thin gloves, heard the sigh of his spirit as it fled to hell. My senses flooded with the sound and smell of the dying beast; I breathed deep of the shit-stench that filled the air.

I had a hard-on like a nuclear warhead.

I saw the Mother scream in ecstasy and tapped on the glass with an offering before retiring to the dark. As a final gesture, I shamed the corpse, displaying his penis, further torment to his kami, *his spirit, as it craves an impossible peace in the afterlife.*

Nice touch, I thought. Then I had a wank, a parting, sordid gift to the corpse.

In the offal and waste, in the gaze of the Mother – our beautiful letch of a Mother – I was purified.

I am man no longer. I am a vessel of Japan. I will end those who betray our land, who betray themselves and our Emperor, and the Mother. There will be more sacrifices. She demands it. My faith demands it. My hunger demands it. My hard-on demands it.

I am changed, utterly.

I, Demon.

Chapter 5

Ito, head of the Ringo-kai syndicate, didn't have any knowledge of the murder at the Invisible Man Club.

Sato, boss of the Maruma-ikka gang, denied any knowledge but offered a speculative name, a possible suspect. A nobody in his organisation who had been expelled for screwing a higher-up's wife on the nights when the husband had been wrestling with a cabaret singer in a Susukino love hotel. All bullshit.

Nakata, Reizo's second lieutenant, is reaching out to gangs in Hokkaido's other cities, Asahikawa and Hakodate, and the smaller outfits in Sapporo.

Suzuki, number one in the smaller Umeda-Abe-ikka outfit, had sounded astonished and flattered to even be considered a suspect. Suzuki barely had an organisation, more a loosely-knit street rabble searching for the next score.

And there's the rub. Every gang in the city – on the island – large or small, the gutter-level dregs and the organised syndicates, is all about the money. At the end of the day, the yakuza life is all business. The likes of Shintaro Ishikawa might bang on about their rituals and doctrines and lineage, might despise the chinks, the Koreans, the foreign gaijin. But the Kanto Daichi-kai boss, Reizo Himura has yet to meet a yakuza who wouldn't do business with little green men from Mars if it brought a healthy profit.

He will not contemplate the unthinkable: this could not be an inside job, a betrayal from one of his men. Inconcievable.

Reizo runs a calloused finger through Fujiko's hair and watches the faint rise and fall of her chest as she sleeps. He lies, fully clothed, next to her on the queen-sized bed in her apartment on the twenty-third floor of a high-rise. The eastern façade of the building towers above a main road and the Toyohira River, but Fujiko's apartment faces west, overlooking Nakajima Park. Below, through the wide, floor-length windows, the park is a palette of autumnal colours, the small island in the central lake ablaze with daubs of crimson maples. Fire and water, he thinks: he and Fujiko. She's baring up well but the images of last night won't leave her for a long time, if ever. The looming Tengu mask. The blood.

Her camisole clings to her body as her breasts rise and fall with each breath, clean ridges of bone straining against her skin, smoother than the silk clothing her. She's too delicate for this world, thinks Himura. Too good. Too decent. She should be a teacher, or a doctor. A mother. She laughs easily, fusses and tends the men when in the outfit's offices. When the boys have a personal problem, they speak to Fujiko. Woman trouble, they consult Fujiko. She never complains, never turns them away. When he ridicules and sneers at the men who pay to watch her from the shadows in the club, she defends them. There are no absolutes in life, she says. Every man who sits in the dark is alone with who and what he is. If she can relieve their solitude for a moment, she will.

She needs him. Such an innocent soul needs a monster to protect them.

A monster to catch a monster: but where to start? His body yearns to let loose a terrible violence.

First things first. He stands and stares through the window across the park and the confusion of high-rises beyond to the hunched mass of mount Moiwa rising from the western fringes of the city, and the trail of smaller peaks that connect it to Mount Maruyama like a broken spine. Somewhere on that peak, Goro Inaba is burying the dead cop. Once in the ground, nature will take its course, devouring the body and corrupting forensics. Even if an early snow freezes the corpse, by the time it thaws next spring there will be little physical evidence left for the blue-shirted bitches of Sapporo Police.

Reizo glances at his Rolex. Another couple of hours until he is due to meet Inaba, get drunk and formulate a strategy to find the bastard who killed that cop.

A couple of hours.

He looks at Fujiko sleeping soundly.

A couple of hours.

He remembers the girl in the Hakodate love hotel, what they'd been doing before the news got through of the killing. He looks to his right at the northern edge of the park, bordering the outer reaches of Susukino. Pockets of neon are already burning through the wan late-afternoon sunlight.

A couple of hours.

Reizo Himura pads from the bedroom to retrieve his phone from his jacket. He runs through a list of female contacts and dials a number in the North Ward of Sapporo. After thirty seconds, a female voice answers, thick with sleep and too many late nights making hostess-talk and smoking cheap cigarettes. In a rushed whisper, he tells the girl he will be at her place in twenty-five minutes, instructs her to make a strong pot of coffee, and not to bother getting dressed.

#

Goro Inaba wants a bath. A scalding hot shower, sluicing off the soap and death-stink that clings to his body followed by a soak in a broiling tub.

He takes shallow breaths but the stench of the dead cop still seeps through the surgical-style mask covering the lower half of his face. The two men with him smoke to kill the smell and stay warm.

After the finger-cutting, Inaba had knelt before his oyabun, Himura, and offered a deep bow, pleading that he be permitted to lead the disposal of the body. There had been a long, heavy silence and Goro had begun to ache, straining to maintain rigid posture in the deep bow.

Had Himura been impressed? Did it matter? Obligation had been fulfilled. Goro Inaba had shown contrition and his boss informed him that he had permission to atone for his negligence by leading the small team who would dispose of the body.

Now Inaba grabs at the bristled hair on the decapitated head, loses his grip and drops it on the plastic sheeting.

'Shit! Was this fucker a cop or a junior-high baseball player? He's got a fifteen-year-old's buzzcut.'

The others snort, cool, affected. Poseur assholes, he thinks. They each carry a couple of heavy sports bags and he grunts at them, 'Put your gloves on before you go any further. And stub those smokes out in a can and bring them with you, just in case.' No point leaving any more of their garbage to choke a fox or squirrel. Hikers in Japan do not litter. No one does, including yakuza at work.

The men nod and strain further up the slope, patches of light snow visible in the weak light through the evergreens on the higher ground.

'Don't worry about tracks,' says Inaba, 'there could be another snowfall tonight or tomorrow. If not, the tracks will fade before anyone else is up here.'

They are on a slope at the western reaches of the cluster of peaks that lie behind Maruyama Park. Only a couple of kilometres from the suburbs, bear roam and few hikers bother to tread.

'Maybe we should have burned all of him, eh?' he shouts as the men pass from view. They grunt a response, forced banter. Some media darling had spouted a pile of bullshit to one of the tabloids, the yakuza don't bury the bodies but burn them. With hot asphalt, of all things, wiping out all trace of DNA. It was fiction. Why burn them when most of the bodies were small-time felons or rival gangsters? Maybe down south, in the vast urban sprawl, it was more difficult to bury the bodies in isolation but up here, with a wilderness on the doorstep, nature could take its course.

The corpse had been taken to a meat warehouse near the racecourse and butchered by one of their contacts in the large wholesale market. Inaba had personally pulled the cop's teeth and cut off the hands and feet to help impede identification. These, along with the clothes, were burned in a stove. To incinerate a full-grown adult would take much longer and require a cremation oven, more time and expense than necessary.

His men have gone. He told them to fan out, walk for fifteen minutes before burying the rest of the dismembered corpse. Let the earth and the small, crawling things that live in it devour the evidence. If they were lucky, a bear would feast on it. It would fuck any forensics.

He grabs the head in both hands.

'Stupid fucker,' he says. 'You stupid, stupid fucker.'

He drops it with a dull thump into the pit dug by his men before they hiked up the slope.

He fishes in the plastic sheeting and chuckles, a dark, disembodied sound. This is like a lucky dip in one of the festival stands that clutter the city parks in June, August and January. Will he come up with a cup-and-ball, a spinning top, a paper toy, a little drum? Nope: a chunk of flesh with a caramel nipple in the centre. Damn, that butcher knows his business.

#

The katana blade gleams in the strip lighting of the kitchen in the affluent district of Miyanomori clinging to the mountains overlooking Sapporo. The city sprawls across the darkening plain below like a concrete virus. Shintaro Ishikawa has finished with the choji oil and enjoys the subtle fragrance of clove as he points the samurai sword away from his heart and sweeps the specially prepared paper along its length in a smooth, practiced motion, cleaning excess oil from the tempered steel. His breathing is soft and controlled, the air whistling through his nostrils. He repeats the motion on the underside of the blade, guard to tip. As he peers down the length of the sword, he sees pockets of neon and LED ignite across the city below, a rainbow concentration centred on Susukino.

His men are elsewhere. He told them not to pick him up this evening. He would make his own way to the entertainment district for another interminable sit-down with Himura and his rabble.

Ishikawa applies the uchiko ball of cleaning powder to the katana blade with gentle taps then cleans it off with the paper, following the same process as before. The steel glints with a wicked brilliance, the weapon a thing of beauty and purity of purpose.

Ishikawa had wanted to pay respects to Fujiko Maki San but Himura had requested he wait until she had rested. Perhaps tomorrow. Shintaro knows Himura feels threatened. Fujiko Maki is a beautiful woman, superior in breeding and manners. She would make a fine lover for Ishikawa and, perhaps, a suitable wife. There have been concerns within his group, and the wider sphere of the Yamaguchi gumi gang, that he has still not married. It is expected of a man of his stature and age and yet it is the one convention of yakuza life to which he will not adhere. Japanese women are the most delicate, loyal and passionate of all females. Truly exquisite. Women to be treasured, not beaten or violated as so many other yakuza enjoyed. They deserve more respect than trophy status while their husbands grunt and labour on young hookers in love hotels and rented apartments. He knows men within Yamaguchi ranks who fuck foreigners, lowbred Thais and Vietnamese and even white sluts while their women – Japanese women! – make a home for their children and manage their households.

He slides the razor-sharp blade back in its saya scabbard with great care. Walking to the lounge, he mounts the sword, horizontal and edge up, above a simple hanging scroll of calligraphy.

To relax for the afternoon, Ishikawa had retreated to his rented home, drunk tea and cleaned his sword, a favourite blade he had brought with him from Tokyo. It was a samurai weapon from the latter half of the nineteenth century with a hilt wrapped in fine silk cords.

Tokyo were undecided about the Hokkaido brutes. Ishikawa had erred toward a rejection of Reizo Himura's advances toward the Yamaguchi syndicate, and hoped a decision would soon be forthcoming from Tokyo and the parent organisation in Kobe. Now he isn't so sure. He has yet to inform his organisation that a cop was butchered on Kanto Daichi-kai premises, and is unsure how to play his hand. Because he is entranced by Fujiko Maki. Could he have her? Would she entertain the thought of his patronage, even marriage? How to navigate a path to Maki San without causing an incident, perhaps a small war? One of the universal yakuza tenets was never to violate the wife of another member. But Himura wasn't a member of Shintaro Ishikawa's syndicate and Maki San wasn't his wife. Ishikawa knew that the Sapporo oyabun had been fucking some slut in Hakodate when his woman witnessed the brutal killing at the Invisible Man Club. Fujiko Maki must know of Reizo's other women, yet she stays by his side. She is no fool, so what angle is she playing?

He remembers a proverb, Teppu shiro o katamuku: A smart woman ruins the castle.

But he cannot help himself. The death of the cop is an opportunity to damage Himura, get him out of the way and take Fujiko for himself.

Another weapon hangs, horizontal, between the katana sword and the scroll. Its blade is a little over thirty centimetres in length, a smaller companion to the katana, a wakizashi sword. The hilt is wrapped in the same fine silks, its lacquered scabbard shining in the electric light. It would have been used for close quarter combat, thinks Ishikawa. He wonders which samurai wielded this particular blade.

Yes, Shintaro Ishikawa is not ready to leave the north just yet.

He takes the smaller sword from the wall with the reverence of a monk with a sacred talisman at a Shinto shrine, and walks to the kitchen to enjoy the view of the darkening city again.

Chapter 6

And so it begins. Two young Westerners standing in front of a convenience store on a wide thoroughfare in Susukino running east to west, downing tall cans of lager. The street is bustling, a constant shunting stream of traffic, legions of taxis among the cars and sandwich-board vans advertising hostess joints and eateries. Downtown Japan after dark, the people alive, the seductive promise of the night, and the temporary joys of alcohol, flushing grey nine-to-five faces with colour and life.

Jackie and Ian walk either side of Megan, heading for a drinking spot and an introduction to her boyfriend, Yuji. Jackie can sense Ian is a little tense. The people, noise and lights swirl around them, the city in perpetual motion. All except the two young Westerners, standing next to a line of parked bicycles on the kerb, taking greedy slugs from their beer cans. As they size up a young woman in a cocktail dress hurrying from the convenience store with an armful of bottles of cheap sake, a drunk middle-aged Japanese man in glasses wearing an immaculate suit approaches them. Megan enters the store to grab a nailfile for a last minute touch-up before meeting Yuji. Her father, entranced by the multi-coloured Aladdin's cave inside, joins her for a gander at the vast array of snacks and bric-a-brac on the shelves. Jackie loiters in front of the store, enjoying the show.

'Aah you American?' The drunk Japanese man leans in close, inches from the taller Westerner's face, an unthinkable invasion of personal space if sober.

'Shit, here we go,' says the shorter, red-haired beer drinker.

'Listen,' says his tall, bespectacled companion, 'we're just having a drink, okay? Go take an English lesson somewhere else.'

The middle-aged man, oblivious to the barb in his drunken joy, ploughs on. 'You aah strong-u. Much strong-u zan Japaneezu. American, desho?'

The Westerners ignore him, supping on their cans of lager. The taller drinker's jaw clenches.

'You like-u Japaneezu beeru, ne? You drinku a lot-o! Strong-u. You is-u American.'

The taller Westerner turns and says, fast and mocking, 'Yeah, I'm American, and I'm strong enough to beat your ass up and down this street, so go pay to talk to some airhead in a club who'll pretend to give a shit.'

The shorter Westerner steps from behind his taller friend and says, 'I'm Canadian. He's American, which is why he's such an asshole when he's drunk. Come on, James.' He touches his friend's arm. 'Leave it, the guy'll drift off in a minute.'

James is not having it. He yanks his arm away from his friend and turns on him. 'Fuck you, Nate. I put up with this garbage all day, every day in my job. Nobody's paying me to listen to this shit in my own time.' He whirls back to the Japanese man who is now inspecting the zip on his trousers. 'Fuck off, you got that?'

The Japanese looks up, his face a mask of mock fury and yells, 'Fuck off! Asshole! Shit!' His pronunciation miraculously improves with each obscenity and a wide grin splits his face, like a toddler who discovered some words with which to shock his parents.

James hurls his beer can in the gutter and squares up. 'You wanna go, bitch?' He stoops down to push his forehead hard against the Japanese man's.

Christ, thinks Jackie, all that bollocks I fed Ian about Japan: never seen a fight. And now some drunk English teacher is going to make a liar of me. He glances behind through the window of the convenience store. Megan is standing in line to pay at the register while Ian inspects the array of pre-prepared lunch-box meals on display. His friend looks younger. Happier. Somehow lighter.

When Jackie turns back to the street, it's all change. James stands with slumped shoulders, head tucked into his collar. His friend, Nate, has set his can down and moved beside him, and holds his palms up in supplication, blethering something in broken Japanese. Three younger men in expensive-looking jeans and jackets surround the drunk man. One has long hair tied back in a ponytail and a wispy goatee like an unfinished sketch. The other two sport spiked, teased haircuts, one dyed blonde, the other silver. The ponytailed man has a low-cut neck on his t-shirt and a fishscale tattoo strains into view above the collar. He stands inches from the taller Westerner. People hurry by, keeping rigid focus on the pavement ahead.

Ponytail takes a step toward James and barks something in Japanese. The young American flinches. Jackie makes out 'Baka ka!' – *asshole!* The silver spikey-haired man slaps the drunk middle-aged man across the back of the head like a disappointed teacher clipping a schoolboy around the ear. The drunk man's glasses shunt askew, one lens teetering on the bridge of his nose. Ponytail bellows, 'Omae wa dare da?' *Who the fuck are you?*

Bollocks, thinks Jackie, I'm on holiday. Take this shit somewhere else.

James is terrified, all but pleading for mercy while his friend, Nate, pursues a hiding to nothing, trying to reason with street thugs.

Then Megan's voice bawls in Jackie's left ear and she is marching across the pavement cutting a swathe through the passersby.

'James, are you causing trouble again?'

The street thugs look at her, amused. The blonde spikey-haired goon mutters something through a lopsided leer. Megan ignores him and goes straight to ponytail, nodding a short bow and pro-ducing a stream of fluent Japanese that takes him by surprise. James looks wretched. Nate is glancing anxiously between Megan and the thugs. Her posture is ramrod straight, composed but on the right side of arrogant and she is playing the goons with feminine expertise, judging by their reactions. They are all magnanimous mercy, alpha male egos intact and handed an out from the confrontation by Megan's scolding of her Western friends like an angry mother.

Then Ian Sparrow wanders out of the convenience store.

Placid, shrewd, calm. The man to talk down the young country boys when they've had a few too many in the local Cotswolds pubs; the panicked father now sprinting across the pavement and barging between three younger, fitter Japanese gangsters and his precious, one-and-only daughter. He gets it all wrong, raising his voice, burning into the street thug's gaze, all glowering eye contact. Ian leans toward the tattooed, ponytailed gangster. He points and yells a warning to back off his daughter. The thug bats his hand away to a yelp from Megan. She clutches her father's arm but he points again, his voice almost shrill, furious in his fear. His daughter pleads, hauls at him, looks to the young Westerners for help. The American takes a step back, relieved to be out of the line of fire. Nate reaches out to Ian but the blonde thug shoves him hard in the chest.

Then Megan remembers Jackie and turns to the convenience store entrance.

Jackie has gone from in front of the large, strip-lit window.

He is already behind her.

He bitch-slaps James hard across the face, hears the flat snap above the clamour of the street traffic. The young man's glasses go flying, bouncing off Ian Sparrow's arm and onto the pavement. Jackie steps in on his right foot and swivels his torso into a punch, driving into the American's side with his left fist. The young man arches his back, cries out and drops to his knees.

'What the fuck?' screams Megan.

The spikey-haired thugs stare open-mouthed.

The drunk, middle-aged Japanese squeals.

Nate drops to his haunches and puts a gentle hand on his friend's shoulder.

Ponytail looks hard at Jackie. His face is impassive. Reflected neon drenches his dark eyes blood red.

People walk by, a couple casting furtive glances as they pass, most diligently oblivious.

'It's done,' says Jackie. He points to the crumpled young American man and nods at the three thugs. 'He's sorry. I apologise, too. Forgive me for taking a liberty but I couldn't see you disrespected.'

Ponytail looks to Megan, the official interpreter by default. Her eyes linger on Jackie for a beat before she turns and speaks in a flat, hushed voice. Ponytail squares his shoulders and studies this new arrival.

'We'll be on our way,' says Jackie, 'before the police arrive. I called them just before I joined you.'

Megan translates. The thugs' eyes flicker at the mention of cops. After a few seconds, each tosses them a grunted parting insult before they amble away with the drunk middle-aged man .

Jackie drops to his haunches next to James and picks his glasses up from the spotless pavement. 'They aren't broken,' he says. 'You either. You'll have a blotch like a smacked arse on your cheek for a wee while and a decent bruise on your side but that's about it. If you piss blood, get it checked out but I avoided your kidneys.'

Megan says, 'You've done this before?' Her voice is a whisper.

'Occupational hazard.'

'Who are you?'

'He's the man who put an end to a dodgy situation,' says Ian. 'Sorry, love. If I hadn't rushed in your friend wouldn't be sitting down to pee tomorrow.'

True enough, thinks Jackie. The only person with the will to follow through had been ponytail. The other two thugs had been enjoying the moment, no intention of causing any real trouble. But when Ian blundered in, he'd forced their hand and ponytail might have decided a lesson was due. So Jackie had stolen his thunder, left the gangster standing with his dick in his hand but honour satisfied. The spikey-haired pair had wilted.

'Here.' Jackie hands the two young men a few Yen notes. 'Get something to eat, go home, take a couple of pain-killers and sleep it off.'

Nate tries to refuse the money but Jackie stuffs it in his pocket and the young Canadian is too frightened to resist. The American, James, has a hunted look in his eyes and touches his slapped face. His eyes are red as he takes shallow breaths. Jackie wonders what it feels like to be so shocked by such mild violence. He passed that milestone long ago. The pair have a short, nervous chat with Megan, say goodbye and hobble off toward the subway station on the corner.

Ian puts an arm around his daughter and hugs her close. 'You know them,' he says.

'I see them around. This is a big city but there aren't that many Westerners and they tend to stick to the same nightspots. They're English teachers, work for a chain of conversation schools. They can be a little weird but they're harmless.'

Jackie doesn't like the look she gives him.

He tries to shrug it off and get them moving. 'I didn't call the police, but another concerned citizen might've. Let's go and I'll buy us all a drink.'

They set off but Megan stays on the opposite side of her father from Jackie and walks in silence. The lights grow brighter as they approach the central crossing, the night sky a pale grey blanket above the blazing light show of the city. Vertical rectangles of signage stream down building fronts like neon rain. They pass a young couple outside a McDonald's. The man is standing, smoking, angry. The girl is perched on the low ledge of the window, crying softly.

#

Yuji is groomed, polite, and handsome. He introduces himself as Yuji Miyamoto, working at a large insurance company, graduate of Hokkaido University. As he offers an awkward hand at the entrance to the izakaya, Ian Sparrow attempts an embarrassed bow, leaving Megan to take a hand of each and introduce the men in her life.

A couple of young men tumble through a toilet door on the left of the lifts, erupting in high-pitched giggles. They freeze for a moment when they see Jackie in the corridor, then walk on. He hears his name and turns. Megan is introducing him to her boyfriend. Her gaze falters when she looks at Jackie. Yuji smiles, his mouth wide, teeth flashing, canines like inverted spikes bracketing snow-white incisors. His features are fine-cut, almost delicate. His jaw is a smooth, tapered ridge framing the generous grin and cut-glass cheekbones. Not quite the picture of rugged masculinity Ian Sparrow had expected would attract his daughter but the strength of his handshake belies his slim frame. Jackie flashes a smile of his own and they enter Bar Seico, a straight-up drinking and eating joint on the ninth floor of this huge concrete slab of a building. They pass a large *taiko* drum on display at the entrance and remove their shoes before being shown to a sunken table with a pit below in which to dangle their legs. All around, groups of people, from teenagers to middle-aged office workers, yell and bray. A white-grey gauze of cigarette smoke hangs in the thick air.

A beautiful young woman comes over to take drink orders while Yuji and Ian eye one another across the table. Megan sits opposite her father, Jackie across from a squirming Yuji. They fall on the small complimentary starter dishes, relieved to have some task to detract from the uncomfortable first step of father and boyfriend taking measure of one another. Yuji has good English and apologises profusely to Ian for his absence this afternoon, then asks Megan for forgiveness in Japanese. She waves it off but Yuji presses his contrition home to Sparrow senior once again, head bobbing, face a portrait of agony. Megan turns to her father with a 'give-me-a-moment' look before addressing her lover with growing irritation but, before she can stop him, Yuji bows to Jackie across the table.

'Jackie San, I am so sorry I did not meet you this afternoon. Please, accept my apology.'

'Of course, Yuji, it's not a problem. It gave Megan and her father a chance to catch-up before Ian met you.'

'You are very kind. I was rude not to contact Megan and explain. I tried to find time but my parents are very demanding.'

Jackie says, 'Well, sure, you're here now.'

The drinks arrive. Ian sends a sliver of pickled octopus skittering across the table with fumbling chopsticks and says to Yuji, 'Is everything okay?'

'Let's order some real food to have with the drinks, eh Dad?' says Megan.

Jackie knows she doesn't want her boyfriend to feel any more uncomfortable, pressured to reveal personal details in the jealously guarded privacy of Japanese society. If Yuji wants to tell them what held him up, he will, but Sparrow senior hasn't taken the class on social and cultural norms.

'Don't worry Yuji,' says Ian, 'we're fine. I just hope whatever happened this afternoon has all been resolved.'

There is nothing behind the remark but the young man's expression freezes. Conflicting thoughts and emotions flicker across his eyes but, after a pause, he sighs and his shoulders slump a fraction. Megan drops her gaze. In Ian asking if anything is wrong, however unwittingly, Yuji feels obliged to explain himself, to justify his absence this afternoon.

'My family is having a problem. I had to go to my parents' house. It's my older brother, Rei.'

Ian says, 'Is he in trouble?'

Megan all but smacks her palm on her forehead.

'I think, maybe, yes, he is. He still lives with my mother and father but last night he didn't come home.'

'How old is he?' says Ian.

'Let's have some chicken, and a bit of yakitori. That's skewered, grilled meat, great with a beer,' says Megan. A valiant attempt to change the subject, doomed to failure.

'Forty-one,' says Yuji. 'He always calls if he won't be home.'

'Good lad,' says Ian, eyebrows raised in surprise at a forty-one year-old checking in with his folks. 'Have you thought about calling the police?'

Megan, running out of options to salvage the evening, turns to Jackie with imploring eyes.

'I'm sure there are a hundred reasons why he didn't come home, Yuji,' he says. He hopes there is more conviction in his voice than his head. 'The police are very efficient in Japan, I hear. I'm sure they'll find him if he doesn't turn up tonight.'

'Not all police are so efficient,' says Yuji with a rueful smile. 'Some are very good people with very little sense – you say *common* sense? Like Rei, for instance. You see, my brother is a detective in the Hokkaido Prefectural Police.'

Chapter 7

The little asshole is crying, his nose streaming with whisky-soaked snot. He smears it on the wooden floor leaving snail trails on the polished boards.

'You'll clean that shit up,' says Reizo Himura.

Cue more bawling and frantic bowing, the drunken dickhead actually cracking his forehead on the floor. Himura gestures to a footsoldier, a ponytailed, tattooed scrapper nicknamed Fox because of his narrow, predatory eyes, to stop the floorshow. The soldier places a placatory hand on the drunk's shoulder, causing him to flinch.

'Have a drink. Calm down,' says Himura.

A low-level ranker hurries off to fetch a tumbler of cheap whiskey and Himura gestures for the middle-aged loser to follow him into the tatami sideroom. Here they are screened from the bustling public area by sliding wooden doors, and the small sideroom is screened off again from the private function room by a sliding shoji partition. The man looks over his shoulder at the collection of yakuza drinking and eating on cushions around a long, communal table, some of their faces already flush with drink. Two of the men who picked him up and squared off with the big foreigner in the street are lighting up cigarettes at the far end of the room. The third, Fox, saunters off to join them. The terrified middle-aged man steps through the open shoji into the confined snug and sits opposite Himura at a small table.

'How's business?' says Reizo.

'It's okay.' The lenses of the man's glasses have steamed up but he is too afraid to take them off and wipe them. 'The summer is past,' he says, 'tourist traffic dips before the winter ski season comes in. People are staying indoors more in the weekday evenings, although this leads to more domestic calls for the uniformed officers.'

'But not the cream of the detective division, eh Yoshida?'

A nervous laugh. 'Oh, I'm just a cog in the machine, Himura San. But you are right, as always. We have more important things to do.'

Like getting a rub down in a cheap soapland and knocking back free booze because you're a leech-cop, thinks Himura. He says, 'I'm sure we all feel safer knowing men like you are on the job.'

The whiskey arrives. Gangster and cop talk shop for a couple of minutes about the principled young sergeant in the small police station in Susukino who's been causing some friction with the local touts drumming up business for the sex clubs on Lilac Street; about the funeral of an old-time gangster, long retired; and they discuss the donation the Kanto Daichi-kai had made to the Prefectural Government's new development project last month.

'And your son, Yoshida, how is he?'

'Fine, Himura San. Doing well. Thanks to you.'

'The fees for a good private education don't get any cheaper, eh? Lucky you can supplement your police wage with a little paid information, here and there. And lucky you don't spend any of that extra income in the soaplands you're so fond of. Sex or drink can be pretty cheap in Susukino if you know where to look, but put them together? Fuck!'

Yoshida nods his head and puts the tumbler to his lips.

'And if your wife found out – shit!' says Himura.

The nodding slows, the whiskey gone, the police detective's eyes on the table.

'Did you ever try our Invisible Man club, Yoshida?'

'Not really my thing, Himura San.'

'It seems it wasn't Rei Miyamoto's thing either. He had his throat cut last night enjoying the view in the club.'

Yoshida's eyes flicker then settle somewhere on Himura's neck. 'Do the police know?'

Himura ignores the irony. 'I thought you could tell me.'

'Nothing. I worked a shift today and no homicides came through for investigation. No missing persons, either.'

'Does the name mean anything to you? Rei Miyamoto?'

Yoshida says, 'Now you sound like a policeman.'

The joke is met with silence. Yoshida drops his gaze to the table and says, 'I'm sorry. Please, forgive me.'

'Miyamoto was a cop. He had a warrant card with the ID in his wallet and a working relationship with my man, Goro Inaba. You,' Himura pours himself a whiskey, ignoring Yoshida, a clear insult, 'still haven't arrested that little shit who's been pushing his own dope outside our place on West 6 for a month. Yet you can afford to get drunk and hassle foreigners on the street, eh? And snivelling won't help you.' He downs the whiskey and slams the glass on the table.

'I'd like to know where Miyamoto was stationed, and the moment he's missed.'

Yoshida bows, his head centimetres from the table top, and says, 'Yes, of course. Sir.'

'Best you get home,' says Reizo Himura. 'Look in on that son of yours and grovel to that harridan you're married to.' He calls out and a stringy young thug slides the shoji open with a hungry smile. As Masa Yoshida leaves, the detective notices the young hood has tobacco-yellowed teeth bar one made of gold with a diamond embedded in its centre.

#

Goro Inaba sees them as he passes Bar Seico on his way to a hole-in-the-wall stand-up noodle bar nestled in the corner of the ninth floor. The dead cop's brother with three foreigners, a girl, an older man and a big-boned fucker, slipping their shoes off just inside the entrance. He's seen the brother before in photographs on the dead cop's phone and a couple of times from afar as he drifted off from meets, the younger sibling approaching his older brother after

Inaba had walked off. Would the kid brother recognise Inaba? Had he caught sight of him wandering through the crowds in the suburban parks they always used for clandestine appointments?

He wolfed the noodles and drank too much tea so he is busting for a piss before he even makes it to the elevators from the noodle bar. When he is at one of the two grime-encrusted urinals in the toilets the big foreigner walks in and stands next to him, unzipping his jeans. Inaba and the foreigner piss side-by-side, staring at a poster for a French maid cafe above the urinal like inmates at a routine prison inspection told to face the wall. Inaba keeps his head down but looks to the left, studying what he can of the foreigner out of the corner of his eye. The man is in a black t-shirt now, shedding layers in the indoor heating, and looks in good shape. Broad shoulders like some of the rugby players Inaba has seen at the university matches he watches on occasion. A flat stomach and powerful arms. He notes a twisted knot of scar tissue on the foreigner's left forearm. Average height but the man has a presence that makes him seem larger, like he fills the space around him.

Inaba finishes first, stepping back and zipping his jeans, eyeing the man from behind. The foreigner's hair is short, not a buzz cut but similar to some of the bitch-cops on the riot squad. A small nick on the pale skin near the shoulder appears for a second as the neck of the t-shirt pulls tight, the man zipping up. Inaba has seen enough knife scars to know the tip of one when he sees it. The man turns as Goro Inaba rinses his hands under the cold tap and the yakuza sees eyes the colour of roasted barley tea and a broken nose, a fraction off-kilter. The mouth is wide – almost generous – but set, as though containing some terrible secret, complimenting the strong features and cheekbones. A hard face, thinks Inaba, but not cruel. Then the man offers a smile and the face takes on a guileless charm. Inaba replies with a small grin and nods, muttering a greeting, before pushing through the door of the toilets into the corridor and striding to the exit at the far end. He takes the stairs rather than wait for the elevator and risk seeing the foreigner again when the

Westerner leaves the toilet. No point in giving the big fucker a second look.

Pure luck, he thinks, running across the gaijin like this.

After walking down a couple of floors he calls the lift and exits onto South 4 Street, the four-lane road choked with traffic. Crossing over, he takes several turns before arriving at the small door to a boisterous izakaya, a place for simple food and cheap drink, next to a towering multi-storey carpark. Weaving through tables thronged with animated groups of drinkers, he walks down a narrow corridor next to the kitchens at the rear and slides open a wooden door.

'Inaba San!'

The chorus is raspy, inebriated. Most of the men have been at the beer, whisky and sake for over an hour and the booze has worked its magic. The men loll around a long table. He sees the usual collection of street trash. Fox is there, knocking back beer and telling some story to a couple of shaven-headed lapdogs. To the right, in the corner, the shoji screened cubbyhole is open and Goro Inaba can see Reizo Himura's right hand resting on the low table nursing a cigarette, the left propped against a half empty bottle of scotch.

He enters the snug and Himura grunts the usual rote greetings while Inaba bows and settles himself opposite his boss.

'You'll be sad to hear you missed Yoshida,' says Himura.

'Sleazy bastard. Fucking detective,' says Inaba. 'The only thing that bent bitch can detect is when his next bung is coming. What did he have to say?'

Himura takes a long drag on his smoke. 'Fuck all. The asshole claims there hasn't been any notice in the last twenty-four hours on our dead voyeur blue-arsed little bitch-cop.'

Inaba nods and calls one of the men outside.

'You knew the dearly departed,' says Himura, 'why do you think his colleagues in central cop-shop wouldn't be ringing alarm bells at his disappearance as we speak?'

'I have no idea, boss. Miyamoto was dirty, like Yoshida. He approached me, had some big gambling debts and wanted to pick up some tax-free income through us. As we know, he was a twisted little fucker too, got off on some weird sex shit and saw us as a way to fulfil his fantasies through our clubs without paying. I think the Invisible Man stuff was just the beginning for him. Maybe he's gone AWOL before on a drunken binge. I don't think he was exactly reliable.'

The *weird sex shit* of the Invisible Man Club had been Goro Inaba's idea. He'd heard stories from a couple of hookers he was banging of what their clients paid good money for – who could have known there were so many repressed little would-be voyeurs out there in corporate Japanland? The gang set up side attractions to capture more of the fetish crowd: ten thousand yen to put your head on a fully clothed young woman's lap and have your ears cleaned, just like mummy used to do; another ten grand to have your hair brushed and teeth cleaned.

Himura set up Fujiko as the main attraction at the Invisible Man. She pulled the punters in, more beautiful and classy than the average Susukino girl, and Reizo slept well knowing his men were keeping an eye on his woman and no one laid a sweaty hand on her.

He glances at the foot soldier at the door then nods at Inaba. Goro says, 'A beer and a shot of vodka.'

'But we don't run any contact brothels. Our stuff is all no-touching fetish shit,' says the oyabun.

'He didn't know that. I hadn't told him: wanted to get him well and truly into us for a lot of money first, so he couldn't back out. That's why I invited him to the club. I was planning to get him comfortable, then take a few infrared shots of him in the dark with his dick out.'

'And, of course, you'd have run all this by me first.'

'Of course, boss.'

'How did you meet him?'

'At a mah-jong game up by the central train station. He approached me, said he knew me from police files. Had a proposition, wanted to work with me.'

'Work with you. Yeah.'

The foot-soldier returns with Inaba's drinks, bows and slinks back to the drunken melee at the long table. Goro waits out the silence from his boss. After thirty seconds, he says, 'I have an idea who might have killed him.'

Reizo Himura gives him a look like an amused father awaiting an excuse for some mischief from his errant son. 'Go on.'

'There's a guy at the mah-jong games, some asshole works in finance. He's a young guy, fit, plays rugby with an amateur team. I've seen him in a couple of local games with the university sides. He could take our dead cop any day of the week, especially if the useless prick had a couple of drinks.'

'*Your* dead cop, Inaba.'

'Sorry, boss.' A quick bow. 'So, he hated Miyamoto. They played at the same table a couple of times, always pissed each other off. The finance guy accused our – sorry, my – police lackey of cheating. When they'd had a couple of drinks, they squared off. The usual pushing and shoving with no intention of throwing a punch. But then, finance guy pulls some shit with a girlfriend, slaps her around a little.'

'How come?'

'Not sure. Maybe his gambling, maybe drinking, whoring. Maybe she decided to hoover while the baseball was on TV. Anyway, she's one of the few who actually calls the cops and the uniformed ass-holes turn up and take a statement. They nod, smile, make the right noises and say their hands are tied because she can't prove he beat her. She shows them a bruise just below her throat and a cut on her head. They say it could have been an accident, a fall, and trundle back to Central Ward cop-shop.'

'Fucking typical,' growls Himura.

'So finance-guy goes crazy and puts her in hospital. Now the cops lift him. At Central cop-shop, who should he bump into but my bent cop. Miyamoto hates him but he's a guy, and he's been tempted to lay one on his lady more than once, too. And he sees an opportunity to get this finance prick in his pocket.'

Himura says, 'Assholes, both of them.'

'Oh yeah,' says Inaba. 'So he puts in a word, testifies to the good character of finance guy and gets him off with a warning. Now finance guy is really stewing because he's got an obligation to my dead cop. Gets drunk and starts gabbing about how dangerous police work is becoming, how many psychos are out there, how bitch-cop should watch his back, Sapporo isn't as safe as it used to be.'

'Bullshit.'

'Exactly. Then I'm at the mah-jong place one night and the finance dickhead is showing off a knife. Says he carries it for protection, especially when he goes to Susukino. The next night, my tame cop tells me the finance guy has been following him.'

Himura looks long and hard at the bottle of whiskey, as though trying to read some elusory truth in the amber liquid. Then he pours a measure for himself.

'Fujiko is in terrible shape. I've barely spoken to her, they've got her so doped up. But she mentioned this psycho asshole tapped the glass of the booth with something when he killed your cop. A pin-badge.'

'A company pin-badge? You think this psycho works for Mitsubishi or something?'

'She was a bit far to see it clearly, and terrified. But when you're terrified, you can see things with amazing clarity. Like that time in Asahikawa.'

Inaba snorts at the memory. There were a lot less open brawls like that these days.

Himura says, 'She thinks it was grey with some kind of white symbol. Mean anything to you?'

Inaba studies his glass as though it holds the secret of eternal life. He says, 'No. Do you have it? I could take a look.'

'It's gone. The men searched the club but couldn't find it so the maniac must have taken it with him.'

Inaba takes a drink.

'Okay,' says Himura, 'let's see where this mah-jong guy leads.'

'You want me to pick him up, bring him to you?'

'I want you to beat the shit out of the guy and ask him the right questions. Do some real damage. If he didn't kill your bitch-cop, he deserves to suffer for beating the woman anyway.'

Inaba nods and mutters the expected pledge of obedience. He drains his vodka and Himura splashes a measure of scotch in the empty glass without asking. Inaba thanks him and takes a sip, then says, 'So Fujiko San is pretty shaken up?'

'Yeah, still sleeping off the drugs the doctors gave her. I shouldn't have been in Hakodate. I shouldn't have been so far away.'

'You weren't to know, boss. How could any of us have known?'

'If I wanted to fuck around, there are plenty of women in Sapporo. Me going all the way to Hakodate for a piece of ass. I must be getting senile.'

'None of us could've dreamed someone would do this on our property, boss.'

'I'm the oyabun of this organisation. I should've been there.' Himura grinds out his cigarette and snatches at his tumbler of whiskey. He fixes Inaba with a stare, eyes black and hard as lacquer, his back ramrod straight, and says, 'And so should you.'

#

I'm making progress, thinks Jackie.

Since returning from the toilet he has noticed Megan softening, reappraising him as he listens to Yuji. Jackie reassures when he can, hits his marks in the old routine as though all those years haven't passed since he was last providing victim support as a police officer. Belfast, Hong Kong, it didn't matter. The principle was the same. In a missing person's case, relatives were confused, frightened, angry. They wanted answers but didn't expect them. Not yet. No, people wanted someone to listen, someone they thought would care, someone who'd seen bad things before and come through the other side.

And Jackie has seen plenty.

He is attentive, pouring beer for Yuji when the young man drains his glass. There may not be a crime and it's far too early to classify Rei Miyamoto as a missing person but Jackie is the epitome of the caring cop, a strong, sensitive, calming presence with a clear head and no-nonsense attitude. With time, the young man opens up, offering small details of his life, his interests. He smiles shyly, and says, 'Rei didn't understand me, Jackie San. There are too many years between us. And he was – is – a Christian, like you. You know, Hokkaido has a higher percentage of Christians than any other part of Japan?'

'I don't go to church.'

'Rei does. He reads the bible. Prays.' Yuji laughs, a flat bark, almost robotic. 'We are a religious family.'

Jackie lets him talk, the beer doing its work.

The young man says, 'I lived in Kamakura for a time. It is a small town, about sixty kilometres from Tokyo.'

'I know it,' says Jackie. 'I've been there.'

A memory.

Jackie had been dispatched by the Royal Hong Kong Police, with another officer and a Japanese interpreter, to liaise with Tokyo police on a drug smuggling operation, Triads and a Tokyo syndicate dealing in amphetamines. He remembers frustration, obfuscation, polite refusal, and a day trip with a polite, straining interpreter to Kamakura. The town had been beautiful, shrines and temples perched on hillsides, small hump-backed bridges, a giant stone Buddha statue. The Westerner's Japan come to life.

Yuji says, 'I studied there. Shinto. I dreamed of being a priest, of living in Kamakura or Kyoto in a shrine. A life of peace.'

'Sounds ideal.'

'Just a dream. It was not for me. While I was there, a couple of tourists were attacked. I remember the shock in the town. The media were everywhere. Police. We Japanese had believed our country was safe, an example to the rest of the world. I believed

Shinto was a driving force behind this harmony. It teaches reverence for life and appreciation of nature but my dream was broken. I felt great shame that people had suffered such violence in one of our most sacred places. I was disillusioned. What was the point in living in a shrine, dancing kagura and selling amulets when violence occurred just outside the gates? So, I left my training and came back to Hokkaido to study in university.'

'I wish some of the folk where I come from had your conscience,' says Jackie. 'What did you study?'

'Medicine.'

'And you work in an insurance company?'

'In Japan, a degree is a degree. It doesn't always matter in what your qualification is.'

To lighten the mood Jackie tells a couple of missing persons stories with happy endings from his days on the job and sees Megan look at him like a schoolkid who's just discovered their teacher is a human being. Jackie as good cop.

Just as well she'll never see the other side of the equation, he thinks. The Jackie who ended the careers of paramilitaries, dealers, gangsters, permanently. It doesn't matter that they deserved it, that they'd have killed him, that they destroyed lives. They'd all ended badly; they all live on in his skull.

I'm on holiday, he thinks.

I'm on fucking holiday.

He glances at his watch – lunchtime back home – and says, 'Yuji, it was a pleasure to meet you. I think I'll head back to the hotel but, if there's anything I can do to help, just ask.' Jetlag is threatening an appearance and besides, it's a time for family and Jackie needs the air. Ian insists on paying Jackie's part of the bill and they arrange to meet in the hotel lobby tomorrow morning. He says a hurried goodnight to Megan.

Chapter 8

Shintaro Ishikawa sips at his sake. These hayseeds can get that right, at least, he thinks. Junmai Daiginjō-shu brand, a special brand which uses rice polished down to less than fifty percent of its original size before it is brewed, and served at room temperature, as requested. Reizo Himura has joined him in a drink but the cocky little shit, Inaba, left shortly after Ishikawa arrived at the drinking spot.

Reizo Himura offers a polite bow at a thirty-degree angle, just enough to display the appropriate regard for the man with which he hopes to do business. Shintaro Ishikawa reciprocates, edging a fraction lower than Himura but stopping well short of the forty-five degrees or more he would have bowed for his own superiors in Tokyo and Kobe. For a time they talk shop, meaningless chat.

Ten minutes later, Shintaro Ishikawa looks through the open shoji partition and sees Inaba check his mobile before approaching his boss. Himura and Inaba mutter but Ishikawa only hears snatches – '...talked about...mah-jong...information.' Then Inaba hurries from the room.

Now Ishikawa, impatient, says, 'Have you made progress in identifying who is responsible for last night's incident, Himura San?'

Himura nods. 'Inaba has identified a possible culprit. You can assure your associates in Tokyo and Kobe that we will deal with the matter.'

'A rival? Someone from another Sapporo organisation?'

'Something much more prosaic. A petty rivalry between deadbeat gamblers.'

'Petty enough to kill a cop? Perhaps Hokkaido really is the Wild West.'

Reizo Himura's mouth contorts in a smile his eyes can't muster.

Bastard, he thinks. Typical patronising Tokyo bullshit. Hokkaido had only been colonised proper in the latter half of the nineteenth century. The people here were pioneers, settling the land and conquering the indigenous Ainu people in the process. Some of the pioneers had seen the Ainu as a proud people with a rich, beautiful culture and smelled a smart business opportunity for trade. Many others had viewed the indigenous people as savages to be tamed, if not destroyed. Some of those in the south considered the Japanese in Hokkaido just as uncultured, lacking in civilised manners and propriety.

'A land of opportunity,' says Himura. 'As a trusted counsellor of your organisation, I appreciate that you have been advising your superiors of the expansion here on our island. The prospects in construction; developments with our near neighbours in Russia; the lax political landscape, fertile in the deepest-rooted corruption. Surely the trivial demise of one dirty cop isn't enough to preclude the largest syndicate in Japan reaping the benefits we can offer here in Sapporo.'

'We appreciate your recognising the power, influence and professionalism of our organisation, Himura San. Indeed, within comparable businesses here in Sapporo, and the wider island, yours is the syndicate in which we see the greatest potential. The Kanto Daichi-kai has a capacity for versatility in the face of unpredictable circumstance. Your 'loose' structure and the relative autonomy enjoyed by your lieutenants certainly bestows your syndicate with a certain flexibility.'

Ishikawa enjoys a brief flicker of pleasure at the fleeting tension in Himura's jaw, the twitch of muscle at the adjective, 'loose'. Fucking sloppy, you knuckle-dragging caveman, he thinks.

'However,' says the Yamaguchi counsellor, 'regretfully, this versatility may stand in the way of a certain compliance our syndicate may require. You wish to work with us but we are a vast enterprise. We have standards of practice with which we require all of the families within our broader organisation to adhere.'

Like fucking McDonald's, thinks Himura. 'Of course,' he says, topping up Ishikawa's sake cup.

Shinatro Ishikawa continues, 'Therefore, it might be expedient to keep me abreast of all developments in this inquest into last night's debacle.'

Swallow that, cocksucker, Ishikawa thinks. There is a danger he could overplay his hand but the undeniable fact is, Reizo Himura's gang fucked up. The oyabun has been shamed by his lieutenants' ineptitude, Himura himself dropped the ball by banging some slut in a city hundreds of kilometres away, and they're groping in the dark when it comes to a culprit for the cop's murder. And Fujiko Maki is traumatised. Traumatised and beautiful and, just maybe, ripe for the picking.

'I will take your wise counsel under advisement, Ishikawa San,' says Himura. He realises he is gritting his teeth. Sanctimonious asshole, he thinks. 'I recognise the great investment your organisation is considering in a partnership with the Kanto Daichi-kai. As you are their subordinate on the ground, I will be sure to communicate with your masters through you, should I have any need to inform them of developments.'

Ishikawa bows, his eyes on the table, his mind on murder – *insolent motherfucker! Subordinate? Masters? I'll fucking master you, you fucker!*

But the Yamaguchi consiglieri swallows it. He'll let it churn in his gut until the day he slices this arrogant shithead's eyelids off. Then he will fuck his woman. Himura is nothing. He, Shintaro Ishikawa, is a white snake, a tiger, a dragon. He is fucking invincible.

'And how is Maki San?' he says. He sits ramrod straight, his eyes smooth black pebbles in the soft light of the small cubbyhole. 'It would be an honour and pleasure to visit Fujiko at this time of distress and offer her what meagre comfort I may.' He can smell the stale reek of Himura's breath as it quickens at Sintaro Ishikawa using his woman's first name. Ishikawa summons a tight smile and says, 'With your permission, of course.'

Susukino district is Oz, Wonderland and Neverland in pulsing technicolour. Jackie loves it.

It isn't the chaos of Wan Chai or Kowloon, or the humid bustle of Bangkok or Kuala Lumpur. There are no cackling, laughing, carousing Cantonese or Thai or Vietnamese crowds sitting on cheap chairs wolfing street food which would put Mayfair fine dining to shame.

But Susukino after dark is a multi-coloured hall of mirrors, the lights like a brilliant tiling above the traffic-clogged streets. Everyone on the streets seems to have a destination, a focus.

Jackie wanders past a girl in a fur coat hurrying to a parked Mercedes. Another girl in hot pants and stilettos hurries by. She has a bruise in a perfect circle on her left knee. A police car, siren blaring, crawls along the wide street, caught in traffic, at no more than ten miles an hour. The driver stops at a red light and inches across the small intersection, then continues at a sedate pace toward whatever emergency awaits.

Jackie turns into a smaller street to discover the mouth of a magical undersea cave, coral and rock in psychedelic shades of blue and green. A dimly lit sign declares prices for a *Rest* of three hours or an overnight *Stay*. One of the love hotels ranged across the city. A harried salaryman strides past. Another turn and the streets narrow and darken. Thick bunches of telephone and electrical wires criss-cross overhead, connected to buildings or lamp-posts, like giant unfinished spider webs. Another man emerges from a door in a smart three-piece and the cloying scent of strong soap thickens the night air. A soapland brothel where a patron pays the house for a bath with a naked girl, then tips for any extra services provided.

Jackie's mind wanders with his whimsical stroll through the narrow backstreets. They say life will grind the sharp edges and mellow the angry young man but Jackie wonders if he hasn't gained those sharp edges as he's gotten older. Would he have handled the situation in front of the convenience store in the same way a few years ago? Would he have been so quick to resort to violence?

The streets and alleys are on a grid but he is getting lost: the city is a dream-maze. Just as well he stuck to tea. He crosses another small backstreet and passes an empty lot, converted into a small car park.

The street is quiet, although he can hear the muted blather of from bright lights just a few blocks away. A couple of black cars are parked in the empty lot and a clutch of cables and pipes snake up a building to his left housing the small door to a quiet grill house, steam clouding the window next to a red hanging lantern. The smell of stale cooking oil clogs the street.

He hears an angry grunt behind and turns to find the two spikey-haired goons flanking their ponytailed comrade, the thugs he had confronted in front of the convenience store. They smile below a mirror set on a post above the car park fence. It distorts them, giving them bulbous insect heads on reed-thin bodies.

Through the Looking Glass, thinks Jackie. He points to the blonde goon on his left and says, 'You must be Tweedledee,' – then to the silver-haired thug on the right – 'and Tweedledum.' Their smiles falter but ponytail is grinning.

Jackie says, 'You'll be the Cheshire Cat.'

The other two look to ponytail and he growls a dramatic taunt, something about gaijin, rolling the words around his tobacco stained teeth before spewing them into the night.

Ponytail switches to English with a heavy accent. 'I am Fox. We are yakuza.'

'Congratulations.'

'This is our street. You stand on our street, you pay money.'

'How much?'

'One hundred and fifty thousand yen.'

A thousand quid. Jackie says, 'I was wrong, you're the Mad-fucking-Hatter.' He takes a step forward to anxious mutters from the spikey-haired thugs – but Fox isn't moving an inch.

'I'm on holiday,' says Jackie. 'My friends are around the corner.'

'Not understand your English,' says ponytail with relish. He puts his right hand in his jacket pocket and his companions' balls grow back.

Could be a knife. Guns aren't scarce in Japanese criminal circles but the local talent don't walk around of an evening with an automatic in their Armani jeans. Firearms are reserved for special occasions and this is just a regular Friday night kicking for ponytail, with the added thrill of doling it out to a Westerner. Jackie needs to retake the initiative and try to face them down. He steps forward, his distorted reflection joining that of the three thugs in the car park mirror.

I was too busy gawking at the 18-rated Magic Kingdom around every corner, thinks Jackie. Too blitzed with jetlag. He had disrespected the local talent by playing the strong arm in front of the convenience store. One of them must have followed him to Bar Seico, then through the streets, calling in reinforcements on his mobile. Jackie didn't exactly blend in.

I'm on fucking holiday.

He says, 'How's the salaryman?'

Fox says, 'Salaryman?'

Jackie makes spectacles with his fingers. He enjoys Tweedledee's flinch.

'Ah,' says Fox. 'He owe us, like you.' The last word is in Japanese but Jackie brushed up on his stock of phrases before flying out. Though he never learned the lingo for put-that-fucking-blade-away, which would have been handy as Fox produces a small tactical folding knife and opens the honed steel from the handle.

Now we're racing through the gears, thinks Jackie. He calls ponytail's bluff and steps within a couple of feet of the three thugs. Tweedledum shifts from foot to foot, half-scared, half wanting to go and get it over. Tweedledee is a statue. His eyes still flit around the street. He could be high but the knot of fear on his forehead says he is sober enough to dread what is coming. Fox is the problem, the true believer.

The knife hovers just over the thug's chest, held side on for Jackie to get a good look at the blade. No glint in the modest light of this backstreet, just a blunt finality in the slim cutting edge.

Jackie bellows, 'What the fuck is that? Are you gonna use it or just stand there like the tall streak of cat piss you are! Fuck you!'

He's trying to bludgeon them with English. The angry foreigner, unpredictable, berserk. A long shot and it almost works. Tweedledum steps back. Tweedledee blanches. Even Fox blinks, the sneer bitch-slapped from his face for an instant.

An instant.

Then he smiles again, yellowed teeth the colour of rotting fruit in the sodium streetlight, and holds the knife out from his body, pointing the tip at Jackie. Silver-haired Tweedledum is rocking back and forth like a runner under starter's orders. Blonde Tweedledee is glancing about the scene madly. His eyes freeze. They bore into that blind spot to Jackie's rear. Tweedledee's eyebrows rise a fraction. Jackie glances at the mirror perched above the car park fence. Another twisted shadow joins the four of them just behind Jackie's back, bringing something to bear on his head, fast. Jackie takes the bottle on the right side of his skull, his head going down as his hands spring up in instinctive protection. He's lucky. The bottle doesn't break with the glancing blow and he twists left away from the strike as he bends, sees the knife flash past his face as he folds. Instinct kicks in, hurling adrenaline to the fore. Jackie's thrown his left jab, still bent low, right hand in classic boxer's guard, at Fox's groin before conscious thought catches up. He barely registered the bottle on his head but he feels his knuckles drive into Fox, missing their target but finding tight-packed midriff, driving the air from the yakuza's lungs and the knife from his hand. The blade sails into the dark.

Jackie knows he's screwed, knows he's one man against at least four, but he throws his head up and back, connecting with bone and cartilage, a sharp pain stabbing his skull where he took the bottle to the head. He hears a muffled cry behind as he swipes at Fox in front, the thug bowed like a crooked old man, and catches him on the right temple. At close quarters he can't muster much power behind the punch but it keeps the pressure on. A girl screams somewhere and Jackie wonders madly if she's wearing hot pants. He takes a knee to the ribs, feels a short burst of pain on impact but sees another kick coming and grabs the foot, sending the figure to the asphalt with a flat smack. Jackie roars, seizing a leg around the knee with his arm and throwing a rabbit punch with his left fist into the groin. He sees a spikey blonde head flash past his face as the man crumples, then launches a vicious kick at Tweedledee's scalp, feels his boot connect and the hard dome of skull snap back on the thug's neck.

His breaths come in harsh, rapid gasps and he's sweating despite the fresh night air. Fox is shrieking, coming at him as someone behind knees Jackie in the ribs again. He wheezes with the blow and the sharp pain of bone on bone. He lands a decent right above Fox's heart, feeling muscle soak up the impact. The ponytailed thug grunts, a hoarse cough, his pill-box eyes widening for a second.

It's Tweedledum who makes the difference. The silver-haired yakuza grabs a crate of empty beer bottles from outside the grill house and flings it at Jackie, forcing him to duck. The crate misses, glass clattering and smashing on the street, but someone's boot connects, the toe-cap smashing flush into Jackie's ear, wrenching his head to the left. The world goes dull and liquid. He folds, stumbles, arrests his fall on impulse with his left hand, the ground cold and harsh on his palm. He realises it's over before they set on him, all knees and elbows until he goes down under the barrage. The blows build to a crescendo, echoing in his head as his ears begin ringing from a boot to his head. The blows begin to blend into one constant, pummelling attack.

Then it stops.

He curls up further, ready for a renewed assault. A shoe settles on his shoulder and shoves him over and onto his back. Then it drives into his cheek, grinding chips of asphalt across his face. His limbs feel huge and heavy. The yakuza stand over him, snarling insults. Tweedledee has a gash across his cheek. Tweedledum spits, a wad landing on Jackie's hair, and he and Fox laugh. The fourth man, the man who got the back of Jackie's head in the face, appears from stage right. His hair is slicked back, a broad smear of blood across his mouth like a stroke of crimson calligraphy, his lips already swollen. He hands a small, slim object to Fox.

The knife.

Fox crouches next to Jackie.

'Now you go to hospital.'

The words are lost on Jackie. His head is throbbing, a timpani beating in his brain to accompany the ringing in his ears. The world softens around the edges of his vision.

'Maybe, you go to grave, neh?' says Fox.

Jackie closes his eyes. No point in watching the blade coming.

The woman's screaming is fading. Maybe it was in his head. He smells the dust on the asphalt and the stink of cooking oil again, then darkness swallows him and he's gone.

Chapter 9

The body was relatively fresh. The cold saw to that. The uniforms hauled it from the freezing current, stumbling in the shallows.

Now the sergeant checks his watch: almost two in the morning. The young couple huddle in the small police station on the western side of the Toyohira Bridge. They are on their fifth cup of tea and the boy still hasn't stopped shaking. His girlfriend has turned to tobacco to steady her nerves, walking to the door and lighting up every twenty minutes. Their ID has her at twenty-two, the boy at twenty-four. The sergeant wouldn't place them over eighteen, most likely in their last year of high school. No doubt all will be revealed when the parents turn up.

A couple of hours ago, the kids had stumbled down the incline next to the road and across the wide, grassy western bank of the Toyohira River. Out walking, they said, but the boy's zip was still open when they burst through the door of the small neighbourhood police station, little more than a glorified police box, perched next to the bridge.

Where are their parents, thinks the sergeant? He called them soon after the kids turned up.

The crime scene team will be down there for some time yet but the forensics aren't going to yield much if the body's been in the water. The wounds will have been sluiced with impurities, the skin scoured by the freezing current.

The kids had run into the police station and babbled of how they had stopped their riverbank stroll for a moment, hugging to keep warm in the cool autumn night. The sergeant could imagine them, love's young dream, locked together in the deep shadows next to the water. The riverbank is wide enough to accommodate cycling

73

paths, tennis courts and children's playgrounds. Tall reeds stand at the water's edge. To the left and right, stacked banks of lights on apartment buildings and neon signage scattered across the bar-graph skyline.

The girl said the couple heard the splashing of someone stumbling in the shallows. She had almost yelped but something inside her closed tight, constricting her throat. The boy pulled at her hand, hurting her, but she could not move. A form was emerging from the tall reeds, almost human. Something on the bridge above cast a weak light for a moment and the kids saw the aberration. It had a furious, glaring face set in a profane scowl. Each eye was a huge, black abyss in deep shadow flanking an obscene nose, long and phallic. A devil, a goblin. Something glinted at its side. Then the light had passed and the girl had snapped, bolting for the incline up to the road, outrunning her boyfriend, almost colliding with traffic as she had sprinted across the lanes. She had still been screaming when she and the boy burst through the doors of the station less than a minute later.

The sergeant had called in a couple of uniforms from the Susukino station and they had gone to the spot where the mysterious prowler had emerged from the reeds. There, they found the corpse. It was floating in the shallows, an ankle entangled in some river grass like a boat moored to the bank. The area was flooded with police, lights set up with crime scene crews in their bodysuits, a helicopter hovering overhead. Uniforms began sweeping the area, detectives began canvassing and a couple interviewed the kids, a female uniform on hand. Both the teenagers had given the same succinct description of the figure they had seen emerge from the reeds.

The corpse was in a bad state according to one of the crime scene boys who had ducked into the station for a piss. A frenzied attack, the head all but severed from the trunk. A mass of lacerations, on the face as well as torso. The work of a monster he had said, out of earshot of the kids.

The sergeant is not a superstitious man by nature. He clicks his tongue and shakes his head even now as he fills out another of the countless duplicate forms required in the labyrinthine bureaucracy of the Japanese civil service. But he can taste the fear of that young couple in the dark, see the pale light cast over the monster emerging from the morass of the black river. The red-faced demon of myth and legend, haunting dreams and persecuting the living. Feared by some, revered by others. The Tengu.

#

Fujiko Maki lays a slim hand on the gangster's shoulder, long fingers brushing the man's thick neck. 'I'm fine, Saburo. I just needed some air and a coffee. Now I'm home, safe and sound, and Reizo need never know.'

Saburo flinches and she feels a pang of guilt. The physical contact does more than embarrass the bodyguard: it frightens him. Reizo is protective of his girl and even an innocent hand on the shoulder could spark his rage, were he to see, or hear, of it. To make contact with the bare skin on the neck, one of the more intimate areas of the body, is unthinkable. But it will go some way to ensuring the man's silence.

'You didn't drink, did you Fujiko Chan? The doctors said you shouldn't, with your medication.'

She smiles, her lips wide and a touch provocative. 'Would you like to smell my breath?' she says, stepping closer. She is enjoying herself, using her beauty, her sensuality. Perhaps I'm still tipsy from the sex, she ponders.

The bodyguard, a young hardcase, steps back. His adam's apple bobs and she hears him swallow, like a character in a funny anime.

'That's okay, Fujiko Chan. I'll be in the kitchen again if you need me. But please, don't leave again.'

'And we don't need to tell Reizo about my little moonlight flit?'

His brow creases. She got back to the apartment some time ago and he is still fretting. The yakuza is torn between fealty to his boss

75

and protecting Fujiko from Reizo Himura's fury, should Himura discover she had disappeared for a few hours.

Fujiko had woken at dusk and made tea. Saburo had been sitting in the kitchen reading a comic and explained that Reizo had ordered him to stay with her for the night. He was only to leave the kitchen to visit the toilet or in the unlikely event that an intruder appeared. Fujiko's personal space – the living room, bedroom, bathing room – were not be breached without Reizo in attendance. She had made him a cup of tea, chatted briefly and gone to the living room to watch television.

The drugs they had given her for the shock of last night had calmed her but she felt brittle, waves of emotion rising in her chest, then washing away like the tide leaving her hollow. Fujiko craved human contact and Reizo's obsessional protection, cosseting yet rarely tactile, didn't help. She took her mobile and texted a number buried deep in the various files and memos in the phone. Fujiko had been using online chatrooms for a year and a half to meet men in the virtual world then arrange clandestine rendezvous. She surveilled the men from a distance and, if they interested her, approached. The sex was enthusiastic, illicit, thrilling and devoid of emotional attachment. She never told the men her real name or her circumstances. The act fulfilled a physical need and for a time made her feel as beautiful and desired as many of the men in the claustrophobic world of the yakuza told her she was.

Tonight she had contacted a shy young executive with a company exploring the possibility of drilling in the northern islands and arranged to meet him at one of the more modest love hotels next to the Toyohira River. Then she had gone to the kitchen and told Saburo that she'd go to bed and sleep off the lingering trauma of the night before. She had made him another cup of tea and brought a laptop for him to play with, then told him to help himself to any food in the cupboards. Fujiko had dressed in the bedroom in a simple gingham skirt, grey sweater and jacket, and waited.

The first cup of tea she had made for Saburo had been straight green tea; the second had contained an added diuretic Fujiko had grabbed from a cupboard. After he drank the second cup, Fujiko sketched the bodyguard's face to while away the time until the diuretic took effect. She was talented but not the artistic genius that Reizo declared. When she heard the toilet door close, she left and locked the bedroom, then padded to the apartment entrance in her stocking feet, taking a pair of heels from the shoe rack. She eased the front door open and slipped into the corridor outside. Fujiko walked to the lift and waited until it arrived before slipping the heels on.

It was ridiculous, this sneaking around like a teenager. Reizo's reaction if he found out, however, would be terrifying. She counted on this to keep poor Saburo quiet, should he discover her escape. He had her mobile number. Fujiko hoped he would try it before calling his boss.

The executive was still in his suit. He paid for a *Stay*, a couple of hours, and they took a room with a massive round bed and Jacuzzi. The young man worked hard, his smooth chest beaded with sweat. But Fujiko was distracted, slipping in and out of focus, the last twenty-four hours weighing on her mind. He noticed – couldn't fail to – and didn't manage to labour to his own climax, never mind satisfy Fujiko. She cooed and smoothed his hair and stroked his ego but she could tell he was wounded when they parted ways at the hotel entrance.

She had wandered back to her apartment building, in no rush to return and deal with her abandoned bodyguard. When she had opened the door of her apartment, Saburo was stunned.

Now, his frown etched deep in his rough skin, he says, 'I will not tell Himura San. I think you should, Maki Chan, but that is your decision.'

'Thank you, Saburo San.'

Fujiko walks to the living room and collapses onto the sofa. Everything is a touch off-kilter, the world tilted since the violence of last night. She checks her mobile, realises it's on silent mode and finds, to her surprise, that the young executive has tried to call her more than twenty times since they said goodbye.

As the hour hand crawls past five in the morning on the small clock tower in the centre of Susukino crossing, the night-people begin to wane in spirit and numbers in the entertainment quarter.

Hostesses and sex-workers gather their personal belongings, some to consummate their shift with a last-minute assignation in a love hotel, others to pick up children from childcare establishments dedicated to the women who work in the salacious 'Water Trade'. Hosts, the male equivalent of hostesses, take late-arriving 'patrons' for pre-dawn coitus or meet off-duty hostesses and sex-workers, serving their needs and fantasies as the women, in turn, cater to their male clients. Taxi drivers doze in their cabs, sequestered in quiet back streets, and businessmen snore in all-night internet cafes, too drunk to navigate their way home or too broke to afford an exorbitant cab fare.

Megan Sparrow sleeps in her one-bedroom apartment, a mile and a half from the bright lights. Her father snores in his hotel room some two miles southwest of his only child, finally succumbing to slumber after his jetlag is trumped by sheer exhaustion. Surrounding them, over two million men, women and children catch a last couple of hours sleep before the sun washes Sapporo in a pale autumn light.

On the slopes west of Maruyama Park, a fox worries a joint of decaying meat. Its teeth have shredded the plastic wrapping. The arm of the dead police officer Rei Miyamoto, brother of Megan Sparrow's boyfriend, Yuji, is a banquet, enough to sustain the animal for days. The fox hears the soft tread and pricks its ears before the torchlight scythes the dark, picking out foliage and bark before finding the scavenger. Its eyes, with their keen night-vision, glow green in the beam for a moment before the fox darts into the shadows, leaving the dismembered corpse to the intruders.

There are fewer lights peppering the banks of the Toyohira River but the red light-bar on a police car roof still illuminates a high wall on the Susukino side of the bridge. Arc lights shine at the water's edge as investigators continue to comb the scene. In two suburban homes, lights will burn into the dawn as worried parents question, scold and hold their kids close, and wonder how they might repair the damage of the teenagers' brush with the fearsome demon, the Tengu.

The sidestreet where Jackie Shaw fell to the gang of yakuza is deserted. The hole-in-the-wall grill house is shuttered and silent. No steam billows through its vent, although the stink of stale cooking oil clings on. The street, like those of the main drag, is litter-free, despite the carousing of a Friday night. The asphalt is untouched save for a couple of stains on the coarse surface: spilt beer on the corner next to the grill house, drying water under the steam vent in the wall, and a darkened patch of blood on the spot where Jackie Shaw lay, hours earlier, as his holiday came to an end.

Let me tell you my story, as far as it goes.

I know you won't interrupt; you're the very definition of a captive audience. What's left of you, that is. Ironic that I sit, addressing nothing more than your bloodied tongue, cut from your screaming mouth when I butchered you by the river – but I don't want to say goodbye to your earthly being, not altogether. It's important to me that we continue our relationship, for a time at least. I'm not much of a social butterfly, see? Wasn't the most popular kid in school.

Not that I want to do any of that sick shit you read in the tabloids, either. You know, the vomit some godless hack spewed over the pages of Shukan Post, *or* Flash *or* Friday *magazines. No fucking your skull or eating your flesh or keeping you in the bathtub for three weeks: I might be a demon but I'm not depraved.*

You weren't my first. There was that worm in the fetish joint. Perverted fuck, he didn't even have his dick out when I cut him. Who pays money to watch a beautiful girl in Susukino, clothed or otherwise, if not to get their rocks off? It somehow seemed even more depraved that he wasn't jacking off behind that thick glass wall so, when I finished, I pulled my gloves tight on my twisted fingers and put his dead dick in his cold hand.

But I had already killed before the Sun Goddess touched my soul last night. The very first time – years ago – it was violent, too. Just like the pathetic wretch some twenty-four hours ago and your slaughter by the river tonight.

That first sacrifice hit back. They fought and scratched.

I didn't know it then but that was the inital step on my path to purification of the defilement of my youth, of my lineage.

That is the essence of our great, indigenous religion, Shinto: purification. The purging of the filthy, earthly lust and deceit and gluttony that pollutes our Japanese soul. A practical purge, and an acceptance of the imperfection of life, that the rituals of purification must be repeated again and again. Indulge, offer the gods a little backhander to makle it all go away, rinse and repeat. No hypocrisy. None of this prayer to a Jewish preacher, no one-time conversion fix-all, no childish battle between good and evil.

No miracles.

Miracles. What a facile concept. Property of a child-like religion with these Christians and their autocratic God with his absolutism and his self-righteous preaching.

Love, forgiveness.

Bullshit.

And the Bible. The only thing that little book of fairy tales gets right is how wicked and craven human beings are. As for the muslims? I despise their pious certitude.

I used to go to the Shinto shrine at New Year, tossed my money at the entrance and made my wish – not prayer, but wish. All that 'what-I-want-for-Christmas', fortune-lucky-dip bullshit they foist on us now. The Shinto priests of today treat the old gods like fucking Santa Claus, as though tossing a coin at a shrine and clapping your hands and squeezing your eyes shut will guarantee you might pass your exams or have a baby or survive the cancer. Our forefathers didn't believe in that shit. To them, Shinto was the grass at their feet, the mountains, the lakes.

Japan.

These modern priests are charlatans. Just like the Christians, and the Jews, and those greasy brown bastards clogging up Ueno with their Islamic religion.

Where was I?

Oh yes, my miracle. Hah!

All those years ago, I killed my first biting, scratching victim and The Sun Goddess smiled on me and I honour her to this day for she is beautiful, radiant, pure: her name means 'shining in heaven'.

The mask I wore when I carved your face, your last glimpse of this mortal world before I hacked your eyes from your head, is my true self. I am a demon, a goblin, a Tengu. Something more than man or beast. A defender of our true Japanese Shinto faith, my friend. I am here to punish the heretics. To punish you and your like.

Yes, I must labour on in this filthy, corrupted plane of existence: scouring, cleansing.

For her.

My Mother, the Mother of us all.

What's that you say? My blood mother?

My blood mother's been dead many years.

She was beautiful. Every boy thinks his mother is the pinnacle of womanhood but she was truly a vision. She went to the forest one day in her best clothes, smiling as though the world had complimented her on her finery and vowed to crown her as its empress. I remember her stroking my cheek and grinding the dirt from my skin between her long fingers. Her hair was piled high on her head. She whispered goodbye and disappeared between the trees. I watched until the last sliver of her red and gold dress was swallowed by the forest.

It was days before the men found her hanging by the neck. She hung herself with her obi sash from a great cedar.

That left me an orphan. Copious drink and tobacco had ensured the heart of the man I had called 'father' had stopped beating one year before. This, in turn, had ensured the sadistic bastard stopped beating my mother. He barely acknowledged my existence. I didn't even merit a raised hand.

It was another man that did for her. The man she truly loved. I heard the story years later. He loved her, fathered me, but his parents stepped in and forbade the marriage. Instead, she had married the drunken bastard I was expected to call father. Her true love, my real father, married a girl from a respected merchant family. My mother's life was dominated by the violent passions of my stepfather, a monster crawling through the world of men. Meanwhile, her first love – my blood father – it's said, had been slowly petrifying in a childless union. Until he met my mother at a summer festival and they reignited their passion with a tempestuous, clandestine affair.

I can't imagine my mother fucking another man.

The affair went on for years until my blood father's wife discovered their trysts. The next morning my mother wandered into the wilderness and ended her life.

Stupid, selfish, hateful bitch.

What a load of sentimental bullshit, right? All the story needs is a monster-slaying boy, or a moon-child or a turtle-ride to the undersea kingdom. Fucking fairy tales.

So my mother's true love, this gallivanting playboy who swept her off her feet, was my real father. He knocked her up then watched that alcoholic brute fill the paternal void for four fucking years and did nothing.

That's the reality of the world, my bodyless friend.

You don't know me, never will. You didn't see my face under the mask. You never hurt me, persecuted or wronged me. You woke up in the morning with a spring in your step because it was Friday. You had a night out and a few drinks – more than a few drinks to judge by your condition when I tracked you. The last thing you expected was for a demonic presence to follow you in the night, drag you into the shadows and cut you open. I could see it in your eyes before they stopped looking at this world and stared into the abyss of the next: you couldn't believe this was happening to you, even as my blade grated against your breastbone and the stench of your entrails filled the cool air.

It could have been anyone. I was hungry for blood. You were there and 'anyone' wasn't.

That's the truth of this world.

There are the lucky, and there are the damned. There are the strong, and there are the weak. The truly strong will embrace their role and hunt the herd. Others will rail against nature and lose their strength as a result to become the hunted.

My mission, my friend, is to use the privilege bestowed on me by Her, *Amaterasu, Mother of Japan, as a predator of men and purge our nation of the weak, the corrupt and the debased.*

A predator of men, and of women.

Perhaps a foreigner.

Or a foreign woman. Yes! An anti-Mother, the ultimate offering for my Mother goddess.

You have my word. Soon, I'll send company to the afterlife. Perhaps next time, a woman to attend your needs. Yes, my friend, I will be sure to send more cowardly, cocksucker kin to reside with you in hell.

#

Chapter 10

The afterlife is full of angry cats.

The spitting sound grows in intensity becoming more female than feline. He has to shatter the serenity of the warm, black womb, to concentrate on swimming up from the depths, and force his eyes open. His eyelids open and his skull pounds in protest. Jackie Shaw winces, sending a sharp twinge of pain through his cheek and lip.

I'm alive, he thinks, it couldn't hurt this much in the next world. *And this world is?*

He's in bed under a duvet, his feet sticking out the bottom where he's snagged the covers. He has a vague memory of hard asphalt and the scent of cooking. There was violence. People were drinking alcohol. Is this a hangover? No, he hasn't had a drink for years.

He smells something real, something tangible. Tatami. A tatami mat.

I'm in Japan, he thinks. I'm on holiday.

The room has three bare walls, a floor-length mirror propped against one, sliding doors for storage in another. An unlit portable oil heater, one of the big ones with a grill on the front like the paraffin heater his parents used to have , squats in the corner. The fourth wall is comprised of a couple of large shoji sliding screens, one of which is drawn back to reveal a girl standing shoeless, the norm in any Japanese home, her back turned to him, grousing into a mobile phone. She's wearing a simple blouse and grey trousers, the kind of uniform found in countless shops and offices around Japan. Her hair is tied up to reveal the chain of a silver necklace around her neck.

Everything looks too tall. At least the pounding in his head is clearing the fug of sleep some.

Jackie tries to swing his legs out of the bed with the ambition of standing on his own two feet. Instead, a stab of pain drives through his left side as his heels thump into the floor. He swears. This is no bed. It's a thick futon flat on the tatami mat floor.

The girl turns and begins squealing into the mobile, frantic, before trotting down the corridor and disappearing through one of the doors on the right. Jackie eases back the covers. He is naked. He rolls onto the floor, manages to prop his aching body on elbows and knees, and straightens like an old man after a fall. In the long mirror, he studies a purple-blue bruise on his left cheek. Happy that there isn't any swelling, he presses tentative fingertips to his head. Not so happy after the spasms of pain, he turns to check the large, angry welts on his left side. Fox: that was the fella's name. Fox and his spikey-haired goons. The bastards gave him a decent hiding. No fresh scars to add to his impressive collection, though. Seems he had a guardian angel to protect him from Fox's knife.

Odds-on that angel isn't the girl he hears yelling from the room at the end of the corridor.

He takes a step to the built-in storage and winces again. Panic burrows into his mind like a maggot and he breathes through his nose to slow the spread of fear. Alone in a strange apartment in an alien city. Naked. A young woman in another room. No idea who she is or how he got here. The first thing to do is get dressed. He takes it slow and makes it to the sliding doors of the built-in storage. Sliding the door open he sees folded clothes, a rolled futon, towels and stacked bedclothes neat, like in a military barracks. No sign of his clothes but he takes a large towel and wraps it around his aching body. He's about to close the door again when he spots something nestled behind the stack of towels. A slim, black shaft like a small umbrella handle.

Shit.

The pounding in his head rises a notch. Jackie reaches in and withdraws the combat knife from behind and under the towels. He struggles to picture last night through urgent pain. The yakuza, the kicking, the smiling thug with the folding blade.

Folding.

This blade is fixed. The design is simple, a dimpled tang with a moulded motif on the edge of the plastic where the blade meets the handle. About eight inches from tip to hilt. Deadly in the wrong hands but not Fox's knife. He wedges it down into his makeshift waistband, feels the cold steel against his skin and slips out of the room. He creeps down the corridor. A set of golf clubs sitting in the hallway near the front door look somehow different. He realises they are for a left-handed player. The girl held her mobile phone in her right hand.

The living room door is open. The girl has finished her conversation and is sitting on a sofa next to the window when he enters. She gasps at the sight of him. Her eyes widen when she sees the network of old scar tissue on his chest and the sprinkling of knotted potholes – cigarette burns – on his skin. He could sit down, try to calm her, but the knife tucked in the towel at his back would be awkward.

An incomprehensible litany of Japanese tumbles from her small, pinched mouth.

'Gomenasai,' says Jackie, 'I'm sorry, I only speak a little Japanese. Can you speak English?'

The girl looks at his scarred body, then turns her eyes to the glass-topped coffee table in the centre of the room. Jackie would guess she's in her late twenties. Her hair is dyed auburn and her make-up is modest bar the heavy black shadow around her sleek eyes. Her cheekbones are strong, set in a square face, just the right side of characterful in a pretty sense. Slim, quite elegant, like a million other young women working in shops and offices around Sapporo. But handling the presence of an almost naked Western man standing a couple of yards away surprisingly well. She's lived a little, he thinks.

'A little,' she says, as though echoing his thoughts.

Lucky, he thinks. The chances of her having any of his native language were low. He says, 'Where am, I?'

'Makomanai area, Sapporo. South of city.'

'Who are you?'

'My name is Aina. This not my place.'

'Whose place is it?'

'My friend.'

'Were you talking to your friend on your mobile?'

'Mobile?'

He remembers the ubiquity of American English in Japan. 'Your cell phone.'

'Yes.'

'You didn't sound happy with your friend.'

'My friend happy?'

'Are you angry with your friend?'

She drops her gaze. 'I don't understand.'

Jackie checks the room. Compact. More polished wood flooring. The wooden door is on his right, nestled against the wall where it swung inwards. The usual TV and entertainment system, a game console, two mismatched sofas and a low glass coffee table on a cream rug. There's a shelf unit with some bamboo trays of bric-a-brac and a suitcase wedged in the corner between the unit and the wall. A poster of Los Angeles on the wall above the TV and a clock mounted on another. A Hokkaido Fighters baseball cap on the floor. He remembers the set of left-handed golf clubs propped in the hallway. This is a man's space. A bachelor. Like Jackie, or Ian Sparrow.

Bollocks, he thinks. Ian.

Jackie sees the time is past nine-thirty in the morning by the wall clock. His friend will have knocked on the door of his hotel room. Checked reception. Maybe called Megan.

And if this is a man's apartment, the owner will be back.

'Aina, do you know where my clothes are?' Jackie says, edgy now he's on the clock.

Her name surprises her and she points to an adjoining door. As he opens it she says, 'But they are dirty.'

'And my shoes?'

'At the apartment door.'

The adjoining room, a utility room, is almost a cupboard. His clothes are folded on top of a washing machine. He keeps the door open as he dresses, taking an age. They can't see each other but he hears her mutter to herself a couple of times. His jeans and jacket are smeared with grime after last night's fight and there is dried blood on his t-shirt but the jacket will hide the stains if he zips it to the neck. He slips the knife into the inner jacket pocket and finds his wallet is gone. His mobile, too. When he walks back into the living room the girl is studying the coffee table again.

'Aina,' he says, 'I'm in trouble. I think you know that.'

'I don't understand.'

'You understand trouble. I can see it in your face. You understand yakuza.'

'Do not say that word.'

'I know you are not yakuza. I think maybe you know them but you are a good person.'

She stares at the coffee table again and he reads something in her expression he can't decipher. His head still pounds, his brain addled. His body aches – *Fuck, Jackie! Calm down and think!*

'I need to get away and I need to call my friend. He's staying at the Prince Hotel. Can I borrow your cell phone?'

She stares at the glass coffee tabletop, shifting forward an inch or two, almost perched on the edge of the sofa.

'Aina, please,' he says.

But she isn't listening. Her eyes are boring a hole through the glass. No, into the glass, as though it were a portal to another, Jackie-free, trouble-free world. Studying the surface where he can see the reflection of downtown Los Angeles, the angle of two walls meeting on the ceiling, the clock.

The clock. She is watching the clock.

Her eyes close. Her shoulders relax. Jackie recognises relief. And then he hears a key in the front door.

#

Reizo Himura hides behind the broadsheet, studying the fine print without seeing a thing. In his mind's eye, all he can see is an image of the girl going down on him in his office in Big-Touch building.

He'd returned to the scene of the murder last night after leaving the small izakaya and a drunk Shintaro Ishikawa. Standing in the bare space of the Invisible Man Club with the stark strip-lighting on, looking through the glass partition at the mocked-up apartment, he'd felt a sickness swell in his stomach. At first he thought it was the whisky, that he'd been gypped by the Russians and it wasn't a twenty-one year old, sherry cask single malt but some Vladivostok bottled piss-water. Then he realised that the bile rising in his throat was disgust. A cop – a fucking cop! – slaughtered on his turf. In his home. And Fujiko. How many nights had she sat in the space on the other side of the glass, doodling her comic sketches or drawing her portraits, while some low-life sat in the dark grunting and straining with his dick in his hand. How had Reizo Himura ended up like this? What did he think he could give Fujiko? He could protect her, provide for her, but that was his limit. She'd never gain respectability unless he could get in on the game in Tokyo or Osaka or Kobe, find a seat at the big table.

Then he'd have real money, the possibility of connections, legitimacy, a shot at a way out.

A girl had walked into the mock apartment to retrieve a forgotten bracelet and jumped when she saw Reizo standing on the other side of the glass. He remembered seeing her around. A new girl. She was short and her lack of height added weight to her figure. Not bad, he thought. Fleshy rather than fat. The nausea had subsided as he stirred and fifteen minutes later he'd been sat at his desk as she knelt before him, taking his mind somewhere far from the cruelty and fear and filth of his life in the yakuza.

Reizo peers over the newspaper. Fujiko is buttering a slice of toast and reading something on the screen of her phone, lying on the table. He senses something is up. The man he'd left with her, Saburo, had been obsequious this morning when Reizo had returned to Fujiko's place at dawn. Reizo had chosen Saburo to watch over Fujiko last night because the soldier didn't go for the boot-licking, sycophantic act that some of the other low-rankers employed. Yet this morning, he'd been grovelling like some of the mongrels Himura detested in the lower reaches of the Kanto Daichi-kai.

Fujiko is as light and airy as ever. Which is wrong. She'd been traumatised by the cop's murder, quiet and withdrawn for much of yesterday. Now she's trying too hard.

'Any news?' she says.

'The Fighters lost again. To Orix. From pennant winners to bottom of the Pacific League in the space of months. They'll be bringing Shinjo out of retirement at this rate.'

'My friend met him once in a nightclub near the Tokyu Hotel. She said his head was massive. It looked like his neck could barely support it.'

'Probably all the work he had done on his teeth.'

Fujiko smiles and takes a bite out of the toast.

'Did you sleep okay last night? Saburo didn't bother you?'

'I didn't hear him. Either he's quiet as a mouse or I slept so deeply his clumping around didn't register.'

'You must have had a good rest,' says Himura. 'You're a new woman this morning.'

'Knowing you're here to protect me, Reizo.' She reaches across the breakfast table and touches his cheek. He's tired after three hours' sleep but the feel of her fingers on his stubbled face gives him a jolt of energy. He's about to tell her what she means to him, how he'll risk everything for her, when someone hammers at the door. Fujiko jumps, then puts her hand to her mouth again.

Reizo Himura stands and kisses the top of her hair, smells citrus and fresh cotton. He flings open the front door and hisses, 'What the fuck are you doing? This is a residential building! Keep the noise down, you idiot!'

Nakata leans forward and whispers, 'Sorry, boss, but you should know there's been another murder.'

Reizo's stubble prickles on his skin and a shiver darts across his shoulders.

'On our turf?'

'No boss, down at the river. One of our contacts at Central police called me twenty minutes ago.'

'Yoshida, I guess,' says Reizo. Imbecile cop. He's only supposed to look into Miyamoto's background, let the Kanto Daichi-kai know when the dead cop is missed. 'I'll kick his ass for interrupting my breakfast. After I finish with you.'

'That's just it, boss,' says Nakata, his head bobbing frantically in a series of small bows. 'The corpse at the river the cops turned up. It *is* Yoshida.'

#

Jackie's eyes flash around the living room. Nothing he can use as a weapon. He grabs the baseball cap and tries to cup his left hand inside. Not much defence if the new arrival has a weapon but better than bare skin against a blade. The girl's eyes are huge, panic draining her face of colour. He steps to the left of the living room doorway and flattens his back to the wall. His head clears as adrenaline drives the aches and pains down. His brain begins debating the age-old question, fight or flight? Either way, he slips the knife from his inner pocket.

A rough male voice barks a stream of Japanese from the hallway. The girl sits rooted to the sofa, her eyes on the open doorway as though she's forgotten Jackie is there. Her mouth is open in a soundless shout.

The male voice bawls, 'Oi!' Then another stream of harsh Japanese. It sounds as though the words must grate against the man's throat, emerging shredded into the close air of the apartment. Then a pause. Jackie left the sliding shoji door of the bedroom open, but the futon is empty. Whoever is on the other side of the wall, in the corridor, will know Jackie is up. The girl's breathing is amplified by the silence. The man in the corridor has taken his shoes off at the front door, his feet silent on the wood flooring. The blood rushing through Jackie's head threatens to drown his senses.

The girl's eyes dart from the open doorway to Jackie to the doorway again. Then stop. Jackie can't read her expression. Fear makes a frozen mask of her face. He's sure someone is now standing just outside the doorway. He eases slowly to his haunches.

He looks at the surface of the coffee table, hoping for a reflected glimpse of the man in the doorway but the angles are all wrong. The girl begins working her jaw, words or a scream caught in her throat. Jackie can smell cologne and the outdoors, autumnal air, on the man's clothes, inches from where he crouches. He stares at the girl, fighting down panic, the urge to spring from his hiding place and run. His eyes sweep the room in desperation – girl, shelves, clock, sofa, TV, girl, window: TV.

TV. A huge flat screen, the power off. A phantom stands reflected in the black screen clutching an object in its hand. Jackie has seen enough trouble in his time to recognise the blurred image of a gun in the man's grip. Left-handed, a southpaw. Has the man seen Jackie's reflection, crouched against the wall?

Jackie lets the baseball cap slip to the floor and grabs it by the peak. The movement is enough to snap the girl from her paralysis. She turns to stare at Jackie and, as an ear-splitting shriek explodes from her throat, he springs up, his legs pistons. He pivots toward the open doorway and hooks the cap over the man's gun hand, glimpsing a revolver as he brings the hilt of the knife down hard. There's a small juddering shock as the tang connects with the man's bony wrist. The hammer clicks: no shot. Empty chamber. Jackie's socks skate on the smooth flooring and his legs go. He drops to a hard landing on his knees. The man slips too, runs on the spot, legs pin-wheeling like a cartoon as he tries to stay upright. Jackie hears another click as the revolver's hammer falls on the firing pin again. No shot. He lets go of the cap and snatches at the man's legs to upend his opponent. His hand is slapped away by a bony knee. Jackie drops his hands to the floor to steady himself as the wiry man collapses on top of him inside the living room. The gun clatters across the floor as Jackie loses his grip on the knife and the tangle of knees and elbows sends it skittering across the polished wood.

The man is tanned and lean, not an ounce of fat on him. He grabs for a hold on Jackie, hauling at the t-shirt, stretching it with a tearing sound. The floor is like a skating rink to their socked feet. Jackie swings a wild haymaker and connects with something hard and hears a hollow thump. His view is a confusion of limbs and torso and flashes of wild hair and he curls on his side and aims short, vicious kicks at the man. They separate.

Jackie gains his feet and makes for the living room doorway while the man struggles to stand. He's just over the threshold when the bastard grabs at his ankle. Not enough to get a grip but tripping him, unbalancing him so his feet go from under him again and he lands hard against the wall of the corridor. The jolt sends a shot of pain up his left side and his head begins hammering again. The girl is still screaming, like nails on a chalkboard. The man is on Jackie's back in an instant.

Jackie bellows, 'Who are you?'

The man squawks a reply in grating Japanese. He's younger than Jackie, all hard muscle and bony joints. But for all his flailing, he is in too close and lacks the heft to get much power behind his attack.

Then Jackie glimpses the knife at his side, lying against the skirting board of the corridor. He reaches out and his knuckles rap against wood and plaster board. He sees the knife flash past him in the attacker's right hand. The man hooks his arm around Jackie's throat and pulls hard, exposing his neck.

Not now, thinks Jackie. *Not now!*

I won't be beaten, cut, body dumped out here. He thinks of his sister back home, his mother's grave, his father's. He wants to visit them again. He wants to chip away at his ledger, see if he can't convince Saint Peter his good deeds outweigh the bad when the day comes, and he's still got some way to go.

But the thug twists, pulling Jackie with him, and hurls the knife behind and into the living room. The blade clatters on the floor out of harm's way.

Jackie roars, 'Fuck!' and throws his weight on his hands, hard against the wall. He hurls himself backwards, his arms straightening with a snap. He takes the man with him, feet flailing as he launches his bulk into the sinewy body behind. They land hard and he hears a flat smack as the scrawny bastard's head hits the doorframe. Jackie rolls left to come up on his knees in the corridor. The man is sprawled, breathing hard, his head propped against the skirting board. The gun and knife are lost.

Fight taken care of, thinks Jackie, time for flight.

He' s almost at the door when the girl bursts from the living room swinging the small knife around like she's swatting a giant hornet, her mind gone to a different place. She sees Jackie and stands in front of the fallen man, protecting him and swinging the blade in wider arcs. She howls a litany of Japanese, her voice shrill and ragged. The stunned man puts a steadying hand against the wall and reaches to take the combat knife from her small fist with his right hand.

His right hand.

His weaker hand.

Jackie grabs the golf clubs propped against the wall by the strap and hurls them at the girl, a couple toppling out of the bag as they slam into her arm. He hasn't got much traction, worried he'll skate on the polished floor again and land on his arse but the girl flinches and turns, swinging the knife arm back and slicing the wiry man's chest just below the clavicle. The pair collide and go down and Jackie half sprints, half slides the last couple of steps to the front door, grabbing a pair of trainers and tumbling out of the apartment as the door swings open.

He runs for the lifts at the end of the long concourse clutching the trainers and utters a silent prayer of thanks that a lift is at his floor. He punches the button and feels the car shudder as he collapses inside. He hears a furious roar and a terrified wail before the doors slide shut.

Chapter 11

The cops hit Reizo Himura's office across the river less than an hour after the courtesy phone call. A bored desk sergeant got one of the low-level rankers on the phone while the senior yakuza on-site was taking a piss and told him he was so sorry to intrude, but that there would be a large contingent of his fellow officers raiding the premises in forty-five minutes or so. Superintendent Genda sent his apologies and was confident that the raid would be of benefit to everyone.

The message was relayed to an older bruiser holding counsel on the Bubble Economy years in Big-Touch Building to a group of younger men, and he contacted Nakata's mobile. The second lieutenant cleared his throat twice before he could choke out the news to Himura as they sat in Fujiko Maki's apartment, still processing the murder of their pet detective, Yoshida, by the river last night. But the expected onslaught stalls as Reizo Himura pours a cup of coffee from the pot. The tumblers and cogs are turning in his brain, his mind feverish as he tries to make sense of the last forty-eight hours.

'What the fuck is happening?' he says.

This is bad, thinks Fujiko. He never swears in front of me for fear of cracking my delicate sensibilities and sending me screaming to the bathroom in tears.

She's been taking small sips of strong coffee, letting the caffeine bite and sharpen her up. It's a waiting game: she has to sit things out until Saburo and Nakata leave them alone, then find a way to tell Reizo what her illicit lover had blurted on her mobile in the early morning when she'd finally noticed his calls. Now, with the news of the raid and Masa Yoshida's murder, Fujiko is desperate to unburden herself of what her latest sex partner had to say after he had bid her goodbye at the love hotel last night. But how could she tell Reizo without incriminating both herself and her lover? Reizo would fly into a homicidal rage. She'd escape unharmed but Saburo would suffer, and god knows what Reizo would do to the poor sap with whom she'd had sex. Not for the first time, part of her wishes she had never met Reizo Himura.

Himura finishes his coffee. No point in rushing. He'd never make it to the office across the river before the raid hit. He makes a call to the premises and gives detailed and strict instructions as to how the men there should prepare for the cops' arrival. Then he calls Goro Inaba.

Silence.

A hiss.

Then a chirping female voice declares the number is out of service.

'Shit!'

'Boss?' says Saburo.

'Reizo?' says Fujiko.

Himura calls Inaba's office at Big-Touch building. The phone rings five times before a pre-recorded message cuts in. Himura hangs up. Goro doesn't bother with a landline at home. Many of them don't, on the off-chance they might slip up and mention something incriminating and the cops are tapping the line.

'Try Inaba's mobile,' he says, pointing at Saburo. 'Put it on speaker.' The man calls the number. Reizo, Fujiko and Saburo wait in silence for twenty seconds. Then, once again, a tinny, bright, disconnected voice declares the number is out of service.

'Nothing,' says Saburo.

'I've got fucking ears, idiot!'

'Reizo! Saburo is trying to help.'

Himura turns on Fujiko and glares. Then his eyes soften and he seems to notice her for the first time. She holds his gaze, challenging him. Chastised, he nods. 'Saburo, I am tired. You are here, and Goro Inaba is not. I appreciate your loyalty and your care for Maki San.'

Saburo, embarrassed, bows fast and deep. When he stands erect again, his neck is flushed.

Where the fuck is Inaba? thinks Reizo. He disappears before the cop is killed in the club, now he goes missing after Yoshida turns up dead and the pigs raid a syndicate property. One of the universal yakuza principles is *do not fail in your loyalty to your superiors*. So where the hell is he when he's needed most? Fucking some whore? Drunk? Or is there another, more insidious explanation?

Reizo Himura dismisses the thought. He made Goro, brought him up through the ranks; even counselled him through a nasty divorce a few years back. Inaba is loyal. To consider otherwise is unthinkable in their world. But, with all the shit coming down, Himura needs his closest man.

'Keep trying him,' he says to Saburo. 'Every fifteen or twenty minutes, on his mobile and at Big-Touch. And send someone over to his apartment. He'll turn up.'

Himura calls various other Kanto Daichi-kai men, rallying troops for a show of force to confront the cops. He instructs Nakata to check in on Ishikawa and his three bodyguards and do what he can to ensure the Tokyo yakuza know nothing of the police raid. Then the second lieutenant is to chase up the tip Inaba gave Himura on the dead cop, Rei Miyamoto's mah-jong rival. Not much of a suspect now Yoshida has been killed but better to follow through. Who knows? The tip might, if useful, restore a little of his faith in Goro.

Himura tells Saburo to sit tight with Fujiko while he drives to the raid rather than waste more time waiting for a man to show up and act as chauffeur.

Almost an hour later, he arrives at the office in Shiroishi Ward on the other side of the river, a brutal concrete two-storey building with a tall granite wall and stone-carved lions perched atop the thick posts of a solid steel gate. Police vehicles line the street and boxes of documents confiscated from the offices are stacked next to a police van as plain-clothed cops wander out clutching more. A smell of burning hangs in the chill air and Himura smiles. The men have been incinerating the good stuff before the cops turned up. He steps out of the BMW as an old woman ambles to a laundrette on the corner, bent double with brittle bones. She nods at Himura as she passes and he returns the greeting with a deep bow. He lights a cigarette. A uniformed cop standing next to a small two-seater police car leans over to his partner and mutters. The partner scuttles over, pushing his glasses up the ridge of his nose and bowing deep.

'Himura San, please remain calm.'

Himura checks the old lady has passed and there are no kids on the street, girds himself with a suppressed sigh, fixes his mouth in a revolted sneer and squints at the policeman. 'Fuck you!' he says. 'I come to your place, ransack the rooms, steal your possessions and humiliate you in front of your neighbours, then you can tell me to stay calm! Fucking cops!'

'We have a responsibility by law to – '

'By law? What law governs the police in this country? You hold suspects with impunity, beat confessions from innocent people! Harass businessmen!' He points to his offices. 'You're the biggest mafia in Japan today!'

'Nobody mentioned mafia, Himura San.' The voice is deep and rasping, scoured by decades of harsh cigarettes and alcohol. Superintendent Genda walks toward Reizo Himura and waves the young policeman away.

'And here comes the fucking oyabun,' growls Himura.

'Let's go somewhere quiet and talk.'

'Like a police cell, where you can beat me with your men standing nearby as back-up?'

'Like your personal office inside, where we can look over some of the documentation here and discuss a course of action.'

Genda gestures for Himura to lead the way and the yakuza boss begins strolling, defiant, toward the open gate. Plain-clothed officers pass them, some nodding to Himura, others scowling. The uniforms avoid eye contact and busy themselves with menial tasks, working hard to appear busy. Inside the gate, his men rush forward, bowing to Himura, begging forgiveness for permitting the police to enter the premises. They shun Genda, focusing on their boss. A salty detective gives one of the men a shove and a bout of pushing ensues, both parties loathe to throw a punch: the point has been made. Outnumbered by the cops, the yakuza can step down with oaths and furious gestures, pride intact and reputation maintained.

At the large glass door to the building, Himura stares down a tall uniform, forcing the cop to step back and offer a small bow before he strolls in. They keep their shoes on. This is a place of business, not a home. Inside the building, Genda and Himura remain silent until they come to the door of the oyabun's personal office. Himura opens the dark wood door and enters first, swinging it shut behind him so that Genda has to stop the wood slamming into his face with his palm.

The superintendent enters and closes the door with a soft click. The room has a simple pale green carpet, several filing cabinets against one wall. Facing the door is a teak desk furnished with a laptop, a frosted window with metal slats on the outside set in the wall behind. Himura settles in a leather chair on the far side of his desk and reaches into a drawer, producing a bottle of Bowmore.

'Not for me,' says Genda. 'It's going to be a long day.'

'Twenty-five-year-old.'

'I'll be reading a lot of fine print while I sift through the garbage we're taking out of here. It's blurry enough without the scotch.' The senior cop is a solid man going to fat. His broad face would be ravaged by his twenty years on the force if it hadn't filled out with good eating and increased desk work. His hairline has begun receding, catching his short greying hair in a pincer movement with his bald spot. He is ten years older than the yakuza boss and ten weeks on the wagon. He feels a familiar warmth in his neck, a nip of desire at the back of his mind. The whisky looks better than Himura could ever know. Too damn good. But ten weeks is ten weeks, and Genda has promised his wife.

'At least have a seat,' says Himura.

A frown furrows the beetling, wiry brows above Genda's sharp eyes. He stands opposite the yakuza boss and shoves his hands in his pockets. The yakuza oyabun shrugs and says, 'Suit yourself.' He pours himself a measure of whisky and says, 'What brings you to my place?'

'You're in trouble, Himura. Masa Yoshida turned up last night by the Toyohira River. Throat cut, tongue removed. Someone did a sloppy job of trying to take his face off, too, by the looks of it. Butchered his chest some, as well.'

'Not our style, you know that. Why would I want to murder Yoshida? He was tamer than a pet shiba.'

'I don't believe you would.'

'So, what's all this?' Himura jerks his chin to the closed door and the raid progressing beyond. 'Did you get a tip-off? You won't find much other than a couple of unpaid parking tickets here.'

'I don't have the time or resources to follow tip-offs with a raid like this. Not with recent budget cuts. I received orders from Head-quarters. Not Centre Ward station, or Shiroishi Central; not city police. Hokkaido Prefectural Police Headquarters.'

'You looking for something in particular?'

'Me? No. But the three suits from Headquarters are. We haven't been told what, just to leave them alone and conduct a typical raid. You know what that means?'

'It means a shit load of trouble.'

'They're Organised Crime Bureau.'

Himura downs the whisky and sits back in his chair.

Genda is old-school, as are many of the cops in senior positions across the force in Hokkaido. He is straight-as-a-dye, not on the syndicate payroll. But he and many less principled senior officers know the system and cut corners to maintain the symbiosis of cops and yakuza that had served the country through rebuilding after the war, the boom years of the Bubble, and kept the peace for decades. The senior cops still made moves like calling ahead before a raid so syndicates could get their house in order and burn anything too damning, leaving a few scraps for show. The police could claim a victory and show off a little contraband, and the oyabuns offered up a couple of low-level lambs to the slaughter, young rankers and no-hopers who'd grasp the chance to do minor time and make their bones in prison. It was all about maintaining a balance.

Genda says, 'With respect, you need to get your house in order.'

'We've been good as gold, you know that.'

'I know we haven't had any complaints from civilians, so you aren't classified "extremely dangerous". I'd bet there might be a few shadier characters around who would disagree.'

Reizo Himura smiles and pours another measure. Anti-yakuza legislation introduced a few years ago had given cops wider powers to prosecute gangs who threatened private citizens, deeming those syndicates "extremely dangerous". Reizo had cut protection rackets and loan-sharking in response.

Genda takes his hands from his pockets and places them on top of the desk, leaning in toward Himura.

'You've weathered the Yakuza Exclusion Ordinance laws, too. I'm not saying you aren't smart. You keep the peace, by and large, and god forbid your sort make way for the Russians and Chinese.' Genda cocks his head toward the door and the neverending dance of cops and criminals in full swing beyond. 'But someone is either fucking up, or trying to fuck you up. And you'll excuse me for saying, in my modest experience, the most likely source is close to home.'

#

Jackie can't outrun the panic biting hard on his heels. Or maybe it's the trainers he grabbed as he bolted from the apartment, at least a size too small, hobbling him. He's surrounded by identical blocks of drab apartment buildings. The cycle path on which he runs is a never-ending belt channelling him – where?

It's like a giant treadmill, he thinks. The top of that apartment block – Christ, they're all the fucking same! – Olympic rings? Where the hell am I?

The pounding in his head drums in tandem to the slap of his trainers on the cycle path like the hangover from Hell.

The man in the apartment. Something familiar about him. What? He'd caught an impression of his angular face and wiry frame rather than a decent look but something had struck a chord. Had he glimpsed him in the izakaya? On the narrow side streets threaded through Susukino?

Shit, Jackie thinks. *Where the fuck am I?*

Was the man in the apartment the man who'd been watching at the plaza when Jackie and his friends drank coffee? Had the man been watching them or was the stalker a figment of an overactive imagination?

Megan and Ian. He has to find a phone and call them. But he doesn't have any money. Can't use a public phone. He doesn't speak enough Japanese. Can't explain what's happening. A cop-shop, that's what he needs. Get to a police station, call the embassy, have the FCO earn their pay. Contact Ian and Megan, let them know he's okay. But is he okay? What time is it? What day? Fucking jetlag.

The train station. There are train stations everywhere in Japan. Walk – run – anywhere in a ten-block radius and you'll come across a subway or train station. Some of them have police offices. Even if he finds one that doesn't, he knows the word for police. Doesn't he? Shit! What was it. *Keisappu.*

No, but *Kei*-something. Come on, *kei...kei...*

Keisatsu! That's it!

He's gonna be okay. Ian and Megan are gonna be okay.

The car hits him, tossing him across the bonnet. He slides over the edge of the metal and collapses onto the street next to the wheels. The car looks huge from the ground and he feels like a child for a second. He sees tyre marks on the asphalt. The driver's door opens and a babbling taxi driver tumbles onto the street, arms reaching for him but holding back from actual contact. Jackie levers himself to a sitting position, his legs hollow with the sudden shock of the accident. He struggles to his feet and brushes his jeans down. Nothing broken, he thinks, a glancing blow.

The cycle path is a couple of yards to his left and he realises he ran blindly onto a two-lane road. A children's playground and supermarket are across the street. Jackie, lost for any other course of action, bows to the driver. The man is older and terrified. He blurts in broken English, over and over, 'Okay? No hurt? Okay?' Cars pass in the other lane while a couple wait behind the taxi to drive past once the coast is clear. A few pedestrians hurry along the pavement. One old man stands in front of the supermarket and stares.

'Okay. Not hurt. I'm sorry,' says Jackie. He shows his palms in placation. 'You take me to keisatsu?'

The driver blanches and something hard sets in his face. The man says 'police' in Engliah and begins a stream of Japanese, his voice harsher, dropping a couple of octaves.

Doesn't matter where you are, thinks Jackie, fucking taxi drivers, all the same, covering their arse at all costs. He shakes his head and taxes his pounding brain as to how he can make this man understand he isn't interested in a tap from his cab. The beating and kidnapping he's endured in the last few hours is another matter. He takes a breath and opens his mouth to explain when the driver's face goes slack, his features almost melting as he takes a step back. Jackie catches a growl of invective in his right ear and smells the sour reek of cigarettes, stale booze and body odour. The musk of a man who hasn't seen his bed for a while.

He turns while the driver begins a frantic series of bows, edging closer to the driver's door. The man standing behind him rubs his cheek with his right hand while his left plays with a US Air Cavalry zippo. His hair looks greasy in the light of day, errant strands escaping from the make-shift ponytail; a couple look stiff and brittle. Perhaps with the same caked blood which stipple the split lip wrapped around a smouldering cigarette. Wraparound shades hide the eyes but the raised brows betray amusement and the damaged mouth curls in a lopsided smile. Three goons straight out of central casting cross the road and flank the man.

Jackie feels the weight of defeat descend. Fox takes the shades off and his smile broadens. He keeps them trained on Jackie as he offers a deep, mocking bow, then orders his attack dogs forward.

#

Thirty minutes later, a different man sits opposite Jackie. Everything feels familiar, despite the short time Jackie spent in the apartment. The coffee table has been righted but the glass is gone, smashed in the scuffle. The clock is still on the wall. The golf clubs are back in the leather bag, now wedged in the corner behind the television. There is a trace of blood on the wall of the corridor where the girl, Aina, stabbed her – what? – partner? Friend? Lover?

The man opposite is older than Fox and carries an air of combustible authority. He fishes a pack of cigarettes from his jacket pocket and Fox, standing by the window, rushes to light it. The man waves him away and produces a cheap plastic lighter, taking a couple of drags on the fag before exhaling the tobacco in a thin grey stream, his square jaw jutting out in a challenge like an open drawer.

Jackie sits on the other sofa, fear gnawing away at his insides like a starved rat. He breathes through his nose to a count of four to stop himself losing it. A vague image of Ian and Megan Sparrow lurks in the shadows at the periphery of his mind. Two bruisers stand either side of him. The smoking man looks like he doesn't need them; like he can handle himself.

'Who are you?' the man says. There's a trace of an American accent in his English.

Jackie nods at Fox and says, 'I'm the man gave your boy that split lip.'

'I hear he had you down last night. Almost cut you bad.'

'He got his licks in.'

'Then your friend, Inaba, turned up and stopped "my boy" carving his name on your face.' The man leans forward and tips ash in a glass ashtray on the floor. 'Again, who are you? And where's Inaba?'

'I've never heard of an Inaba in my life.'

'I find that hard to believe considering you were wearing Goro Inaba's shoes when we picked you up running around the old Olympic village. Your shoes are at the door. This is his apartment.'

Jackie's boots are now one of several pairs lined up neatly at the small entrance. His are set apart at the end of the line, in quarantine. He says, 'Would the man in question be about five-nine, thin, deep tan out of season; messy hair, maybe in his late twenties?'

'Twenty-nine.'

'Well, he's sporting a knife wound above his heart.'

The man on the sofa takes a long drag on the cigarette, sharp eyes appraising Jackie with renewed interest. He thrusts his jaw forward further and Jackie sees he has an impressive underbite. The man's skin is darker than many of his countrymen with the crevices set hard in his face. Jackie would bet his leathery complexion is thanks to long hours in the scorching sun and harsh winters of Hokkaido's great outdoors. The man runs a large hand through his slicked hair and says, 'You tell me who you are and why you're here or "my boy" will finish what he started last night.'

'Okay,' says Jackie. 'My name is Jackie Shaw. I'm on holiday. I was out in Susukino with a couple of friends and we ran into three of your men giving a local and a couple of Western kids a hard time. I'm sure Fox has already told you about it.' At the mention of his name, the gaunt yakuza turns.

'I went to an izakaya with my friends,' Jackie continues, 'and left early for a stroll before I went back to my hotel room. Your boy and three of his mates jumped me in a quiet street. They gave me a kicking and I passed out. When I woke up, I was lying in the bedroom down the hall and a mighty pissed off girl was in this apartment squawking down her phone at someone. Your Inaba turned up with a gun, a revolver. He pulled the trigger twice on empty chambers. We had a shoving match. The girl cut him by accident in the confusion and I bolted with a pair of his trainers. Or sneakers, if you prefer American English.' He doesn't mention that Goro Inaba was familiar. He's sure he recognised the mess of hair, the brownstone complexion, the sharp bone structure.

'And your friends?'

'I'd have thought they're a bit worried about me, seeing as it's almost lunchtime and I haven't been back to my hotel.'

The man takes another drag on the cigarette and stubs it out in the ashtray.

'But enough about me,' says Jackie. 'You're a yakuza. These men are yakuza and, judging by the arse-licking, I'd bet you're their boss. Your man Inaba has broken a few house rules. Gone rogue.' He gestures around the room. 'Maybe he's using. The furniture in here is functional at best; he doesn't even have a suite, just mismatched sofas. A man making the kind of money a yakuza pulls in could easily afford better unless he's shooting his profits into his veins.' Jackie looks at ponytail, then back to the authority figure opposite. 'This fella Inaba steps in and stops a kicking for some random foreigner last night. What's that all about? Have you asked Fox over there what happened while I was lying in the street for the taking?'

The yakuza boss sits back in the sofa and locks his fingers across his flat stomach.

'Goro Inaba is my right hand man,' he says. 'He turned up just as my men were about to cut you and yelled at them – Fucking idiots! Knifing a foreigner! Did they want to bring the whole police force down on us? He was right. Hokkaido makes a lot of money from tourism and Sapporo has an American consulate. The last thing we need is that kind of trouble. He sent my men away. Goro Inaba said he would get you cleaned up, shove some money in your pocket, check your wallet and have a taxi take you back to your hotel. That's the last anyone from my organisation saw him.' The man leans forward and offers Jackie a smoke. Jackie shakes his head. The man shrugs and lights up again.

'My organisation is the Kanto Daichi-kai. You would call it a gang but for us, it is a family.' The man's eyes glaze for a moment. 'When one of our family disappears, we worry. I sent Fox and a couple of his "brothers" over to see if Inaba was home, if he was okay. What they found was a lost gaijin bumping into taxis and yelling at the driver. I was already on my way over. And here we are.' He splays his arms wide, then balances the cigarette in the glass ashtray before placing his hands on his knees and bowing.

'It is a pleasure to meet you, Jackie San,' he says. 'My name is Reizo Himura and I am oyabun of the Kanto Daichi-kai. Please think well of me.'

Chapter 12

Megan can hear her father's rapid breathing on the back seat of the people carrier. He sits on her right, furious with terror, grinding his teeth and shifting his hips like a restless child on a long car journey. On her left, the gangster's stale breath assaults her nostrils. The thug reeks of tobacco and tooth decay.

The driver glances at her in the rear-view mirror, his eyes like polished black prayer beads. His expression changes with each shadow that slopes across his face: now angry, now confused, now resolute, now guilty. Is the last a result of the hard slap he gave her, the fact that he terrorised a father and his daughter with a gun less than an hour ago? She doubts it.

The sprawling suburbs of Sapporo gave way to ragged country-side a while back. Now they pass forested hills and flat lands scarred with haphazard farming and shack-like houses. Some distance off on the right, a great shaft of rock shears through the forest to a jagged peak. They're heading south. She's travelled this road before, to Jozankei hot spring resort.

Her father had called her in the morning, worried about his friend, Jackie. The Irishman hadn't met her dad for breakfast and reception hadn't been able to call him in his room. Jackie, her father told her, had been in trouble before. He could take care of himself but they were a long way from home, and her dad couldn't help but worry. There was a darkness in Jackie, he'd said. Might not that darkness act as a magnet, drawing other, more malicious characters? Megan had suppressed a sigh and told her father to catch a cab and come to her apartment. They could figure things out over a cup of tea. She could always call Yuji and, if it came to it, the police. She was a pragmatist. This talk of darkness, of evil, was nonsense. A sign of her father ageing.

Then the three thugs entered her apartment building with her dad, and she was confronted with a very real manifestation of the darker corners of human nature.

Ian Sparrow knows he's almost panting but his fear is racing ahead of conscious thought, climbing higher than the jagged peak the car has just passed. Fear like he's never known. Fear for Megan. Not the past, irrational terror that Megan-as-excited-toddler might sprint into a busy road; or the dull fear in his gut as he stared at the ceiling above the bed in the wee small hours, vague notions of what dangers might befall her as the student Megan enjoyed the nightlife of the big city. This is the very real fear of bad men, inches away, hurting his little girl and the fear that now, for the first time, he can't protect her.

He had called the lift and one of them, the man with a bandage on his hand, rode up with him, passing the third floor on their way to the seventh. As Megan opened the door, the blonde man with the cut on his face, appearing from nowhere, shoulder charged Sparrow into the hallway and drew a gun from his jacket pocket. Megan yelped. Ian called her name. The thug pointed the gun and put his fingers to his lips. Sparrow grabbed his daughter's arm and pulled her to him. The goon called someone on his mobile as he held them at gunpoint. When his bandaged companion arrived back from the seventh floor ruse, they listened to the thugs' guttural exchange.

Megan stares at the big country unfurling by the car window and thinks back to the snarl of the men as they congratulated each other on the success of their plan.

Megan remembers her father, panicked, gabbling at them.

The men barked, 'No English!'

That was their mantra.

'Who are you?'

'No English!'

'What's happening?'

'No English!'

'What do you want?'

'No English!'

Megan had sat mute, stunned by the sudden violation of her home. Her father clutched her arm and whispered that he recognised the blonde one, had seen him last night outside the convenience store, that he was one of the three thugs who intimidated her friends. She had studied the man. Her father was right.

'Please,' she said, 'we don't understand. My father is on holiday, visiting me. We don't want any trouble. Take what you want.'

The Japanese stopped them short. A foreigner, a woman, speaking their language. Then a mobile phone rang, and the bandaged man had an animated conversation with an angry voice on the other end of the line.

The thugs killed the call and waited. Megan prayed that someone had heard the commotion, seen the shady characters enter the building. Should she scream? Throw something, try to break a window? Megan was furious with herself for not putting up more of a fight.

Thirty minutes later the goons' slim, gaunt leader strode into the room. Beads of sweat hung on his forehead. There was a bulge in his t-shirt just under his left shoulder and specks of something dark had seeped through the cotton. The leader handed his mobile to her father and Megan heard a woman speaking in faltering English on speakerphone.

'You go with these men. If cooperate, you are okay. Go down to car. Get in and they drive. Okay?'

Ian Sparrow, belligerent, said, 'And if we don't cooperate? What then?'

A bewildered silence.

The obvious questions spun around father and daughter. Who were these men? What did they want? And the perennial question asked by victims of crime: *Why us?*

The answers were an impenetrable mystery, like the truth of events in the morning after a booze blackout.

Megan took the phone and said they understood; they wanted no trouble. The yakuza took her and her father's wallets and mobile phones. A black people carrier, tinted windows drawing a veil over the interior, had been parked in front of the building.

Now, as the faint buzz of a bi-plane passes somewhere overhead, the blonde-haired thug gazes out of the window, then snorts and swallows something thick in his mouth. His fingers brush the small laceration on his face, the result of some street brawl no doubt. Megan hears a soft moan from her father on her right. She turns to him and Ian Sparrow offers his daughter an apathetic wink. He is bearing up and she wonders, not for the first time, what he saw and did when Megan was a young child and he was a soldier. The third yakuza – for she knows they must be yakuza – in the front passenger seat rubs his bandaged left hand and plays with the car radio. The driver grunts an order and the passenger fiddles with a cigarette packet, earning a sharp rebuke for his fumbling. He hands the smoke to the driver who lowers the window and lights up.

'Very civil,' whispers Ian Sparrow.

'No English!' The driver and blonde thug shout in unison.

Megan, her nerves frayed to breaking point, snaps, 'He's thanking you for putting the window down. Shouldn't your code of chivalry appreciate that?' Her voice is almost a screech. Her Japanese is a smack across the face and the three gangsters balk. The blonde thug on her left raises his hand in delayed anger but the driver stays him with a grunted, 'Oi!'

She glares at the gangster beside her and feels her dad shift position, his weight straining against her.

'Tell your father to relax,' says the driver, 'my friend won't hurt you.'

She translates.

The gaunt driver meets her eyes in the rear-view mirror and says, 'I promise you, if you and your father do what you are told, no harm will come to you. In a few days, you will be free to go. I know that's hard to believe right now but I can only give you my word.' He takes a drag on the cigarette. She whispers a translation to her father.

The driver says, 'We'll be travelling for another couple of hours. If you want to pee, let me know.' He takes another, long drag on his cigarette and flicks it out of the car window. 'My ex-wife isn't a smoker and hated the smell of cigarettes. I want to spare you the second-hand smoke.'

The dark eyes search her out in the mirror again. They are hooded. The man looks tired, thinks Megan. More than tired, dispirited.

The gaunt yakuza rolls his head on his thin neck and nods a brief bow, his eyes on the road once more.

'I'm sorry for your troubles,' he says. 'Forgive me.'

#

Reizo Himura squints through a pall of cigarette smoke and repeats, 'They are gone.'

Jackie says, 'Something's wrong.'

'You are not as important to your friends as you thought.'

'No. I know Ian. He'd be checking his phone constantly waiting for my call.'

'There is poor reception in the mountains, or some of the underground shopping malls, or in the larger beer halls.'

Himura had called Ian Sparrow. It was no kindness, Jackie knew. The yakuza had an enigma on his hands with a missing lieutenant and a beat-up gaijin in his top man's apartment. Did he believe Jackie's story? And the girl, Aina: the mention of her slashing Goro Inaba had darkened the man's stark gaze. Why trust a gaijin who had already marked a couple of his men? Perhaps any corroboration was welcome so, when Jackie had asked Himura to call Ian, the gangster had played along.

Ian's phone was dead.

Himura had called the front desk at Jackie's hotel and sent a couple of men over for a face-to-face with the receptionists.

Ian was gone.

Sparrow had left a message for Jackie to call him whenever he could and headed over to his daughter's apartment. Now Himura is on his mobile with his goons. His goons are at Megan's place. They ring the doorbell, knock and finally break in.

The apartment is empty.

Jackie says, 'Can your men see anything unusual in the apartment? Signs of a struggle?'

'And what are signs of a struggle?'

'Take a look around,' says Jackie, pointing to the broken coffee table. Himura stares at him. Jackie bobs his head and says, 'Please.'

The oyabun snaps a few sentences down the line in Japanese. They wait. After a couple of minutes, he says, 'Nothing.'

Jackie feels something sickening and familiar rise in his gut, creeping toward his chest. If he doesn't control it, it'll erupt from his mouth in a scream – *Trouble. Violence. Darkness.*

His past, distant and recent, rushing up to ambush him. Again.

'Does that thing have Skype?' he says, nodding to Himura's mobile.

'Of course.'

'Put it on and tell your men to sweep the apartment with their camera. Let me see the screen.'

The eyes flicker in their sockets and a scarlet flush rises in Reizo Himura's cheeks. He says, 'You are not the oyabun here. Remember who the fuck you're talking to or I'll cut your gaijin throat.' The men idling around the room, picking up on the cold anger in his tone, shift position.

I don't have time for cultural awareness 101, thinks Jackie. But he swallows his frustration and says, 'Of course. I didn't mean to disrespect you but I'm worried for my friends. As you would be for your men. I hope you can understand.'

Himura glares for a beat. Then he barks into his mobile and kills the call. His fingers work the screen and a different ringtone chirps. The yakuza holds the screen to his face, growls a command and hands the mobile to Jackie.

Jackie looks at a shaky image of a small apartment. There are glimpses of a well-kept room with a television, sofa and bed. A laptop is on the duvet. The camera is moving too fast, offering impressions of the space rather than a picture for study. Cramped, clean, mundane. Another yakuza is leaning against the wall, bored. Jackie sets his mouth and wills the thug holding the phone to slow down and stand still. 'Could you ask your man to sweep the room more slowly? I apologise, but I can't concentrate if he moves so fast.'

Himura nods and leans toward the phone, giving a command. The others can't understand, thinks Jackie. None of them speak English. That is why I'm getting away with this. The men don't know what we say, don't know their master is taking his lead from a foreigner. Jackie bows, appreciative, to help Himura preserve pride in front of his subordinates. The image improves, clarifies. Jackie sees nothing strange.

'That's enough,' says Himura.

Jackie bows again. 'One more thing, please. If you could ask your men to focus on the floor. Slowly.'

The yakuza boss finishes a smoke and grinds the butt in the ashtray, hard. He orders his men to scan the floor of Megan's apartment with the mobile camera. The living space is carpeted and immaculate. Not much of a job to vaccuum such a small space. The corridor is spotless pale grey linoleum. Except –

'There!' says Jackie. Himura leans over to check the screen. The area around the apartment door has a series of faint marks. Scuff marks. Boot and shoe prints. The camera follows the corridor to the carpeted living area. The marks stop a few inches before the carpet begins.

'Someone was inside the apartment with their shoes on,' says Jackie.

'Your friends are foreigners. They might wear their shoes indoors.'

'Megan has been here for a year. Her boyfriend is Japanese, she'd follow the Japanese customs. We all had to take our shoes off at the entrance to the izakaya last night so Ian knows the form and his daughter would tell him to take his shoes off in her place anyway. And look.' He points at the screen. 'There is more than one set of prints. There was a group of people in that apartment but I'd bet no one walked as far in as the carpet. It's too clean.'

Himura peers closer at the screen. His men are fixated on the mobile too. The oyabun looks up at Jackie.

'Are you a cop?'

'Not any more. A long time ago.'

'And now?'

'I'm on holiday,' says Jackie, 'with my friends. At least I was.' The disquiet in his gut flares again. 'They've been taken.'

With the words out, a calm settles on him. He leans back on the sofa and takes a deep breath.

Ian and Megan. Goro Inaba. Coincidence? Reizo Himura has lost his lieutenant; Jackie has lost his friends. He looks to the ceiling and makes his peace with the fact that, for now, he'll be shaking hands with the devil to save a couple of lambs.

#

Shintaro Ishikawa catches himself bowing at his desk as he reports to his superior in Tokyo, the phone at his ear, and thinks, What the fuck am I doing, bowing at a telephone? But he keeps his voice supplicant, soothing the old man's ego and oiling the rails of Ishikawa's personal advancement, professional and carnal.

He clears his throat as he clears his mind of the fantasy of Fujijko Maki lying naked on his bed and says, 'This is my humble opinion, Oya San. Himura's organisation is the largest syndicate in Hokkaido. He has varied and strong ties with law enforcement and government at a city and prefectural level. By forging alliances and manipulating many smaller operations, he has done much to maintain a stability and peace in Sapporo. Susukino does not solely belong to the Kanto Daichi-kai but they are the largest operator in the area. As a result, they enjoy modest business arrangements with the Russians. Of course, whether we would wish to pursue that particular avenue further, bearing in mind how volatile the Bratva can be, is another matter.'

The voice on the line grunts, 'So, so.'

Eat shit, thinks Ishikawa. You send me up here to work with these barbarians while you sit on your decrepit ass in Ginza getting blown by five-hundred-dollars-a-night foreign whores, and all you can say to my report is "so, so"?

A cry in his head punctures his anger: the image of Fujiko Maki, back arched, legs locked around his waist convulsing in climax as she calls out, 'So! So! Yes! I'm cumming!'

His face flushes, his crotch stirs. He says, 'Your judgement is unimpeachable. You were perceptive and wise as ever to explore these possibilities in Hokkaido. There are further avenues to be exploited in the Northern Territories. While the Russians hold the northernmost islands, the Kanto Daichi-kai links with their fraternities are of great value coupled with their political connections within Hokkaido itself. It would provide possible access to the oil and gas exploration project on Sakhalin. There are minerals and rare metals on some of the other islands. Perhaps, most importantly, the strait between Kunashiri and Etorofu does not freeze in winter, providing year round access to Vladivostok and the Russian Pacific Fleet. There are many young sailors and whores sitting out the long nights in port: a vibrant market for our heroin and methamphetamine operations.'

The eighty-three year-old vocal cords of the Tokyo oyabun creak higher in interest, 'So?'

In the fantasy, Fujiko Maki's voice lowers to a satisfied purr as he lays his head on the soft pillow of her belly, her long fingers tracing the knife scar on his crown, buried beneath his hundred-dollar haircut.

'However,' he says, 'I regret to inform you that there are issues with Himura San's management of his organisation.'

'So?'

'There was a killing in one of his clubs two nights ago. A man had his throat cut in a fetish establishment. The man was a police officer being courted as a potential source within the Hokkaido police. No culprit has been found although one has been suggested by the first lieutenant, Inaba. Clearly, this matter must be dealt with before we could consider any formal arrangement with the Kanto Daichi-kai. It may be expedient to encourage Himura San to give me a larger role within the syndicate, in order to close this matter with the professionalism that his men appear to, regrettably, lack.' To close him down, thinks Ishikawa, and enjoy his woman.

The frail voice on the other end of the line hardens. 'It might be expedient not to presume my course of action, Ishikawa San. You are my advisor and your counsel is greatly appreciated, but you are not a policy maker. And you are no longer a soldier.'

Ishikawa bows until his forehead is a fraction from his desk and breathes a rushed, profuse apology. He is glad that he is alone in the room, that his men aren't present.

Old bastard, he thinks. The only policy you're concerned with now is who's going to wipe your ass and how much you can squirrel away for your idiot son.

The voice on the phone says, 'Do not underestimate these people. They are descended from hardy stock. Their ancestors forged a life in a harsh, unforgiving countryside, crossed vast mountain ranges. Give Himura San some time to rectify this infringement of his territory and business. Observe. Nothing more.'

'Of course, Oya San.' – *Shit drip! Lech! Cowardly old fart!* – 'I am, as always, your devoted son and servant.'

They exchange the usual formalities and end the call. Ishikawa places the receiver in its cradle and looks around at the bare concrete walls. A scuttling in the corner gives lie to the fallacy that Hokkaido is free of the cockroaches that plague the south.

The gambit was worth a shot. Push his boss to lobby Himura, give Ishikawa a foot in the Kanto Daichi-kai organisational door. From there, he could have dismantled the syndicate from within, deposed Himura and rebuilt the Sapporo outfit, moulding it to his own desires. And Maki San. He could have shown Fujiko how a true yakuza could fulfil her needs, protect her and glorify her. He logs out of his desktop and stands, his body lithe and responsive. He takes care of it, oils and tends it as he does his swords. No longer a soldier? Fuck that doddering old goat with his whores and his Viagra, and his pride.

Ishikawa takes the metal pin-badge, grey and white, from his pocket and turns it in his fingers, studying the emblem from several angles.

Fuck that doddering old goat back in Tokyo!

He slips the pin-badge back in his pocket, goes to the door and thrusts it open, startling the bodyguard playing with his mobile on the other side. This building is the largest property owned by the Kanto Daichi-kai, the hub of the syndicate and they sit in its bowels. Grey concrete corridors wind like intestines past storerooms, waste disposal areas and Ishikawa's makeshift office. Ishikawa and his men are in the shit-hole at the end of the world.

No more.

'Get the car,' he says. 'We're going to visit Fujiko Maki San.'

Chapter 13

The three black BMW saloons come to a halt in front of a metal-framed walkway roofed with scratched perspex. The drivers ease themselves out of the cars and open doors for their superiors. Reizo Himura exits the BMW with a practiced grace; Jackie is awkward and laboured in comparison. In the car behind, another yakuza enjoys a level of deference. A wired, agitated looking man with hunted eyes. Nakata, Himura had said, his second lieutenant. Fox and his silver-haired acolyte unfold themselves from the third car.

The walkway is wedged between a clapboard house and a concrete two-storey apartment building with a thin sliver of weed-choked hardscrabble dirt struggling to pass as a garden. A sign next to the walkway sports a Japanese kanji character, like an un-dotted "j" hooked by a scribbled sickle.

'Please,' says Himura, gesturing for Jackie to follow as he steps through the metal arch under the perspex. The men stroll behind, six in total. The same number stand around the cars chatting and laughing, Fox scowling among them.

They come to a wooden sliding door set in a crumbling concrete wall. Following Himura, Jackie steps through into a small lobby lined with lockers in which they place their shoes. There are two more sliding doors of frosted glass, one with a red, shoulder length curtain displaying Japanese characters, the other, a blue curtain. They duck under the blue curtain, and enter an open room with a couple of benches in the centre of a tatami floor. The air is close with the scent of matting in the humid air. What look like oversized pigeonhole units cover the left wall. The wall on the right is a tall partition with a gap between the upper edge and ceiling. At the far end of the space is a wall of frosted glass with another sliding door set in the centre.

Next to the entrance through which they passed is a polished wooden box-like platform, not unlike a miniature pulpit. Himura nods at the small, hunched old woman perched in the platform reading a newspaper. Her face is the colour and texture of dried pear, her shoulders crooked as though gravity were exacting a toll for her longevity.

'A bandai platform,' says Himura. 'This is one of the only public baths left in Sapporo that has one. Most of them have a simple front desk now. I'm not a sentimental man but sometimes there's just no need to lose the old ways.'

Nakata produces a thick wad of yen, handing it to the old woman. As the men begin undressing, she nods and leafs through the money. There is a sign taped to the glass of the door, a cartoon image of someone with a tattoo refused entry to a similar establishment. They are in a sentō. A traditional bathhouse. Jackie visited one in Tokyo with a Japanese detective. Like all public baths in Japan, this sentō has a ban on tattoos. He points at the sign.

'Are you welcome here?'

Chuckles ripple around the men when they grasp his meaning.

Himura eases out of his shirt and says, 'Like so much in this country, it's all for show. An American college kid shows up on his gap year with a tattoo of a sports team on his arm, he won't get further than this room.' Himura's shoulders and chest are covered in an intricate mosaic of demonic heads, oriental clouds and cherry blossoms, framed by thick cords of knotted rope. 'But you really think any of the baths in this city, or any other, are going to refuse us entry? It's a social contract. We don't show up at any popular tourist hot springs or plush hotel spas so they don't lose their reputation and the small, neighbourhood places like this let us bathe because it's good for business.'

'And the other punters? The regular people?'

'Katagi no shu,' says Himura, his chin jutting. 'The "People under the sun": that's what some yakuza call *regular* people. The regular people have a saying about us. "Dealing with the yakuza is like feeding a tiger: stop feeding it and the tiger will eat you." I guess they figure, ignore the tiger and it will go away.'

He turns to shout something at one of the men and a blood-red carp flexes across his shoulder blade, glaring at Jackie with a huge, furious eye, the skin pimpled, almost scaly, around it. Three of the men are covered in body art save for a thin strip of uninked skin from groin to throat. Designs cover Nakata's arms and shoulders. The other two have no tattoos.

'I thought you'd be covered head-to-foot,' says Jackie, 'being the boss man.'

'I got these when I was young and foolish. It was seen as a duty by the old boss. I don't enforce it with my men. It has its advantages: it's still expected by many so it sits better when I do business with other families if I have at least some tattoos.' He smiles. 'Take your clothes off.'

We're taking a bath, thinks Jackie, while my friends have been kidnapped.

Kidnapped. His memory crashes through: a squalid barn. A disfigured, heavy wooden chair. Ropes biting into his wrists. Cigarettes searing his skin, a belt striping his shoulders, the buckle gouging. A knife. A drunk murderer drinking tea and eating sandwiches while Jackie bleeds and sweats and prays. Back then a girl had been kidnapped, a girl Jackie had sworn to protect. He was taken and beaten, goaded, tortured. But the girl is safe now and the men who took her, the men who tormented Jackie, are gone, cold in the ground.

A year on and Ian and Megan have been taken but, rather than cigarette burns and knife scars, he's going to have his back scrubbed with the local talent.

But this is Japan. These people won't be hurried. They will do whatever they need to in their own time and they will do it right. And what choice does Jackie have but to play along? He can't go to the cops. He has no ID or money. He's lost his wallet and mobile. He thinks of Yuji Miyamoto and wonders if the young man's brother has turned up.

Jackie offers a small nod to Himura and eases out of his coat. 'Well, it looks like we're in business,' he says.

Himura offers a hand. Jackie takes it.

#

They stew in two deep, tiled baths, each twenty foot by twelve. The temperature is ferocious, broiling the men as they groan and grunt and chat. A couple of gangsters sit on the edge of the pools with small white towels on their heads. All have a well-practised masculinity, gruff, insouciant, fraternal. They showered before entering the baths, scrubbing their naked bodies, the tattoos stretched and contracted, and washed the soap away with buckets of scalding water. The carp on Himura's back seemed to glare as the cloth stretched the oyabun's skin and muscle. Jackie caught them staring at his scars when he hauled his t-shirt over his stiff shoulders. One of them pointed to the knot of discoloured, twisted skin on his forearm and Himura asked if Jackie had had a tattoo.

'Yes,' he said, 'a mistake. When I had it removed, the ink had its revenge. Marked me in a way I can't wipe clean.'

No one had asked about the berserk network of knife wounds on his chest. Jackie has a romantic notion as he stews in the steaming water, of yakuza from long ago, crouching on a clay floor sporting traditional topknots, soaking in pine tubs.

'You aren't uncomfortable?' says Himura.

'Fucking boiling. Throw a couple of spuds in here and you could serve me with a bit of marie rose.'

Himura's face twists in amused confusion and surprise. He says, 'You aren't American. Where are you from?'

'I'm Irish. Northern Irish. Not that that means much to you.'

'I know about your problems. I.R.A. All of that. I have an interest in divided countries.' Himura splays his arms along the tiled rim of the pool. 'What happened?' He eyes the network of ragged scars across Jackie's chest and shoulders.

'One of my countrymen thought he'd try and divide me from my skin.'

'Cigarette burns and knife work. It is very poor.'

'In his defence, he was drunk. Think of them as tribal scars. Made by the other tribe.'

'And this man. Where is he now?'

'Roasting on a spit with the devil's skewer up his arse.'

'This means he's dead, right?'

'Aye. Yes.'

Himura looks into Jackie's eyes as though he's just realised there's something worth exploring in them.

'You are very calm. You were in a street fight last night, woke up in a strange place and had another fight – and your friends have gone missing. Now you are naked, sharing a bath with gangsters.'

I have probably killed more men than anyone in this room, thinks Jackie.

He says, 'When you're a cop, you learn interrogation techniques. You come at a suspect from a supposed position of power. They are in your territory, the police station. You do your best to control the interview.' He gestures to the men scattered around the bathing area. 'I wouldn't say I'm the man in power right now, would you?'

Himura smiles.

Jackie says, 'So all I can do is bide my time. You want me for something. Maybe you need me. I'm shit-scared that something's happened to my friends but it looks like your man, Inaba, could be involved.' A couple of the men glance over at the mention of the name, then resume their posturing. 'You say he saved me because violence against a foreigner is bad for business. Maybe, maybe not – but he turned up at the apartment with an empty gun and threw a knife out of reach when he could easily have cut me. I'm betting he wanted to scare me but keep me in one piece. I'm betting he's got my friends and I'm betting he doesn't want to hurt them, either.'

Himura nods.

'Not so sure your intentions are all that honourable, though' says Jackie.

Himura looks around at the other yakuza. His chin moves in slow circles as he grinds his teeth, like a cow chewing the cud. 'These are good men,' he says. 'They are honest and loyal but now, they are confused. They feel betrayed. We have a code of honour and Inaba, by his actions, has broken it. He has disappeared, perhaps kidnapped your friends. Many yakuza are outcasts and misfits. They come from broken homes, or lower classes, or immigrant families: Chinese and Korean. They find brotherhood, success, structure in the family of the organisation. When one of their own abandons them, they are unsettled. Lost.'

Jackie gazes at the opaque rectangles of light swimming on the surface of the water and the distorted tangle of legs glimpsed below. 'So much for the tourist brochure,' he says. The heavy sarcasm in his voice raises a couple of heads again.

Himura fixes him with a hard stare.

Then the yakuza boss smiles. 'Okay. They are criminals but they are mostly good men. However, there are other parties involved, associates from Tokyo, who I don't trust. And then there's the competition. We had an incident a couple of nights ago that could be seen as an opportunity by the other organisations in Sapporo. I need to sort out this problem with Inaba. To regroup and strengthen my hand again.' He runs his fingers through his slicked hair. 'I, too, believe he has your friends, and I believe he wants you, too. I think it's linked to the incident I mentioned. I think it is good to keep you around for now as my guest.' His mouth splits in a grin to reveal irregular, small white teeth, like bone chips embedded in his dark gums. 'Now I know you were a cop you may be able to help me.'

'And what about the real cops? Would they be happy to know a foreigner was your guest? What if someone at my hotel calls them, reports I haven't been around?'

'You're free to go. See what kind of reception you get from our wonderful police force. A beat up gaijin with wild stories about the yakuza and kidnappings. No wallet. You are a foreigner with no identification and bloodied knuckles. In their eyes, you are a bigger menace than us because they don't understand you. Many of the cops here will take our word over yours because we are Japanese.' He closes his eyes, still grinning. 'Besides, it's been less than twenty-four hours since you were seen at the hotel. And you haven't been involved in any illegal activities since you joined us. Although, before that, you did assault a taxi driver and cause a public disturbance after you fled a crime scene still showing "signs of a struggle" with blood on the walls.'

Jackie smiles too. Smart bastard. Bloody hell, he thinks, I've missed east Asia.

'Okay,' he says, 'I think we can help each other.'

#

She is scared. Shintaro Ishikawa wants to reach out and touch the cool silk of her cheek, run his fingers down the naked sweep of her neck.

Himura's man says, 'Should I call Himura San?'

The fool is hunched in deference, a hulking counterpoint to Fujiko Maki's easy beauty and grace.

'That won't be necessary, Saburo,' she says. 'I'm sure Ishikawa San wouldn't be here if there weren't a compelling reason and I'm sure he won't stay longer than is expedient.' She bows to Shintaro Ishikawa. 'My apologies but I am still somewhat drained by the events of Friday night.'

'Of course,' says Ishikawa. He turns to the local thug. 'Some tea.'

He suppresses a cold fury when he catches the brief nod from Fujiko. These peasants continue to deny his authority, deferring to a woman before a representative of the Yamaguchi gumi syndicate. The ignorant oaf will suffer when Himura is gone. Fujiko will honour Ishikawa's authority after a more pleasurable education.

She shows him into a living room hung with sketches of local landmarks. In the corner, next to the window overlooking Naka-jima Park and the western peaks, sits a drawing table and various art materials. She gestures for him to sit on one of the cream sofas. Then she folds her long legs, wrapped in skin-tight jeans, onto the sofa on his right.

'To what do I owe the pleasure of this visit, Ishikawa San?'

'I am concerned for you. The trauma of what you witnessed on Friday. Terrible. For such a rare and gentle woman to be exposed to that violence is outrageous.'

She repositions herself on the sofa. It is his comment that is out-rageous, in the home of an oyabun's woman. He enjoys her discomfort and tries not to stare at the soft curve of her hips as her slender weight shifts. Fujiko keeps her gaze lowered, looking at the table in front of the sofas.

'Your concern is very much appreciated,' she says. This is a vio-lation, his presence in her home. She is not married to Reizo but Ishikawa should never presume to visit her without Reizo present.

'Have you seen Goro Inaba San recently?' Ishikawa's voice is low, soothing. Almost conspiratorial. The answer should be no, he thinks. Inaba hasn't been to the Big-Touch building since yesterday. The last most of the men saw him was at the small drinking den last night and Ishikawa had seen Himura's second lieutenant, Nakata, in the parking lot before driving over. A brief exchange, a mention of the Yamaguchi syndicate name, a couple of probing questions about Himura's whereabouts and the weak-minded idiot blabbed that Inaba has disappeared and his oyabun is out search-ing.

'I have not seen Inaba San personally,' says Fujiko. 'But I believe Himura San was talking with him this morning.'

You're lying, thinks Ishikawa. *Himura is searching the city for him as we speak. When we are together, I must chastise you for your deceit.*

'I see,' he says. 'Then I would advise Himura San to proceed with great caution in his dealings with Inaba. Something has come to my attention that shocks and saddens me. I believe it sheds light on the culprit of that terrible incident two nights ago.'

You bastard, thinks Fujiko. *If you know anything that might help in the search for the killer, you should have contacted Reizo directly.* 'While distressing,' she says, 'I am sure Himura San will be most grateful for any intelligence that might resolve the issue.' – *I wish he would cut your unscrupulous throat, you pompous Tokyo asshole.*

She sees Saburo standing in the doorway holding a tray and feels a warm rush of gratitude that, for a moment, no matter how fleeting, she won't be alone with this monster and his secrets.

Ishikawa inspects the tea and small dorayaki pancakes filled with sweet red bean paste. He tolerates the lumbering bodyguard for as long as it takes Himura's goon to serve them, and is irritated when Fujiko asks the thug for an update as to where Himura is. As the man makes to leave the room, she tells Saburo to call Himura and inform him Ishikawa awaits him in her apartment. Her eyes are a fraction wild. Ishikawa watches a vein pulsing in her exquisite neck, fascinated. He fancies he can see the contours of the glands and muscles, flexing and straining in her throat. He feels himself swell and stiffen. He summons the image of Goro Inaba, jostling obscene notions out of his mind.

'I regret,' he says, 'I cannot stay. Please tell your man' – his face sets for a moment – 'it is not necessary to contact Himura San. I will see him this evening.'

He sips at the tea, his liver-like tongue slipping out of his lined mouth. The cha is hot and bitter.

Fujiko channels her revulsion – *he's a reptile, not human!* – into numb composure.

She takes a confection and nibbles. The pancake and thick, sweet paste melt in her mouth but turn to ash at the sight of Ishikawa attempting a smile.

'If you are busy, Ishikawa San, I would not presume to keep you.

I am sure you have much more pressing matters than to sit with me. It is true, women lack the strength of our men but, in time, I will reconcile the events of Friday.' *So, noble samurai, superior, great and strong paragon of Japanese manhood, get the hell out of my apartment!*

Ishikawa reaches into his jacket pocket and produces a handkerchief. A small metal object nestles in the material with an emblem engraved in the setting. She stares at the plain outline of the oblong oval symbol with two small lines jutting from its tail. The object is unmistakable. A pin-badge, grey with a white symbol. A foul brown crust of dried blood covers half the badge.

As Ishikawa lowers his head he watches Fujiko, enjoys the flutter of recognition and confusion on her face.

My god, when you are frightened! How you'll look under me, dominated! I'll tear you apart: I'll possess you!

He says, his voice a touch thick, 'This morning I went to Inaba San's office in Big-Touch building. I wanted to discuss some terms related to our possible patronage of the Kanto Daichi-kai. I took the liberty of trying his door when he did not answer me. It was unlocked. I entered and noticed a handkerchief, much like mine, on his desk. A corner of the handkerchief was a rust colour.' He manages a melancholic smile. 'I have been a yakuza long enough to know blood when I see it. Forgive my indiscretion but I opened the handkerchief and found this inside. I suspect the emblem has connotations with the police. It concerns me as to Inaba's motives for dealing with the cop.'

Fujiko swallows. She remembers the Tengu demon – *it looked at me. Stared at me. Tilted its head like I was an insect to be studied. The window: it tapped the window* – the blood, the dull violence of the boot hammering the glass. *My god! It's his. The dead cop's.*

Ishikawa leans forward in concern. His jaw works as though he is willing himself to offer some words of comfort but they are caught in his throat, stymied by emotion.

'I am sorry,' he says. 'I know Inaba and Himura San were close,' – *She's fucking carnal! Wrap this up before you lose it and take her here, on the fucking sofa!* – 'I must go but please, keep this badge and show it to Himura San.' His mobile buzzes in his breast pocket. 'Excuse me.'

A short text from one of his men. Himura is climbing out of a car parked across the street from Fujiko Maki San's building. Shit, he thinks, I could have planted the seed of doubt deeper with a couple more minutes. Still, the die is cast. With luck, he has laid suspicion of police collusion at the missing Inaba's feet. The first step in dismantling the Sapporo outfit's hierarchy. He takes a last look at Fujiko Maki, memorising the sight of her long fingers, the smooth curve of her hips, her tight mouth. Her haunted eyes.

Then he stands and, bowing, leaves the room. Himura's man stares at him for a beat before remembering his place and offering a bow and a muttered farewell. Ishikawa slips on his shoes and waits as the man opens the door for him. It is only when the lift is settling at the lobby that the last trace of his erection withers and dies.

Chapter 14

As the car eases to the kerb, Reizo Himura's mobile trills with a J-Pop ringtone. He listens, then grunts a few words in Japanese. They idle next to a large park rimmed with tired looking trees who have given up in the face of encroaching winter. Himura kills the call and turns to Jackie.

'A loose end. Inaba suggested a salaryman as a possible name for the first killing on Friday night. My men just paid him a visit at his office. He broke his leg on Thursday in a company soccer game.' He sniffs. 'It was a long shot anyway.'

A bit like going on holiday and getting stuck in the middle of a mafia murder-fest, thinks Jackie. He'd sat in the plush pod of the BMW and listened to a chronology of killings and deceit. A bent policeman gets his throat cut in a twisted fetish club on Friday night. The working girl is the sole witness; another dirty copper turns up dead, cut to ribbons by the river sometime last night; the local talent's second-in-command goes AWOL but manages to fit in a quick dust-up with Jackie, after saving Jackie from adding to his collection of scars in a Susukino back-street; Jackie's friend and his mate's daughter are missing – *Christ! Ian and Megan* – and, in the midst of some maniac in a Halloween mask carving up the Bad Apples of Sapporo city police, there's a power-play in progress between the local colour and a major syndicate from down south.

Jackie can glimpse the peak of a mountain through the rabble of balding trees on his left, a cable car creeping toward the peak. No doubt full of tourists, catching the view of the city in all its autumnal glory.

A holiday, he thinks. Next time he'll go for a package deal.

Himura steps onto the pavement. He gestures for Jackie to join him. A line of cars has already formed in the busy downtown traffic as the BMW blocks the lane on the far-left but no one honks or yells. A police car sits five vehicles back, waiting for things to start moving again. Another Kanto Daichi-kai man joins them and the BMW glides into the smooth flow of traffic once again. They are here to introduce Jackie to the witness to the first murder, the girl working the fetish club. Himura's girl.

Himura touches Jackie's elbow and points to an apartment block across the road. There are lights a couple of hundred yards away but Himura's man strides into traffic to clear a path for his oyabun.

'Is he Moses?' says Jackie.

'Moh-says?'

'Doesn't matter.'

The volume of traffic keeps speedometers low but there are still a couple of emergency stops as they walk over to the building entrance. As the low-ranking yakuza reaches for the console next to the smoked glass door, the panel slides back to reveal a slim middle-aged man in an immaculate suit with a murderous look in his eye. Neat hair, thick neck, sharp cheekbones framing a hawk nose and tight-set mouth, lines crawling from the lips like cracks in concrete. His dark gaze burrows into Jackie as though he has seen a glimpse of some terrible truth in his eyes. They stand for a moment like boxers at a weigh-in. Jackie has seen the look many times, in uniform and out, in Belfast, Hong Kong and elsewhere. Hatred crosses all borders. They face off for a couple of seconds before the man remembers himself and turns to bow at Himura.

Jackie catches snippets of their back-and-forth, their voices rasping. The Sapporo oyabun clenches his fist. The middle-aged man is ramrod straight. Old school, thinks Jackie, like the Osaka and Tokyo boys who used to fly in for confabs with the Triads back when he worked the HK beat. Their top men held themselves with the same controlled arrogance. This bastard could be standing in a sentry box at Buckingham Palace.

Then each yakuza takes a step back and bows. The middle-aged man strides away from the apartment building.

The entrance hall is spare and plush, all marble effect pillars and soft lighting. A large urn in a corner holds an ikebana display of bamboo leaf and purple flowers. Two banks of metal mailboxes are set in the walls to their left and right, the lift ahead, opposite the glass entrance. A broom and pan are propped in the corner. Jackie and the yakuza walk to the lift in silence and Himura's man punches the call button. Then Himura punches the lift door with a hard right and a low metallic roar echoes from the shaft. Himura lunges. He grabs the broom and goes to work on the mailboxes, hammering at them with animal snarls as thunder-cracks echo around the minimal space. The broomhead splinters from the hardwood shaft. The violence locked within the man charges through his body, through the broom handle like a makeshift kendo stick, and into the metal boxes, warping under the ferocity. It lasts for ten seconds. Then Himura winds down, breathing hard, shoulders heaving, and hurls the broom shaft in the corner. As it clatters to the floor, the low-level yakuza rushes to pick it up, fetch the broken head and return them to the corner.

The lift arrives.

As they pass the eighth floor, Himura says, 'Shintaro Ishikawa. Our *guest* from Tokyo.'

'Sumiyoshi-kai?'

Himura looks impressed. 'No. Yamauguchi gumi syndicate.'

'Aren't they based in Kobe?'

'They're everywhere.'

As they glide past the twenty-first floor he says, 'He knows that Inaba is missing.'

'How?'

'I told Nakata to deal with him, keep him out of this for as long as possible. Nakata let slip that we're searching for Inaba. I'll bet the coward pissed his pants at speaking with a top Yamaguchi man and told him everything.' He clears his throat. 'I'll start searching for your friends. I have an idea where to start: the girl from Inaba's apartment, Aina.'

As the lift settles at the thirty-fifth floor and the doors glide open, Himura says, 'You are about to meet Fujiko Maki. She is more than one of my girls. She's *my* girl.'

Jackie says, 'You let her work in the club?'

'Many of my girls don't fuck. They are hostesses, they flatter and flirt; or they provide non-contact stuff in the fetish clubs, like Fujiko.' He stops, his face intense like a child convincing an adult of their innocence. 'And those that do sex, do so of their own accord. None of the trafficking shit the competition are into.'

Jackie, lost for a response, says, 'That's good to hear.'

Himura is encouraged. 'No kids, no strays, no Thais or Filipinos or Vietnamese sold in a village for the price of a hot meal. Only Japanese girls who are happy to sell their bodies.'

Jackie wonders if anyone, in their soul, is truly happy to sell their body but he nods as they arrive at a door and Himura's man raps three times. Another bruiser opens up and blanches for a second at the sight of Jackie before Himura introduces them.

'This is Saburo, one of my best men,' he says, interpreting his own words into Japanese. 'I trust him to keep my woman safe. He is a loyal and honest yakuza.'

Saburo nods, a ghost of a smile on a man-child face.

They slip off their shoes and enter a bigger, more open apartment than Inaba's place in the Olympic Village. They pass a kitchen, a bath and shower room, and a couple of closed doors Jackie assumes are bedrooms. A door at the end of the hallway opens to reveal a well-appointed living room with a view of the park below. A beautiful woman sits on one of two sofas set at a right angle around the table.

Jackie plays it stoic, offering the woman a bow, holding her eyes – burnt coffee beans set in the pale apricot of her skin – all the way. The woman's eyes widen a fraction, then settle, the folds of the lids flickering. The teardrop of her philtrum perches above a small mouth with full lips, which twitches as he holds his bow. The ridge of her jaw strains. She looks proud, perhaps arrogant. Spoiled.

The woman stands, unfurling an elegant, lithe figure in t-shirt and jeans. Reizo Himura speaks to her in Japanese, the roughneck edge of his voice gone, then turns to Jackie. 'I spoke Japanese for the benefit of my men. Maki San speaks English.' He doesn't acknowledge the woman, even as he says her name. Instead, he performs a slight bow and, keeping his eyes on Jackie, says, 'Maki San, this is Jackie Shaw, from Ireland. He is going to help us with our current problem.'

Jackie looks back to the woman but her eyes are now trained on the floor.

'Jackie, this is Fujiko Maki. Please think well of her and show her respect. She is my one true love. She will be by my side until the day I die.'

#

They blindfolded Megan and Ian as they passed the concrete husk of an abandoned hospital, the once-red cross faded to the colour of spoiling salmon. They turned on to a track and, finally, the crackle of an earthen lane strewn with debris. Led, still blindfolded, from the car Megan stumbled over twigs and sticks and heard branches sway in the breeze as they hauled her over knobby ground choked with grass. She heard her father wheeze behind. They walked for what felt like an age. Rough fingers dug into her arms. The ground became thick with grass. They were guided up a short, steep incline and Megan's head was shoved down and held, like a prisoner being hustled into a police car, and the world went quiet. A door shut. The blindfold was removed as an electric light flickered to life. They were in a dust encrusted room of wooden walls.

She sits in the room now, a bare bulb leaving the corners in shadow, next to her father on a torn leather sofa.

Opposite, two of the yakuza sit at a plain wooden table under a boarded-up window, on what resemble outsized primary school chairs. The gangster with the bandaged hand and the one with the spikey hair smoke and read tabloids while the leader is out. A revolver lies on the table between them. A film of dirt speckles the floor and a smell of damp earth like the stink of a grave smothers the room, competing with the cigarette smoke. The men did not bind Megan and her father. She supposes they see no threat: a young woman and, to them, an old man, unarmed, disoriented and isolated. A small television, the screen dead, and a radio sit on the table. An unlit wood-burning stove sits in the corner, the metal chimney disappearing through a cobweb-strewn low-beamed pine ceiling. Another door sits in the wall to the left.

A cabin.

'With that window boarded up it's like a bloody tomb,' whispers Ian Sparrow.

'The horror-movie light doesn't help.'

Spikey-haired thug shoots them a murderous look but Ian continues speaking. 'I wonder what Jackie's up to.'

The thug hurls a cheap plastic lighter at Sparrow and yells at him to shut up in Japanese.

'You shut up!' Megan screams back. 'This is my father! He's been a soldier, a loving dad and a better man in life than you'll ever be so show some respect to your elders and betters!'

The yakuza's eyes go wide and he pushes his chair back from the table. 'Faaakk you!' he screams, the flat English vowel a screech. Then, in Japanese, 'A fucking gaijin doesn't deserve my respect, and neither does his loud mouthed bitch!'

The bandaged thug smiles with hungry eyes, like a schoolboy who scents a playground scrap.

'You're animals,' says Megan. 'Where is your precious tatemae – your 'face' – now? You scorn a man old enough to be your father, denigrate a woman and let your true, vile emotions show through. You are weak! Where is the great yakuza stoicism? Your bushido code? No gi – no integrity; no jin – no benevolence; no rei – no respect.' As the thug stands, knocking over the chair, she says in English, 'Fuck *you!*'

Ian Sparrow flinches at Megan's curse, then struggles to stand as the yakuza grabs the gun from the table and comes at them. The bandaged goon shouts. The spikey-haired yakuza points the revolver at Megan. Ian sits back on the sofa and leans in front of his daughter, staring down the barrel.

The gangster spits. 'I am burakumin! My father was a butcher; my mother was a tanner in Kansai! They fled to Hokkaido to get away from your fucking integrity and benevolence! I'll fucking kill you both!'

His finger tightens on the trigger, eyes wild. The scrape on his face drains white as the skin around the wound flushes red. The bandaged thug giggles as Megan sucks in air, ready to scream.

The door implodes. The hanging waterproof slaps off the wood and the driver, the leader, walks in and bellows, 'Oi!' as he slams the door shut. The spikey-haired man jolts backward and bows to the doorway. The leader holds a plastic bag of groceries in each hand like a furious parent come home to find the kids at mischief.

He glares at the spikey-haired thug and says, 'Sit down.' His voice is tight.

The gangster bows a couple more times and returns to the table with as much shredded dignity as he can muster. He sets the gun down. His bandaged partner stares at the table.

The leader sets the bags on the floor and barks at the two goons. They grab a bag each and slip out of the room.

'I am sorry,' the leader says in halting English. He gives Ian Sparrow a deep bow and turns to Megan, speaking Japanese. 'Please translate: My name is Goro Inaba. Those two idiots are Jun, with the bandaged hand, and Kenta, with the temper.' He walks to the table and grabs the revolver with his left hand, a chair with the right, and brings both over to sit opposite father and daughter.

'You don't have to worry about this,' says Inaba. He opens the cylinder and holds the gun barrel up toward the ceiling.

Ian sparrow states the obvious. 'It's empty.'

Inaba says, 'Some gangster. A revolver with no bullets.'

Father and daughter stare at the weapon.

'Don't be frightened,' says Inaba, 'be smart. You are alone with three men. We are younger than your father and stronger than you. Hokkaido is a very big place. Every year hikers disappear and people go missing in the wilderness. If you run, you will die out there in the mountains and forests. And we have knives.'

Megan's eyes seem to swell in her face and, for the umpteenth time, she questions why they have been taken in her head.

Inaba's voice is velvet. 'We will feed you and keep you as warm and comfortable as possible until we can release you again. Through that inner door is a small toilet and kitchen. You can use the toilet and wash in the kitchen sink but – I am sorry – one of us must accompany you. Once we have what we want, you will be free. Translate.'

Megan explains the situation to her father. She turns to Inaba.

'Why have you done this? Why take us?'

'You'll have answers in time.'

Ian Sparrow, Jackie still on his mind, asks if the yakuza knows his friend. Megan interprets.

'Your friend? The big man?' Inaba touches his chest above his heart. 'I don't know who he is, or where he is now, but I get the impression he can look after himself.'

After Megan translates, her father smiles. 'He isn't that big but I can see how you'd think he is. He could have given blondie that mark on his cheek,' he says, thinking of the bullying Kenta.

Megan wonders who Jackie Shaw really is. Are they here because Jackie Shaw did something to this gangster? Is Shaw looking for them, coming for them? Will he put his brutal talents to work in freeing Megan and her father?

'In any case,' says Inaba, 'your friend is of no importance now.'

Megan gives herself an inward scolding. Jackie Shaw as some avenging saviour was a ridiculous thought. False hope will get them nowhere. And Yuji, what of him? She wonders if his brother has appeared. She wonders at how fast a life can be kicked off its axis and spun out of control.

If she could get in touch with Yuji somehow, he could tell his brother Rei about their plight: at least get the police involved. But how can she reach him? Her mobile phone is gone and they are watched constantly. She doesn't even know if Rei has turned up.

Tired and furious with fear she snaps, 'What do you want?'

The yakuza says, 'You don't need to worry about what we want. Only that we get it.'

'I worry when my father and I are kidnapped and taken to a dirty shack in the middle of nowhere. When gangsters scream at me with guns in their hands, empty or not, and threaten me with knives.'

'I didn't threaten – '

'We've seen your faces. You are yakuza. You'll kill us because we can identify you to the police.'

'No one is going to kill – '

'You've had a fight with my dad's friend. You'll want revenge. Oh God! We're in Japan! No one will ever find our bodies! My mum won't know what happened to us and we'll be on the news! "A British girl and her father have disappeared on the island of Hokkaido in Japan." There'll be campaigns to find us! The only person who can say anything will be that Irish lunatic! We'll be all over social media and people will say terrible things about us!'

Silence.

She realises her entire tirade has been in fluent Japanese. Ian Sparrow gapes at his daughter as though someone has replaced her with a bilingual doppelganger.

Inaba is in awe.

A clang from behind the inner door breaks the impasse and his eyes soften. He smiles and says, 'You've seen too many gangster movies.' Inaba drops the empty revolver on the floor with a rude clatter. 'I can't even afford bullets for my gun and you think I'm some crime kingpin. Meanwhile, Goofy and Donald are out in the kitchen putting the fucking groceries away.' He shakes his head in wonder. 'No one is going to die here. As for the police, they are the people I'm contacting. With luck, they will be here in twenty-four hours. Have a cup of tea and calm down.' He bows to a bemused Ian Sparrow again and mutters an apology for the surroundings, his men, even his language. Then he turns to Megan and offers another bow.

'Please tell your father what I've said. He is worried for you. I understand his concern,' he says. His eyes glitter. 'I am a father too. Please, translate.'

Chapter 15

The leaves sigh in the breeze, the last, faint breath of life before the death of winter envelops the mountains with snow. As they walk, the wind rallies for an exhausted charge, thrashing Fujiko Maki's skirt about her calves and drawing a squeal as she clutches the hem.

Jackie walks to a small stone figure squatting by the narrow dirt path and crouches, sending a fat, thuggish crow flying. The statue is of a small bald Buddha. Someone has placed a red bonnet on its mossy head and draped a cream crocheted shawl around its shoulders. The statue is waist high, one of several they have passed as they wander up the path on Mount Maruyama.

'There are eighty-eight of them,' says Fujiko. 'People bring them warmer clothes as the winter draws in.'

Her English is almost flawless, better, even, than her lover, Reizo Himura. She pulls her overcoat tight around her, trapping the long skirt below. It is cold on the low mountain, the fallen leaves snapping like desiccated paper underfoot.

Jackie says, 'Any reason why there are eighty-eight?'

'Eight is a lucky number in Japan. Some say these statues hold the souls of dead children and that is why people dress and care for them.'

'Is that true?'

'I doubt it. I'm not religious but eighty-eight is an important number in Buddhism, too. Something about enlightenment.' She giggles. 'Only the yakuza manage to give the number eight negative connotations. The name *yakuza* comes from a card game where the worst hand is eight, *ya* short for *yattsu*, nine, *kyu*, and three, *za* for *san*.'

'The losers hand, yeah. The outsiders. I've seen the movies.'

She rolls her eyes. 'Oh God, don't get me started on Takeshi Kitano.'

A wheezing from behind reminds them they aren't alone as a sweating bodyguard follows at a discreet distance. Another is hauling his bulk a couple of yards behind. The men are bored, out of earshot of a conversation they couldn't understand anyway, not having any English. Jackie and Fujiko begin walking again. They have come to the slopes of Maruyama at Fujiko Maki's request. She didn't want to discuss the horror of Friday night in her home. They've been through the murder once already.

'It's a lot to deal with,' says Jackie, 'witnessing a murder.'

'I didn't actually witness very much. As I told you, a foot kicking the glass, blood splatter, the mask. That's it.'

'No glimpse of the man's face?'

'Nothing.'

'A slouch, the way he moved his head?'

'Nothing.'

'Whoever did this probably knew the layout of the building. Can you think of anyone who works there who'd have a reason to do this; someone who seems a little strange, withdrawn?'

'No one.'

'The cut on the victim's neck, was it slanted, like this?' Jackie slashes the air in a diagonal line.

'I never saw the body. When the lights came on I was on the floor. I collapsed.' She pulls the coat tighter. 'The men wanted to spare me the horror of seeing the corpse and took me straight to hospital.'

She plays a good game, thinks Jackie. Delicate, demure. Does that Japanese thing of covering her mouth when she laughs; walks on a dirt mountain path like she's on a catwalk. But she talks about seeing a man butchered two nights ago like it was a judo match on TV and there's a hardness in those dark eyes like polished quartz.

'Who was the victim?' he says.

'A cop.'

'I know that, but I just realised, I don't know his name.'

'To Reizo and his men, a cop is barely a person.'

Jackie says, 'And you?'

Fujiko looks at the path. 'To me,' she says, 'he was a foot kicking at the glass and a spray of blood. I never saw any more of him than that.'

'The kicking,' he says, 'which foot was it?'

'I'm sorry?'

'You saw the victim's foot kick the glass, maybe twice. Which foot was it? Was it the same foot each time?'

'I'm sorry,' she says again, 'I don't remember. I was frightened. It was all a blur.'

'But you remember the mask, the tapping at the glass. I know it's hard to think of that night but it could be important.'

She shakes her head, her hair veiling her face. 'I don't remember.'

'You said the dead man was wearing boots.'

'Yes.'

'Not shoes, boots. You remembered that detail even though it was dark behind the glass. He moved fast, his kicks were violent. Can't you remember which foot?'

'I'm sorry,' she says, her voice rising, a touch shrill. Her fists clench and the catwalk strut takes on a petulant aspect, a semi-stomp. Jackie stops walking. She turns and catches his look, then softens. Her voice becomes small, her eyes wounded. 'I was very frightened. Alone.'

Jackie shrugs and begins walking again. She blinks and follows at her own pace. When he forges ahead she calls from behind.

'The left. I think it was his left boot.'

'Good.' Jackie waits for Fujiko to catch up before strolling on. The bodyguards walk and smoke about fifteen yards behind. The forest around the trail is closing in, becoming dense as the light is failing. The path takes a steep turn. Something flits to their right through the trees, a black blur blocking a sliver of light. Jackie listens for the shuffle of feet on the carpet of leaves or the crisp snap of a tread on dry wood. Nothing.

Fujiko says, 'Is something wrong?'

Are you having me on? he thinks. What a question. I'm walking through the woods thousands of miles from home with a Japanese gangster's beautiful girlfriend, investigating a cop-killing.

'I'm not sure.'

Was that another dark blur ducking behind a caramel tree thirty yards ahead? The jet-lag is kicking in again. Dusk is creeping up on the city and it's only breakfast time back in the UK. Christ, I'm tired, he thinks. He rubs his eyes. They're hot and itchy, despite the autumn chill. He's going crazy, seeing shadows everywhere.

He says, 'Let's head back.'

They walk down to Hokkaido Shrine in silence. The great sloping roof of the entrance puts Jackie in mind of a giant pronged samurai helmet. As they stroll down the long gravel path leading from the shrine to a huge red Torii gate and their parked car beyond, Fujiko says, 'You are quiet. Are you okay?'

'I'm tired. I'm worried about my friends and I hope Himura has some information to help me find them.'

'Friends are very important to we Japanese.'

'Friends are important to everyone.'

'Goro Inaba is my friend. And Reizo's.'

'Well,' says Jackie, 'I can't say we're all that close.'

Fujiko stops and turns to face him. The two bodyguards halt some distance behind.

Jackie thinks she's one of the most beautiful women he's ever seen.

'Do you think,' she says, 'I am safe?'

Jackie looks into dark doll's eyes.

'As houses,' he says.

She frowns. 'Your English is funny, like another language.'

'You're safe. You have men watching you, protecting you, and a lover who is a powerful and dangerous man.' Her eyes are swallowed in shadow as she lowers her gaze and twilight surrenders to night. 'Both victims were police officers, both victims were male. The first victim was in a specific place, difficult to access in a building full of paying customers and hardened criminals. He was murdered for a reason; the second victim being another policeman indicates there's some kind of connection. If this man kills again, no offense but I don't think you're his type.'

Of course, he thinks, if the objective is to get at Reizo Himura his woman is fair game. Or they could be dealing with a full-blown psycho who just happened to butcher two cops on successive nights. It happens.

She steps close to him and glances back at the two bodyguards, now a couple of inky smudges in the early evening gloom. He feels the soft touch of her fingertips on his knuckles. She holds his hand for a moment and says, 'Thank you.'

'What would Reizo think of this?' says Jackie. He glances down at her long fingers enfolding his hand, then over to the bodyguards, smoking and chatting.

'Reizo was with another woman when that man was murdered in front of me. It's an open secret.' Her forefinger traces a circle on his skin. Then her hand is gone, fingertips brushing his as she steps back.

'Everyone has secrets, Jackie,' she says as she turns to the Torii gate, a sombre arch against a slate grey sky. 'Perhaps this will be ours.'

#

Sunlight stripped the city of its midnight allure and laid it bare. In the daylight hours, monotonous apartment blocks towered above small, misshapen houses, a bric-a-brac of living space crammed together a foot or two from one another. Susukino was a tired old whore without the neon rouge on her spoiled, haggard façade.

As night falls, the city waxes into a labyrinth of endless, glittering promise. Jackie, Fujiko and the bodyguards walk the broad pavement of South 4, passing under a shining cliff of LED and through a simple glass door. The punters aren't out in force yet. A metal plate next to the lift declares they are standing in Big-Touch building.

'It's still early,' says Fujiko. 'Most of the clubs and bars won't open for another hour or so, at seven or eight.'

'And what time will they close?'

'Sunrise.'

Like in the building where he'd spent a couple of hours with Ian, Megan and her fretting boyfriend Yuji, there was a collage of business plaques on the wall: Club Spider, G-String High School, Club Model. Club Invisible Man.

One of the bodyguards takes a call on his mobile and they wait in the building entrance, looking across at an LED display of a girl in high school uniform smiling with a soft drink can in her hand. The bodyguard finishes the call and nods to Fujiko, speaking in a reverent hush.

She translates, 'Himura San cannot join us at present and sends his apologies. However, he believes he has made progress in his search for our missing colleague and your friends. We should go to Club Model on the fourth floor.'

They file into the lift, the squat bulk of the bodyguards pressing against Jackie to avoid physical contact with their oyabun's woman. He thinks of her touch at the shrine. On the fourth floor they file out of the car and pass through a sliding door into a lounge bar with alcoves, leather sofas and chintzy tables. An art deco bar occupies a corner and there are prints of various Japanese comic book covers on the walls.

Filing through a fire door next to the counter they enter a harem.

Dolls line the walls like guests at a macabre costume party. A dead-eyed policewoman in blue PVC mini-skirted uniform and leather boots is propped in the corner next to a lifeless cheerleader with a UCLA sweater and flared skirt. A forever smiling blonde in

Disney pajamas leans next to a rack of outfits, her arms reaching for the ceiling with plastic rigor mortis. There must be thirty of them, unblemished cream-coloured rubber skin and huge vacant eyes atop a nub of nose and small mouth. They look impossibly smooth, the silicone too perfect. Repugnant.

'What the fuck is this?' says Jackie.

'The staff of Club Model.' Fujiko smiles.

A small figure sitting at a formica table in the centre of the room wraps her arms about herself, as though bullied by the corpse-dolls. The living, breathing woman from Inaba's apartment. She is crying. Fox stands next to her, hands in pockets. His hair is loose and teased on top. He licks his lips.

Jackie says, 'Aina.' He looks at Fujiko. 'Who is she?'

'Inaba's ex-wife,' says Fujiko.

There's a plastic chair across the small table from the woman and Jackie takes a seat.

He says, 'Have they hurt you?'

'No.' Her voice is small, a faint echo of that which he'd heard in the apartment.

'And Goro?'

'I don't know.'

'You cut him with a knife. How bad was his wound?'

'Wakanai. Not understand.'

The Japanese wakes Fox up and he snarls something at the woman who shrivels in her seat. Fujiko's voice drifts across the room, as smooth and flawless as the rubber bodies surrounding them. Aina speaks with her. Fujiko says, 'She bandaged the cut and Inaba San left the apartment. He met two other yakuza and they got out of Sapporo.'

'With my friends?' says Jackie.

Aina nods.

Jackie says, 'Who were the other yakuza Inaba went away with?'

'Not understand.'

Fox runs his fingers through his hair and Aina flinches. Jackie notices a faint pink flush to her cheek on the left side and wonders if Fox's hand left the mark. He sits straighter on the chair.

'I know you understand some of what I say, at least,' says Jackie, 'but to save time, Fujiko will translate.'

Fox drops his palms on the table with a smack and Aina squeals. He glares at Jackie and says, '*Maki San*. Not use first name. *Maki San*.' His voice is slow and deliberate, as though talking to a child or idiot. Jackie looks from Fox's hands to the smirk in his eyes and wonders how fast he can smash the gangster's face off the tabletop. Fujiko says something and the thug straightens and bows to his boss's woman.

Jackie and Aina talk through Fujiko. Goro Inaba left Sapporo with two other Kanto Daichi-kai members. When Aina reveals their names, Fox yells and kicks a blonde hard in the stomach, toppling the mannequin with a soft clatter. One of the men with Inaba is Tweedledee, cohort in Jackie's kicking in the Susukino sidestreet, real name Kenta. The other is Kenta's brother, Jun. Inaba called Aina at a rest stop and told her to lay low for a couple of days. He told her about the two foreigners he'd kidnapped. In English, she says, 'But he will not hurt them.'

'Where did he call from?' says Jackie.

'Nakayamatoge. It is the top of a mountain. There is restaurant there. A gas station.'

'You don't know where he was going?'

'I'm sorry.'

Jackie turns to Fujiko. 'Where would he be headed if he called from Nakayamatoge?'

'There are many places he could go. Niseko, Kutchan, Rusutsu. Then there is Lake Toya and the south coast.'

He doesn't expect an answer but, if you don't ask, you don't get. 'Why is he doing this?'

Aina shakes her head. Fox cuffs her and she yelps. The chair clatters across the floor. Jackie drags the table a couple of inches as he launches himself at Fox, grabbing the gangster's throat and driving the skinny bastard back with the momentum of his charge. The yakuza's face turns scarlet and spittle flecks Jackie's cheek. Fox's head cracks into a plastic skull as Jackie bulldozes him into a cheer-leader, pulls his face close and headbutts the fucker for good measure. Jackie smells sweat and fags and sour booze and sees the fear in the pin-prick eyes. There's screaming somewhere and a scraping of metal as a door opens. He grabs a handful of teased hair. The screaming is louder now, echoing around the room and he realises Fox is shrieking with the women. He smashes the yakuza's face into a grinning plastic mask with a coal-black bob. Then he's lost in a swirl of shouts and yells and arms grabbing at him, dragging him off Fox. The bobbed doll has a crimson smear across her face.

Jackie's ragged breathing slows, and a throb of pain in his skull from the headbutt kicks in. His legs go and he sits with a heavy thump, taking down a couple of staff from the club still clinging to him. Fujiko stares, appalled. The taste in Jackie's mouth is as bitter as his expression. He's sick and tired of women looking at him like he's an animal.

The bar staff stand back like keepers surrounding an escaped beast. Fox is on his knees, forehead pressed to the floor, arms wrapped around his stomach. He looks like he's withdrawing into himself like Aina as she sat at the table.

Aina.

Forgotten in the melee she sits aghast at the violence. Her swollen eyes look cadaverous under the spare strip-light. Jackie stumbles upright to calls from the bar staff and lurches to the table. Tentative hands reach for him but none touch, as though he might bite if they get too close. Before he says a word, Aina babbles in hurried Japanese. Fujiko translates.

'She is very frightened. Please understand. Her ex-husband has always been reckless but she is afraid of what he has done, what she might be dragged into. And her family. She doesn't know any-thing other than he has your wallet and phone and that he took your friends somewhere south, near Uchira Bay. She is so scared because the police are somehow involved: a dead policeman. Goro knew him. His name is Miyamoto.'

'Stop.'

Everyone turns to Jackie. He sits in the plastic chair opposite Aina and looks at the ceiling.

'I am sorry,' says Aina in English. 'I am sorry. Please. I am sorry.' Like a Buddhist mantra.

'No,' says Jackie. 'You did nothing wrong.' He has a shot at a smile but the result chases any remaining colour from her face. 'This policeman: do you know his Christian name?'

'Christ-o?'

'His first name. Like Tom with Tom Cruise, or Will with Will Smith.'

She looks to Fujiko. For help? Permission? He keeps his eyes on Aina. He doesn't care what Fujiko thinks or does right now.

Aina says, 'Rei. Rei Miyamoto.'

Jackie stares at her but sees Yuji in his mind's eye. The quiet, polite young man fretting over his brother in the izakaya last night. Jesus, less than twenty-four hours ago.

'Did Goro Inaba ever mention the name Yuji?'

'He not talk about "business" with me. We meet only when he come for – ' Aina blinks, looks at Fujiko again and speaks through the oyabun's woman. 'We kept in touch after we divorced. He visits, helps me with money. But we are not close. He might have mentioned the name Yuji but I do not remember.'

'So the brother isn't involved,' says Jackie, thinking out loud.

'I am sorry. Please, I am sorry.'

Irritated, he says, 'Stop. You're fucking sorry, I get it.'

'I want to say,' says Aina, slow and deliberate in the unfamiliar language of English, 'I am sorry for the action of my ex-husband.' She nods in satisfaction at finishing the apology. 'I am sorry for your friends. When you find them, please tell them.'

Jackie, no longer listening, rubs his throbbing head.

Chapter 16

The man slaps the woman across the crown of her head to gales of laughter. His friends grin and berate her. She's stout and plain with a bowl haircut and black-framed glasses. She stares at the floor as the man lifts his leg and shoves her thigh with the sole of his boot. His friends cluck and fuss but the smiles are intact. More braying.

Shintaro Ishikawa doesn't feel like laughing.

A fucking gaijin!

He can't comprehend what the fuck Himura is doing. The redneck bastard already allows slovenly, loose standards in his group. But to sully the great, Japanese institution of their brotherhood, the yakuza, by bringing a fucking gaijin into their affairs was like spitting on the flag.

His men sit in an adjoining room in his Sapporo home watching a comedy show on a national channel. A gaggle of prat-falling comedians slap and kick the fall guy – or girl on this show – for her idiocy. His men drink and smoke and laugh as the humiliation continues, joining the howls of the studio audience.

'Turn that shit down!' he says.

They flinch and one scuttles over to the remote, bowing and scraping. The fawning obeisance irritates Ishikawa.

'No! Turn it off! And get out of my house! I don't want to see you until the morning!'

One begins reasoning that they'd neglect their duties if they didn't stay at hand for their supreior but he tells them he will contact the office in Tokyo to absolve them for the night, and he'll fetch the swords hung on his wall and cut their balls off if they don't get the fuck out of his home. They back away, bobbing their heads like scolded dogs and are gone.

What is Himura up to?

Ishikawa knows the Sapporo oyabun isn't like many in the ranks down south. The Yamaguchi gumi syndicate does a brisk trade with the nationalist groups in Tokyo and happily employs their members as muscle when cheap labour is required. The War Flag of the Imperial Army hangs next to the emblem of their syndicate in many of their offices. Himura couldn't care less.

But to see a white-skinned lug with a yakuza oyabun is unthinkable. To watch him enter the home of Fujiko Maki, intolerable.

Ishikawa grunts and scratches his armpit, then walks to the living room and takes a sword from the heavy hooks skewered in the pale, bare wall.

#

Megan and Ian speak in whispers as the gangster and his spikey-haired companion guzzle cans of lager and watch the small portable TV, a relic from a lost civilisation in state-of-the-art Japan.

Kenta, the spikey blonde, scares them. Occasionally as they whisper he shoots them a murderous look before taking a long drag on his beer. If the leader, Inaba, weren't here they fear Kenta would give in to his vicious, alcohol-fuelled hatred.

Inaba looks bored and restless, turning his beer can in his hands. A couple of times he's cursed the reception as the TV has threatened to give up the ghost.

Why are we here, thinks Ian Sparrow. Why us?

The three yakuza don't use mobile phones although they probably all have one. The clear impression of a phone can be seen in Jun's hip pocket, no doubt turned off to ensure they won't be traced. Ian glances at the TV screen. 'And I thought our telly was bad,' he whispers. 'Do they pay a licence fee for that rubbish?'

Megan nods. 'They do say comedy doesn't translate.'

She feels for her father. Marooned on the other side of the world, reduced to an infant: with its three scripts of kanji, katana and hiragana, often blended together, the non-Japanese speaker can neither read nor write, never mind converse in the language. Everything is a mystery, every trip to the supermarket a fresh adventure. She could see her father's ignorant fear as she spoke, argued, and yelled with their captors. Like adults fighting in front of a child.

She takes his hand.

'We'll be okay, Dad. Like they said, a day or so and they'll let us go.' She doesn't believe a word but clings to the lie in the hope she might will it true somehow.

'The angry one,' says Ian, 'he said a word. *Bura*-something. What was he talking about?'

Megan lowers her voice, almost breathes the term. 'Burakumin.' She checks for reactions among the three men across the small room. Nothing. 'I don't know a huge amount about it so don't quote me. It's not discussed very much here. They're like an underclass. The people who do the dirty work like butchers, you know, working in slaughter houses and the like. Society considers them unclean. There's some discrimination. The blonde one said he was one of them. I think his father was a butcher, his mother, a tanner.'

'And he's an angry young man.'

'His family were originally from the Kansai region, down south. The family came to Hokkaido to escape discrimination.'

On cue, Kenta shoots father and daughter a filthy look and wanders off through the inner door. He slams it behind him as Jun chokes and convulses with giggles. One of the TV comedians has knocked the girl's glasses off with a swipe. Inaba rises from his chair with a smooth grace. He carries it over and sits opposite Ian and Megan, less than a foot away. Leaning in he says, 'You might want to keep your voice down when you discuss the burakumin.'

At his suggestion, Megan translates as Inaba confides. 'They're brothers, these two. It's true, their parents were tokushu buraku, but it isn't the word that's the problem, it's the way people say it.'

Like *gaijin*, thinks Megan. The word itself means outsider: it's when some dickhead on the subway says it like it's a disease that you come to despise the term.

Inaba goes on. 'These buraku, like Jun and Kenta – not so long ago people were saying they were hinin: non-humans. They've been segregated, outcast, discriminated against, you name it. These guys' family home was covered in hate-graffiti back in Kansai. Their father lost his job and couldn't find another because employers used private detectives to investigate the family. Soon as they knew they were buraku, their father's chances were shot.'

'So they came to Hokkaido,' says Megan.

'Like all of us Japanese up here, they're a kind of immigrant. The indigenous Hokkaido people are the Ainu and there are precious few of them left. Japanese families came here to seek fortunes, escape prejudice, bury secrets. Some of the old attitudes came with them. In comparison to down south, Hokkaido is the San Francisco or Amsterdam of Japan, an open society. But it's still Japan. Family registers are just as important here as they are in Tokyo or Kyoto. People look into Jun and Kenta's backgrounds and doors close. Women cringe at the thought of marriage. But the yakuza,' – he looks at the floor and nods as though there were a mirror at his feet and he concurred with his reflection – 'well, if you're an outcast, all the better.'

Inaba waits patiently as Megan finishes translating. The toilet flushes behind the inner door. Kenta shuffles into the room and rejoins his brother at the table.

Inaba gives Megan a searching look. She meets his gaze, irritated with herself as her face flushes.

'You're pretty,' he says. 'How old are you?'

Her father stares from her to the man and back again.

'It's okay,' says Inaba. 'I only wonder because I'm trying to imagine my daughter at your age.' He produces a leather wallet stuffed with cash and fishes out a small laminated card. On it, a pretty girl in pigtails grins with a soft toy under one arm. Kids and adults mill around in the background of an amusement park. 'Tokyo.' Inaba smiles. 'Yakuza go to Disneyland, too.'

Ian says, 'She's a little beauty.' Megan translates. Inaba bows and mutters in stilted English, 'Thank you. Her name is Emi.'

The little girl holds an adult hand in her small fingers. Megan says, 'Where's her mother?'

'Sapporo.'

'Does she miss you?'

'We're divorced.'

'Your daughter, I mean. Emi.'

'I think so. I hope so. We have some time together every couple of weeks.' The yakuza taps the card a couple of times. 'We are lucky men, your father and I. A daughter is a rare gift. I have great respect for your father.'

She snorts. 'You hold us here. Your men bully and frighten us. One of them almost struck my dad and yet you say you respect my father when you don't know him. How can that be?'

'Because he raised you,' says Inaba.

Megan's face turns scarlet.

'I need to pee,' she says.

Inaba stands and tells Megan and Ian to follow him, informing the brothers at the table he's going to watch the gaijin as they piss. Jun waves a hand, glued to the TV screen. Kenta drinks from his can of lager, following Megan and Ian with his eyes until the rough wooden door shuts behind them. They stand in a dingy corridor with a bare bulb struggling to bring light to the dark space, like a mineshaft with its soiled wooden floor, ceiling and walls. No windows.

They pass the kitchen on the left, clean despite the grime of the corridor, with a small rectangle of nailed wooden boards over what must have passed for a window. It's like a Wild West theme park, thinks Megan – *Come See the Old Prospector's Gold-Rush Cabin*. Further down the corridor, past a couple of closed doors, they come to the traditional Japanese toilet, an evil-looking cubicle with a porcelain trough in the floor and another boarded-up window. A cluster of coats hangs on pegs on the corridor wall opposite the toilet door. Inaba flicks a switch and another bulb crackles to life. He gestures for Megan to enter. She straddles the trench in the floor as her father and captor crowd in the doorway in a conspiratorial huddle.

Inaba bows to Ian, then says to Megan, 'Before you piss, please listen. Tell your father what I say later, there's no time to translate now.'

She nods. The flush has drained from her cheeks.

'I am in trouble. I had a "friend". Now he is dead. He was murdered – not by me, but I panicked and ran. In order to deal with the police and get out of this trouble, I need leverage. So, we took you and your father. I'm sorry but when you need some hostages, a gaijin trumps a Japanese every time.'

#

What the fuck is this? thinks Jackie Shaw.

A couple of arseholes are slapping a woman around on the TV while a studio audience roars with laughter.

No one is laughing in the tatami room. The heating is cranked up and a slick spill of oily sweat sucks Jackie's t-shirt to his back. Reizo Himura sits cross-legged in quiet fury behind a low lacquered table under a painting of a smouldering volcano looming over a lake. Very apt, thinks Jackie. All that's missing is steam coming out of the yakuza's ears.

They'd blindfolded him in the car and, upon arrival at their destination, guided him through various sliding shoji doors. When they removed his blindfold, the boiling crater in the picture was the first thing he saw.

Fujiko Maki kneels in a corner, her calves tucked under her body, her head bowed. Two goons stand either side. Another stands to the left of Himura. Jackie recognises him from Fujiko's apartment. Fox, cleaned up and hair tied back in a loose ponytail, sits opposite his boss at the table. Jackie stands next to him. The floor below Fox and Jackie is covered by a plastic sheet. Never a good sign, thinks Jackie.

Jackie tries not to stare at the plastic sheet at his feet. His limbs seemed to drain hollow when he saw it. Fox, he's learned, is a street boss for the lower rank-and-file and a recruiter among the bososzoku motorcycle youth gangs. So not only has Jackie rearranged the face of one of Himura's men, he's humiliated a yakuza NCO. Which means he's humiliated the boss.

A ripple of laughter drifts from the show playing in the next room. Somebody turn that shit off, thinks Jackie.

On cue Himura barks an order and a goon rushes to kill the TV.

Jackie hooks his thumbs in the belt-loops of his jeans. He doesn't know where to put himself, feels like he's back in Mr Reid's office, ready to be balled out by the headmaster for sending a football through chemistry one's window. He knows he should sit or kneel, show deference but – *fuck it!* If he's going to take a hiding or worse he'll start off on his feet.

Reizo Himura is rigid. His hands are placed on the smooth tabletop. His eyes are shark-black in shadow. He speaks.

Jackie listens without hearing, the stream of Japanese a babble as he runs through scenarios of how the violence will play out, how he might limit damage, in his mind. Assuming the most he'll come away with is a severe beating. Assuming he'll come away from this at all. But he must. For Ian and Megan. He has to do something, try to help them, find them. God knows how, but God loves a trier.

Fujiko's sing-song chirping teases his mind back to the here and now. He hears his surname.

Himura slams his palm on the tabletop.

Fox flinches.

'On your knees.'

It takes Jackie a second to register Himura has spoken in English. He answers, 'No.' His voice is thin.

'On your fucking knees.'

From behind, Fujiko says, 'Please, Jackie San.'

At a gesture from their boss, two of the goons walk over to Jackie and grab an arm each. He closes his eyes for second – *Here it comes.*

A shin at the back of each kneecap has him on the plastic with a muffled thud. He smells strong aftershave and a copper tang from Fox, inches away on his left. He tries to stand but a man on each shoulder keeps him down. Fox is whimpering, a soft, keening sound. Fujiko breathes fast, almost panting. Another hand shoves his head down almost to the floor. Padding footsteps draw near as Himura rises and walks around the low table to stand behind Jackie and Fox.

A sweet scent seeps through the close air. It smells like incense. It smells alien to Jackie. A confounding blur of Japanese swirls around him, three voices jabbering at once. The herbal scent of tatami competes with the plastic, incense and cheap-smelling aftershave in the heavy air. His gut is hollow and he has never been more aware of how alone he is. The terrible babble of the yakuza rises in pitch, Fox joining in with a bleating cry, Fujiko shouting in panic. Thick, hard fingers yank Jackie's head back, exposing his throat. He waits for a blade. He doesn't want to die, feels a heavy sadness descend, can't cry for the fear pressing down on his gut. There's a moment when he thinks he's already been cut, but his head is wrenched to the left and he watches as Himura plunges a slim, clean blade into the nape of Fox's bowed neck with a small sound like a popping pea-pod. Himura grabs Fox's ponytail and hurls the man onto the plastic sheet. His boss – his yakuza father – leans over and sets to the dying gangster with short, stabbing thrusts into stomach and chest. There's a wet, tearing sound, a harsh gasp from Fujiko, a whispered, 'Fuck!' from Jackie. Fox's t-shirt shreds as he battles to force a scream from his twisted mouth. With a sigh Himura throws his elbows into the attack, blood coating his hands. Jackie's eyes are wild as he watches the slaughter, smells the awful butcher's stench, feels the heat as a man's insides are exposed, hears the piercing, cyclical scream, not of Fox but Fujiko in the corner.

Then it's done.

Himura curses. 'This shirt is ruined,' he says.

He rolls his shoulders, lays the blade next to the steaming corpse on the plastic sheet, and steps from the room.

Chapter 17

'You never saw a man killed before.'

Himura lights up a smoke and punches a button for a higher floor in the building. As the car shudders upwards Jackie has an image of ascending from Hell.

'You mean butchered,' he says.

He's been silent since they shoved him onto the plastic sheet next to Fox's body and began clearing the room. He wonders if Yuji's brother died like that, eyes wide with terror as his life spurted from his insides.

Himura says, 'It is better than a bullet. There is more honour in Fox's death.'

The yakuza bodyguard from Fujiko's place, Saburo, is stoic – but Jackie saw a shadow of something like fear behind his eyes in the tatami room. Jackie had been led, blindfolded, down corridors and outside to a car then driven to the Big-Touch building. The Big-Touch building, where Jackie handed Fox a beating. Fujiko had been with them in the car but entered the building by a different entrance. He hasn't seen her since.

Come on, thinks Jackie as they stand in the service lift, front it. Neutral, that's the way he's always played it with the maniacs.

'What happens to me?' he says.

'You're going to visit the scene of the crime.'

'I think I just left it.'

'Come on. You aren't a cop anymore.' Himura smiles, the fag wedged in his mouth. He's calm; the blind fury of the attack on Fox has drained him. Or sated him. 'We're going to the Invisible Man Club. You can take a look at where our first bitch-cop was killed.'

The lift settles and they emerge onto a nondescript corridor with a number of doors, windowless and plain, each with a small plaque to the left.

'And no punishment for me? I beat Fox in front of Fujiko and Aina...'

'You'll be dealt with later,' – a drag on the smoke – 'at least that's what I told my men. You see, we have a code. You know, samurai, bushido. There are a few universal rules for yakuza that cannot be broken.'

'Honour among thieves, right?'

'Right.' A sideways glance. 'Japan is a pretty rigid place. For a Japanese, anyway. People like rules, regulations. They like a definite place in the, what do you say? Pecking order. They like to be given boundaries and told what to do. Even outlaws. Fox broke our code. He messed with another member's family. He picked Inaba's ex up from her workplace, slapped her around, threatened her.'

'An ex-wife. Barely a member of your "family".'

'Inaba's still in so she is connected. Lucky for you, his transgression outweighed yours.'

'He slapped her around. Couldn't the punishment fit the crime?'

Himura squints at the floor. Saburo shifts his weight from left leg to right. Then Himura smiles and says, 'Yes, I think I understand your meaning. Perhaps I was a little excessive. I'm under stress.'

They walk down the corridor. Saburo knocks on a door on the right. A young woman sits on a staircase a couple of yards down the coridor, engrossed in a mobile phone covered in beads and glitter. Her nails are violet talons and Jackie wonders how they can navigate the mobile screen.

The door opens and Jackie, Himura and Saburo enter a cubicle with a counter and window like a train ticket office. A blind is drawn over the window so staff and patron can't see one another. Jackie scans for a camera. After a brief exchange, a metal inner door opens and they step through into a bare concrete space like a large prison cell, with a wall of glass on one side. There is a second door a few yards away below a fire exit sign. The space is bright with strip lights and Jackie sees a sparse apartment, like a film set, through the glass wall. He imagines a punter sitting in the dark and shakes his head at what some people will pay for.

'Didn't whoever was in the front booth think it was strange that two customers entered the room together?' he says.

'They swear Inaba brought the cop, left him at the door and went out. There was no second man.'

'I didn't spot where your camera is hidden at the entrance.'

'There isn't one. We are yakuza, this is Japan. Who would try to rip us off? They'd have to be crazy.'

Exactly, thinks Jackie.

He says, 'Rival gang?'

'We own the entire building. There are cameras in the entrance, next to the toilets, in the corridors. But at a place like this, anonymity is all for the customer. There are security locks everywhere, however.'

'Why didn't someone shut the place down when the attack began?'

'We didn't know what was happening. The door is thick steel. The girl at the entrance desk couldn't hear anything. There is a camera on the apartment space, where Fujiko was sitting, but the dickhead who should have been monitoring was taking a shit.'

His last, wonders Jackie.

'By the time we knew what had happened the fucker in the Tengu mask was gone. It was a mess.'

'And Inaba was in charge?'

'Inaba was missing.' Himura picks up a foil ashtray from a corner and grinds his fag out. 'Could Inaba have done it?'

'Killed the policeman? Unless he's ambidextrous, I doubt it.'

'Ambi-what?'

'The killer held the victim while he cut, probably grabbed his head and pulled it back to expose the throat. He held the victim with his left arm and cut with his right, like this...' Jackie mimes the action. 'The victim kicked at this glass with his right foot, indicating the pressure on his body from the killer's grip was coming down on his left side. That suggests a right-handed cut with the knife. The cut is the more important act. Holding a struggling grown man in position takes a lot of strength but the crucial element is cutting deep and well. Your killer is right handed. Inaba is a lefty.' Jackie crosses his arms. 'The golf clubs in his apartment, his grip on the gun. Inaba is left-handed.'

Himura raises a skeptical eyebrow.

'It wouldn't stand up in court,' says Jackie, 'but I'd say your second-in-command is innocent of murder. This one, at least.' He unfolds his arms and points. 'The killer must have entered and exited through that fire exit.'

'We thought so but the door to the fire stairs can only be opened from in here.'

'So the killer somehow found his way to the stairwell, away from the public areas. Then someone wedged the door open. I can't clear your boy Inaba on that one yet. '

Himura grunts. 'Anything else?'

'Looking at the room, no. It's been wiped clean, evidence erased. Forensics aren't really my thing anyway.'

'We will have customers in here in a couple of hours.'

'The show must go on, yeah. Did anyone take photos of the body?'

'A couple of my men, yes.'

'Can I see the pictures?'

Five minutes later two hulking bruisers march into the concrete room in cheap-looking suits and offer their mobile phones to Jackie. He scrolls through images of the dead policeman – the dead brother. Blood spilled down the man's chest like a toddler's soup, head lolling back on his neck at an impossible angle, penis exposed in a cold, lifeless grip. Rei Miyamoto, sibling of Yuji.

Jackie says, 'Did he ejaculate?'

Himura juts his chin forward, his eyebrows furrowed.

Jackie says, 'Did he cum?'

'Come here?'

Jackie mimes masturbation. 'Did he finish?' He spreads his hands wide like a zealot preaching. It'll be interpretive-fucking-dance next, he thinks.

'Ah!' Himura's chin protrudes so much it looks about to dislocate. 'Star shot!'

'Good enough,' says Jackie.

'Maybe, yes.'

'Maybe?'

'He had something on his hands, dried. I think, maybe...what you are talking about.'

'And where are his hands now?'

'Somewhere in the mountains.'

'And not connected to his body either, I guess.'

Jackie studies the photographs again. 'The semen – the "star shot" – isn't the victim's. You might gain an erection when asphyxiated – strangled – but not when your throat is cut. And he's an adult policeman. He wouldn't want to get his trousers dirty if he was having a wank, would he? He'd most likely have tissues or something.'

'We provide tissues for our customers,' says Himura with pride.

'Five star service. I'd bet the killer masturbated when he committed the murder, maybe even ejaculated unintentionally during the act and his "star shot" splashed the victim's hand.'

'It was rape?' says Himura, his face aghast.

'Doubtful. No other signs of sexual activity.'

The yakuza sags with relief.

'Do you have more contacts in the police?'

'Of course,' says Himura, his face like a teacher with a slow child.

'Reach out. Tell them where the body is buried. Have the cops dig it up and test for DNA. If we're very lucky and there hasn't been too much degradation, they might just get a profile from the,' – he grimaces – '"star shot".'

'You really think so?'

'It's worth a try.'

'There is a cop,' says Himura, 'Genda. I'll call him. Anything else?'

'Did the victim have a phone on him? If so, I'd like to take a look at it with you. It might help.' And it should have Yuji's phone number, he thinks.

Himura shakes his head. 'It's gone. We think the killer took it, if there was one.' He gestures to Saburo and makes for the door. 'Want a drink?'

Jackie kills the screen on which the image of Rei Miyamoto's corpse is displayed and hands the mobile back to one of the bruisers. 'I could murder a cup of tea,' he says.

#

Inaba looks at the small snapshot from his wallet, the only surviving photograph he has of Emi, his three-year-old daughter. He remembers the birth, seared in his memory for the rest of his days. All the violence and sleaze and darkness of a life in the yakuza paled in comparison to his emotions that night: his fear for Aina as she cried out in pain; his impotence throughout the torturous labour; the joy and terror at the first sight of Emi, bloody and screaming in the midwife's hands. The tears, the joy, the vastness of the moment and yet Emi, Aina and he were, in that breath of time, the only three living things on the face of the earth.

It had been in the city of Abashiri on the east coast, as far from Sapporo as they could manage. Aina's family lived there and she had gone to them months earlier in order to keep the pregnancy secret from the Kanto Daichi-kai. Even then, cracks were showing in the marriage. Aina was determined to insulate their child from the yakuza life and Inaba lived in a Susukino apartment while his wife and daughter stayed with his in-laws, three hundred kilometres away. The men gossiped, Reizo Himura pried and, six months after Emi's birth, the marriage died. But not Goro Inaba's hope.

He came to agree that his daughter never be touched by the life he had pursued. Further, he came to a resolution – he would leave the Kanto Daichi-kai, wash his hands and cleanse his conscience.

Perhaps they could be a family again. If Aina couldn't rediscover her passion for him as a husband she might grow to love him as a father to their child. She was temporarily transferred back to Sapporo by her employer, leaving Emi in her parent's care. So he had made plans, approaches, risked his life to engineer an escape route. Then fucked it up. His ex-wife had been traumatised by the fight with the foreigner in his apartment, had shaken and spat and cursed him even as she sobbed and reached for him with the knife slash across his chest. Where was Aina now? Had Himura found her? What had they done to her? And Emi. She was with her grandparents in Abashiri. Would she see either of her parents again?

Yes.

He'd move heaven and earth, like the quakes that rocked the country and the typhoons that razed whole towns. He'd make this work if he had to tear through the entire syndicate to hold Emi once more.

But the killer, the maniac in the Tengu mask, was another matter. Did he know of Inaba's deception? Is that why he had cut Miyamoto's throat? This psychopath was that most feared of concepts in Japan, the unpredictable loner. The time would come to address that problem, though. First Goro Inaba has to get his plan back on track.

An image of a pin-badge flashes through his mind's eye. Grey and white. Himura had said that Fujiko saw a grey badge with some kind of white symbol when the killer tapped it against the glass. But how could she be sure? It was a fair distance; she was crying, panicking. And the badge is nowhere to be found, probably in the killer's possession.

He looks at the sofa and the foreign father and daughter, Ian San and Megan Chan. He likes them, what he sees of them. He can't tell the girl the truth of Rei Miyamoto's death. He can't tell her that Rei Miyamoto had told him about her, about her studies at university; that Inaba had leaned on a contact, into the Kanto Daichi-kai for three million yen, at the university to get her address. That because of Rei Miyamoto's confidences in their yakuza-cop clandestine meets, Inaba had the means to find and abduct her, along with her hapless father. He'll spare her that.

Jun and Kenta are playing cards at the table, Jun's scowl almost a parody of concentration. Inaba knows Kenta is suffering withdrawal from the use of his phone. Inaba tells them he'll be back and reminds them not to use their mobiles, not to give the cops a chance to trace them and storm in without providing the immunity they all crave.

'How long will you be out?' says Kenta.

'I'm not sure.'

Kenta looks pleased and sneaks a look at the foreigners. Inaba feels a ripple of unease cross his shoulders. Nevertheless, he walks to the door and offers the foreigners a reassuring nod before he slips out and into the desolate gloom.

#

I can smell her, she's so near.

She passes by with a brute of a man, flitting from Big-Touch building to a waiting taxi. The brute leans through the window on the front passenger side and shouts an address over the scream of an ultranationalist van crawling along South 3 Street. The address is unfamiliar but in the North Ward of Sapporo, an area I know. The automatic door swings shut and the taxi joins the flow of lost souls in this most degenerate of neighbourhoods. The brute walks off.

I pat the shoulder bag. In it is my true face. The Tengu's face.

The Mother's image remains in my head. Hair gathered on her crown with a simple tortoise shell clasp. Her tall reed of a neck straight and proud. She wears a blouse and light jacket. Pencil skirt. Heels. But something in her face, a rawness around her eyes ...

A robust blonde passes me with a pitying smile, as though I deserve her sympathy. Probably some Russian whore. Fucking foreigners. Like that burly bastard the Mother entered the building with a couple of hours ago. Slouching beside her like an attack dog on a leash.

The blonde has a nice ass, though.

Foreign women.

But I am the Mother's hound; I am her agent of chaos. I will follow mother, stand guard at the address I overheard the yakuza bawl at the taxi.

Someone will come to the address and then the Tengu will do its work. The blood will let fly with my seed. Rebirth.

I walk east toward my car, stacked in a high-rise lot, behind the blonde and admire her ass, its vigorous dance as her wide hips sway. Japanese women are so delicate, so feminine. But foreign women: so wanton and powerful. So ample.

Fucking foreigners.

Chapter 18

A red light brings the car to a smooth halt. Jackie gazes through the window at another row of concrete and steel buildings, small windows set in sheer, prefabricated slabs.

After ninety minutes or so, Saburo had entered the small office and waved for Jackie to follow. They'd walked a couple of blocks and climbed into a black Lexus, Jackie in the back seat.

Now the yakuza is silent as they pull away from the traffic lights. Saburo makes no attempt to speak English, or acknowledge Jackie's meagre Japanese. When his eyes glance at the rear-view there is a hint of resentment. The car glides north until they hit another small cluster of neon and LED, and a knot of taxis. Couples totter on the pavements, some drunk. The Lexus continues through a busy crossing, past a four-storey bank of signage burning bright, restaurants bedecked with red lanterns, a karaoke place emblazoned with burning kanji characters. At a Kentucky Fried Chicken, they turn off the main street into an alleyway. The alley is deserted and dark.

Saburo brings the car to a stop next to a windowless structure with five floors fronted by perforated sheet metal, as though someone has hammered out a giant colander and nailed it to the building. A dimly lit sign clings to the edge displaying the word "Hotel" in English. A neon heart glows a seedy red on the side.

'Love hotel?' says Jackie.

Saburo says, 'So desu.' Yes.

He clambers out and together he and Jackie enter the love hotel. Inside, Saburo speaks to a shadow behind a windowed front desk, a blind drawn behind the glass. A female voice replies and they pass through a fire exit next to the lift and climb five flights of steps. There they emerge from the stairwell onto a spotless corridor with a purple and pink patterned carpet. Numbered doors line the walls and Saburo knocks on 5F. The door opens and Saburo stands back.

Jackie waits. The yakuza tilts his head – *go inside.*

Jackie extends a hand – *you first.*

They stand there like a bad comedy sketch, willing each other through the door. Jackie will be damned if he cracks first. Fuck them, he thinks. You want polite, deferential Japanese manners? *Knock yourself out, big lad.*

'There's a draught in here, Jackie San. Come in and close the door, please,' says a soft voice.

He looks to Saburo for a sign that this might not be a point of no return but the yakuza fixes on a spot somewhere around the fire exit to the stairs, a hard stare of resentment in his small eyes. Jackie takes a breath and plunges through the door.

Thick carpet. A spacious room with a large sofa opposite a huge flat-screen TV set on a wooden unit. Tasteful muted cream tones on the painted walls and a large king-size bed, an earth-coloured frame running the length of the wall above, criss-crossed by stylishly haphazard stalks of bamboo. Through an adjoining door he glimpses a hot-tub. At the far end of the room, a large window overlooks the surrounding low-level buildings; further south, the skyscrapers of downtown trail from a sky pregnant with low cloud, like glow-sticks embedded in grimy candyfloss.

Fujiko Maki stands with her back to the view, almost a silhouette, the curvature of her body outlined in shifting pastel tones from the lights of the pleasure houses a block beyond.

She says, 'Sit down.'

Jackie makes to remove his boots but Fujiko says, 'You can wear shoes here. It's a hotel, not a home.'

He sees her heels and walks to the sofa but remains standing.

'Why are we in a love hotel room?'

'Reizo owns this building and another next door. We thought it was a good place to keep you out of harm's way, in North Ward. Away from Susukino.'

'Why not in one of the organisation's offices? Or a private house?'

'This hotel is anonymous. A place only for lovers.'

She walks toward him. Her tumbling hair, simple white blouse, charcoal skirt and the clean sweep of her calves are a smooth reveal in the soft lighting. Her smile seems to morph from warm to hungry to vulgar and, for a moment, Jackie wonders if he has been drugged, is hallucinating. No. But he can't focus as she walks. The modest lighting gives an impression of her rather than a clear picture. When she's a foot away, he still can't decide what the twitch of her lips reveals but she takes his left hand in both of hers and drapes herself on the sofa, dragging him down.

'Funny,' says Jackie, 'the guidebook said the Japanese aren't big on physical contact with strangers.'

'Are we strangers?'

'You don't know what football team I support.'

'Is that what was here?' she says, pushing his sleeve up to reveal the gnarled skin on his forearm. 'A sports team tattoo? I didn't think you would be so...um...the word is mundane?'

'The truth of it was a hell of a lot more mundane.'

'I thought of getting a tattoo. Many yakuza women have them. It would have been small. A mask used in a traditional play, of the Bride character. I wanted it to be somewhere private, where only Reizo would see. Here.' Fujiko crosses her left leg over right and leans on her right hip, easing her skirt up until the lace trim of her lingerie peeks out under the gathered hem. Her skin is faultless, her legs strong despite their sleek lines, a shallow furrow under the long muscle on her naked thigh.

He can't lie. Jackie feels a rush of hunger, wants to reach out and touch her. Taste the forbidden fruit.

'But Reizo refused,' says Fujiko. She gathers the skirt further, revealing a midnight blue triangle of lace cradled between her inner thighs before smoothing the skirt over her legs again. 'A yakuza woman should be tattooed traditionally, on her back at first.' She shudders. 'Reizo dislikes them anyway.'

The traditional method was a slim blade attached to a shaft of bamboo, hand-held by the tattooist, stabbed into the skin, hooked under and pulled out at an angle over-and-over, thousands of times over many days, months, years. It was arduous, painful, a torturous rite of passage. Jackie rubs his scar.

'Do you think he was right?' says Fujiko. 'Or perhaps here was better.' She unbuttons her blouse and pulls the left collar down and away. Her breasts are small and when she leans forward he glimpses a caramel nipple below the loose cup of her brassiere.

He knows he's being played but ... *Christ! Oh, Christ!*

'Why flaw the flawless?' he says, his voice thick. He feels like a sleazy idiot.

'Thank you.' She offers a ghost of a bow. Leaves the buttons open. 'I like you, Jackie San.'

'Just Jackie.' It's like he's waiting for his voice to break, a gawky adolescent again.

'I like you, Jackie. The men in the organisation, they see me as a mother or sister.'

You're kidding yourself there, thinks Jackie.

'Reizo treats me like I'll break if he uses strong language. The customers? I don't want to know how the customers think of me.'

Thank God you can't see what's going through my mind right now, thinks Jackie.

'You, Jackie, you treat me like a human being. Like an equal, and that is very rare for a woman in Japan, especially in the yakuza life. So, as an equal ...'

Here it comes. The show-and-tell has to be leading up to something.

Fujiko tucks her legs under her and turns to face him on the sofa. 'As an equal, I can tell you things that I can't share with the others. Show you things, like this.'

She reaches in the pocket of the blouse and produces a metal pin-badge. She opens his hand and she sets it on his palm. Jackie looks it over. A simple oval with two lines continuing from one end of the shape.

Fujiko says, 'I guess it is company pin-badge. Almost all companies have these in Japan. Do you recognise the design?' Her voice doesn't hold much hope.

Jackie turns the badge one-eighty degrees on his palm so the intersecting arcs lie horizontal. He says, 'Ichthys. A fish. Not a company insignia; a Christian symbol. Where did you get this?'

Fujiko frowns, determining a course of action. 'I can trust you? We are friends?'

'Aye, yin and yang.' He looks at her brassiere, framed by the white cotton of her open blouse, and shakes his head.

Her composure flickers for a moment before she decides to plough on.

'I think this was taken from the body of the dead policeman. The first one killed at the club, in front of me. The killer tapped the glass with it that night, taunting me.'

Somehow, she doesn't seem as upset as before, the delicate wallflower act abandoned. And with her newfound brass, she reveals the source of the badge, and the yakuza woman fronting it out behind her willowy mask.

#

The arrogance, thinks Genda, expecting a police Superintendent to dance to his tune. And the snot-nosed little shit a good ten years younger than he.

Damned bureaucrats.

He sits back in his chair and looks out the window of his office at the reference grid sprawl of Sapporo.

Reizo Himura had called him on his office line. A surprise contact but nothing compared to the incredible story that followed. A dead officer, murdered on yakuza premises twenty-four hours before the bad apple, Masa Yoshida, met his end by the Toyohira River. The body buried in the mountains behind Maruyama. An internal investigation conducted by the Kanto Daichi-kai. In the course of the syndicate's search for the murderer they received a tip on a possible DNA sample on the dead officer's corpse. Genda, interested and ready to investigate the murder of a fellow officer, promised to look into it and decided to take Himura's personal number.

Now their meeting at the raid earlier today made sense. Genda had recognised an edge to Himura when they spoke at the oyabun's offices across the river. More of an edge than usual, at any rate. Did the mobsters commit the murder? It had to be considered but didn't make much sense. There was no angle to killing a cop, never mind on yakuza turf, and certainly no money to be made. And why provide the tip-off of where the body was buried if the bastards had something to hide. Himura seemed genuinely eager to find the killer and genuinely shocked at the death of the cop. With over twenty years of reading gangsters on the clock, Genda thought Himura had been taken aback when told today that the Organised Crime Bureau were in on the Shiroishi offices raid.

That raid made sense now, too. A quick call to a personnel sergeant, who joined Genda's golf club last year, at Headquarters and the dead officer's file was pulled. Rei Miyamoto. One of their boys had been executed on Kanto Daichi-kai premises, so the Organised Crime Bureau engineered the Shiroishi raid and came along for the ride. The detective who had picked up his call at the OCB offices kissed Genda's ass. Genda pulled rank and balled him out a little. The detective scurried off and returned with a superior who concurred that, yes, Officer Rei Miyamoto was missing and a search was ongoing. Then Genda dropped the facts – a tip-off had informed him Miyamoto was dead, his dismembered corpse buried at the following grid reference in the mountains.

Silence. Dissembling silence.

Genda knew before the Bureau man started babbling that they had Miyamoto's body already. Someone else had beaten Himura to the punch with a tip-off. The OCB had already examined the corpse, the OCB man said. No, the family did not know but, now that the regular police had knowledge, the parents and surviving sibling would be informed. No, forensics had been of little use as the body had been removed from the scene of the crime, had lain in a shallow grave and the corpse may have been tampered with beyond the obvious dismemberment. Hair was present on the body but could not be analysed as the roots were not intact.

'And the semen?'

'Excuse me, sir?'

Genda hoped his tired smile seeped through the receiver. 'There was semen on the victim's hand. Surely forensics picked it up. Or the examiner? It would have been dry, tight skin. There could have been more elsewhere.'

'I...I don't...I am not aware of any developments in that respect. Sir.'

'I'd advise you reassess the situation and have the samples analysed. Low copy number DNA testing could take less than forty-eight hours. I'll check back periodically. It may be inadmissible as evidence by now thanks to degradation, perhaps some cross contamination, but it'll open doors for investigation.' And besides, he thought, we don't even have a national crime intelligence database. He despaired at the bean-counters in the National Police Agency but the DNA was a lead, however slim. They might get lucky. Every avenue had to be exhausted.

'Excuse me, sir, I apologise but I do not have that kind of authority.'

'No. Your ranking officer, Watanabe San, does. Give him my regards when you submit the testing request. Let him know I'll see him on Thursday for dinner with the Assistant Commissioner.'

'Apologies, sir. Of course. I will request authorisation for the testing forthwith.'

Then he had a thought. Genda had no love of Reizo Himura or his ilk, had been as straight as a policeman could in his years of service. True, the Sapporo outfits were generally manageable and consistently predictable but he would not countenance any of this romantic bushido garbage. The yakuza weren't disaffected modern-day samurai, they were pimps, pushers, traffickers, thugs. Now it looked like Himura had the unthinkable, an informer in his ranks. Someone who had tipped the OCB off about the body and maybe called in the raid. If Genda could get a name, or what the Organised Crime boys were looking for at the raid, he could use it as leverage. Keep Himura in line. A tame yakuza for a change rather than a rotten cop.

He bluffed it out, barking orders down the line. Genda was to be given the name of any OCB source in the Kanto Daichi-kai and the target material in the Shiroishi raid.

Then he cut the detective off mid-sentence, his left hand reaching for the desk drawer as his right slammed the receiver in its cradle. He had turned down the offer of a scotch with Himura at the raid, had been on the wagon for a while, but one glass of Nikka wouldn't hurt at the end of a long day.

No, he had done well, resisted temptation until now. He needed a clear head for the work to come. And a good night's sleep.

He had been shouldering his bulk into his trench-coat at the door of his office, ready to head for home and a decent bath, when his phone rang. The Senior Commissioner, top National Police Agency official in Hokkaido Prefectural Headquarters, barked down the line. A career bureaucrat, the Senior Commissioner was an administrator with no investigative experience despatched by Tokyo to oversee the Hokkaido force. He was young, brash and made no attempt to understand actual police-work. He had no working knowledge of crime or criminals, motives or investigative techniques. And the Senior Commissioner enjoyed making key decisions in big cases, overruling officers who'd been on the job for decades.

And so it was with Genda. The Senior Commissioner declared DNA testing would be permitted with his blessing – and fingers crossed for credit to be taken in any breakthrough, thought Genda – but Genda was to desist from interfering further with OCB business and attend to his own responsibilities. There would be no source name, no further information regarding the raid. Then the prissy little shit had hung up on the twenty-year Superintendent.

Now the outer corridor is dark and Genda calls Himura on his mobile. He explains he will have a result on the DNA sample in time and text it through as soon as he receives the news.

'Thank you, Genda San. Perhaps this is the beginning of a fruitful working relationship,' says Reizo Himura.

Genda says, 'Don't call me again. I'll contact you.'

He keys his home number into the mobile. His wife answers and he flinches at the expectancy in her voice. He tells her that something has come up. He'll be home late, in a couple of hours. She tells him she understands and they say goodbye.

Then Superintendent Genda shrugs out of his trench-coat and settles his ever-increasing weight on his chair with a sigh. He opens the desk drawer again and pulls out the bottle of Nikka whiskey and a small glass. The twin bushes of his eyebrows meet as he frowns in concentration, wiping the glass with a handkerchief, his tongue clenched between his teeth, his breath whistling through broad nostrils. Then he grunts – *pompous little NPA shit! Damned bureaucrats!* – and pours a generous measure of liquor.

#

I remember a girl, pretty with large ears that stood out like flaps when she tied her hair back. Those ears caught the light on summer days. The cartilage seemed to burn like a paper lantern. She loved a movie, a cartoon with a princess and a monster in a castle. The princess kissed the monster and he became a handsome prince.

Western bullshit.

The girl in the story was white; the prince was white. The story was closer to the truth when the man was a heaving, raving, hairy brute, his huge snout twisted in rage. That's the true face of the foreigner. Like the repulsive asshole holed up in that filthy love

178

hotel with the Mother. A misshapen animal, like the ugly freak on the beer can labels. The kirin.

That was it, the movie title: *Beauty and the Beast.*

Well, I have my own beast, growing inside me. It kicks at my guts and demands another delivery. Like all births, it will be painful and bloody, with screaming and tears. But the Mother, Amaterasu, shall have satisfaction. And after, the demon will retreat inside me until she bids it unleashed again. It is restless. One day soon, it will devour me.

There should be a last sacrifice before I am gone – the revelation came to me as I watched the love hotel. As I imagined that blonde, Russian whore in Susukino, inside the hotel with me.

I know now.

It will be a foreign woman.

The final victim should be a Honnari. The anti-Mother. A demoness consumed by jealousy for the beauty and purity of our Japanese women.

A foreign bitch.

First, I will gut the foreign man/animal in the love hotel; then, I will slay a foreign demoness. I know just the witch with which I will complete my transformation to pure Tengu. I will gut her, eviscerate the cunt.

On that day, I shall take the Mother with me to paradise where we can fuck in the heavens and she can care for me and I will lay my head in her lap and she will stroke my hair and clean my ears and cut my nails and cook my meals.

Yes, a foreign woman. I know which one. Young, fresh. I know which one. I know which one. Soon ...

That girl with the ears was cute, back when I was younger. I wonder where she is now.

God, those ears were fucking huge! Like Minnie-fucking-Mouse!

The blade is ready. The mask is ready. The bag is at my feet. The smell from the garbage behind this American fast food place is a *primer for the stench of the big Westerner's spicy fear when I cut him in the love hotel.*

Are they fucking? Is the Mother naked?

It is time. I will deal with the thug who arrived with the foreigner first. Quick, clean. Then the Tengu will feed, the Tengu will be satisfied, the Tengu will feed.

I cannot fucking wait.

Chapter 19

She's on her feet and screeching. He can't understand a word. An unbroken aural scrawl of invective tearing the air around him. Jackie winces.

Fujiko stamps to the bed and hurls her handbag on the duvet. She punches the mattress then clutches the criss-cross bamboo display above the headboard and shakes it like the bars of a prison cell.

Like a fucking toddler throwing a fit, thinks Jackie. He ploughs on.

'It's true,' he says. 'You knew this, you should have gone to Reizo – shite, gone to someone. If another person dies because of this Tengu maniac, you take some of the blame.'

He's building to a rant, knows it but – *fuck it!* It feels good.

Fujiko shrieks again, the smooth lines of her body now all sharp angles. Jackie hears the occasional "fuck" and "shit" peppering the furious Japanese. *Well, good.* It'll harden the precious wee princess, a few home truths. And well dare Saburo walk through that fucking door or he'll cop it. Full in the face with a haymaker.

Jackie rides a surge of anger and stands from the sofa – *Sleaked wee girl, playing her games while people are dying; while his friends are missing!*

First, she told him she got the ring from the sour-looking yakuza who squared up to Jackie outside her apartment building. Ishikawa. How did he lay hands on it? The story about finding it on Inaba's desk is mad-dog shite, has to be. The Tokyo yakuza was on the scene before Inaba showed up and five'll get you ten he pocketed the badge himself. Or was Ishikawa the nutcase tapping it on the glass after he'd slit Rei Miyamoto's throat? Did he duck downstairs, dispose of or hide the weapon and saunter back up with his men? Were they in on the murder?

Then Fujiko told Jackie that the delicate wee flower called up her fuck-buddy, wheedled her way past the goon outside and had a tumble in a love hotel down by the river. All this while the second cop was carved up by the same river. Then she went for a dander and returned to her apartment to a torrent of texts and calls from lover boy. It turned out he'd seen some joker with blood on his clothes skulk up the incline from the river and shove a Tengu mask in a shoulder bag. A positive ID and she'd been sitting on it, scared her gangster boyfriend would find out she'd been grabbing a little salaryman arse on the side.

Jackie says, 'Call your lover. Now. Did he take a photo on his phone? If not, get a description to Reizo. Or the police.'

Fujiko blinks away tears, perhaps of rage, perhaps frustration.

She says, 'I like to draw. I sketched the pictures in my apartment. When my *friend* described the Tengu man, I drew a likeness. Like the police artists in movies.' She pulls an envelope from her handbag. 'This is the picture. This is Tengu man. I can't tell Reizo.' She shakes her head, hair clinging to the tears on her cheeks. Her voice goes small. 'You don't understand.'

Bollocks, thinks Jackie. Tears. He's always crumpled at a woman's tears. But he can't help himself. He wants to sting her, wants the higher ground.

'I understand you cheated on your yakuza lover. I understand that you held back the best chance of catching a killer to save your own skin. But this is not all about you.'

'Maybe it is.' She looks at him askew, as though something has been revealed. 'For you, Jackie San,' – her voice dripping with sarcasm – 'maybe it is *all* about me.'

He drops onto the sofa again. The best he can muster is a mumbled, 'Fuck off.'

'Fuck off? Fuck *me*, is that right? You are jealous, Jackie San.' She glides across the carpet on her heels, catwalk style, the envelope in her long fingers. 'You are angry because another man fucks me, yes?'

The verb sounds brutal, harsher than the screaming tantrum. She stops, her knees an inch from his splayed legs as he sits below her. She tosses the envelope on the floor.

'And Reizo? You are jealous of Reizo?' The fingers reach down the front of the skirt. 'You should not be jealous of Reizo.'

Jackie says, 'Reizo? I'd rather not be a cuckold.' He hates the petulance in his voice. He met her only hours ago but despises the truth in her words.

She doesn't understand his rebuff but sniffs and shrugs. She leans forward, her blouse divulging the midnight blue brassiere and the small secrets of her breasts. Her fingertips hook the hem of the grey skirt and lift it, the material gliding up the sweep of her thighs until it is no more than a rumpled belt. The dark lace of her lingerie traces the smooth sweep of her pubis. Her hands disappear behind her back. Jackie hears the soft buzz of a zip and, a moment later, the skirt drops to the floor.

He breathes out a long sigh. Fujiko straddles his legs and sits on his lap, her knees either side of him on the sofa. He burns, deep down, and Fujiko's dark eyes glitter as she feels him swell.

She says, 'I thought English are gentlemen.'

'I'm not English.'

'So, I remember. You are Irish. Irish are drunkards.' She smiles, almost predatory.

'People have told me that wherever I go,' says Jackie, 'and they're usually drunk when they say it.'

She grinds into his hardness with her hot weight.

'You are a good little Catholic Irish boy?' she says, her eyes flickering closed.

'Wrong again.'

His hand stabs forward and his thumb traces the nub of her jaw bone below her ears as he draws her to him, hungry. Their teeth clash as their mouths lock and she says, 'Oh.' For a beat, they are mismatched pieces of a jigsaw. Then they find each other.

Shiori stares at the textbook but sees a horror show play across her mind's eye. She has had a strong imagination since childhood, lived her life in her head. It helps with the job. Receptionist at a love hotel has its advantages: the drawn blind over the window of her desk gives her an anonymity she craves at college. She is a shy girl. Some say pretty, but awkward. Fiercely intelligent. A star student at Hokusei Gakuen University in the School of Humanities. She has embraced the religion of the university's founder, the American Presbyterian missionary Sarah Clara Smith – so, while the part-time work in the hotel pays the bills, the seamy complexion of the business doesn't sit well with her. Neither does the sinful nature of her employers.

The thuggish man who growled through the window at her desk was one of them. He had slipped into her cramped workspace and barked an order for a pot of coffee for a room upstairs. A brute of a man. Thus, the horror show in her head. What do they do up there on the floors above? What wickedness? What evil? Another advantage of the blind over her window is the peace to pray. For her soul and those of the men who pay her salary, men she knows must be yakuza. She thinks of the woman accompanying the thug, like a model or one of the TV personalities her brother watches at home when he should be studying for his university entrance exams – if he isn't careful he could end up like the gangsters who frequent the hotel. After Shiori had delivered the coffee, the yakuza had left the hotel. Then the brutish man had returned over an hour later with a foreigner. American, like Sarah Clara Smith? A Presbyterian? Not likely if he is associating with her employers.

The tap on the glass startles her. Her yelp is like a scream in the confined box. There is a monitor to her right, the electronic eye of the camera set in the ceiling above the entrance hall. But the camera is broken and no one has bothered to mend or replace it. In Japan, in a yakuza-run love hotel, there is little need.

Another harsh tap on the partition of her counter. She fumbles with the textbook, knocking it to the floor with a flapping of pages like a startled bird.

Why am I afraid, she thinks. This is Japan. And North Ward, not Susukino. Her mobile is in her jacket. Her jacket is hanging in the small office out back. The phone on her left is service only, an exclusive line connected to the rooms above. If she's quiet, she can pad to the locker room door, slip inside and call home, just four blocks away. Her father will come, her brother. But why is she afraid? Why is a worry of cold fear at work in her stomach?

'Excuse me, can I help you?' she says.

There is a door to the left of the window and desk. Locked. The handle clicks. The knob rotates, makes a small noise of complaint at the lock, and eases back to its resting position.

Again.

Again.

Twice more like a predator scratching at a hen house latch. Shiori breathes hard, the sound ragged in the close air. She clamps her hand over her mouth. Profane and awful images race through her mind as she stares at the drawn blind over the counter window, her imagination wild at the thought of what might lurk behind.

A small scrap of paper crawls from the slit opening under the counter window.

No fingers, no shadow of a hand but something fine, perhaps metallic, at the very edge of the paper pushing it through the slit. She reads a scrawl in pen.

Gaijin: room number.

Not a question. A demand.

Her fingers rest just under the guillotine-like window blind, next to the paper. Her imagination betrays her again and she imagines the glass scything down, slicing her fingers off. Shiori drives the image away with a prayer. Her unvarnished nails brush the paper with its black scrabble of kanji characters. Then a strong hand darts through the window slit and seizes her, the dry film of the vinyl gloves firm as they crush her fingers. Her other hand flails, triggers the blind. It rockets up with a clatter. Through the glass, the evil takes form.

#

Her eyes flicker at the the confusion of scars on his chest. Fujiko's lashes draw closed and she leans forward, her hair cloaking the ruined skin, and kisses his face. His jaw. His neck.

Jackie clamps down on his lust and lets the touch of her lips, the tickle of her hair nourish his desire. The urgent farce of hopping and hauling, unbuttoning and unzipping is over. He's naked on the sofa. Fujiko straddles him again, in heels and brassiere. She sits hot against him, he hard against her pubis and the lowest scope of her belly. Her breath is quick, scorching his neck as she grinds against him.

He reaches behind her, finds the clasp of the brassiere and wills it to open. It comes undone with a pop and Fujiko draws her arms together, allowing the straps to slip down her body. As her mouth moves to his shoulders, Jackie twists around her and kisses her side. He has a notion of snakes entwined.

Her skin is sheer, but for a cinnamon blotch above the lower tip of her left shoulder blade, like spilt barley tea. The birthmark has a texture like goosebumps. Fujiko shudders when he touches and then kisses it.

They unravel and face one another, she resting on his lap, ready. She closes her eyes again and Jackie studies her lids, the delicate lines of the folds. Fujiko places her long fingers on his shoulders as he takes her in his hands. She levers her hips up, her body over him for a moment. Then she descends, slowly, and they begin their dance.

#

The corridor closes in on Saburo, then opens out again, expanding and contracting with each breath. A panic attack? Now? What kind of a yakuza am I? he thinks.

The kind that stands by while his boss's woman, his "mother" by another name, entertains a fucking gaijin in a love hotel. He can't believe Himura San countenances this.

Then again, Saburo can't believe the Kanto Daichi-kai ever took him in, ever gave him a home and purpose. All he had known before the approach from Nakata San, the second lieutenant, had been rejection, abandonment or punishment. Rejection from a father who'd pissed off to Hiroshima with a taxi driver's wife and shacked up in Kure City. Rejection from a mother who worked night shifts to pay the rent and was ashamed of her teenage son's arrest for a phone scam fleecing pensioners out of their savings. Abandonment in a Juvenile Training School near Hokkaido's north coast, a detention centre where his low IQ and susceptible nature were exploited by inmates and officials alike.

And the punishment. There were two officials in the juvenile centre, a bowl-cut bastard with bad skin and a handsome fucker with a pencil-line moustache. They forced ice baths on the boys in minus twenty-degree winter. They humiliated the teenage inmates, making them wear paper nappies or prohibiting toilet visits until they pissed themselves, then forcing their friends to wash the soaked clothes. And they wrapped a bed-sheet around Kazuyuki – Kazuyuki, who had given Saburo an ear when he was lonely, covered for him with the older boys when he cried and didn't want to leave his room – and began choking, choking. They shoved a will in Kazuyuki's straining face, forced a pen in his groping hands and told him to write. Told him he would die there, in that cell. When Saburo's friend's tears and snot blotted the page, bowl-cut twisted the sheet tighter while moustache got his cock out. They didn't see Saburo, quiet, watching in the crack behind the just-open door. Bowl-cut got off lightly with a broken jaw and three snapped fingers. Moustache retired early with a fractured skull, broken nose and cheekbone, and the joy of pissing into a bag for the rest of his life. Thanks to Japan's juvenile criminal laws, Saburo was never named and couldn't be transferred to an adult prison. In a few years he was out – but not before another boy had reported his performance to Nakata. Nakata recruited Saburo. Saburo gave his oyabun, Himura San, absolute devotion. Perhaps more so, he worshipped Fujiko Chan. He hadn't been with many women. His mother had loved him, he knew, and her shame and rejection at his arrest had cut deep to the point where he was almost afraid to connect with a woman, lest he disappoint them and disgrace himself.

Fujiko Chan had encouraged him, counselled him, mothered him. She was beautiful, intelligent and she gave of her time and attention to him, Saburo, a punk who'd never amounted to anything. In return, he gave his loyalty and protection to the point where his boss had all but appointed him her personal bodyguard.

She trusted him; why did he not trust her?

The gaijin was dangerous. Was that why?

Perhaps. Or perhaps he'd smelt a smell he knew well on Fujiko Chan when she'd returned to her apartment the morning after the tame bitch-cop, Yoshida, was murdered by the river. He can smell it now, sweet and citrus with an underlying chemical tang. It infected the sex shops, Touch clubs and DVD shops in Susukino. It stank out the Invisible Man Club at the end of business, when the withered little cleaning lady had finished with her mop and sprays. It cloaked the corridors of love hotels. Like this one. A chemical detergent, strong enough to wipe the cum and desperation from the places of business that traded on vice and lust and loneliness. A faint trace of it had been on Fujiko's clothes when she returned that morning.

How can he voice his suspicions to his oyabun?

How can he not?

But he knows he must tread carefully. *Look at what happened to Fox.*

He catches a flash of something red in his peripheral vision and turns to see the glaring face of a demon standing next to him.

Saburo has always imagined the Tengu in traditional wooden clogs but this one is wearing expensive looking brogues, polished to a brilliant shine. He wonders for a second why he didn't hear the demon approach. Then he feels a sting like a papercut on his belly. He seems to deflate and blood is soaking his shirt. It wets his trousers like the piss of the boys in the juvenile detention centre. It seems to drain from his limbs so fast he can barely raise his arm to go for his pistol, some cheap Russian piece of shit. When the blade cuts to his bone he feels the razor edge of the steel grind against the tendons under his palm and he realises his right hand won't be holding anything. Ever again.

He collapses, sits against the corridor wall. The Tengu looks down at him, furious. All in black save for that red face, the blood-sullied sword in its hand. Saburo opens his mouth to shout, give some warning. The gaijin looks strong. Maybe he can protect Fujiko. But the blade swipes Saburo's throat and his mouth fills with liquid iron. The Tengu tilts its head and moves to the door, a card key in its sword-free hand. It slides the key in the lock of the door. The door leading to Fujiko and the gaijin.

Saburo's head sags on his chest. He stares down the slope of his body to his splayed legs, his leather shoes. Too slow, he ponders. Too slow to react. Too slow to save Fujiko or himself. And the last thing he'll know before he dies is that damn antiseptic stench of the cleaning detergent in the love hotel. The pain comes in a tsunami and he despairs that he won't die before he has to suffer for a long time. His blood is saturating the carpet. As his conscious thought slips away, he muses how no amount of detergent will get that shit out.

Chapter 20

Fujiko is moving faster now, Jackie bucking against her from below. The smooth sweep of her body sways as her hips pitch and roll, her breasts shining with a film of sweat. Jackie's stomach is hard and tight as he strains to keep control. He wants to lift her, carry her to the bed and finish there rather than the sofa. He wants some control. But she won't surrender, braces her slender arms against his shoulders, crushes against him as she rides. Her mouth is drawn tight. Her small, urgent moans gain pace as she fights to not call out and alert Saburo on the other side of the door.

Jackie has forgotten about the yakuza in the corridor. Far from home, in this room, Fujiko is all. Sweet release from the chaos beyond. As they build to their climax he feels his body lighten. The darkness locked in his head, all the bad people and places in his life – in him – he's ready to pour it all out. He feels a shudder in her thighs, hears a tightening in her throat. She leans close and he breathes the sweet scent of her hair. Her hot breath scalds his cheek. His own breath roars in his ears. He barely catches the soft click, takes precious seconds to register someone has opened the door of the room. Fujiko slows her grinding, looking at him. Fear then anger trouble her fine features as his attention shifts.

Jackie leans, Fujiko wrapped around him, to see who is standing at the door, watching. His mind is plummeting from the crest of pleasure even as his body still works to a climax. He expects to find the bodyguard, Saburo, standing behind Fujiko. Or Reizo, seething, hands balled in fists. Or wrapped around a weapon.

Fujiko twists on his lap and strains to see the intruder. Her sharp cry is a sobering slap.

A lean figure stands in the doorway. His hands are by his sides, sheathed in vinyl gloves. The right clenches a slim, wicked short sword. The left clutches a blood-soaked cloth. There is a terrible violence in that grasp, the cloth drenched in the awful consequence of the blade's work. The figure's face is a brilliant scarlet. The eyes are tarnished gold, pinpricks of darkness in their centre. The nose is like a monstrous cock, as though aroused by the naked lovers before it.

Fujiko babbles a confusion of Japanese.

Jackie catches a word.

'Tengu.'

It's a trigger. The masked figure comes at them and lunges as Jackie pitches forward. The blade spears the back of the sofa as he and Fujiko land in a sprawl on the floor. He's still inside her as they lie at the feet of the demon, the assassin raising the blade high above his head, ready to scythe down. Jackie grabs Fujiko in a bear hug and hurls their clinched bodies over like a barrel, the splay of their legs enough to tip the demon, its arms raised high, off balance. The Tengu collapses in a heap with a roar, the blade hitting the carpet with a soft thump.

Jackie and Fujiko separate. She gags and moans. As the Tengu struggles to his feet and reaches for the blade, Jackie sees a slim film of blood on its edge. A scarlet seam has opened on Fujiko's back, from the lowest rib to the wing of her shoulder blade. Her hands knead the carpet and Jackie smells her hair again as he takes her under her arms and lifts her, shoving her to the corner as the Tengu recovers the blade. Jackie runs his hands down his belly, his naked flanks, feels sweat and slick body-hair on his exposed skin. He smells sex in the room and steps to the side, away from Fujiko, as the Tengu takes a fighting stance. The assassin is rigid in his plan of attack. Jackie catches a transferral of weight, the left hip rising, the shoulder dropping a second before the lunge. He throws himself to the right, his shin bashing the sofa, the impact lost in a swathe of adrenaline and lands on his belly. He scrambles to his feet, his back exposed.

The Tengu is recovering its balance from the lunge. Again, Jackie smooths his sides with his palms, checking for a tear in his naked body. His hand comes away red. He's been cut. No. It's Fujiko's blood, not his. He backs away as the Tengu changes its grip on the hilt of the blade.

Jackie shivers, adrenaline and fear leaking through his pores. He feels the soft tickle of the carpet on the soles of his feet. His breathing is shallow and he hears Fujiko crying in the corner. He wills her to open the door and crawl outside but her mind has gone to another place. The Tengu is pacing again, assessing angles for a fresh line of attack. The assassin has a warm, laundered, chemical smell. No need to rush: it holds the killing blade, the courage born of anonymity and the comforting cloak of clothing. The deliberate movement, the control, is a spiteful contrast to the awkward stumble of Jackie's legs, the bird-flutter of his heartbeat, the coursing fear in his hollow arms. He's against the bed now, the top of the mattress against the crack of his arse. His hands find the duvet. The assassin grips the short sword two-handed and advances, closing the meagre distance in fast strides, and attacks with a diagonal stroke. Jackie pivots backward, throwing his body up on the bed as the blade finds his skin and bites, drawing its razor edge across meat and sinew. His foot flails and catches the Tengu on the side of the head. The mask shunts across the assassin's face and the bastard yells.

Jackie, sprawled on the bed, sees his naked body in the ceiling mirror, sees the slim cut in his right thigh. A glancing blow. Lucky bastard, he thinks.

When he struggles on to his side, the Tengu is fiddling with the mask, righting it. Jackie has a glimpse of a shock of shining black hair. He scrambles on the bed, rumpling duvet and sheets, reaching for the bamboo lattice above the headboard. The Tengu roars and swipes with the short sword, butchering air as Jackie collapses against the lattice. He grabs a knotty pole and heaves. No give, the rod rock solid, fixed above the bed. He whines, 'No!' like his voice is breaking and yanks at the bamboo.

The Tengu flails with the sword, its blood up. Jackie falls backwards and tumbles off the far side of the bed as the blade splinters bamboo and shears through wall plaster. He lands in a heap and hears the fast thump of the assassin's feet running around the bed. He's still on the floor as the polished shoes loom into view and aim a vicious kick at his head. He twists his torso, catching the blow on his shoulder. Another on his bare spine. The blade comes down. He rolls. The tip catches his flank, just above his arse on the right and he cries out. Panic more than pain, although sweat stings his wounds. The blade comes down again, clattering off the bedside table as the Tengu abandons a plan of attack in a berserker rage.

Jackie hauls at the duvet and throws it over himself. He hurls his body at the attacker, feels the slim heft of the blade through the fabric, then a bite in his skin. But he's in close, no traction for the Tengu, the wound a shallow slice above his kidney. He lurches into the attacker like some ridiculous monster, cloaked in the duvet and they collapse in a seething tangle of limbs on the floor. Jackie catches a blow on his head. He punches, kicks, thrashes like a schoolboy in a playground fight. He grunts as he stabs out with his feet, his naked body grazing the carpet, his legs extending more and more as he slides from the heaving duvet and the killer within. Separated from the Tengu, he clambers upright, the gashes in his skin tearing at his nerves. Before, the world was he and Fujiko coiled together; now it's he and the demon, locked in a different dance.

The assassin emerges from the rumpled duvet like a goblin from under the bed. The short sword still grasped in its hand, the mask staring with unmoving malice. Again they pace, Jackie tiring, shivering. He feels like a seam is splitting in the fabric of his body and his torn skin is opening. Like he's unravelling.

Fujiko screams, once. The screech seems to echo around the room. I'm naked, he thinks, ready to be butchered like a fucking beast. I don't want to die. Oh Christ, please.

He takes a step back and something gnaws the sole of his foot. Splinters on the carpet. Bamboo splinters from the shredded wall display. A hard, fibrous bamboo rod lies across the floor and sofa. The ends are sharp needles, cruel slivers birthed by the Tengu's blade. Jackie lunges, almost fumbles it, then his hands find purchase and he raises the jagged staff.

The mask juts forward and a low murmur comes from behind the scowling demon's face.

A laugh.

The killer comes at Jackie fast, the blade arcing through the air, slicing the rod. Jackie's braced for a blow but barely feels the blade scythe through the bamboo, halving its length. He twists right as the killer brings the sword up again and almost goes over on his ankle. Jackie steps back and his foot catches Fujiko's calf, tripping him. He stumbles across the room, co-ordination gone, and goes down hard, his spine glancing off the TV unit. He calls out, legs wide on the carpet, exposed. His back feels shredded from the fall. He clutches the splintered shaft of bamboo like a lifeline. The Tengu bellows, the sword raised at a right angle to the killer's body, ready to thrust and pierce bare skin, spear muscle and tissue and heart. Fujiko shrieks. It sounds wrong, displaced.

Her slender frame rises behind the Tengu, clutching the other half of the broken bamboo shaft. As the demon thrusts at Jackie, she swings the pole, a glancing blow on the bastard's shoulder. Enough to jar the Tengu's arm. Enough to send the blade past Jackie's face and through the flat screen of the TV. Enough to shock Jackie into action. Enough to startle his arm into launching upward, the jagged tip of his bamboo rod driving the edge of the demon mask against the skin of the killer's neck, spearing the assassin's throat. There's a wet gasp, as though the killer is taking his first breath for a long time, and a brace of knuckles mash Jackie's eye, the vinyl glove slick on his sweat covered skin. His head cracks off the wooden unit as a knee smashes his face. His hearing dulls, his limbs wading through thick mud. Something hot and wet hits his chest, a blood-slicked gloved fist, and he grabs it, snarls, clamps it in his teeth and bites down. The taste is foul, synthetic, then salty and metallic. Another hand clouts his skull and his head snaps back on his neck. He hears a feminine yelp, the sound of something crumpling on the carpeted floor and an enraged bellow. He glimpses the Tengu convulse, clutching at its throat. The killer stumbles to the door and falls out of the room.

Then there is quiet, save for the hammering of his heart, the quickness of his breath and the whimper of his naked lover somewhere beyond his exhausted reach.

Part Two

Part Two

Chapter 21

Jun looks from the gossip magazine in his bandaged hand to Megan, to the image of the American actress on the page again. She and her father are tired – she guesses it's late in the night – and this has been going on for some time. Jun is like a child with a new game but she summons a weary smile and cocks her head in a jaunty pose.

'Yeah, you look like her, too.' He shows her the face on the page. A paparazzi shot of a young Hollywood actress. She looks nothing like Megan but Jun is convinced they are doppelgangers.

'I thought all foreigners looked the same,' she says.

Jun laughs. 'Not the pretty ones.'

Pretty. There is something in Megan Chan's high brow, the smooth curve of her neck, that is closer to beauty. He likes the softness in her voice when she speaks to him. Some women affect the same quality in their speech when they talk to him like a child. Megan addresses him with kindness, but as an adult. A man.

Like Shouko used to.

Shouko. A name from the past. Pretty, flirtatious, smart. She had beguiled Jun with her intelligence, her knowledge of books and language and other countries. He had been excited in ways he had never experienced before by her pretty eyes, her smile, the swish of her skirt, the slim lock that refused to stay put in her styled hair. She had been coy but affectionate, giving him small gifts and much time. Kenta had goaded Jun, told him she was using him, told him he was nothing more than a puppy to amuse her, that she would drop him as soon as some university student showed a glimmer of interest in her. So he had stalked her. He watched her as she met friends and sat in coffee bars or noodle shops.

It had been a dim night, the city silent, smothered by snow. She had sensed someone following her. Shouko had run across a street in panic and slipped on the sleek surface of the impacted snow and ice. The taxi had not been doing more than twenty but it was enough. Jun discovered later, the driver had called an ambulance then found a photograph in her wallet, a sheet of small shots from a Print Club photo-booth of Shouko with a young man, a heart drawn in marker on the back with a phone number written in the centre. A kanji character too. *Kareshi*. Boyfriend. The number was Jun's. Thank god his mobile had been on silent at the time. And he had stood behind a bank of snow watching her die as the driver called the number on the photo, his number, his phone vibrating in his pocket while Shouko went as still and cold as the ice sculptures in Odori Park.

Jun looks from the girl holding the mirror for her father as the older man works on Inaba to Kenta skulking in the corner. His brother, devoured by his own weakness, like their mother.

The foreigners are good people, he thinks. Shouko would have liked them. She loved all things foreign. Funny, he hasn't thought of her in years.

Jun chews on his lips as he flicks through the magazine. He clicks his tongue in frustration at his clumsy fingers and the restricting bandage, then displays a studio portrait of a nineties Sean Connery. Megan laughs. Her father, too.

Kenta, sitting at the table reading a tabloid, scowls and mutters.

Inaba ordered the TV turned off to save power from the generator and, when Jun pleaded and Kenta moaned, he confiscated the set, taking it with him as he left on another errand.

Megan has no idea of the time – the boarded-up windows a constant taunt – but her body clock is telling her it's night; her father, addled by jet-lag, is saucer-eyed as he looks at Jun. How long has Inaba been away? wonders Megan. How many beers has the angry gangster at the table, with his detonation of bleached blonde hair and streetfight scar, drunk while his brother plays with the gaijin?

How much hatred will it take until Kenta takes some of that loathing out on her and her father?

She thinks of Yuji.

Has his brother, Rei, reappeared? She likes Rei. He was always a little uncomfortable in her presence, withdrawn as though he had some secret she must not discover but he was polite and thoughtful. She had been surprised to hear he was a Christian; he was shocked to hear she did not believe in God, had thought all Westerners were Christian at heart. He'd even made it something of a mission to evangalise her. He had given her a Japanese bible as a gift, a small bookmark embossed with a cross and a couple of other religious items. It had irritated Yuji, she knew, but Megan had found it sweet. She knew Rei's intentions were good and her father still had a lick of the old C of E running through him like a message in a stick of seaside rock. Yes, she hopes Rei has turned up.

Yuji isn't particularly close to his parents. If his brother is still missing, he probably feels terribly alone. In the time Megan and he have known each other he has been a comfort to her and brought solace when she felt isolated and homesick. Always attentive and affectionate. The antithesis of the old national male stereotypes, with an inner strength that gave him a certain dignity, although it lent him an aloofness. Now, with his brother missing, Megan cannot give something back, can't offer comfort and understanding.

And Inaba's story: incredible. The brothers, Jun and Kenta, in on Inaba's plan. She feels like she's living in a gangster movie.

She had been led to believe the laws of Japan were inviolable, including the creed of its mafia – but here were the brothers and the plotter-in-chief, Goro Inaba, turning on their boss, colluding with the police. Inaba had told her he was working with the Organised Crime Bureau as an informant. There was trouble and he got scared. Then Jackie-bloody-Shaw stepped in and had a confrontation with the yakuza called Fox, one of the men Megan had spoken with in front of the Susukino convenience store, and Inaba panicked and grabbed Megan and her father. Inaba had told her that Kenta had been there when Shaw had fought with Fox in a side street, and that they had found a hotel receipt in the Irishman's pocket. Kenta and Jun had gone to the hotel and discovered Ian Sparrow was staying and had left word for Shaw that he had gone to visit his daughter. A connection at city hall immigration had given Inaba details of Megan's university and current address – a chilling indication of the extent of yakuza influence. And so she and her father had been abducted. Now, claimed Inaba, he and his companions could keep Megan and Ian safe and use them as insurance against the police screwing the three gangsters over. Jun and Kenta had turned against their boss, sickened at his actions toward, and disregard for, Jun and joined Inaba. Her father had wanted to press the matter of Jackie Shaw but Inaba had abruptly ended the discussion and left the cabin.

A chill settles over Megan's shoulders. Another sign that it is night.

She and her father had whispered about the coats hanging opposite the toilet, whether there might be something inside a pocket they could use to escape. A long shot but at least it kept their minds active. Prodded by the cold, she checks that Jun is engrossed in the magazine. She lays a hand on her father's arm and says, 'I'm going to try for the coats.' Before her dad can protest she leans forward and says to Jun in Japanese, 'I think I need to pee again.' She repeats the sentence to her father in English.

'Okay,' says Jun, to himself as much as her, then calls to his brother, 'I'm taking the girl to the toilet.'

He stands and hitches up his trousers. Megan gets up from the sofa as her father reaches for her hand. Kenta springs from the table and says, 'No. I'll go.'

Jun says, 'I can do it.'

'I don't trust her.'

'She's going for a piss. What can she do with her knickers around her ankles?'

Kenta walks over and takes his brother's wounded hand in both his. He squeezes. A muscle twitches in Jun's jaw.

'I'll take her,' says Kenta again. He releases the bandaged hand and slaps his brother on the shoulder. 'You're too young to see a gaijin naked, anyway.'

Megan shivers and lays a hand on her father's shoulder. He looks wretched. She remembers a similar look on his face during the divorce, remembers her shock at how the man who had always seemed so large, so strong, so in control, could look so broken. She had hated her mother for a time, had yearned to leave her and move in with dad – screw the courts. She'd hated her mother more for the insinuations, hints and comments seeded throughout their screaming matches that Ian Sparrow, her revered father, had had someone else. That he had neglected her mother for another woman.

Bullshit.

Bullshit! Stop the maudlin reminiscing and get back in the game.

Megan follows Kenta through the connecting door. Beyond the main room, the cold has taken a firmer grip. At the end of the dingy corridor Kenta stands aside and gives her space to squeeze into the cubicle. She eyes the coats hanging behind his broad shoulders.

'Aren't you going to turn around?' she says.

'Why would I?' He turns on the light.

Megan mutters in English, 'Wanker.' Then she unfastens her jeans and drops them with her underwear, holding them suspended between her booted ankles just above the filthy floor and grime-stained porcelain trough below her. She squats and looks away from the yakuza.

After a couple of seconds Kenta says, 'You think Goro Inaba is your friend?'

Megan says nothing.

'You think he's our friend? My brother and me?'

He hawks up a wad of something thick and spits the phlegm at her feet.

'Answer me!'

'No,' she says.

'No.' The yakuza lights up a smoke, vindicated. 'You see my brother's hand? The boss of our syndicate, Himura, did that with a dagger in punishment. My brother took the heat for Inaba's fuck-up and that's what he got for his loyalty. Jun's my blood but he's a fucking idiot. There was a crisis within our syndicate a couple of nights ago. Inaba was nowhere to be found. Off seeing that kid of his and his ex-wife, giving the mercenary bitch more of his hard-earned money. That's why he's fucking broke. More fool him.' He takes a drag on the smoke. 'Then he goes to grab noodles with a piece of ass. So there's this crisis while he's slurping noodles with some skank. The way our life works, someone has to take the blame and it should have been Inaba. But my brother felt, as Inaba is his senior, he should save his superior's blushes. Thought he'd lose his little finger and gain some leverage with the boss's right-hand man. Except the boss is a cold bastard and ruined his whole fucking hand instead.'

Kenta tokes on his fag and says, 'Yeah.' The word is long and drawn out like the film of grey smoke seeping from his mouth. 'The bastard Himura couldn't even remember Jun's name. Least, that's what Goro said.'

For a moment his eyes are lost in another time and place.

Megan tries to clear her mind. She can't pee with this thug standing here.

'Your friend, the big gaijin, was a problem,' says Kenta. 'Thanks to him you're being kept in this hole.' He coughs. 'Another member of our syndicate, Fox, wanted the big gaijin after that little display with you and your father in front of the convenience store.'

Megan stares at a rust-coloured stain on the floor and sees Jackie Shaw in her mind's eye, slapping and punching her American friend last night before her father met Yuji. Her father is right; the Irishman is not that physically big but he has a presence for sure.

'Fox went looking for your friend,' says Kenta. 'Found him, too.

Wandering Susukino. Bad luck for your friend. I'd texted Inaba, let him know. The gaijin took a beating. Fox pulled a knife, ready to cut him. I knew it was trouble. The cops grow a set of balls for a while when a gaijin is hurt.' He finishes the cigarette and flicks it against the wall in a small shower of sparks. 'Inaba turned up just in time, tracking my mobile. Pulled rank and balled out Fox, told him we didn't need the attention a maimed gaijin would bring after our little syndicate crisis. Of course, we – Inaba, Jun and me – needed to protect the big bastard and you. We thought we could use you to keep the cops honest and on side. Our future survival depends on the cops now. So Inaba took your big friend to his apartment. Inaba was still scared after the syndicate trouble, trying to work out what he should do.'

Then Kenta talks about the fight in Inaba's apartment, Jackie Shaw's escape and Inaba panicking then grabbing Megan and her father.

'With that gaijin bruiser on the loose, Inaba had to act fast. If the gaijin went to the police he'd eventually lead them to us and the Kanto Daichi-kai would know he'd been working with the cops. We have plenty of sources in the National Police Agency and it might leak that Inaba was a rat.' Kenta looks her up and down, the dark seams of his eyes settling on the flap of blouse hanging over her crotch as she squats. 'So we have to keep you and your father under wraps until Inaba contacts the right person in the cops, and they bring him and Jun and me in.' He smiles a yellowed smile and spreads his arms as wide as he can in the dingy space. 'And here we are.'

The yell from the other room is loud enough to startle Kenta and Megan almost falls over in surprise. Kenta hisses, 'Fuck!' and runs down the corridor. She hears the door slam, raised voices, whining and raging in Japanese. She doesn't hear her father.

She struggles upright, zig-zagging her knickers and jeans up her thighs and hips. The sounds of argument coming from the main room intensify, voices cracking as they holler. Dad, she thinks, what have you done? She wants to run, to hurl the door open and go to her father. Instead, she tiptoes over the gobs of Kenta's phlegm on the tiled floor and steadies herself with a hand on the coats hung opposite.

The coats. One of which might contain something useful.

From beyond the door at the end of the corridor she catches snippets of vexed Japanese: 'What do you expect?'; ' – not my fucking fault if – '; ' – just because you're older doesn't – '; 'Not fucking now!'

She begins rifling through pockets. Her fingers conspire against her, fumbling with fear. There are three coats, a leather jacket and two heavy, winter jackets. The leather jacket has something soft and papery in the side pocket on the left – a crumpled cigarette pack; two plastic lighters in a breast pocket; an empty Hello Kitty keyring on the right side. Then she feels it through the padded fabric of the second jacket. A rectangular slab.

A mobile phone.

From the main room: 'I don't give a fuck if you're hurt, you bring this shit on yourself!' 'Fuck you, asshole! At least I don't have hair like a Chinese lesbian!'

The mobile catches on the pocket lining for a second. She gives it a short tug.

'I'll slap you senseless you little shit drip!'

'What, looking like a Korean faggot in a soap opera?'

The smooth, rounded corner of the phone comes away from the nylon lining with a soft rip. Its bead encrusted strap snags on stitching.

She pleads in a whisper, 'Please, oh please.'

Kenta rants from beyond the door, 'Get a fucking grip, you ass-sniffing little pervert, and watch the old man!'

The phone leaps free of the pocket, black and gleaming in the stark light of the bulb. A small character, a cute baby bear with a melon on its head, dangles from the end of the strap. The screen is dead, the power off.

At last she hears her father. He yells a warning, 'The door!'

She shoves the phone back in the coat pocket with a soft clack of beads as the door opens.

Kenta barges into the corridor, filling the narrow space with his bulk and fury. Megan fiddles with her jeans buttons in the toilet doorway. Her fingers tremble and her pale pink cheeks are florid. She flinches as the yakuza marches down the corridor, raising his hand. He delivers a full-blooded right hook to the coats on the wall and yells out as his knuckles bang against the hardwood behind.

'Is my father okay?' says Megan.

Kenta snorts and shoves her toward the main room in answer. She leaves the coats behind but holds tight to the knowledge of the phone and a lifeline to Yuji, to the police. She prays that her father is unhurt.

#

Genda is drunk. The alcohol sends scraps of memory, good times, floating through his consciousness, settling him deeper in the chair. This sturdy seat, a loyal servant for the last five years, has never felt softer, quicksand for his considerable arse. When his mobile phone rings, he tuts with annoyance at the shattered reverie. It takes him seconds that feel like minutes to find it nestled under a sheaf of papers.

'Genda,' he says. He hears his own voice, thick and sluggish. For god's sake, don't be my wife, he thinks.

'Genda San, is this a bad time?'

'Watanabe San. No, no. I was just relaxing.'

'Please pass on my apologies to your wife for calling you so late.'

'Of course, of course.' A thought seeps into Genda's whiskey addled mind. He had used his friendship with Watanabe San, senior officer to the OCB detective he had spoken to an hour or two earlier, as leverage to force the issue of DNA testing. Genda says, 'I was just talking about you this evening.'

'So I understand. A rather disturbed Inspector mentioned you had a conversation with him several hours ago. The DNA was an interesting discovery. How did you come upon it? If you'll excuse the pun.' A high-pitched chuckle.

Silence. Moments for Genda to think, rearrange the fragments in his memory. 'The raid on Kanto Daichi-kai premises across the river. You knew about that, of course.'

A grunt of assent.

'I was there, Watanabe San. I had a discussion with the oyabun, Himura. They want to know who the perpetrator is just as much as we do. Bad for business. He gave me the DNA tip.'

'And you believe him?'

'Yes.'

'Well,' – Watanabe non-committal – 'it may be helpful. Inadmissible you know, but another angle is always welcome.' A pause.

Genda moves papers around on his desk. Neither man speaks for ten seconds or so, a soft white noise on the line lulling Genda to sleep like a newborn.

Watanabe breaks the impasse. 'Genda San, I called your personal mobile for a reason. We've been friends as well as colleagues for some years.'

'Yes.'

'Please think well of me, Watanabe San, as I think well of you. Thank you.'

'Please, please,' Genda's voice is sleepy, accepting the sycophancy, the accolades, on autopilot, 'think well of me, too.'

Watanabe says, 'I am sure you agree that experience is all in our occupation. Indeed, in Japan. It is what makes us Japanese unique, this respect for seniority, for elders.'

'We Japanese, yes.'

'It is truly regrettable, that the Senior Commissioner for Hokkaido does not show the same accord and respect to his most experienced officers. Well-intentioned as he may be.'

The little shit, thinks Genda. *Officious little asswipe.* 'No doubt,' he slurs, 'the Senior Commisioner acts in his own best interests. I mean, in the interests of the NPA.'

'No doubt. However, I believe you had a couple of queries regarding the circumstances of our work with the Kanto Daichi-kai. And of the work of our officer, Rei Miyamoto, so tragically murdered a couple of nights ago?'

'Yes, yes.' Sleep, thinks Genda. Must sleep. *My god, this chair is more comfortable than a Susukino whore's ass.* The last time he paid for ass was the last time he got drunk. When was that?

Watanabe says, 'The Senior Commissioner has little stomach for organised crime investigation at present, Genda San. So,' – more air sucked through teeth – 'nothing is being done regarding Miyamoto's death until the Senior Commissioner has considered all options. Orders of the top brass in OCB.'

'Nothing?' A shaft of sharp reason pierces the slow stream of whiskey-induced daydreams in Genda's mind.

'Everyone has to wait on the say-so of the Senior Commissioner before making any move and he doesn't like to be disturbed of an evening at home.' There is an edge to Watanabe's voice now.

Genda says, 'And the dead policeman? Miyamoto San?'

'The DNA test will be completed. We should have results in less than forty-eight hours, perhaps tomorrow. Rei Miyamoto's parents have been informed of the death. We cannot find the brother at present: the parents said he often works late. We will speak with him face-to-face later. A couple of detectives will stay on assignment, researching background. The Senior Commissioner will be here in the morning to liaise with the press office and then we shall see.'

Genda thinks: the matter will be contained; the family managed; and the Commissioner will blow hot air up the media's ass until some teenage J-pop star gets busted for indecent exposure and everyone forgets about a dead cop.

He says, 'The Senior Commissioner has no interest in yakuza business at present? Do you think he'll cut the source within Kanto Daichi-kai loose?'

'The source has run.' Watanabe sucks in a lungful of air, then speaks with resolve, as though he has taken a tough decision. 'However, regarding the information you requested – please understand only the small core of officers working Rei Miyamoto's case are privy to all the information. However, I do have some, limited intelligence. I believe someone must know the truth and I am concerned that records will be lost, files misplaced or destroyed. But please, you must swear you will never reveal where you heard what I am about to tell you.'

'I swear, Watanabe San. You can trust me with your life.'

'Genda San, do you have a pencil or pen at hand?'

'One moment.' Genda searches his desk, scattering papers and files. *A fucking work desk and not a pen to be found!* Irritated, he pats down his pockets. Then he stops. He says, 'Why tell me?'

'Frankly, why not? The source risked his life. A good policeman died.'

He's drunk too, thinks Genda. Here we are, two befuddled old cops, passing secrets on the phone late at night, angry and spiteful at the officious little shit who waltzed up the ranks with his civil service exam grades and his political connections. So sad. Modern Japan, where age and seniority mean nothing to the young. He finds a ballpoint pen behind his desk phone and contemplates stopping off in a local shot bar for a last drink before a taxi home.

'I'm ready' he says, leaning back in the chair with a protracted groan. 'Fire away.'

Chapter 22

The wail brings him around.

A siren?

Human?

Both.

He opens his eyes to see his torso, spattered with blood and his legs splayed on the floor. Half propped against the sofa, her face masked by hair, is Fujiko. She is still naked but now Reizo Himura is crouched by her side clutching a handgun. The siren passes somewhere in the streets outside as Himura wails. Fujiko smacks him hard across the cheek and he falls on his arse, inadvertent slapstick, and drops his pistol.

Jackie catches an impression of Fujiko's face as she peers through her curtain of hair, a moustache of blood linking her nose and lips. She raises her arm. She holds Himura's dropped gun. The men with Himura, huddled in the doorway, begin imploring. The pistol looks huge in her hand, threatening to drag her thin arm down with its weight. Himura crosses his legs in the lotus position.

He grunts at his men, 'Silence!'

Slow with effort, Fujiko's arm pivots, the gun pointing at the floor, the door and then Jackie. Himura turns to him and a look of comical surprise washes over his brutal face – as if he hadn't noticed the bloodied, naked man lying slumped against the TV stand.

Fujiko's arm is taut, knuckles white as she grips the pistol. In the dreamtime of the moment Jackie takes it for granted that he will die. After his struggle with the Tengu killer it seems somehow inevitable. Then Fujiko's head drops and the pistol follows suit. Himura is on her in a moment, arms encircling her but loose, as though embarrassed by her nakedness. He, not she, cries out when his fingers find her wound, the slash across her back. He whispers in her ear as a couple of yakuza approach Jackie.

They cluck and gabble. Jackie looks up, winces at the pain stabbing at his skull, and sees the slim blade of the short sword suspended above his head, lodged in the flat-screen, like Excalibur awaiting Arthur. The men take an arm each and lift him from the floor.

Himura stares at him, perhaps through him, his face flushed as though drunk. His eyes are dark slashes torn in his crude face, as impenetrable as Fujiko's. A yakuza fetches the crumpled duvet and drapes it around Fujiko. Himura's jaw works as it juts forward, chewing the cud. Chewing his options. Jackie remembers the yakuza tenet through the ruckus of aches and confusion tearing through his brain – never violate the wife or children of another mobster. What had he done if not violate the woman closest to the boss – the father – of the syndicate? They are both naked. It doesn't take a genius to do the maths. He lets the men at his sides take his weight as he sags, reconciling with the fact that he is now truly fucked.

Himura barks orders in quick succession. The men tighten their grip on Jackie's arms.

Fujiko speaks, her voice cracked. When she talks every man listens. Himura works his jaw again, staring at the floor. Jackie hears Saburo mentioned. The men nod. Fujiko pauses. Himura's eyes go to the clock on the wall. Fujiko speaks again. She is giving orders. Reizo Himura takes a moment, giving Jackie a hard stare. Then he nods and the men lead Jackie to the door.

In the corridor, Saburo lies dead, a large blot of dark blood encircling his corpse like a bull's eye. The men hurry toward a fire exit. Jackie shivers, feels exposed, the only naked body in the group as he is led on. He hears Fujiko speaking with a calm patience and the soft shift of the duvet wrapped around her slim figure. Another man hurries up behind and wraps a sheet around Jackie. Jackie trips, almost falls. Himura is on his mobile. They go through the fire escape and down one flight of steps. For Jackie the going is torturous, his battered body screaming for respite. They pass through a connecting door on the other side of the stairwell and into another corridor.

More stairs to basement level. An underground car park. Into a Toyota estate. The car grumbles to life, then glides through the concrete cave. They emerge onto a different street. Parallel, Jackie thinks, to the side street with the love hotel. As they pull out onto a large avenue running north to south, he hears wailing again. This time, he is sure, it is the sound of sirens.

#

Genda passes the bar as a woman in a mini-skirted blue PVC police uniform screeches with laughter outside, a mobile phone clamped to her ear. Her hair, straw-like in colour and texture, hangs in a tangle of knots. The Superintendent tuts as he lurches to the kerb and waves an aimless hand in the air. He checks his watch: almost one in the morning. There should be a few taxis around.

Drunk, belligerent, he has arrived at the conclusion that the Organised Crime Bureau is comprised of driven little weasels who failed the civil service exams and dreamed of a fast-track to the illustrious, bureaucratic heights of the NPA. Or drop outs who'd fucked up so badly in regular uniformed work, they'd been farmed out as tea-boys and paper shufflers in the lost cause of bringing the yakuza to bear. There were a few decent, obsessive police like Watanabe, with a healthy respect for the yakuza capacity for violence, and who refused to accept the criminal fraternity as a thread in the fabric of Japanese life. But, in his inebriation, he considered those cops very much the few.

The yakuza syndicates might be as established within Japanese society as the civil service itself, as the governing political party they helped build and promote; they might have their badges and official magazines and television interviews and their grip on the construction and finance and entertainment industries, but they were still a blight. Drugs. Loan-sharking. Prostitution. Human trafficking. Blackmail, violence and murder. The business of yakuza inc., one of the largest corporations in Japan. Scum.

Genda regrets drinking so much whiskey.

He knows the name of a gold-plated rat in the largest Hokkaido syndicate now, thanks to his frined, Watanabe. Details of a planned deal between the kanto-Daichi kai and Yamaguchi-gumi organisations. The contents of a folder confiscated from Kanto Daichi-kai premises. And an official embargo from the top of the Hokkaido office of the National Police Agency on the use or spread of any of the information surreptitiously supplied by his drunk and very pissed off friend.

Information worth a great deal of money to the Kanto Daichi-kai boss, Reizo Himura. For Superintendent Genda has not only the name of the Organised Crime Bureau source, Goro Inaba. He not only knows that Inaba had a child, kept secret from his the members of the Kanto Daichi-kai organisation. He also has a vague idea of the rat's location, a hundred square kilometre area in the south of Hokkaido, triangulated through matching the location of several public phones from which Inaba called OCB offices. A large area – but still valuable information for Reizo Himura. Himura probably knows if Inaba has any history in that area, family, perhaps an old property where he could hide out.

Genda could feed information to the gang boss, perhaps sow the seed of doubt within the gang and engineer a fissure deep enough to shatter the organisation and cause some damage to the Yamaguchi bastards, too. Yes, Genda could play the game and see how the organisation might tear itself apart, and torpedo Tokyo mafia involvement. But could the yakuza, thinks Genda, even one syndicate like the Kanto Daichi-kai, really be eradicated? Every trace destroyed?

Was he a true believer?

An alternative was to hand Himura his rat. Give him Inaba, curry favour and earn the highest value currency in Japanese society – debt and obligation.

Or perhaps he could broker a way out for Inaba and save a life.

But what if he couldn't protect Inaba? He had learned from Watanabe that the informer was a father. What if Genda were responsible for a little girl losing her daddy? Was he, childless and locked in a stale marriage, prepared to take that chance?

Whatever it is, he knows he must do something with the intelligence. Watanabe unburdened himself of the knowledge in an alcohol-fuelled stream of information like a drunkard's piss. Now the intel is swirling through Genda's mind, demanding an outlet. His hand drops to his side and he executes a shaky turn to take in the police-costumed woman again – but the door of the bar is swinging closed, smothering the sound of jazz, chat and laughter. Genda comes to a conclusion.

Only one thing to do, Superintendent, he decides. Check your wallet, gird your loins and have another drink.

#

Dim shadows and the impression of sounds and smells swirl around Jackie Shaw. The now familiar smell of tatami matting. A notion of Olympic rings; a dream-maze of identical streets and Jackie running, running and getting nowhere. Pretty women named Aina, beautiful women named Fujiko. Familiar emotions, his fellow travellers of fear, rage, regret. And his old acquaintance, despised yet insistent, bound by blood – violence.

He won't open his eyes, won't be dragged from his dark cocoon. His body is curled, fetal. His head is sealed from the outside world, a tomb. He remembers. A reel spins; the projector in his mind throws old images on the memebranes of his eyelids. Impressions of city streets. Cracked pavements. Crude paintings of masked killers on walls. Hard men strutting, planning, bullying. Beatings. Shootings. Belfast in the old days.

Something sharp and sour in his mouth now. He moans, rolls over. Hears a soft whisper of feet on the floor. The image in the theatre of his head flickers. The reel changes.

People he must protect. People he must stop. People he failed. The cold abbatoir of violent memories. So much violence. Throwing punches. Pulling triggers. Thrusting knives.

He strikes for the surface of his mind.

#

As he lies, his eyes flutter and he catches a clean, pure scent near his prone body. Feminine. Light. Comforting.

#

He cries out when the hand strokes his arm. His eyes open. Fujiko is kneeling by his side, wrapped in a yukata robe, a finger to her lips.

She whispers in Japanese.

He says, 'Thank you.' He isn't sure why.

She places those long fingers over the duvet on his chest and kisses him deep, slow and long. Then she stands, lithe and elegant but not Fujiko. Another woman, the coloured scales of a tattoo showing above the low neckline of her light robe. The woman touches her lips and gestures to the corner. He is in a simple room with one wall of shoji doors, tatami flooring and the futon on which he lies. His clothes are folded in the corner.

The woman pads to the corner with small steps.

'Do you speak English?' he says.

'Little.'

'Did you just kiss me?'

'Kiss?' Her face does a good summation of childish surprise. Her hair is shorter than Fujiko's, died light auburn with a black spider of roots as she bends to pick up a bowl and some dressings. Jackie's mind is still clawing its way back to reality after the eddy of memories.

He says, 'Where is Fujiko?'

'Fujiko?'

'Maki San. Fujiko Maki.'

The woman says, 'Hospital.' Then she folds the duvet covering his wounded body down in careful, methodical movements.

'Is she okay?'

'Okay.' She draws in a breath at the sight of his bloodied, makeshift dressings. He is still naked.

'Is it bad?'

'Okay.' She mimics the act of rolling.

Jackie rolls over, feeling slow and old and decrepit. He remembers the jolt of his spine as it cracked off the TV unit in the love hotel. The woman's fingers are delicate on his skin. She helps him roll onto his back again. 'Like this,' she smiles, miming clawing the air with her long, manicured nails. 'Your back. Scratch. No deep.'

She changes the dressings, swabbing the wounds on his thigh, his hip, his side. When she works on him she is utterly focused, her touch a balm. He feels his limbs grow heavy and his eyelids succumbing to fatigue. He thinks she says, 'You strong, neh?'

He tries to open his mouth to answer but cannot muster the energy. Before the black envelops him, he hears the woman slip out of the room, the shoji screen of the opposite wall gliding shut on a quiet respite in the savage story of Jackie Shaw's troubled life.

#

Reizo Himura breathes deep as though sucking on a cigarette, counting the seconds as his rage settles. Seconds that afford Shintaro Ishikawa – Tokyo mobster, Yamaguchi syndicate respresentative and psychopathic-Tengu-fucking-killer – precious moments to put further distance between himself and the righteous fury of Himura. The murderous bastard had sat with Himura the night after the cop was slaughtered in the Invisible Man club; hours before the crazy fucker had sliced Masa Yoshida by the Toyohira River. And now he has cut Fujiko, almost killed the gaijin, and run from this apartment where Himura himself set him up.

The city of Sapporo glints through the windows of the spacious kitchen. Himura visited this Miyanomori property to give the official stamp of approval when the Kanto Daichi-kai rented the house for Ishikawa before the Tokyo Yamaguchi sent their man north. He had been here twice more for tea and gift-giving. In the living room, the Samurai sword is mounted above the hanging calligraphy scroll. But the short sword is gone. It sits in Himura's office in Big-Touch building. His men had yanked it from the love hotel flatscreen television. The young girl on the front desk was commended for calling her employer rather than the bitch-cops. She feared her employers, he knew, but understood they could protect her.

Himura digests the evidence. The short sword that cut Fujiko belongs to Ishikawa. The sword used in the attack at the love hotel.

Ishikawa is the Tengu.

Shintaro Ishikawa had access to the service areas in Big-Touch building, where the first cop was murdered at the fetish club.

His motive? Perhaps he wanted to discredit the Kanto Daichi-kai. Perhaps he was just fucking crazy.

What Himura can't understand is, why not kill the girl on the love hotel's front desk? Ishikawa had slaughtered two police in the Tengu mask and had no qualms about ending Saburo but let the girl live. He locked her in the small office out back. Locked her in with the outside phone line and access to her mobile, the stupid asshole. Probably some old school yakuza chivalry bullshit – never harm women or kids. *But they can farm them out as whores for the salaryman drones*. And why did Ishikawa murder the cops? Did Ishikawa know Rei Miyamoto when no one other than Inaba had heard of the man before? Did Ishikawa know Himura's tame cop, Yoshida?

The men are keeping their distance. They are wary of Himura's explosive mood. And they are shamed.

Fujiko Maki, the oyabun's woman, with another man. A foreigner. The father of the Kanto Daichi-kai cuckolded by a gaijin. It won't be easy to come back from this humiliation. The rivals will find out and revel in the news.

And there was the Yamaguchi-gumi syndicate. Not that it would matter once he'd killed their man. The death of Shintaro Ishikawa could spark a small war despite the circumstances. Yet it was unavoidable. Reizo Himura must claw back a semblance of pride. Shaw had fucked Fujiko, that was clear, but Ishikawa could have killed her. That demanded an answer.

But the bastard has run.

Himura's mobile rings. The voice on the other end is rushed and tells him Ishikawa's three men have disappeared too.

More questions for Himura. Had they participated in the killings? Had they known what their superior was doing? Had the Yamaguchi bosses in Tokyo sanctioned all of this in an attempt to destabilize his organisation, take him out and fill the vacuum?

Careful, he thinks, that way leads to paranoia.

He'll call the Tokyo top men, allude to the situation and feel them out. Ishikawa has gone rogue, but Himura can act more decisively with the backing of the Tokyo syndicate. Perhaps he should fly down for a face-to-face after he has resolved the Inaba issue. After he's dealt with Shaw.

He stifles a yawn. It's late.

The mobile trills again. He must change the ringtone. That J-pop song is a couple of years old now. A sign of his age.

The voice on the other line is reedy, difficult to hear over the background clamour. Irritated, he snaps, 'I can't hear you. Who the fuck is this?'

A woman. He doesn't recall the name.

'Where are you?'

A bar. One of the syndicate's, a five-minute walk from the Toyohira Bridge. Not far from where Yoshida's body was found.

'Go outside. It's too noisy.'

Himura hears shouts, laughter, then the jangle of a bell on a door and the wash of traffic. The girl is drunk but coherent. Himura listens. An excitement rises, coursing through him. Then he kills the call and barks to his men.

'Get the cars. We're going back to Susukino.'

Chapter 23

The Brothers Grim, as he's come to know Jun and Kenta, see him as a liability now and that suits Ian Sparrow just fine. He knew they had considered him an old fart before Megan went on her recce to the toilet so it didn't take much to confirm the thought with a tumble.

While Megan had been out in the corridor with Kenta, Ian had played the lookalike game with Jun. The thug had brayed and slapped Ian's shoulder and swore the older Englishman was the spit of Sean Connery, Clint Eastwood, even George–bloody–Clooney. He'd faked the laughs and suffered the bruiser's bad breath and waited for Megan. He was scared and angry. The isolation was getting to him. When Megan spoke to the brothers in their own language it felt as though his own daughter was a stranger – wrong, he knew, but to be the oldest in the room, ignorant and ignored, was to feel helpless and, worse, obsolete. So he sat and simmered in his resentment and let it cloud his bloody judgement until he remembered his girl was out there in the corridor searching for a lifeline. A way out.

He went for a pratfall, tripping and smacking his head on the edge of the tattered sofa. All very Benny Hill but, to his amazement, it did the job. Jun began yelling like he was scared. Scared of his brother, perhaps, or the leader Inaba. The gaunt, controlled Inaba had been approachable, even kindly spoken: Sparrow and his daughter were valuable and the fact that the Englishman had gone on his arse had the bandaged lout Jun throwing a fit. Then the brother, Kenta, arrived, apoplectic. The two began bawling at each other and it went from Benny Hill to The Young Ones. After a quick shouting match, Kenta turned back to the door and Ian, quiet until then, blurted out some nonsense to warn Megan. Now she sat by his side again, watching the brothers argue.

She had found a mobile phone. Now doubt consumed them. Was the power off or was the phone broken? Was the battery dead? The frustration of not striding across the room, down the corridor and settling the issue was a silent torture. They were living in a vacuum. They craved sleep but oblivion wouldn't come.

'I don't like how they keep pointing at you, Dad,' whispers Megan.

'They just think I'm a burden, that's all. A senile old nuisance.'

'You're still in your fifties, for God's sake.'

'That's ancient to a couple of Mensa candidates like these two.'

'Yeah,' says Megan. 'The other one, Inaba: he's a bit different, isn't he?'

Sparrow isn't sure he's comfortable with the tone of his daughter's voice.

'He's a gangster, same as them. The fact he's got a couple more brain cells and a civil tongue in his head doesn't mean he's any different at the end of the day.'

He watches her smooth forehead drop, her eyes harden. 'You mean tough, amoral, given to bouts of unpredictable violence. Sound like anyone else we know? That *you* know?'

Ian's voice softens and he's kneeling by the oatmeal coloured sofa in their old house back in England again, a toothbrush in his hand, coaxing Megan to let him clean her teeth before bed. It's almost eight, bedtime, but she's clutching some storybook with a mouse on the cover and playing him beautifully – 'Read me a story, Daddy. After a story, Daddy. Daddy stories are best. I love you, Daddy.' Incredible, he thinks, that her features are older – more of her mother now in the sculpted nose and piercing eyes – but her expression is the same as the two-and-a-half year-old who captivated him all those years ago.

'Megan, Jackie Shaw is what he is. He'd be the first to admit that he's far from perfect. But sometimes there can be a couple of sides to people, and we don't always get to choose how we turn out. All you can do is try to control the darker parts of you.'

'So he's schizophrenic?'

'That's not what – '

'I know. I'm being facetious, dad. But I don't buy this crap about not choosing what kind of person we might be.'

The Brothers Grim are gabbing, animated, a couple of inches from one another. Ian rubs his face with his rough hands.

'Look at me,' he says. 'Divorced. An absent father for stretches. A comfortable but dead-end job.' He frowns. 'Don't be too quick to judge Jackie. He was a policeman in Belfast. It was a terrible place to be a copper back then.' A flicker of muscle works in Megan's jaw. Nothing's changed, he thinks. If she doesn't like what you have to say, it's all creaking signs and tumbleweed.

'Jackie came to the farm a couple of years ago after some trouble in Belfast looking for a quiet life, a bit of peace. We got to chatting and I found out he'd been in the army, Royal Irish Rangers, before the police. Only for a short time, when he was a kid really, but it was something we shared. We were a couple of ex-squaddies.' He shakes his head. 'Thank God, that's all we had in common. He's seen some shite, I can tell you.'

Megan flinches. He's always been careful about swearing around her. The brothers needle one another across the room and something cracks, the timeworn wood of the cabin straining against the cold.

Sparrow looks at her. She's still his little girl. He feels he still needs to protect her from so much.

Megan opens her mouth as Inaba opens the outside door and whatever thoughts she had are lost to the plaintive moan of the wind. Inaba looks from the brothers to the father and daughter, two families camped on opposite sides of the grubby room.

Ian Sparrow holds his daughter's hand tight and draws strength from her. He knows: he is not resentful, or alone, or helpless. He is proud. Proud of Megan's strength as she spoke with Inaba, her defiance as she yelled at Kenta, her ease in dealing with Jun. As Inaba approaches the brothers, she looks at her father and her face softens. She is the child-Megan again, the toddler who used to stare into his eyes, searching for something.

She says, 'You're my father and, right now, there's no one else I'd want to be with. You keep me strong.'

She takes his hand in hers and gives it a squeeze. He smiles. She's still playing him after all these years, still indulging the old man.

He says, 'I love you, Megan.'

#

'I love you, daddy.'

The girl places a hand on his chest. He's feverish, burning up. The hand is cool, almost reptilian but the girl is attractive, if a little hard. Used, thinks Genda.

But, *daddy?* He doesn't have a daughter, or a son. It's one of the reasons he's been able to commit to the job, to keep a clear head and operate without compromise. And, if he had a daughter, he can't imagine she'd look like this with a bad dye-job, trowelled on black eyeliner clogged around hard eyes. There is something re-signed in the dead space behind her detached gaze. He's seen the look before. *When? Where?*

And why is she naked except for that dumb plastic police cap cocked back on her head?

He can't think straight, can't see straight either with this furnace in his chest and arms. He shouldn't be so hot. Not when he's naked, too.

Then it comes to him, the look. He's seen it in the faces of count-less working girls in Susukino from his years busting illegal casinos, sex parlours, yakuza hostess bars.

Satisfied with his recollection, he smiles. The girl purrs, then giggles, thinking his pleasure is a result of her own endeavours. Let her, he's too tired and addled to set her straight. Instead, Superintendent Genda closes his eyes, relaxes his beetling brows and lets the cool fingers of the naked prostitute go about their practised work.

Chapter 24

A line from a hymn, of all things, comes to Jackie as he opens his eyes.

Dancing on a Friday. The sky turning black. And the devil.

Reizo Himura is squatting in the shadows like a childhood bogeyman. Jackie struggles to sit up and lean on his elbow. The sun is up, a wan light filtered through the bamboo blinds.

'Penny for your thoughts,' says Jackie.

'I don't understand,' says Himura. 'I don't understand this phrase. I don't understand your accent. I don't understand why you were naked with Fujiko. I sent you to that room for your own protection. It was a safe place – I thought – and you repay me by shaming me, and her.'

'Your idea of safety is taking me to a public hotel in the yakuza-mobile and posting a goon on the door outside the room. And your Fujiko isn't the paragon of virtue you'd like to believe. She started whatever happened in that room before Halloween-boy turned up.'

'She is emotional. She can be unstable.'

'Runs in the family?'

Himura's head cocks back like the hammer on a revolver and he stands, slow. Jackie pushes himself upright in response, a flash of pain in his side.

He says, 'Fujiko Maki is your sister.'

The air in the room is even thicker than the fug in his head. He's thrown the dice and played the hunch. Time to follow through.

'Do your boys in the gang know that? Or the big players in Tokyo?'

Himura leans back on the wall. 'You talk shit,' he says. 'You were naked with the oyabun's woman. My woman. I should kill you now.'

'You could try. I was naked as the day I was born when the Tengu fella had a go, too. And yet, here I am.'

'I don't want to fight you now.'

'Great minds.'

'Why do you think this about Fujiko, that she is my sister?'

'You went to her in the hotel room but your arms were rigid and your arse was higher than a duck diving when you held her.'

Himura's broad features sag, bemused.

Jackie takes pity and explains, 'When you held Fujiko, you looked uncomfortable. Your body was at a distance from hers. You weren't used to touching her naked and didn't want to. She sleeps with other men and hides it from you but out of fear, not guilt.' He places his hand on his side and feels the ridge made by the blade in his skin. 'When we were together in the room, she closed her eyes. There are small scars on the lids: she's had surgery to create a fold in them. Without that fold, they might not be a kick in the arse off yours in shape.' He bends for a robe lying next to the futon, holding Himura's gaze all the while. 'We kissed. Our teeth clashed at first. I touched her face, below the ear. There's a small seam in the bone of her jaw. I'm no expert, but I'd have a punt on her having some cosmetic surgery on her jawline. Let's say she had a slight underbite before.' Himura shakes his head, confused. Jackie pushes his own jaw forward in explanation.

'With the underbite, her bone structure would be a lot more like yours. And then there's the birthmark.' Jackie reaches around under his own armpit and points to the lower area of his shoulder blade. He winces as his scars protest. 'You have a carp tattoo. The skin is mottled, dimpled around the eye. Fujiko has a patch of similar, discoloured skin in the same region. It could be a coincidence but, taking everything together, the two of you are blood.You love her for sure but she's as untouchable to you as to your men.'

Reizo Himura pushes his back off the wall with an ease that gives Jackie pause for thought and takes a pack of cigarettes from his hip pocket. He takes two from the pack and offers one to Jackie who shakes his head. The oyabun produces a zippo with a dramatic flourish and drags deep on the tobacco as he lights his Marlboro. Then he stabs at the air with the fag, the glowing butt aimed at Jackie's chest.

'There is an old Japanese saying. Only death will cure a fool.'

'Or a smoker,' says Jackie.

'Your mouth is as smart as your head, Irishman.' Himura walks to the corner and kicks the folded stack of Jackie's clothes across the floor to the futon. 'Get dressed.'

'Where's your sister now?'

'Fall down seven times, stand up eight, neh? Another Japanese saying. You don't give up, neh?' Himura walks to the screen door and gestures to the clothes. 'I like you. It is a shame, what has happened, Jackie San. I cannot save you after your actions. I cannot save you from yourself.' He takes a drag on the cigarette and contemplates the tip. 'I say this and then it's finished. You do not talk about this again.' He reaches around his back and produces an automatic handgun from his waistband. 'No one will understand you anyway, my men don't understand English. But if you repeat what I say outside of this room, I'll kill you on the spot.'

Jackie says, 'Looks like you're going to kill me anyway.'

'Yes,' says Himura, his small eyes sad. 'But not here. Not yet. Get dressed.'

He holds the gun in a loose grip as Jackie begins dressing.

'You are right, Irishman. Fujiko is my twin sister. We were born on the northern island of Sakhalin. Our parents died when we were young children and Fujiko was adopted by a family in Sapporo. I wasn't wanted and went to a boys' home. I met tough kids and learned to survive. It was good,' says Himura, nodding his head with conviction. 'A good education. When I was a teenager, I left the home and joined a bosozoku street gang. Then I graduated to the yakuza. I gained power in the Kanto Daichi-kai and searched for Fujiko. Our organisation has many connections in Hokkaido. A civil servant gave me the register of my sister's new family. When she saw me...' He rubs his eyes with the back of his hand and says again, 'When she saw me ...'

Jackie buttons his jeans.

'Fujiko is very smart,' says Himura. His voice regains depth and grit with each word. 'She had been to a good school. She went to Hokkaido University. She spoke English and taught me the language. But she is delicate. Her strengths are also her weaknesses. She is trusting, kind, perhaps gullible. My world is dangerous and now we were together again it was easier to protect her if I kept her close. I introduced her to the Kanto Daichi-kai. If my men thought she was my woman, she would be untouchable. I set her up in the fetish club so she would be surrounded by my men. A simple job, no nudity, no touching.'

Jackie grimaces as he eases his t-shirt over his torso. 'She was like a pin-up girl in a dirty magazine. You set her up for voyeurs to letch over from the shadows. You made your sister an object.'

'I made her a goddess and I kept her safe.'

'Like you said, untouchable. Except she wasn't happy. She had lovers.'

Himura examines the trigger on the automatic and says, 'She is an adult. If I didn't know and the men didn't know, it was no matter. "Not knowing is Buddha". In English you say, "Ignorant is ..."'

'Bliss.'

'Yes. When the Yamauguchi agreement went through, I would have had the money and influence to get her out of this life and find her a good husband. An honest husband. And my responsibilities would have ended.'

'You don't trust her to find her own man? What century are you living in?'

Himura says, 'This is Japan,' as though it is enough; as though a gaijin cannot – will not – ever understand the intricacies of the anointed isles.

Jackie says, 'She's strong willed, your sister. She wanted me. She got me.'

'You were a very stupid mistake. Like I said, my sister is emotional. The last few days have been very hard for her. Saburo, her guard, was soft and she used this. Now the men no longer trust her. She betrayed me with a gaijin. Now I cannot protect her like before. She cannot be seen as my woman.'

'But she can't be seen as your sister, either.'

'And you,' Himura peers at Jackie down the handgun sights, 'you are a problem.'

He reaches into his back pocket and produces a crumpled envelope. The envelope Fujiko had in her delicate hands before sex. Before the Tengu.

Himura says, 'What is this?'

Belligerent, Jackie says, 'I don't know.'

'It was on the floor of the hotel room. Fujiko drew it. I know her style. Who is he?' Himura stands and waves the envelope like he's swatting a fly.

Jackie sighs. 'She told me a friend saw the face of the man under the Tengu mask after the second murder by the river. She drew a sketch from the description.'

'She was lying. The Tengu is Ishikawa.'

Jackie raises his eyebrows.

'Ishikawa was the one who attacked you in the room. We went to his place. The sword used to cut you and my sister was his. He wore the Tengu mask.'

'Why would Fujiko make a sketch of the man her friend saw remove the Tengu mask if was Ishikawa? She'd have just said his name when she talked to me.'

'So whose picture is in this envelope?'

'I don't have x-ray vision, do I? You've already seen it. Open it so I can get a look.'

'Don't push me, Irish,' says Himura. He steps close.

'Open it.'

There's a knock on the door. Shouted Japanese.

'We will talk about this later.' Himura shoves the envelope back in his pocket and waves Jackie, now dressed, to the sliding screen door. 'Out. And remember, you say anything, Irish, I'll kill you.'

Four men slouch in the corridor. They straighten when they see Jackie emerge from the room, and mutter guttural insults and curses. There is a clock on the wall. It is almost midday. Himura pushes Jackie and barks in Japanese. He shoves his handgun back in his waistband and cuffs Jackie across the back of the head, then shoves him again to a rumble of approval from the goons. Two of them grab Jackie's arms and drag him along the corridor, then halt and point to his boots. They watch as he struggles into them, then slip their own shoes on and kick him out a door and into a small garden, moss-carpeted islands of green speckled with petite purple flowers, a small, sinuous tree anchored in the centre.

They enter an annex through another sliding door, a wooden frame with squares of glass down its length, and wait as he hauls his boots off again. After slipping their shoes off, the men hurl Jackie down a hard wood corridor to a sliding shoji. The shoji is opened by a kimono-clad woman revealing a tatami room. She bows as Jackie enters and waits for the yakuza to file in behind before leaving and closing the shoji behind her.

Jackie recognises the room. Himura slaughtered Fox here. The men stand against the back wall. Himura sits under the painting of the smouldering volcano next to the lake and motions for Jackie to sit on the tatami opposite, the low wooden table separating them. Jackie is relieved to see the plastic sheeting is absent. The sword wielded by the Tengu in the love hotel is on the floor next to Himura.

'This room has seen a lot of blood.' Himura pulls the automatic and weighs it in his hand, then points it at Jackie's belly. The men murmur. Jackie feels his chest expand and contract, expand and contract, each breath taking more effort as though the testosterone, heavy in the room, is clogging his lungs. Then Himura places the gun on the table and picks up the short sword, drawing the blade from its scabbard. The cutting edge is tarnished by crusted blood, the essence of Jackie and Fujiko melded on the steel.

Jackie's legs already ache in his cross-legged position on the floor as Himura lays the sword on the table next to the gun.

Himura speaks in Japanese, then English. 'If your crime against the Kanto Daichi-kai was not so serious, I could accept your little finger as punishment – but you broke one of our most important tenets. You violated our trust and one of our women. The only answer for that is death. When the time comes, I will let you chose a bullet or a sword.' He places a fingertip on the table. 'There is more honour in the blade.'

Jackie says, 'Like Fox? I didn't see much honour in his death.'

'Yours will be quick. For all your sins, you protected Maki San. You deserve to die like a man, at least.'

The dark gashes of Himura's eyes flare for a moment at the shuffles and whispers from his men, their unease at the mention of Fujiko's name.

'First, there is the matter of your friends. I now know, they were taken by my first lieutenant, Goro Inaba. I know where they are. We will go to them. I will deal with Inaba. My men will take your friends to Sapporo, to safety.'

Jackie remembers Inaba struggling to gain his footing as they wrestled in the man's apartment, the snapshot image of his build, hair, a fleeting impression of the features. Now he knows – Inaba is the man who watched him, Ian and Megan in the pedestrian plaza as they sat and laughed and drank coffee. He'd stood next to Jackie at a urinal on his night out, when Jackie met Yuji Miyamoto. It had been surveillance of a target.

Himura snaps his fingers and unleashes a stream of ragged Japanese at his men.

'Tea,' he says to Jackie. 'We are gangsters but we aren't uncivilised.' He strokes the blade of the sword and says, 'You did protect Maki San. You helped search for Inaba. You deserve some answers.' He snaps at another thug. The goon hurries forward, bowing, and hands Himura a decorative envelope, holding it in both hands as though made of crystal. Inaba takes out a sheaf of photographs and lays them on the table facing Jackie, above the handgun on the polished wood.

They show a heavy-set Japanese man in late middle age naked on a futon with a girl. The girl is nude, her bony shoulders working as she stimulates the older man. He looks addled with drink, his eyes small and red. In two shots, the girl laughs at the limpness of her lover. A PVC police cap is set at a jaunty angle on her head.

Himura says, 'This is Superintendent Genda of the Hokkaido Prefectural Police. He fell into our lap last night while you were sleeping off your injuries. The girl is one of ours. Genda went drinking in a local Susukino bar. One of our men was in the bar with his girlfriend, who you see in the pictures. She had finished a shift at one of our cosplay clubs. Our man called me and we set this up in a room above the bar. Genda was very drunk. He talked a lot.'

'About my friends?' Jackie's voice is tight with expectation.

'Yes. Goro Inaba was working with the cop murdered at our fetish club, Rei Miyamoto. He was giving Miyamoto information on the Kanto Daichi-kai, files and operational details of our business. He was what the Americans would call a fucking rat.' Himura fishes for his cigarettes.

Jackie swallows a surge of liquid excitement in his guts. Ian and Megan are within reach. Inaba is a police informer, which means it was in his interest to keep the two innocent foreigners alive. With his police contact dead, he needs to prove himself to the cops in order to secure protection with the authorities.

'Inaba has a daughter,' says Himura as he sparks up a fag. 'I did not know. Apparently, he did not want her to be a part of our world. He hid her from us. Because of her, he turned to the Organised Crime Bureau. The idiot thought it was a way out and a chance at a new life with his family.'

Jackie has heard the story before. Republican and loyalist terrorists in the bad old days in Belfast had turned to the security forces and offered their services as assets, trading insider knowledge for the hope of relocation, a new life and a clean slate.

Himura says, 'Inaba introduced the cop, Miyamoto, to the club. After he was killed, we dismembered the body and Inaba took a couple of men to bury it near Mount Maruyama. Then he called the OCB and gave them co-ordinates to dig it up. Your idea about DNA from a star shot – semen? – is being checked out by the cops.'

Jackie says, 'And my friends?'

'Inaba took them after you escaped from him. I guess he wanted collateral with the cops.'

'Makes sense.'

'He called in a tip that there were some files in our office across the Toyohira River as proof of his association with Miyamoto to the cops. They raided the offices and found the files.'

'What were the contents?'

'I don't know.'

'You're the boss.'

'This is a big organisation, Hokkaido-wide. I can't know everything. It makes it more difficult for the bitch-cops to prosecute.' Himura's mouth puckers like he's tasting something sour. 'That is why I have lieutenants,' he says. 'Superintendent Genda was out of the situation ... out of the ...'

'Loop.'

'Yes. It was Organised Crime Bureau only. But the cops have politics. Someone got pissed off and talked to Genda. Genda celebrated with a bottle of whiskey, then went for another drink in the bar. We found him.'

Jackie says, 'Where are my friends?'

'Here.' Himura points above his head. 'This painting is of Lake Toya. Goro Inaba knows it well. He lived there for some time, when we had an interest in a resort hotel on the shore. That is where he and your friends are. He is holding them with two more disloyal bastards, former members of our family.'

'They're holding my friends at the lake?'

'Nearby. The cops know he's somewhere in the region but it's a large area. Inaba calls them from public phones. In a hotel in Toya

Onsen resort, near a temple at the camping grounds, in Rusutsu town. On the coast. They're looking in a hundred-or-so square kilometre radius. Farms, towns, resorts. The cops are fucked.'

'But you know exactly where he's hiding out.'

'Yes. There is a property there we used to store contraband. Inaba went there regularly when he was overseeing an old hotel investment in the area. Then the volcano of 2000 hit and Toya was evacuated. There were emergency crews everywhere, cops, even the Self Defence Force. The area was declared out-of-bounds. We thought the cabin was wrecked by the volcano and wrote it off. But Inaba dated one of our girls last year and they went to Toya for a spa weekend. They got drunk and he took her to the cabin one night for fun, still had a key, the sly bastard. The girl told Fujiko and she mentioned it to me. At the time, it didn't seem important. The area around the cabin is still a no-go zone, closed to the public. Inaba taking a girl there was like teenage kids going to a haunted house. I thought nothing of it and never spoke with him about it. I doubt he knows I'm aware he was there.' He licks his fingers then pinches the glowing embers of the tip, killing his cigarette. 'He must be there.'

'And that's where you're going.'

'You will come with us. Some of the way.' Himura lifts the short sword from the table and slides it back in its scabbard. 'There are many large mountains between Sapporo and Lake Toya. Very good locations for hiding a body. You will never reach the lake – but the countryside on the way is very beautiful. I am glad you will see some of it before I kill you.'

Chapter 25

Goro Inaba measures his chances against the brothers in a scrap. He could take Jun with ease in a one-on-one, more so with the injury to the man's hand. Kenta is a coward by nature. But if the two came at him together could Inaba win? The foreigner might help but he is an older man, out of shape.

Kenta is a coward but he is desperate. The syndicate gave him a role and an army of brothers to back him up should there be trouble. He knew his place. Now, on the run, a rat, he feels exposed and disoriented. The system, the hierarchy, the comfort of following orders is gone and Inaba knows the blonde-haired shithead is taking his fears out on the weakest target at hand, the foreign father and daughter.

Inaba's insurance.

He had suspected the cops would try to cut him adrift with Miyamoto dead and so it proved. The polite refusal on the phone, the condescending thanks for his work, how society owed him a debt. Then he dropped the bombshell. He had two foreigners – not hostages, no. The girl was connected to Officer Miyamoto via the dead cop's brother. It would be great a tragedy if anything were to happen to the Western father and daughter. The world's media would savage the Hokkaido police. So Inaba was keeping them safe in a secret location.

Silence on the other end of the call.

Then a new voice came on the line, urgent and deferential. The OCB might be able to arrange immunity and protection for Inaba. Yes, there may be a possibility of a fresh start. Relocation was not ruled out.

So many grey areas, so little concrete assurance. So few facts. But Inaba knew it was the best he would get.

However, if an arrangement were made, said the mewling voice, it was a one-man deal. Jun and Kenta had not worked with Officer Miyamoto or passed on information. They had not paid their dues.

Yes, thinks Inaba, Kenta is a coward – but if he and his brother knew they were now adrift, disowned by the police, they would turn on Inaba.

'Shouldn't you call the cops again?' says Jun.

'Not yet. I told you, the acting Superintendent won't be available until after lunchtime.'

'But there must be more of the fuckers you can talk to,' says Kenta. His skin is bloodless in the dim light of the cabin.

'I had one contact. That's it. I told you both before.'

Jun opens his mouth, an elusive idea eager to get out before the bug-zapper of his IQ sees it fried. Before he can speak, the foreign girl asks if her father can piss. Kenta, eyes on Inaba, mutters to his brother to go with the older man. Jun's mouth hangs open for a moment, then he nods and gestures for the father, Ian, to follow him through the door and down the corridor to the toilet.

'Inaba San,' says Kenta, his eyes darting to the girl on the sofa, 'we can't stay here forever. Last night – early morning – I woke up, cold, desperate for a smoke. Everyone was sleeping. The gaijin, Jun, you. *Everyone*. If either of the English had woken up, they could have slipped out and escaped. We're tired and stressed and there are only three of us to guard two prisoners.'

'A woman and an old man.'

'We joined you because you swore we could damage Reizo Himura and get us out clean. To do that, we need the cops. You swore you could take this all the way. So why are we sitting on our asses on a smoking mount – ?'

'Hold your fucking tongue.' Inaba's face flushes. 'How many of us, our type, do you think turn on their syndicate? Turn to the cops? Next to zero. How many cops do you think know yakuza, or are on a yakuza payroll, or drink with a yakuza? Do the math. The OCB limit contacts with people like us to protect our anonymity. To protect us.'

237

'People like us. Rats.'

'We did what we did out of honour and loyalty to our families. My daughter, your brother. There's no real honour in being a yakuza, you know that.'

Despite the words a small grub of doubt and guilt gnaws at Inaba's gut for a moment. Kenta nods, convincing himself of their cause with each arc of his thick head, and looks at the girl again. 'Do you think their friend is looking for them? The big bastard?'

'Does it matter? How would he ever find us?'

Kenta scratches, distracted, at his face and neck, leaving red nail marks on the small scar given him by the big gaijin. His leg shakes with agitation. Inaba has never seen Kenta using but he's beginning to wonder.

Kenta says, 'The Kanto Daichi-kai is a pretty big outfit. You'll have been missed, being top of the tree and all. The men will suspect something. But my brother and I – do you think Himura San has even noticed we aren't around?' He rubs his eyes, red and sore, and wipes his sleeve across his forehead.

Inaba steps close. He can smell something foul on Kenta's breath, sees up close how haggard the man looks, how the skin is swollen and almost bruise-dark under his eyes. The bastard is in bad shape.

'When the bitch-cop died, your brother stepped up for me. Every eye in that room was on him when Reizo Himura stabbed him through the hand. The oyabun may not have remembered his name but others will. You were with Fox when he met the big foreigner. That story will have been passed around the bar a couple of times by now.' Inaba moves closer still, taking shallow breaths to counter the stench of Kenta's breath. 'When I disappeared you can bet Himura pulled every man he could in to search the city. You know how it works, we're a family. Everyone knows someone and the chain is wrapped all the way around the fucking syndicate. You'll have been missed. Jun will have been missed.'

He places a fingertip on Kenta's forehead. The skin is clammy. 'You'll have a fucking target on your head, same as me. Just be sure the right fucker has your back. You never know whose finger might be on the trigger.'

Megan watches, out of earshot. Inaba dominates the bullying thug and she's glad. But there's a desperation Kenta's eyes, something animalistic that she fears. She prays Inaba can handle him.

It had been a long night. She had held her father's hand until she felt the burning urge to pee again and went to the toilet chaperoned by Jun. The bandaged goon had surprised her, offering a measure of respect in his slight, hurried bow and had turned his back while she squatted over the porcelain trench. He had even rummaged for a presentable towel with which to dry her hands after she washed them in the kitchen. When they returned to the main room, Inaba was gone and Kenta was standing over her father seated on the sofa, mocking him. Sometimes his voice rose, questioning her dad in Japanese with disgusted condescension – *Are you a dirty old man? You are a filthy old shit, aren't you? I'll bet you'd like to watch while I fuck your whore English daughter, right?* Then Kenta had tired of the torture, spat on the floor and wandered back to the table, rubbing his eyes and scratching at his neck.

Later, she had dozed. Her father's words came to her in her half-sleep, his defence of Jackie Shaw – *All you can do is try to control the darker parts of you.* She remembers her mother's inferences that her father had given his love to someone else. Some part of her wondered if that might, after all, be true.

When they woke, a weak sliver of light crawled through a crack in the bottom of the door. Inaba was silent as he ate fermented beans and supped instant coffee. Then he left again. She willed him to return as time stretched and Kenta, sluggish and disinterested when they awoke, had grown agitated and aggressive again.

Now, she watches Inaba and Kenta argue and thinks of Yuji. Her cheeks glow for a moment, her eyes lower. Her belly is hollow.

They had been close at times, had explored one another's bodies, had lain awake talking until first light but hadn't yet made love.

239

Now, with a cold, corrugating acceptance, she knew they never would. This was the first she had thought of him in hours.

Megan swallows, looks away from the yakuza across the room. She digs the heel of her hand into her eyelids too hard, then turns and glances at the door to the long corridor and her father beyond.

Ian Sparrow stands with his back to Jun and, behind the yakuza, the coats hanging in the corridor with a mobile phone lying snug in a pocket. He wants to piss but can't with the phone weighing on his mind.

'Japanese toilet-o isu difficult-o.'

Ian, a million miles away, doesn't register the words for a second.

'Sorry, English-u no good-o.'

'No,' says Ian. 'Your English is fine.' He looks over his shoulder.

Jun points at the porcelain toilet, the trench in the floor. 'Japanese toilet-o, English-u toilet-o, different-o.'

Ian smiles. 'Yes.' At a loss, he turns back to straining for a piss.

'My brother, he – uuuh ...'

Ian turns again and Jun mimes a spreading wet patch on his crotch. His face is contorted with the effort of speaking English. 'He do this, bed-o. We are chibiko. Child-o.'

Ian smiles.

'My brother ...' Jun mimes a frightened face, sucks his thumb and whispers, 'Mama, mama.'

Ian says, 'Scared.'

'So, so,' says Jun, eager, pointing at Ian like he has the winning guess at charades. 'Scared-o. Bad-o dream-u.'

Ian tries to imagine the vicious blonde thug as a frightened little boy, his big brother settling him in the darkness, maybe hiding the soiled sheets from a testy parent. His own piss comes in a spattering stream and he steps back from the toilet as splashes ricochet.

Jun says, 'My brother is-u still-u child-o. Child-o is hidoi.'

Ian, watching the toilet, feels a tap on his shoulder. He turns to see Jun in another pose, his face scrunched, savage, his hand stabbing forward as though thrusting a needle, an evil grin splitting his crude features. Jun says, 'Hidoi?'

'Cruel?'

Jun considers. The word will do. 'Cruel-u. Child-o is-u sometime cruel-u. My brother, cruel-u. But-o, not-o bad-o. Nature.' A troubled shadow shrouds his face and he frowns. When inspiration strikes, Ian expects a lightbulb to pop above the yakuza's head.

Jun says, 'Not-o personal-u.' He smiles, guileless, his eyes bright with a conspiratorial glee. 'Sparrow San, good-o. Megan San, good-o.'

Ian zips his jeans, follows Jun to the small kitchen and washes his hands. Jun is repeating, in sing-song intonation, 'Not-o personal-u, not-o personal-u, not-o personal-u ...' Ian tries to stifle a smile. Then a rough, calloused hand juts forward. Ian takes it and they shake, Jun's free, bandaged hand giving Ian's shoulder a light pat.

'Yoroshiku onegaishimasu,' says Jun.

Ian, baffled, says, 'Thank you,' then, 'arigato.'

#

Genda soaks in the bath, wishing his wife would leave the house for her coffee morning date. Her restrained disdain had been bearable. This wasn't the first time he'd fallen off the wagon and crept home at midday, the smell of whiskey on his breath and a drinking-hole-tobacco reek clinging to his clothes. He could reconcile his betrayal of their marriage with time. But the girl had been a plant, a professional whore. He had been manipulated, intoxicated, stripped and sucked but couldn't remember a moment of the nightmare seduction.

Surely he was barely culpable.

It was the indignity he could not stand. A Superintendent, a real cop, not one of the political lackeys or corrupt parasites who riddled the system. A principled man – that was Superintendent Genda.

Lying naked in a yakuza whorehouse getting a blow-job from a pock-marked Susukino pro. And the undeniable truth of the matter was, it was his own fault. He had a tipping point with alcohol, always had. He'd indulged himself, let his ego take hold with the warm glow of triumph at Watanabe's confidences, the possibility of influence over a yakuza boss – *the* yakuza boss on the island of Hokkaido.

Stupid. So, so stupid.

They had sobered him up with some chemical shit enough to show him the photographs. Good god! A video, too! They told him Himura had been there, watching, for a while. Told him all that he had said. He watched the sagging, foolish old idiot on the screen, his fleshy body splayed, the PVC cap bobbing at his crotch as they girl knelt to his left. He had admitted – *old fool!* – that there were more details in the safe in his office. Things he had written down but couldn't remember now regarding the files confiscated by the OCB in the raid. They had told him to go home, make his excuses to his wife, clean up and go to work. Open the safe. Call a number. Fill in the blanks in his story. They had told him they owned him now.

His wife calls out: does he want her to buy something particular from the supermarket? She will stop off at the Jusco store next to Soen station after her coffee date with her friends.

He shouts not to worry, he can't think of anything he needs at present.

For god's sake, leave, he thinks.

He'll have to get out of the bath soon, have to dress and catch the subway and go to the office. He'll have to forsake his ideals and condemn the men hiding out in the south of Hokkaido. But he cannot stand the thought of seeing his wife before he leaves. He fears that he might tell her everything. That he might destroy everything.

There's a clatter of keys being grabbed from a table – 'I'm going, see you later!' – and the door of the apartment slams shut. Genda sighs, grips the sides of the tub and hauls his tired, defeated bulk from the water, the sweat on his cheeks mingling with his tears.

#

I am starving. My knife is clean. There is no blood on the steel.

The Tengu is unsated.

It has whispered in my ear of its obsession, its craving for the foreigner.

The love hotel. A desperate place for some. A place of deceit, of lust, of business. Clandestine. And an indictment of the cancer eating at the very core of our country. Young couples rutting in a decorated cell under cartoon characters. Seamy rooms with schoolgirls cutting class, playing video games and eating American junk. Rooms of Japanese theme park imagery, our people fucking under a plastic torii gate, a woman with a vibrator shaped like a Shinto shrine rope. What the Christians or Jews or Muslims would call blasphemy.

And so, Japan needs the Tengu. Tormentor of false prophets, mortal bane of heretics. Defender of the faith. Of the Mother.

And so, this gaijin. This defiler of the Mother.

The foreigner was so close.

I was so close, waiting. Ready for him to leave, ready to approach the hotel and tear him apart as he walked out the door before he could climb into whatever car might be waiting for him. But he never walked out that door. Some thugs went in; one came stumbling out. No one else. Another exit, I guess. The foreigner lives.

No blood for me.

So I had to fuck instead. If I couldn't satisfy the Tengu, my body needed appeasement, to give me the strength to contain this terrible spirit. The girl was poor. I paid over the odds and she chewed gum, kept her socks on, studied her nails when I needed encouragement. I caught her reflection in a glass cabinet door, checking her mobile phone as I worked away behind her. The young: so typical. No sense of customer service. So I beat her until her face was ruined, at least for a week or so, and showed her my blade. I whispered in her ear – a small shell, not like the large-eared beauty of my past – in the Tengu's voice, its words, not mine. She cried. Her snot was a thick stream from her broken nose to her swollen lip. She pleaded. The Tengu got hard and we used her again.

That is nothing to what awaits the foreign bitch.

The demoness.

The anti-mother.

First was the man, the gaijin. The penultimate step on my journey of metamorphosis to become the monster.

Now he's gone, out of reach.

But there is the foreign cunt. Connected to the big gaijin bastard. A female Honnari.

When I cut her heart from her body, I'll hold it as it beats its last. When I kill the anti-mother, I will be complete.

Pasty big-assed whore.

Part Three

Chapter 26

The man, clad in black robes, bows deep and slow. The widow returns the gesture, struggling to hide her irritation. Masa Yoshida was neither a good spouse, a good father, or a good man. As far as she knows, he was a barely competent policeman. As she stands opposite the priest next to the high outer wall of Ryukoji temple, awaiting the other mourners, his widow sees a black limousine approaching.

A yakuza car if ever I saw one, she thinks. Bitterly, she wonders if her husband washed and waxed it for his former benefactors.

She realises she has allowed a scowl to trouble her face in front of the serene priest and adjusts her features accordingly.

Before the limousine passes, she surreptitiously checks what she can of her dress and make-up in the reflection of its gleaming tinted windows and offers the priest a meek but brave smile.

#

A boy in his early teens stands on the pedestrian bridge over Route 230. His father will pick him up at the petrol station on the corner a hundred yards away. He has finished school early; the funeral ceremony of the father of his friend, Yoshida, is today and the young teenager has the afternoon off school to attend.

He sees his father's Suzuki pull into the petrol station, a huge black beast of a car passing as his dad drives into the forecourt. For a moment, the young teenager thinks the black limousine might be ferrying his friend to the ceremony at Ryukoji temple. It looks like the kind of vehicle you would drive to a funeral. It has death written all over it. Then he realises it's going the wrong way, heading south away from the city centre.

How many people die in Sapporo each day? he thinks. He starts for the steps down from the bridge, eager to climb into the Suzuki next to his dad.

#

A university student tuts as he slices the golf ball and watches it soar into the huge netting around the enclosure. To his left, the Toyohira River meanders and, past the far bank, the Olympic stadium nestles in a depression within a hill in the park, like a shallow manmade volcano. He stands on the third tier of the clubhouse, too hung-over to bother with his seminar, too bored to sit at home playing his game console.

The one downside of taking another day is that he won't see the English girl, Megan San, in his seminar group. One day he'll work up the gumption to speak to her.

The limousine catches his eye, glinting in the pale sunlight in his peripheral vision. It glides south on Route 230, passing the driving range. He's seen similar cars in Susukino and broad men in sharp suits unfolding their stocky frames from within as chauffeurs open doors. The road south led to mountains and lakes. Out in the wilds, he supposes, is where the bodies are buried.

#

An older man places his pen on a small counter, an inch above his clipboard and check-sheet at a perfect parallel. Order is everything. He is approaching retirement and fears the day when he wakes with no employment obligations, each day a blotch on a blank sheet. For now, though, he signs off on another car ensconced in the slim multi-storey lot wedged next to the apartment building in Misumai, the last, urban neighbourhood in the southern reaches of Sapporo. He leaves his small booth and lights up a Seven Stars unfiltered. Route 230 slithers past, an endless procession of Hokkaido's five million souls, encased in metal, plastic and glass.

The limousine appears like a large predator cutting a swathe through smaller Toyotas and Hondas, bossing the road. He'd been a mechanic at Chitose air field, done some work with the Americans on their F-86 Sabres at the USAF base there in the mid-fifties and seen a few politicians visit in cars such as the long, black, sleek cruiser that glides by as he regains his breath. Not much political about the men who used to bring the cheap black market cigarettes on flatbed Datsun trucks, though. Tight punch-perms. Tattoos. Scars and nicks on their hands, their arms, their faces. Bad bastards.

He catches a distorted, syrupy image of himself slink by in the black metal chassis, the smoked windows. Then he turns away.

The older man reaches in his pocket, fiddling with a small tin. He tuts, opens the lid bearing the legend, 'Smokin' Clean', and grinds the cigarette out as the limousine forges south. Then he breathes the harsh autumnal air and walks back to the mundane comfort of his booth.

#

Jackie Shaw sits facing the inner back window of the limousine, watching past Reizo Himura's shoulder as the cluster of buildings, the last of Sapporo, are swallowed by overgrown brush. Then all is hardscrabble land, tattered shrubbery and knotted trees.

'Have you ever been in an earthquake?' says Himura.

'I felt a couple of tremors when I was in Tokyo,' says Jackie. 'Felt the building swing on the seventh floor of a hotel.'

'How about a volcano? Ever seen one go up?'

'No.'

'I remember when Mount Usu erupted, back in 2000. I was in the town of Otaru, one hundred kilometres away. The ash blotted out the sun. There was no cloud, just a blanket of darkness over the island. Like the end of the world.'

To left and right, mid-sized peaks slouch by as Jackie looks at the wake of the limousine. They cross a bridge spanning dense autumnal woodland, twisted tree limbs reaching for the crash barrier on either side, and the view opens up. Larger, steeper peaks rupture the forest. An enraged landscape tortured by elemental forces.

'Children are frightened by these natural events, the earthquakes, volcanoes, typhoons,' says Himura. 'They are frightened because they cannot control them. But as the people here age, they accept there is power beyond their control in the land.' He leans forward and places a hand on the chain of the handcuffs around Jackie's wrists. The metal bites into skin. The men sitting on either side of their oyabun stare at the view unfurling outside the limousine. The man next to Jackie on his right plays a game on his mobile phone, the superhero figure on the phone strap dancing with his efforts. Himura looks into his eyes and says, 'You are going to die, but you are not frightened.'

Don't you believe it, thinks Jackie.

But he says, 'I've been here before.'

'Such a shame,' says Himura. He looks out the window, as though he cannot bear to see the cause of such crushing disappointment. 'You are a survivor, Irishman. There's no honour in killing a survivor.'

Back in Sapporo, the yakuza men made a show of jamming handguns in shoulder rigs. Jackie spotted a Colt and SIG Pro among the pistols. The gamer on his right has a tactical knife strapped to his hip, too. They haven't looked at him, haven't acknowledged his presence since the car rolled away from the large house near Maruyama Park. He sits in silence, speaking when spoken to, Himura addressing him with sporadic questions. The man is morose.

Jackie feels the handcuffs gnaw at his flesh and tries not to dwell on Ian and Megan: there lies the way of madness. And Fujiko. She must be in hospital. He thinks of her moving against him. Enveloping him. He hears her shriek as the blade seared her back. He wants to ask after her but Himura won't hear her name in front of his men. The answer will be a beating or worse.

It's a balancing act to clear his head. Impossible, but he's learned to fill some of his headspace with details. The odours, the suits, the slabs of gold wrapped on meaty fingers, the pocked face of the man on Himura's left. Jackie is desperate to live. Desperate to act. To do something; advance, claw ever closer to his friends: find them, protect them, get them home. But he must wait. Keep the mental thread taut and ready to seize an opportunity, to lash out. He flexes his hands, forcing the cuffs tight, staying alert.

The limousine devours the miles. They pass through the hot spring resort town of Jozankei, a clutter of crude, brutal multi-storey hotels blighting a beautiful wooded valley. As they drive on the road climbs and the landscape opens. The ocean of trees is dappled with mustard yellows, faded browns, fiery crimsons and evergreen, the highest peaks flecked with snow.

They crest a peak, an observation deck and trinket shop at the roadside, and Jackie sees a Romanised sign, Nakayamatoge. He remembers Inaba's ex-wife, Aina, saying Inaba had called from there before Jackie pummelled the yakuza, Fox. As they descend the twists and turns of Route 230, Himura says, 'Are you a Christian?'

'I believe there is a God,' says Jackie, taking in the vast, cockled beauty of the landscape. 'I'm Northern Irish. It's a contractual obligation.'

Himura scowls with incomprehension and shakes his head. 'Do you believe you will go to Heaven?'

'Bets are off on that one.'

Jackie watches Himura's face knit in exasperation and says, 'I don't know. I haven't been great on the sixth commandment.'

To more vexation in the yakuza's expression, Jackie says, 'I have blood on my hands.'

Traffic thins the further south they drive. The land flattens, the odd hulking mountain in the distance. They pass dilapidated barns bandaged with crude sheets of corrugated iron, abandoned farmhouses of blistered concrete with collapsed roofs and ramshackle outhouses. Remote pockets of neglect and failure, dying a slow, solitary death amid the hard seasons.

Himura's mobile trills. He answers, grunts, and kills the call.

'Ishikawa,' he says. The men look up for a moment. 'My men are searching the city but they can find no sign of him. His soldiers, either.' The men in the car fade out again at the spoken English.

Jackie says, 'Where could they go?'

'This island is big, most of it empty. They could be anywhere. They could be on a fishing boat headed for Honshu, but I don't think Ishikawa will go home to Tokyo. What he has done is unforgivable. When I inform his boss it could kill our merger but it will leave him a marked man. The Yamaguchi-gumi syndicate will disown him. They'll send their postcards out to all the other syndicates soon, letting everyone know he's been kicked out.'

'What if he comes after you?'

'He has three men. I have over a hundred.'

The cuffs work their metal edge into Jackie's flesh. 'Ishikawa's men must know something is wrong now they've had to run. He probably won't have contacted Tokyo. He knows he's fucked with his own organisation. Why would his three men still follow him?'

'Why not?'

'He's crazy. If he told them what happened, they'd be committing professional suicide. Can't join your gang, can't go home to Tokyo.'

'Another of our rules,' says Himura. 'Do not fail in your obedience to your superiors. Ishikawa is their superior. I don't expect you to understand.'

'Glad I won't disappoint.'

'It's called chugi: duty and loyalty. It doesn't make sense to you but it's what we have.'

Could be worse, thinks Jackie. At least when these boys have a principle they see it through to the end. 'Were his men in on the attack at the love hotel?'

'You would have seen them. But he is their boss, he has already

252

acted. Perhaps Ishikawa has lied to them and made you the bad guy. Or me.'

'When will you tell his bosses what he's done?'

'The Yamaguchi? Fuck them. When I'm ready.'

Big words, thinks Jackie. Always big words when little men are scared. Ishikawa isn't the Tengu killer. At least not the same Tengu who murdered the second cop by the river. If he were, Fujiko would have recognised him from her lover's description or Himura would have after looking at her sketch. He doubts the oyabun believes Ishikawa is the true Tengu either, but, out of options for the moment, Himura is focusing on catching the man who slashed his sister. Jackie curses the goon who interrupted them back in the tatami room, back when Himura had waved the envelope in his face. If only Jackie could get a look at Fujiko's drawing, not that there was much chance of him recognising the face.

Himura gazes out the window 'I want Inaba,' he says. 'I want to know what he's told the bitch-cops. Then I will let the Yamaguchi know what is happening and how much this whole fucking mess will hit them.' He shakes his head. 'Don't worry, your friends will not be harmed. I have enough problems. I will simply get my answers from Inaba. Then he and his bastard partners will die. Like you.'

They glide through arable land. It's been a couple of hours since they left Sapporo and he tells Himura he's desperate for a piss. Himura laughs.

The limousine turns onto a narrow, cracked single-lane road plunging through the forest, then dwindles to a dirt track. They come to a stop outside the crumbling concrete husk of an abandoned hotel, a child's nightmare ghost house, the blackened walls swallowed in patches by dying leaves of the surrounding trees. As they clamber out, Himura's mobile sings again. The oyabun takes the call, crooks his head away from the small clutch of men and wanders twenty yards away, his voice low.

Jackie smells damp earth and feels the dry-cough nip of broken concrete and dust in his throat. His cuffs in front, he pisses. The four men accompanying their oyabun loiter. They shove hands in pockets, trouser legs twitching as they fidget. They rub noses, scratch thin moustaches and shuffle feet.

Himura barks in Japanese, the phone call over.

He strides toward Jackie and tries to grab him by the hair, loses grip on the short cut, snatches a fistful of his canvas jacket collar and hurles him toward the broken shell of the desolate hotel. Jackie falls, grunts, arches his back as a vicious kick connects with his side. They lift him, and shove him into the dank shadows of the ruin. Inside there is plaster on the floor, scattered roof tiles, mould-blackened sofas. Jackie sees a rotting wooden counter split down the centre, a rust dappled bell still perched on top. The ruined lobby. He notes two doors to either side of the stairs in the squalid lobby, both shut.

Something cracks under Jackie's foot.

Himura says, 'Stop.'

The men stand behind Jackie. The deserted building is a tomb.

Jackie hears the rustle of clothing, the soft suck of metal and plastic clearing leather holsters. A couple of grunted words, perhaps insults. Feet approach. He feels a hard circle press on the back of his skull, imagines the muzzle nudging his scalp.

It seems obscene to die here. A bullet through the head, surrounded by desolate woods in a broken concrete shell, a monument to failure. How many times can a man be close to death before the cards finally fall and he is gone? How much of this can the mind stand? Jackie is wired, yet exhausted.

I've been a bastard, he thinks. I've had to be. To survive, to protect mine, to stop the evil of others. I've neglected family. Kept a distance, damaged relationships and abandoned lovers. But I've survived. Endured. Was the pain and death and torture all for this?

Jackie thinks of his sister and her family, Sunday dinners together on infrequent trips home. Thinks of his ma and da under the rich, green-clad earth of County Down, so far away. He's adrift, solitary, has been for years. But here, in this place, he is truly alone. He is nothing.

Catch yourself on, Jackie-fucking-Shaw.

He doesn't want to die, but he'll not break down in front of these worthless bastards.

He says, 'What's fucking keeping you?'

They're scared. Soft. Life's been easy. A yakuza in Japan? – *Cushy fucking ride. Well, let's move things along.*

Jackie throws his head back and feels the hard sudden weight of the handgun as his skull slams into it before the pistol careers away and clatters on the broken stone floor. He lashes out with his heel and connects with shin bone. He hears a tight yell and turns, sees Reizo Himura crouching, his empty gun-hand going to his shin, his pistol somewhere behind him. Himura's men rant. Two of them raise their guns, eyes wide with fear and madness, the whites burning through the shadows.

Then someone seizes the day and fires.

Chapter 27

Sudden tearing, ear-raking noise.

Muzzle flashes.

A scream.

Babble. Yelling, growling, mewling nonsense. The flat slap of pistol shots in the dead space. Himura's men fire toward the outer door, aim wild at four flitting silhouettes that merge with the shadows in the doorway, muzzles flickering. Jackie's breathing is a roar in his head, his eyes blinded by the white-light of the dying sun framed in the outer doorway, the cuffs still gouging his wrists. The battle is chaos, wild shots splintering wood, biting corroded walls. He moves at a crouch, half running, boots crunching on debris, slabs of plaster and fractured tiles. He hears a roar from behind, someone calling for Himura. A volley of shots and Jackie is down. A stumble. He lands on his shoulder, a shard of glass stabbing his jacket, tearing through the fabric. No wound.

Two of Himura's men are on the ground. One is a couple of feet from the outer door, his arm waving in the air. A silhouette runs forward and puts two rounds in his chest. The other is splayed on a blackened sofa, not moving. Another of Himura's men is about ten feet away, fumbling with his clip, botching a reload in plain view. A silhouette fires three rounds, rapid, two yards away. The shooter cannot miss, the target drops. The last Kanto Daichi-kai man crouches with no real cover. Someone has a revolver. Jackie hears the full-throated roar of its fire, louder than the snapping of the semi-automatics, as he struggles to his knees.

Something tears at his leg.

Himura lies at his feet, nails dug into the flesh above Jackie's ankle. The yakuza boss is on his belly, mouth working, lower jaw thrusting forward. Tears in the bastard's eyes.

Jackie whispers, 'Where's your gun?'

Himura blethers in Japanese.

'The pistol? Where's your fucking gun?'

The last of Himura's men is dancing left and right, six metres from the shooters, snapping off shots, barrel jerking like he's in a Jimmy Cagney flick. Jackie grabs Himura's arm.

'Get up!'

More gabble.

'Get up, ya useless bastard, ye!'

Himura struggles to a crouch. The silhouettes gain definition as they creep through the rotting lobby. Three are young, their faces twisted and frantic. The fourth is Ishikawa. A thick wad of dressing is taped to his neck where Jackie caught him with the splintered bamboo shaft back in Sapporo. Himura's last man fires, arm thrust far forward, stance all wrong. Yet somehow he gets it right. His target flinches, a bullet tearing into the cheek. The knees buckle. Himura's man moves forward and follows up with a couple more rounds.

Jackie and Himura run, bent low, for the connecting door by the lobby counter. The revolver hollers, three barks from a pistol close behind. They hear a furious shout. Himura runs through the connecting doorway. Jackie glances behind. Himura's last man is down and Ishikawa and his shooters are standing around their fallen comrade. Ishikawa's man is wounded, sitting, clutching at his face. Ishikawa slaps one of his men on the shoulder and points to the doorway. Jackie throws himself through the opening, his ankle cracking off the hanging door. Two shots snap at the frame, another hits the far wall. Jackie and Himura run through an office space, a table upturned by the wall, wiring scattered across the floor. The next doorway is open, the door gone. Part of the outer wall has toppled outward. Sharp air and the scent of wood and grass rushes to meet them. They jump through the collapsed opening, Jackie stumbling on concrete scree, and sprint for the treeline, twenty yards off.

The woods are a tangle of flaking trunks and trailing weeds. Low bushes mushroom on the forest floor, hiding twisted, tripping roots. Their feet snap twigs and brush clumps of fallen leaves. So much noise, so easy to track. Himura is slowing ahead of Jackie. Then they clear a huddle of tall larch and the earth tilts. Their feet scrabble and the ground disappears. A shot follows them over the ridge as they plunge downward into tumbling rock and earth, broken branches raking their skin as they are swallowed by the clawing, twisted forest.

#

Superintendent Genda sweats as he stares at the receiver in its cradle and leans back in the chair. The same chair in which he drank most of a bottle of whiskey last night. The chair in which he listened to Watanabe condemn him. The fool.

The drunken, loose-lipped old fool.

He catches his reflection in the empty glass on his desk.

Genda stares at the haggard, crooked features of a beaten man.

Watanabe was no doubt staring into his own abyss in his own office, his own phone cradled on his own desk. He would be mulling the fact that he had blabbed to his old friend – dependable Genda, solid Genda – about Goro Inaba and his secret child and his betrayal of the Kanto Daichi-kai. The betrayal that Genda had confirmed to Reizo Himura. And while the police began a discreet sweep of the southern regions of Hokkaido, several hundred square kilometres, Himura had thanked Genda and told him he knew exactly where Inaba would be holed up.

This morning, the contents of the file the OCB had confiscated from the Kanto Daichi-kai offices in their raid emerged through a hungover haze. Watanabe had sent the contents to Genda's mobile. Genda had called Himura and sent the information on to the oyabun's phone.

Then Watanabe called, all contrition and morning-after regret, and dropped the bombshell. The good news was the DNA result had come through faster than expected. The bad news: the Senior Commissioner had another reason for burying the dead officer, Rei Miyamoto's, investigation. A reason communicated to the ranking officers in the OCB at a staff meeting an hour ago. Two reasons, in fact: a father and daughter, British, taken hostage by Inaba. The yakuza rat had informed the OCB during a phone call. Only those connected with Miyamoto's running of Inaba had known. The investigators had kept it that way until they could get hold of the Senior Commissioner, who threw a fit. He stamped on any leak of the foreigners' involvement until things could be verified and a head start made on locating them. One of the two, an Englishman named Ian Sparrow, had been visiting Sapporo with his friend, a Jackie Shaw. After a few calls to Sparrow's hotel, the nervous front desk staff had confirmed that the guests were booked in for the remainder of the week but had not been seen by hotel employees since they went out a couple of nights ago. It appeared Shaw was missing, too. The girl hadn't been seen at the university for a couple of days, her apartment was empty and there were signs of someone entering her place.

Now the Governor is fretting and directives are circulating throughout the Hokkaido National Police Agency. The discreet sweep in the south of the island is ratcheting up to helicopters and coast guard patrols. The Special Assault Team is on standby at a heliport in Muroran. The Sapporo uniforms are on the hunt for this Jackie Shaw and the Senior Commissioner is pissing in his pressed pants. The media blackout continues, the lackeys in the national press following orders and banking the cheques. But the NPA cannot – will not – allow foreign nationals to be killed in a yakuza feud.

And Superintendent Genda has led the most notorious yakuza boss on the island straight to the foreign father and daughter's location. Himura will confront Inaba; there will be violence. A crossfire ...

Genda could have picked up his phone and called upstairs. He could have told them of the whole mess, of Watanabe's drunken call, his own fall from grace with the Susukino whore. Perhaps the NPA could round up known faces in the Kanto Daichi-kai and try to sweat out of them where Himura was headed to take retribution on Inaba. At least Genda's conscience would be clear. But his wife, his career, his pension, what of them? He could be prosecuted. Prison was a living hell for convicted cops.

Instead, he had called Himura and given the yakuza boss the DNA result. Himura had killed the call and shut down his mobile before Genda could pursue the issue of the foreigners.

Genda has not been to a Shinto shrine for years. Sankichi Shrine is a short walk away. Perhaps he can throw a few coins in the saisen box and pray that, by some miracle, his colleagues might stumble upon the gaijin before Himura gets his hands on them. Pray that the gods of Japan might intervene to save a couple of Western heathens.

Then again, perhaps he'll lock his filing cabinet, pull the blind over his office window, have his PA take any incoming messages, and go for a drink.

#

Jackie checks for broken bones. He has a pain in his side and his wrists are a mess. The cuffs have slashed his flesh. But his limbs seem to have survived the fall intact and his head is clear.

He peers up the steep incline, a sharp gorge of scree and broken tree limbs, forty foot high or more. He and Himura tumbled down like ragdolls, landing in a thick carpet of bamboo grass. The late afternoon sky is a papery white. Four heads appear at the upper rim of the gorge. They fire a couple of shots but, at this range, with the fading light, their aim is haywire. A stream meanders at Jackie's feet. Reizo Himura is lying in the water, his eyes closed, steam rising from a wound in his side. Trees press in on all sides. A cool stillness lies heavy on the forest floor save for the soft babble of the stream. The bobbing heads at the rim of the gorge disappear.

So there it is.

He can do a runner.

Ishikawa and his men will have to skirt the ravine and pick their way down here. It could take them maybe fifteen minutes. Maybe five. Jackie doesn't know this terrain but they don't either and he can run, put distance between himself and his hunters and leave Himura to the wolves.

He kneels by the unconscious Himura and takes a closer look at the injury. Nasty, a sucking wound. He grabs the man's wrist to find a watch. Unbroken. He nods in thanks to the heavens and fumbles with the clip, fingers cold with the stream water as the temperature drops. There is a sound of breaking wood and shifting scree somewhere above; the hunters picking their way. Jackie's fingers slip. Himura's arm falls in the water. Jackie curses. The watch comes free. He rummages in the man's jacket and comes up with a wallet. Cash, credit cards and some kind of ID. No key for the cuffs. He curses again. He searches through Himura's trouser pockets, muttering like a lunatic.

'Bastarding arsehole.'

Small change. A ticket stub.

'Wanker.'

A handkerchief.

'Bollocks.'

Something worries the bamboo grass in the trees on the other side of the water. Each sound is a thunderclap in the quiet of the forest.

Jackie looks to Himura's feet. Expensive boots. Nickel lace hooks. A small nickel brand plate set on the side of the boot heel. Thank God for the Japanese obsession with brands: the nickel plate could be a makeshift handcuff shim. He finds a small shale stone by the stream and chips at the nickel. Something straggles in the branches of a silver birch. He flinches and scrapes a knuckle. Probably a bird.

The plate comes loose at the edge. He wedges the shale in the opening and pries it free, drops it, panics. He scrabbles around his body and finds it on the ground next to his knee.

His voice is a hoarse whisper. 'Come on, Jackie boy. Any chancer can break out of cuffs with a shim.'

Anyone with time and practice. How much time has passed since the hunters left the upper ridge of the gorge? His fingers shake. He breathes slow. A voice calls out. A raw squawk, some frantic bird. He works the nickel between the locking mechanism and the teeth of the cuff on his left wrist. Then he tightens the cuff. *Just one notch, no more, come on Jackie ye hallion, ye.* He fumbles and tightens by two notches and the cuffs spit the nickel out. It falls on the ground.

'Shite!'

Maybe five minutes have ebbed away. Maybe ten. Precious seconds wasted. He searches, frantic and finds the nickel on the edge of the bank by the stream. Another fraction of an inch and it would have been away in the current, headed for the wilds. He picks it up, breathes slow and inserts it in the cuff again.

Now, tighten a notch. Just one notch.

Is that the sigh of feet in grass, the shush of hands pushing branches aside? Have more than ten minutes passed?

Just one bastarding notch!

He shakes his head. As he tightens the cuff, he pushes the shim in, wedging it. He hears a soft sound like the click of a magazine inserted in a handgun. He closes his eyes, time for prayer. The cuff opens with another click, the teeth and mechanism of the cuffs separating. He lets the cuffs hang from his right wrist. Releasing the other side can come later. Now, the watch.

They were driving to Lake Toya and turned off. Toya is south. Jackie opens his left hand and lays the watch flat on his palm, horizontal to the ground. He checks the long patches of shade on the ground, walks to the slim shadow of a tree branch and estimates the position of the sun as best he can, pointing the hour hand in that direction. He bisects the angles of hour hand and twelve o'clock pip counter-clockwise – due south.

South towards Ian and Megan Sparrow. Jackie's crusade now. He listens. The forest is quiet, the stream a thin gurgle. Time to go.

Except he can't. No more than he can roll Himura over and hold his face in the water, push down on his thick skull and drown him.

'God spares us,' his da used to say – 'God spares us, we'll win the league this time next year. God spares us, your sister will have finished school.'

God spares us, thinks Jackie, looking at Himura lying, dying in the stream.

God spares us, it'll be dark soon. The forest will come alive, every shadow a threat, every sound an assassin ready to pounce. And the memories, bodies that can't be unseen, murder scenes from his days on the job. Bad men Jackie has ended. Guilt and remorse thickening with the darkness. Best not to add Reizo Himura to the roll call of repentance.

So Jackie jumps up and down, his body screaming in protest, to ensure there is nothing rattling or jangling in his pockets, no sound to carry in the black quiet of the forest. If he tucks the loose cuff into the chain it should help kill any clinking until he works it off. He unties the laces of Himura's right boot, a resolve setting in.

A splash, somewhere up the stream. Hard to tell how far. The laces undone and boot free, Jackie pulls Himura's sock off and soaks it in the water. He hears more splashing and hoarse, angry words, the rustle of men clambering through undergrowth. Drawing near. He packs the sock in Himura's sucking wound as best he can and drinks from the stream, not knowing when he'll have another chance. Then he kneels and levers the dead weight of the unconscious Himura across his shoulders. A shout comes to him from the forest like a warning shot. He catches movement in the trees no more than forty yards off.

He runs, slow and awkward at first. Momentum builds and he follows the stream, hears the shouts, the spattering of boots in shallow water behind, the harsh locomotive rhythm of his breath as Ishikawa's revolver roars once. Then Jackie veers south, and plunges into the tangled forest, feet hurling dead leaves before him as he runs.

#

'Please, don't go.'

'You'll be safe. Kenta is a bully but he won't hurt you or your father. He is scared of me. He knows if he harms you, I'll kill him.'

Inaba means it. Megan can see that in his level gaze, the easy confidence with which he says the words. Her cheeks redden and something cold and fluid settles in her belly. Her father studies her face and she sets her expression as neutral as possible. Ian Sparrow takes her hand, sitting next to her on the sofa.

'If you need to use the toilet,' says Inaba, 'ask Jun. If you are hungry, too. Leave Kenta be and he won't bother you.'

The brothers sit at the table, Jun reading a comic, Kenta staring at the floor. He is sitting on his hands but his legs are shaking, scrawny knees bouncing. Megan has an image of a mousetrap, the hammer straining at the catch, eager to spring forward and snap a neck, split a spine.

Inaba walks to the door of the cabin, checks Kenta's vacant expression and eases himself into the darkness outside.

Jun says, 'Anybody want a cup of tea?'

Ian says, 'I wouldn't say n – ' but Megan jabs him with her elbow.

'No thank you,' she says. In fact, she would love a brew, would love something stronger. But she doesn't want her father and she to be alone with Kenta right now, even for five minutes.

Chapter 28

When he was a kid, Jackie was walking in East Belfast and his mate said a big fucker in a balaclava, gun in hand, was jumping out of a car. Total bollocks, but they were away like a lilty, pure adrenaline. His legs had taken on a life of their own, almost hollow with the charge of fear and mad elation. He feels that charge again, driving through fallen leaves and bamboo grass, the dead weight of Himura on his shoulders threatening to pitch him face first into the forest floor. He hears yells, curses and the crash of boots through undergrowth behind. The ground cants down, the slight decline giving Jackie momentum. His bearings are screwed, just endless larch and pine, the forest a multi-layered cage, the trees its bars. He stumbles through thickets of threadbare bush. His breath rushes in his ears, his lungs burn. The light is fading.

No shots. Are the bastards low on ammunition? Conserving their bullets? How far behind are they?

He wills the gloom on. Darkness brings its own problems but it will even the odds.

Something changes.

The racket of feet in the undergrowth is muted. The yelling stops. Then a frightened cry, perhaps at a stumble or grasping branch. One shout. One voice.

The hunters have separated. Fanned out.

The ground clears, sudden space startling Jackie, throwing him off balance. The clearing is a narrow, rough path beaten through the trees. He stumbles at a crazy cant and Himura's weight shifts to his right, dragging him down. His shoulders scream in pain. His body betrays him and he falls, Himura's legs tangled with his, tumbling down a shallow bank on the far side of the trail. Himura comes free, rolls and drops into a tight crevice in the ground at the foot of the bank. To Jackie it looks like a creek but there is no splashing as Himura disappears inside.

Jackie sprawls on the patch of open ground at the foot of the bank, a couple of yards from the crevice, exposed. The hammering of footfalls races nearer, then slows on the dirt path above. He listens to the harsh rasp of the hunter's breath, the yakuza hidden from view. Jackie smells the graveyard scent of damp earth and moss. He grabs a thick wad of lichen and jams it in his mouth, the taste foul, smothering the rasp of his own ragged breathing, soaking his clouds of breath, like smoke signals in the waning light.

He clutches the loose handcuff and creeps toward a thick cluster of giant fuki plants on his right. The gloom presses down on him. He waits for a shot. He waits for total, endless black

to consume him.

The yakuza is whispering on the path above, perhaps goading himself on. Jackie lies on his belly and crawls under the plants. As his foot slips under the canopy, he sees movement in the gathering dark. The hunter is inching down the bank, side on.

Jackie remembers the Royal Irish Rangers, the training. The smallest sliver of white skin or equipment can shine like a torch in a forest at night. He scrapes the lichen from his mouth and smears it on his face. He scoops earth and, watching the yakuza pick his way down the slope, smears it on his face and hands, too. He tucks the loose handcuff down his sleeve and draws his jacket over the cuffs.

The yakuza is wearing a watch with a white face and Jackie catches flashes of a necklace at his throat. The man reaches the bottom of the bank and stands in the small clearing, peering in the near dark. His body language screams fear but his hand clutches something, pointing it at the trees, then up the bank, then at the fuki plants. At Jackie, lying in the dark below the massive leaves. Jackie imagines the pressure on the trigger, the brilliant flash in the murk. His pulse races. He leans back in his hide and tells himself the man can't see him, that the yakuza is scared, aiming at shadows. Then the man takes a step toward the plants. His arm is rigid, holding the gun in his hand far from his body like he's offering a snack to a feral dog. Then the man stops and takes a two-handed grip on his pistol, setting his feet apart.

Please God, don't let him see, thinks Jackie. It must be impossible in the darkness under the fuki. The yakuza is like a kid staring under the bed, wanting to see – yet dreading the sight of – a monster. But if the bastard gets too antsy and shoots, even if the bullet misses the report will echo for miles. Bring the other three.

Jackie and the man are less than ten feet from one another, the yakuza standing, Jackie on his back, praying.

We could stand off like this until Revelation, he thinks, and the bastard won't see me while the sun is down. But Jackie needs to piss and he can't hold his nerve for ever.

Something scurries on the other side of the creek. The forest is coming alive with the fall of night. The yakuza starts, swings the gun to cover the forest to his left. He takes a step back. His heel catches on something and he stumbles, grunts then gasps. Then his imagination gets the better of him and the yakuza takes a step up the shallow incline, ready to make for the path above. Jackie relaxes and stretches an inch, careful not to disturb the fuki stalks. He'll haul Himura from the creek, move slow, try to find the north star in the snatches of sky above the trees and move on. Survive.

The hunter is halfway up the bank when Himura moans.

The inky smear of the man in the heavy gloom stops mid-step like a child playing a game of statues. Himura's moan is a banshee wail in the still of the dark forest. A small sound escapes the hunter on the bank.

Jackie slides his feet behind his arse in the mossy dirt, slow. The yakuza will bolt or shoot but, either way, the decision is made. Jackie will have to launch himself from the undergrowth and quieten him fast. Or die trying.

Himura whimpers something in Japanese that tilts the scales for the figure on the bank. The man begins stepping down toward the clearing again. He moves toward the creek like a gliding phantom. Jackie tucks his feet under his body, the toes of his boots digging into the earth like an awkward sprinter ready for the gun. The figure is a couple of feet from the crevice, about six yards from Jackie's hiding place. The soft rustle of the hunter's feet slows.

Jackie explodes from the undergrowth with a hoarse snarl, a mad dog, arms outstretched, teeth bared in a wrenched, filth smeared face. He closes fast, target taking shape from shadow to man with each step. The gun is by the hunter's side, then over his face. A soft cry. The yakuza points, the muzzle bears on Jackie. Point blank. A brilliant flash. Another. Two quick shots, the angry rasp of the gun preserved for a beat by a flat echo in the trees. Searing pain – Jackie's face on fire as he barrels into the man, the two landing with a mutual gasp in the dirt. Hands clutch and scratch and Jackie's nails find the gun hand, tearing at the wrist. His head takes a weak punch as his fingers scrabble like an angry spider. The man's hand jerks and the pistol is gone. Jackie hurls his head into the yakuza's face and feels a stab of pain as his temple smashes into cartilage. The man yells and Jackie claps a hand over the man's mouth and drives his fist into the yakuza's eye, his knuckles glancing off a smooth brow. He hears a wild, beast-like growl and realises it's himself. He tries to drive his knee into the yakuza's bollocks and misses. They are tangled like lovers.

He pins the man down under his weight, and tries to lever himself up on his knees. His hand clamped on the hunter's mouth, the bastard's teeth gouge at his flesh as Jackie's other hand tries to push through the fucker's breastbone. Jackie's own teeth clench and something sharp carves his side under the armpit. The wanker has a knife. Jackie rolls and kicks, the moss catching on his jacket, his cheek blazing, side stinging, mouth dry. The hunter draws back and onto his knees. He screams for help, voice cracking like a pubescent kid, the cry shattering the dark curtain of forest. They'll come now, the other three. They couldn't be so far they haven't heard the shot or the shout. And Jackie will never see his friends again. His family. Home.

A knot of anger cramps Jackie's guts. It unfurls gnarly fingers, spreading fury and hate to his nerves, his clenched hands, his hackled shoulders.

He comes at the man in a berserker rage, scrambling on hands and feet, back arched, pivoting. He feels the flat of the blade on his hip, grunts and scythes with the open handcuff. The serrated metal teeth gash the man's face across the bridge of his nose. Jackie slashes again, dragging the jagged metal along the yakuza's knife arm and digging into the wrist. The knife falls. The man cries out. Jackie drives an elbow into the yakuza's mouth and hisses, 'Shut up!' The man thrashes, slapping Jackie on the shoulder, cracking him on the cheek but Jackie kneels by his side and hooks the open cuff into the man's mouth. He yanks hard. Jackie fumbles in the moss, nicks his finger on the knife and grabs the tang. Then a red fog rises and he is thrusting the blade through the man's flesh, skin popping like a skewered hot dog. Jackie smells blood, feels hot piss on the man's jeans, and levers his left forearm over the yakuza's throat. He gets close to the man's face, still shanking with the knife, and spits and curses at him. Seconds stretch to an eternity. Then the fury is passing with the dying man, the desolation of killing already taking hold. Jackie sees drops on the hunter's head and the red fog clears to reveal his own desperate tears. His mouth works in a silent plea to the dying man. The thrashing body slows.

He drops in the dirt at the sharp crack of a snapping branch. A shout. Then another. Two voices. Jackie eases his body up and clamps his left hand over the yakuza's mouth for the last time, then tilts the head back to sever the exposed windpipe. But the man is gone.

The rich bass tone of Ishikawa rumbles somewhere near and the grasping beam of a torch reaches through the trees. Jackie scrambles for the creek, hauling the corpse with him. Ishikawa's voice is close. The torch darts above Jackie's head, finding a birch trunk on the other side of the creek, locking on the silvery skin. The beam trails down its length, almost bathing Jackie and the corpse in light. He reaches the lip of the crevice. The corpse topples into the fissure.

Himura stirs on the dry creek bed as the body collapses on top of him. The torch light sweeps the dark above Jackie's head, but now he is lying on his belly at the lip of the creek. A fleeting scrap of memory comes to him of watching some war film with his dad as an escapee lay exposed at the wire, searchlights raking the night and sirens wailing.

Ishikawa's torch beam must reflect on the pale skin of Jackie's neck as he sprawls on the moss. Can't they see him? Haven't they crested the shallow bank behind? Jackie inches his hand to the edge of the crevice and something hard and angular brushes his wrist. The dead man's gun. *For the love of the Good Lord above, the fucking gun.*

The torch beam locks on the ground on the other side of the narrow creek as he snatches the pistol and drops, feet landing on a body. Himura sighs and Jackie feels for his face, covering the mouth as Ishikawa barks somewhere above. The narrow dry creek bed reeks of blood and piss. The torchlight darts around the top of the trench and the voices from somewhere above hush. A bad sign. The men must have seen the creek in the clearing and be whispering in debate.

Jackie shoves the knife he took from the dead yakyuza in his belt. It's small, tactical. The gun is polymer frame and feels like a semi-automatic. His face stings. He could have had it shot off, rather than burned from the muzzle flash. I'm a lucky bastard on that one, he thinks. If that luck holds there'll be a full magazine in the pistol, maybe fifteen rounds minus the two that took the skin of his cheek off.

The torchlight dies.

Jackie gets in Himura's face and shows him the gun. He doesn't know if Himura can see it in the dark. Then he steps on the back of the dead man and feels a cold, sick swell in his stomach at the thought of his handiwork.

Kill it. Time for that later. Eyes on the prize. Draw them away from Himura.

He moves at a crouch, putting space between himself and the bodies. The cuffs swing. He hears movement above. Jackie imagines Ishikawa holding the higher ground at the edge of the bank, two scouts moving on the crevice. After twenty seconds, he straightens his knees, a two-handed grip on the handgun held low at his crotch, muzzle pointing at the ground. He pauses, smears more dirt on his face, praying they will be focused further down the creek trench and miss the bob of his head. His eyes peer over the edge of the trench, his breath roaring in his inner ears. Dark, almost total dark, the forest a vacuum of light now. He holds a conversation with himself in his head – *Should have listened to my da and eaten more carrots.* Then a shape moves. Now two, pockets of deeper black on the bank, descending. Jackie can't focus and squeezes his eyes shut – *Shit!* Pinpricks of light dance in his vision.

He raises the semi-automatic and lets his arms rest on the ground at the ridge of the crevice, aiming on instinct. The pistol's fixed open sights are useless in this darkness. He puts pressure on the trigger, two flat cracks, thunderous in the dark, recoil, two flashes like massive fuses blowing. Jackie's already moving when they yell and open up, pumping rounds blindly into the night. He sprints, the cuffs jangling. Noise doesn't matter now, he needs to draw their fire. He grabs a fistful of mossy ground, hauls himself up the side of the trench and levers his torso onto the flat ground above, his legs dangling in the crevice. The hunters fire again, bullets smacking into leaves and branches behind him, and his bowels seem to drop for a second. Then he's up, running for the cover of the forest opposite the bank at a crouch. He goes down next to a threadbare trunk at the treeline and kneels on his right knee. He points the muzzle in the direction of the bank and fires off a round, pauses a couple of seconds and fires another, then moves a couple of yards.

Come on, you bastards! Follow the muzzle flash.

He sees a cluster of bursts of light, like bulbs popping, men-shaped shadows strobe-lit for an instant as the hunters fire. Frantic commands carry in the quiet, any critters laying low as man goes about the age-old dance of murderous combat. Jackie creeps sideways, left hand out, feeling for trees and bushes. The men follow. He hears them break the treeline somewhere behind. Jackie stops, leans against a trunk, aims in the direction he came and fires again, an orange flare in the black. He hears a curse then a short fusillade of shots. Nearer.

That's it, boys. Come you on ahead and we'll have a good oul' barney.

Then he stumbles and lands in a grasping tangle of dry branches that claw at his face and neck. The shouts of the hunters become more urgent. He catches the sound of snapping wood, nightmare-close in the shroud of darkness. He grabs at a birch, gains his feet and runs deeper into the black woods. The pursuing yakuza fire again.

Now the bullets nip at the dirt at his heels.

Chapter 29

Goro Inaba returns first, cupping his hands and blowing as a chill blast of night air sweeps the cabin. Megan, Ian and Jun look up like dogs at the return of their master and Inaba kicks the door shut with his heel. He walks the length of the room, three pairs of eyes on his face, then stops in front of the door leading to the toilet and kitchen and turns to Jun.

'Where's your brother?'

'Excuse me,' says Jun, bobbing his head in supplication, this dog scared of a beating.

'Where is he?'

'I'm sorry, Inaba San, I couldn't stop him.'

Inaba walks over to the table where Jun has been reading his comic, a rags to riches story of a noodle chef who becomes the greatest in Japan. Goro stands over him and says, 'Where – is – your – brother?' like he is dealing with the village idiot.

'He went out,' says Megan, 'about ten minutes after you left.'

'I didn't ask you,' says Inaba, eyes still on Jun rubbing his bandaged hand.

Megan feels a pinch in her knuckle, her father's grip tightening on her hand.

'Please understand,' says Jun, 'my brother is under a lot of stress. He isn't thinking straight. He – '

Inaba strikes out with his boot and the chair clatters from under Jun. Jun lands on the wooden floor with a high-pitched yelp. Megan gasps in accompaniment. Jun bobs his head faster, frantic, begging forgiveness.

Megan says, 'It isn't his fault.' Her father squeezes again and lays his palm on her shoulder, whispering for her to stay quiet.

Inaba kicks the chair across the floor, ignoring her.

'How long has he been using?'

'Please, Inaba San.'

'How long?' The last word is a roar.

Jun looks at the floorboards and places his hands in his lap. 'As far as I know, eight months.'

'How long since his last dose?'

'Maybe two days.'

Ian looks to Megan, his expression questioning. She says, 'Kenta is using drugs.'

'Yes-u! Drug-u!' yells Inaba in broken English. 'Junkie! Speed-o!' He draws his boot back like he's taking a penalty and drives a hard kick into Jun's spine with a hollow thump.

Megan says, 'No!'

Ian says, 'Wait.'

Inaba reaches down and grabs a fistful of Jun's hair, then slings a punch into the side of his head. Jun takes it, silent. Inaba winces and clutches at his chest. Megan jumps up, jolting her father's arm. Inaba whirls on her and bawls, 'Sit down!' in Japanese, his eyes wild with pain and rage. Ian puts himself between his daughter and the yakuza and raises his palms. 'Sit down, Megan.'

'Listen to your father,' says Inaba.

Megan sits and says in Japanese, 'Amphetamines?'

'What?' says Inaba, voice sharp with irritation.

'The drug: amphetamines? You said "speed-o".'

'Yes.' Inaba places his boot on Jun's head and shoves, savage.

'Can he get them around here?' Megan asks, her voice tight.

'You can't buy a can of beer for a couple of kilometres.' Inaba bellows. He produces a small ivory object from the inside pocket of his jacket. A blade flicks out.

Megan moans, 'No.' Her father grabs her, hurting her, something in his face she has never seen before.

Inaba grits his teeth, yanks Jun's head back by the hair and saws through a thick thatch with the blade. Jun's eyes scrunch closed, his mouth set, his head wrenched with sharp, brutal jerks. The hair comes free and Inaba scatters it on the floor. Megan strains against her father. He thrusts her back into the sofa, blocks her view with his head and softens his gaze. He mouths, 'It's okay. It's okay.' But she knows things are very far from okay. She hears grunting, the scrape of boots on the wooden floor, the slap of skin on the tabletop. A cool lightness flutters through her and she imagines Inaba holding the terrified Jun, forcing his hand onto the table; the knife poised above the little finger, the blade biting into skin, working through meat and gristle. A soft, wet sound, then a dry crunch as the knife splits bone and the finger joint comes away. She says, 'No. Daddy, no,' blinking the hot salty tears away.

Ian Sparrow hears his daughter from a place and time long gone, running into her bedroom in the wee small hours, her head hot and damp to the touch, sweating out a nightmare. He does what he did then, holding her, cradling her, whispering everything is okay, that he's there, that she's safe. Trying to convince himself as much as his daughter. And failing. She pushes him away.

Inaba has wrapped Jun's necklace around the brother's finger, stopping the circulation, watching the colour begin to fade. He remembers the tatami room, Himura, Ishikawa and the rest looking on, Jun staring at the knife on the table, ready to sacrifice for his wakagashira, his superior. The look of astonished betrayal on Jun's face when Himura speared his hand. Then again when their boss summoned them both, could not remember his foot soldier's name and dismissed Jun with an irked wave of an arm.

Inaba catches movement to his left. The father and daughter, holding one another. He thinks of Emi. He hasn't held her anywhere near as much as he would like. He would take such strength now from her small arms around his neck, her little fingers on his shoulders, her pillow-cheek on his.

He rubs his eyes, knuckles digging into the sockets and says, 'Shit.'

He straightens his back, releases Jun's finger and pats him on the shoulder. Jun balks. Inaba walks to the chair, rights it, and gestures for Jun to sit. As Jun mutters a string of apologies, Inaba nods. Inaba slips the knife into the inner pocket of his coat and pulls another chair from the table. He sits next to Jun, rubbing the wound on his chest. Megan heaves one, great sob and laughs.

Inaba looks at Megan and her father, dark crescents under his eyes, and scowls. Fucking cops have been dicking him around all day. He chops the air with his right hand and bows to her father, apologising in Japanese for not speaking English, the daughter automatically translating. 'I've been talking to the police. I drive to different locations and use public phones. We're close to a deal, to getting you both home.'

Jun, staring in supplication at the floor, looks up.

'You must understand,' says Inaba, 'you are our leverage. We come from a place where the police can't be trusted.'

Inaba swallows the sour spittle of guilt, his face creasing in loathing. Loathing for the useless ignorance of the bandaged idiot at the table, for Jun's devious addict of a brother, for himself selling them out for a slim shot at a future with Emi.

When he had called the OCB last, the wheedling voice on the line had told him the original deal was made with Inaba and Inaba alone. With his case officer, Miyamoto, dead, he was damn lucky to have it honoured at all. Then they asked where he was holed-up with the two foreigners.

An image had flashed through Inaba's mind of the third foreigner, the man he had tangled with in his apartment. What had happened to the big gaijin? The cops had not mentioned Megan and her father's friend. Was he lost in the city? Dead?

Inaba had deflected with the cop on the line and demanded some written proof that he would be given protective custody, a new identity, a future. The grinding behemoth of Japanese bureaucracy was working on the paperwork and he was told he should check in again in the morning when progress will have been made. Then the cops could arrange a meet to sign the papers. No emailing, no electronic files. Just pen to paper in the presence of Inaba's lawyer and two healthy gaijin in the tender loving care of the National Police Agency. Two yakuza brothers in custody, their death warrants signed with sentencing to prison where they will probably be shanked by Kanto Daichi-kai serving time. And Inaba, the rat, identity erased, embarking on a new life. Of what? A blissful home, re-united with his estranged wife in the marital bed, daughter dreaming peacefully down the hall in a small provincial town? Perhaps, even, the warm, beach strewn shores of Okinawa? Or a bitter solitary existence in some shoe-box in a dead-end town out in the sticks, driving a forklift or standing on an assembly line on a night-shift, spending his wage on booze and hostesses, his daughter a thousand miles away, her memory of her father fading with each new day, each new friend made in school? He shakes his head, exhausted. Should he summon the energy to tell Megan of his work with the dead policeman, Rei Miyamoto, and the deal struck?

No, he won't mention Miyamoto's name. He will spare her that.

Because Goro Inaba knows the OCB cop was her boyfriend's brother.

And how much does Megan San know of her boyfriend, Rei Miyamoto's brother's, weaknesses? That he was a regular at the Invisible Man Club, that he was into the Kanto Daichi-kai for a couple of thousand in gambling and blackmail debts? That Rei Miyamoto had used his connection with Inaba to try and bury his brother's secrets before he, himself, was buried in a shallow grave in the mountains beyond Maruyama? That he knew of her very existence, her studies at university, because of Rei? That it was Rei who unwittingly led Goro Inaba and the brothers to her door?

No, he spares the girl that sordid little story.

Inaba leans forward on his chair, Jun sliding from his vision, and rests his elbows on his knees.

The door opens. Kenta staggers in.

He is hunched, a hand across his stomach as he kicks the door closed behind him.

'I'm glad you're here,' says Inaba. 'I was just about to explain what's happe – '

'There are a lot of cops out there,' says Kenta. 'I walked down to the town. There are uniforms along the waterfront. Patrol cars in front of the big hotels. Even a fucking boat on the lake.'

'Formality,' says Inaba, smothering his anger at the idiot blabbing details of the area in front of the gaijin. 'A show of force from the NPA but the Organised Crime Bureau are calling the shots. We're so close to a deal.'

'Oh yeah? That's good to know.' Kenta's shirt is caked with something dried, a milky-white spatter pattern on the pink cotton. He notices Jun looking at the stain. 'I was hungry and grabbed some noodles in a ramen bar. They didn't sit well in my gut.'

'You were sitting in a fucking noodle bar?' says Jun. 'What if the cops had come in and seen you like this?'

'Fuck you, little brother.'

'Listen,' says Inaba, 'we're almost there. The cops are drawing up a deal. In the morning, I will go and sign it. Then I will lead them back here and we can all get out of this filthy fucking shack.'

'See?' says Jun, his voice cracking with child-like hope. 'See, Kenta? We're going to be okay.'

'Why are you going to sign the deal?' says Kenta, reptilian eyes on Inaba. 'It's for all three of us, right? Why can't we go too, Jun and me?'

Inaba says, 'Someone needs to stay with the gaijin. They are our insurance. We can't take them to the meet with us. Only when we have the agreement do the cops get their hands on them.'

'You trust the cops?' says Jun.

'You trust him?' says Kenta. 'What's to stop the cops tearing up the immunity deals once we give them the gaijin?'

'My lawyer,' says Inaba.

'Your lawyer?' Kenta's face blanches with a dramatic double take. 'You got a lawyer?'

'Don't we all? Every yakuza has a legal leech hidden away, don't they?'

Jun says, 'Do we?'

Kenta says, 'Fuck you!' His voice withers with his body and he seems to fold in on himself, his mouth puckering as he doubles over. He gasps.

Inaba makes to stand.

'Kenta!' says Jun.

Kenta straightens as though someone has pumped air into his shrinking frame. 'This stinks. You were working with the dead bitch-cop for months before you brought us in on your scheme. Ready to fuck us over along with Himura and the rest of the syndicate until you needed help. Until you grabbed the gaijin. Now we hear you have your own lawyer cutting deals. Deals for you.'

'For *us*.'

'Bullshit! Lawyers work for the people who pay them and only the people who pay them.'

'I pay him to work for all of us.'

'With what? You said it: your gun doesn't have fucking bullets. You're broke. All your money goes on your ex-wife and kid. You're using the gaijin and, once they've served your purpose, you'll drop them just like us. A rat's a rat.'

Jun opens his mouth, finding the words and pats Inaba's sleeve. 'That's bullshit, right? We're in this together, right? Yakuza brothers?'

'You moron,' says Kenta. 'There is no yakuza now, not for us.'

'You're hurting,' says Inaba. 'Maybe I can get you a fix. Ease the pain.'

Kenta glares at Jun and says, 'You bastard! You fucking told him!'

'I didn't need your brother to tell me. It's obvious. Anyone could see you're suffering withdrawal.'

Kenta stares at the father and daughter on the sofa with hunted eyes. His skin has taken on a spoiled quality like bad meat, darkened bibs of sweat on the armpits of his t-shirt.

'I'll try to get something for you, something to get you well. Let me see what I can do,' says Inaba.

I could make it to town in thirty minutes at a jog, he thinks. Call OCB, tell them to hurry the paperwork up, warn them I'm losing control of the brothers. Grab some meds from an all-night pharmacy and pass them off as harder drugs to Kenta. Keep him quiet.

Kenta says, 'You walk out that door, I go with you. We're in this together? From now on we stay together.'

Jun frowns, lowering his heavy brow over his eyes like a pair of blinds. 'What about the other gaijin?' he says.

Inaba and Kenta say as one, 'What?'

'The other gaijin,' says Jun, 'the big one. We haven't even thought of him. He could have gone to the cops.'

Inaba says, 'And told them what? He was beaten unconscious in Susukino and woke up in an apartment. He had a fight with a man and ran. He won't come after us – he wouldn't know where to start looking. Forget him. All we have to do is sit tight, sign the immunity deal and deliver *these* gaijin unharmed.' He nods toward Megan and Ian. 'All the cards are on the table.'

'What if Himura got to the other one?' says Jun.

'What if he did? The big foreigner doesn't know about any of this. He doesn't know who we are. For all we know, he isn't even in the country anymore. Like I said, forget him. Let's get some sleep.'

Jun's jaw is working as he chews over what has been said.

Kenta shudders.

Megan clutches her arms, doubt tapping at her shoulders. She, like her father, can sense a shift. Blood is blood. Inaba is losing the brothers.

'I think Kenta is right,' says Jun, savouring each word of his revelation.

Inaba says, 'You don't need to think. I'll handle that department.'

'Don't talk down to my brother,' says Kenta.

Jun nods, oblivious to Inaba's patronising words. 'One of us should go with you when you sign the papers. Whoever it is can sign for both us. Then you bring the cops back here for the foreigners.'

Inaba shakes his head. 'No. The police have been dealing with me. You'll spook them.'

'What's to spook?' says Kenta. 'We're part of the deal anyway.'

'It's about trust. I was working with them. I have a damn code-name. I meet them. I sign. I lead them here.'

'They trust you,' says Jun. 'You told them about us. So it makes no difference if one of us is there.'

'It's the cops. You know how fucking sly they can be. They make a living ruining lives. It makes them paranoid.'

Kenta says, 'So they *don't* trust you?'

'Speaking of paranoid.'

'How about your lawyer?' says Jun. 'We could call him. Understand the deal before it's signed.'

Inaba, furious in his guilt, snaps, 'You can't write in crayon over the phone.'

The trigger is pulled.

Kenta roars, 'Don't talk down to my brother!' He runs forward, grabs the pistol from the table and brings it down hard on Inaba's skull.

Megan cries out at the thick crack, the vicious spasm of Inaba's head snapping forward on his thin neck. Inaba's eyes go wide, his strong features stupid with shock. Kenta strikes out again, a terrible calm on his face, Inaba's head jolting at a cruel angle. Jun sits back in his chair like a frightened child. Ian Sparrow clutches his daughter, trying to get between her and the yakuza. Inaba, stupid with the blows, moves slow, reaching inside his jacket.

Jun bolts off his chair, grasping at Inaba, whining, 'No, no, no, no!' He trips, collapses into Inaba and they clatter into the table. Kenta goes slack and drops to his knees. Jun reaches out to his brother. Megan screams.

Inaba lies on his back, his head under the table and the small ivory tang of his flick knife standing proud of his gut, the blade embedded in the muscle and sinew of its owner's scrawny stomach.

Chapter 30

Jackie lies in the dirt, his heartbeat violent, like a fist pounding on the ground. For a mad second he fears the men out in the dark will track him through its vibrations on the forest floor. He sprawls on his belly in some spurge. Blend in to the colours and shapes around you, that was basic fieldcraft. The Rangers taught that slow movement was less visible, less likely to attract the eye. Get down low to scout. On your belly you had a better view of anyone lying in wait, were less visible.

He can hear every bastard creeping around out here. Critters rustling in the bamboo grass, small claws scrabbling at bark, wings battering through autumn leaves in the upper branches of the birch and spruce. Each noise winds him taught as piano-wire. He'd shoved the pistol in his waistband to avoid firing off a round with the jitters.

How far has he come from the dry creek? Are Himura and the dead yakuza still lying in the narrow crevice? He eases forward through the spurge, the soft swish of his clothes on the leaves loud as waves crashing on a shore in the still of the night forest. The handcuffs are gone now, thank God. He had worked at them care as he lay in the dirt. He reaches a tree and stands slow His joints crack like a thunderclap. He winces then presses his back against the bark, the branches enfolding him.

How long he stands, he has no idea. He can't orientate. The North Star is somewhere high above, hidden by the forest canopy. The moonlight struggles against the tattered rags of pine, spruce and larch. It is cold but he can't see the cloud of his breath in the black night.

A snap. Something heavy.

Bear? Were they roaming in this area? If so, they could all be fucked – he, Ishikawa and his men.

The shuffle of crisp leaves.

Abrupt silence.

A branch reaches out and strokes Jackie's face, ignites his senses like a nitrate flare. He's back in the love hotel for a beat, smells the same warm chemical scent. Someone inches away, in a laundered shirt. Jackie slides his hand up to his waist. His fingers close around the handgun grip. The viscous dark presses in on him.

Movement.

Something creeps from Jackie's left. Perhaps three feet away. He can't miss at this range. He raises his arms in a two-handed grip, his limbs touching then leaning on a long branch, moulding to its shape. He peers for the fixed open sight on automatic reflex, front blade-rear notch, and realises it is useless in this dark. The shadow freezes.

More sound. Something stepping through tall undergrowth. The shadow waits. The forest is still, a paralysing vacuum. Then the shadow waves in recognition to an unseen comrade. It reaches out, feeling for branches and trunks like a blind man. So close now. Jackie blinks and feels a trickle of sweat bother his cheek. Scenarios reel through his mind. Hide and sit it out, let the men walk on, then move, put distance between himself and them – fuck Himura – and run at first light. Or fire and thin their numbers, add another statistic to the body at the creek.

But the shadow in front of him is a man, not a statistic, who reaches out like a kid in a game. Blind man's bluff. The fingers brush a brittle branch, the tree giving with the touch, trailing the needles. They graze the muzzle of Jackie's pistol. The shadow turns with a rasp of breath.

Jackie fires.

White hot flame in the dark. Two sharp cracks, a huge sound. Short recoil, the gun barely bucking in protest. The figure there one moment, gone the next. A cold fluid plunge in Jackie's gut. Shouts, cries, the thunder of running through straining grass. Jackie steps from the tree, stands over the fallen shadow and fires another bullet into the black oval of the head. An answering crackle of gunfire erupts to his right, rounds flying wild. There is a confusion of yells and more running, clambering, snapping wood. A heavy thud and a grunt then a yelp.

Jackie crouches, moving backwards in short steps, changing direction should his heel snag on something. The others could be yards away or out of range. With a cruel elation he thinks, *another one down*. He'll have thrown the others into confusion. Two urban gangsters lost in the woods. He catches the clean scent of detergent late and ducks on instinct as a cloud of flame and heat flares close to his right with a blast like a right hook to the head and he knows Ishikawa is there. Close.

Bastard! If only the bamboo spear had pierced deeper in the love hotel room. Finished him there and then.

The crackle of pistol fire to the left, Ishikawa yelling. Jackie fires twice, the semi-automatic spitting flame in front, two cartridges out the side. The blanket of trees is strobe-lit for an instant and he sees the silhouette of a hunched man ten yards off to his right.

Jackie runs.

He runs into a slapping, gouging tangle of branches and spins away, his heart galloping. He hisses in terrified fury, clawing back control. Slow down, cautious steps, he thinks. Listen for the enemy. There are hushed voices somewhere. Disjointed talk. Blabbering to themselves, lost in the blackness. Like him.

Blend in.

He sees the dense, inky bulk of a fallen giant. A pine, upended, roots torn from the earth, left exposed to the elements like the tendrils of some dead monster. He crouches below them. He waits.

The forest has been shocked into an uneasy quiet by the violence. Two men dead in these woods. No time for remorse. What had Himura called Jackie? A survivor. Better not make a liar of the man.

What is out there. Man or beast? A demon? A Tengu? What was

the creature on the beer bottle? A Kirin. What other gods and monsters and devils stalk these ancient woods?

Catch a fucking grip, Jackie Shaw – your head's away! It'll be banshees and fucking faeries next!

He has seen plenty of monsters in his time, none of them fantastic. He sent a few to rot in prison. Sent a few to Hell.

How many bullets left? Jackie doesn't want to eject the magazine and count by touch. Too noisy.

Get out of your head! Move!

The land before him lightens to jagged shards of a deep midnight blue between the black trees and Jackie comes to a small clearing. He skirts the open ground, waiting for a scrap of cloud to pass and finds the North Star. The clearing tapers to the east and he edges his way along the treeline. The cold is seeping through, slowing him. Everything aches. His cheek stings. Then he sees a light.

Far off, as small as a firefly ahead and to his right. The chill in his belly is a cold rage, the light a target. Whatever it is – whoever – he moves toward it, faster, clumsier than he should. He ducks back into the trees, grazes a bark with a loud scratch, grits his teeth and closes on the light. He raises the handgun. The light is very low to the ground. It illuminates a thin cloud of breath rising from a black pit in the earth. Jackie moves on and drags some bamboo grass with his boot, raking it across the forest floor. The light disappears. Then it's back, floating in the dark like a restless spirit above a crack in the ground.

Jackie sprints the last couple of feet, loses his footing and scrabbles like a baseball runner sliding to the plate, collapsing over the lip of the creek and landing hard on two bodies. He grapples with an arm, hears a weak grunt and clasps his hand over a mouth.

Reizo Himura's eyes dart around the creek bed.

'Shut up,' spits Jackie, 'and turn your phone off! It's lit up like a fucking beacon!'

Chapter 31

'Noppera-bō,' says Kenta, curled by the wall.

'He says you're a ghost,' says Inaba, his voice thin, mouth twitching in pain.

Megan musters a smile for her father, Ian holding the mirror by her side as she threads the needle. Ian and Megan kneel by Inaba, the wounded yakuza sitting on the floor with his back against the sofa. Across the room, Kenta's arms are wrapped around his stomach. His face is the colour of sour milk. He clutches Inaba's knife in a shaking hand. Jun paces the cabin's wooden boards and worries.

'Look in the mirror,' says Inaba.

The glass is flecked with grime, an infestation of mould in the centre of the glass. The ugly cloud obscures Megan's face.

'Noppera-bō,' says Inaba. 'There's an old story of a man walking at night on the Akasaka Road, back in the Edo era. It was misty but he spotted a young woman crying with her hands over her face. He spoke to her but, when she dropped her hands, her face had no features. It was blank. Like an egg.' He pauses, holding his breath, a wave of pain breaking then washing away. 'The man ran. He saw a glow in the distance and made for it. It was a noodle cart with an old guy selling soba. The man told the old guy about the Noppera-bō, the faceless woman. The old man listened, then wiped his face. When his hand came away, his features had disappeared. He was Noppera-bō too.'

'Creepy story,' says Megan. 'What happened to the man?'

'How the fuck should I know?'

The needle prepared, she hands it to her father. He gives the mirror to her.

Inaba slides down the sofa until his body is prone on the floor, his head on his rolled jacket. 'Hold the mirror up,' he says, 'I want to see your father working.' Megan positions the mirror over Inaba's gut.

The wound is nasty but not deep enough to have penetrated the bowel. No chance of sepsis or septic shock – but Ian Sparrow knows it must bloody hurt. He thinks of the last time he stitched up a wound. Then it had been Jackie Shaw. He concentrates on keeping his hand still. The shakes irritate him; he is pissed off at his own fear. Not understanding a word spoken between these goons and his precious daughter doesn't help.

Sparrow hadn't thought, just reacted when he saw Inaba on the ground with the knife in his belly, the thug Kenta driving his boot again and again into the man on the floor. Jun was screaming at his brother. It was the cruelty that set something off in Ian and he had launched himself at Kenta, Megan's scream tearing at his ears. This man on the ground was their best hope – maybe their only hope – of getting through this ordeal and Sparrow had grabbed Kenta and felt the younger man's wiry strength. Kenta had tossed him aside. Ian had landed badly and wrenched his back. Still, it had flicked a switch in Jun. The bandaged hand had reached out and the yakuza had grabbed his brother and hauled him away from the battered Inaba. Then Kenta had seemed to shrivel. He had snatched the knife from Inaba's gut and retreated to the corner like a guilty child, staring out at the room with baleful eyes, suffering in his private hell of withdrawal.

Ian grasps the needle, blinks a couple of times and sets to his task.

Jun thinks, *Noppera-bō. Bullshit!*

The English girl is too beautiful to be anything other than flesh and blood. Beauty, in Jun's experience, was all too mortal, not like the spirits and ghouls of Japanese myth and legend. His mother had been beautiful, once, before she was shamed by Jun's uncle and his gambling. Before she drank the dishonour down deep in her belly and pissed it out on sheets the youthful Jun changed each morning. He had watched the shame and cheap sake and spirits eat away at her, claiming her teeth, her looks, her liver and, finally – mercifully – her life. His father had died when he and Kenta were toddlers. As the oldest, Jun had shielded Kenta from their mother's moods, her scabrous temper.

They need sleep, difficult with the stress of violence and the growing chill in the stale air.

His brother calls to him, waving him over with a blood-encrusted hand. With a weary resignation, Jun goes to him. Blood is blood.

#

Shintaro Ishikawa pulls his coat tight around his body against the cold. Two men dead. At least, he presumes they are dead. He heard both call out in the darkness. That was the last he saw or heard of them. He has one left, his Tokko Tai-cho, his best soldier. The man lies somewhere in the undergrowth ten yards away, waiting for his master to move. Ironic that the Tokko Tai-cho was the violent vanguard of a yakuza family, the first into battle in any war. The very name meant Kamikaze Squad Leader. And yet here is Ishikawa's man, still alive while his comrades are dead.

In this, the soldier has failed to honour yakuza doctrine.

They are now exiled. An unsanctioned attack on another yakuza organisation, no matter the reason, will not be tolerated. The Yamaguchi-gumi will never take them back. All he has known for most of his adult life is gone. But were not many of the greatest Japanese men of action who bucked the system? The great Sakanoue no Tamuramaro who perpetrated genocide on the Emishi tribes of the north, all for the further glory of his emperor, Kanmu. The former governor of Tokyo, lambasted by liberals, who declared the Rape of Nanking was a Chinese fiction; acknowledged that old women who could no longer reproduce were useless, sucking resources from the country; who compared Westerners to the animals they are. Even that governor's friend, the novelist – arse-loving madman that he was – died with the honour of fighting to restore the divinity of the emperor, committing seppuku.

Ishikawa waits.

He thinks of the girl on the front desk at the love hotel in North Ward, remembers the terror on her face and feels something spark deep down. He rubs his crotch and then pulls the coat tight again. The girl had been young with the pure unpainted beauty of a shrine maiden. He had let her live, locking her in a back room. He could sleep well knowing he had displayed such benevolence, and preserved honour for himself and his syndicate, in sparing such an exemplar of youthful Japanese womanhood. And she'd never identify him thanks to Tengu mask, so there had been nothing to gain in her death.

Perhaps he should have let things pan out. He had spotted the pin-badge lying at the feet of the murdered cop in the Invisible Man Club and pocketed it before Inaba came on the scene. Passing the badge to Fujiko Maki, seeding doubts about Inaba with the story of discovering the badge on the wakagashira's desk – it could have paid dividends if he had let things run their course. But when he saw the gaijin in the lobby of Fujiko's building, something within Shintaro Ishikawa had snapped. When he then bullied one of Himura's soldiers into revealing the gaijin was hidden at a love hotel in North Ward with Fujiko, he had been left no choice. Honour had to be satisfied. For a foreigner to be in such a place with the exquisite Fujiko could not stand so he had purchased a Tengu mask from a cheap souvenir shop, taken his wakizashi short sword, and gone to exact bloody judgement on the Irish filth who sullied Ishikawa's future woman with his very gaijin presence. Then he had opened the room door and found them. Together. Naked.

His neck hurts. The drugs are wearing off, some concoction given him by his men. Amphetamine and painkiller and who knows what – but it had driven the pain down to a low hum of discomfort, enough to keep him sharp through the night hunt. Enough to drive him on. Now the ache is again rising in his neck and with it, anger. The gaijin is a devil. Ishikawa chastises himself. Why had he not brought a gun to the hotel room? Why not put a bullet in the bastard's head, clean and simple. Ishikawa had been too clever, mimicking the Tengu Killer, hoping to cloak the gaijin's death in the trail of destruction wrought by the masked killer.

To fight with a blade again – it had been magical.

But he had fled before he bled out on the love hotel carpet. Had left his own sword in the room in his panic.

Now the foreigner is trying to draw them further into the dark forest, disorientate them. Ishikawa and his man must regroup. They have an advantage in weaponry. Ishikawa's soldier has a luminous compass and can navigate in this black night. If they are careful, he knows they can find and kill the Irishman: they are Japanese, after all, and superior. Should the Western mongrel survive until morning, they can track him in daylight. Ishikawa's man has done some hunting in the mountains around Nagano.

Ishikawa would bet that Himura is with the Irishman, wounded. He had seen the vague outline of the Sapporo oyabun lying at the bottom of the gorge near the derelict hotel, seen the gaijin flit between the trees, Himura slung over his shoulders like a sack of rice. Yes, Himura is hurt bad. A realisation dawns on him: the Irishman drew them into the forest away from the creek. Himura may be lying there, waiting for his pet gaijin to return. That is where he and his man will go. They can kill Himura and rethink their strategy.

He creeps forward and whispers to his soldier, a black wraith emerging from the tangled blanket of the forest floor. The man cups his hand over the luminescent dials of the compass. Seconds pass. Then he bows, a flicker of movement in the darkness of the forest, and they move, threading through the labyrinth of trees.

#

The dead yakuza in the dry creek bed had rendered a cigarette lighter, a clip of yen bills, a wallet stuffed with credit cards, a packet of condoms and a mobile phone. A jacket to drape over Himura in addition to the oyabun's own coat to keep him warm in the cold night air. A Rolex and a miniature kanji charm on a necklace. The dead man also had cufflinks in a hard plastic capsule tucked in an inner pocket. Jackie had taken the battery from Himura's mobile while the man lay on the creek bed preoccupied with breathing.

Now, Jackie is summoning the will to heave the wounded Himura on his shoulders again and move on. The priority right now is survival. Keep moving and find a hide of their own to sit out the night.

Galvanized, he kneels by Himura and begins turning him over. The man groans. Jackie closes his eyes, tilts his head back to the dark heavens and throws together a rough prayer. He stuffs moss into one of the dead yakuza's condoms, pulls aside the makeshift bandage on Himura's wound and begins packing it with the rubber. He is surprised at the heat of the wounded man's skin. A bad sign – infection could have set in. Himura whispers in Japanese, startling him.

'Shut up! I don't understand you,' rasps Jackie.

'You make a dying man speak English.'

'So don't speak. Just stay alive.'

'You should know,' hisses Himura, 'the DNA test ... the result is fucked.' Himura is eager to spit out the words. 'The cops are fucking useless. They don't have a database. They can't do much with results when they get them.' He gags, a cold rod of pain driving through his chest. Jackie places a hand on his shoulder. Himura takes a moment, then whispers, 'Genda called when you took a piss outside the hotel. The cum on the dead cop's leg – the killer shared twenty-five percent of the cop's DNA.'

A scramble somewhere in the forest.

'We have to move,' spits Jackie.

'There's more.'

'Later.'

Jackie clasps his hand over Himura's mouth and feels hot breath. Himura wrenches his head away in panic as something sharp stabs at his cheek until Jackie grabs his hair and yanks his head back.

'It's a stick,' he spits. 'Bite down on it.'

The sharp point grazes Himura's jaw and then his mouth is filled with the damp, bitter taste of rotted wood. Jackie breathes in deep, the cold air stinging his throat. The smell of earth and wood assails him. He's cold, sore and thirsty but begins levering Himura onto his shoulders, staggering like a weightlifter. Then he lurches along the dry creek bed, following its winding furrow, hoping it will take him south to Lake Toya, to Goro Inaba. To his friends.

#

The soldier yakuza stops Ishikawa with a hand on his chest. He squints at a subtle shift in the depth of darkness up ahead.

Ishikawa squats and the man creeps forward, merging into the shadows. The rustle of clothes seems impossibly loud in the still and Ishikawa worries the gaijin devil might pick his man off: then what will become of Ishikawa? Will he summon the courage to destroy the Irishman? If Ishikawa can slaughter the bastard, if Himura is dead, there might be a chance he could still claim Fujiko Maki. Indeed, it may bend her to his will should he show her benevolence and forgive her the blasphemy of the hotel room in north Sapporo. They could run, perhaps to one of the smaller Okinawan islands. Ishikawa has money squirreled away. He could conceal Fujiko Maki's shame within marriage. Were not compassion and benevolence key tenets of Bushido, the samurai warrior's code? And her secret shame would tie her inextricably to him. She would be his. To possess.

He starts as the hand touches his wrist.

His man whispers. All clear.

They thread their way down to the patch of open ground. His

man gestures to the dry creek. A body lies at the bottom. Ishikawa feels a spike of excitement but when they clamber into the hole, it is one of his men. The corpse's coat is gone and trouser pockets empty.

Ishikawa's man whispers, 'They've been here, Ishikawa San.'

Ishikawa sucks air through his teeth and touches the dressing on his neck. *Ishikawa San?* The arrogant little fucker should address him as Aniki – older brother – whether they are in this stinking shit-hole together or standing in a boardroom.

'So, kodomo,' he says, stressing the word *child*. 'We move on.'

'Back to the old hotel? To the car?'

'No. Into the forest. Himura cannot live to bear testimony to our actions. The gaijin must die for murdering our family.'

'Perhaps – '

'Your brothers lie butchered. Dishonoured.'

A sound of wings flapping explodes somewhere in the darkness. Something moves through the forest. Something large.

'Could be a bear,' says the footsoldier.

'Bullets kill higuma just as well as gaijin. We move.'

Himura's man bows, a sharp snap of his neck, and they follow the thread of the dry creek bed through the dark forest.

Chapter 32

Kenta spasmed, cracking his head off the wall. Inaba roared as Ian Sparrow flinched, the needle stabbing into soft flesh. Megan screamed. Jun stood rooted to the floor, midway between his brother and the huddle of bodies by the sofa. Then he scuttled over to Kenta, arms outstretched like a faith healer calling on the power of the Almighty. It went on for a minute before Kenta went slack and sighed. Then he slept with thin, shallow breaths.

Ian had gone back to work on Inaba's stitches.

Now Inaba, patched up, sprawls on the sofa next to Megan and her father, T-shirt drawn down over his stomach wound. He rubs the other dressing over the slash in his chest.

Kenta calls out, his body arching, legs rigid. His eyes open and stare through his brother when Jun rushes to him, crouching, fussing, imploring.

'Nightmare,' whispers Inaba.

Kenta, his head lolling back, focuses on Jun. He nods as though he's come to some resolution, then turns and punches the wall.

Jun grabs his arms.

Kenta swats him away and the brothers' howls ricochet around the room. Megan screws her eyes shut and tucks her chin on her chest; her father pulls her close and they sit with Inaba on the sofa feeling sordid as voyeurs. The family drama seems to last for an age.

Then Kenta slumps, spent.

His face is clad in a film of sweat like he's stepped from a sauna, his tongue darting around drawn lips. His eyes close.

'He needs water,' says Inaba.

Jun, head bowed as though in prayer, doesn't move.

'Jun, he's dehydrated. He needs a drink.'

Jun raises his thick head and turns to face them. His eyes are red, his cheeks shining. A thin cord of snot runs from his nose to his twitching mouth. Megan takes a gentle hold of her father's arms and eases them from her shoulders then stands, slow and cautious, like she's facing down a wounded animal.

'I'll get some,' she says. 'You stay with him.'

Jun drops his eyes to the floor and nods. He is still staring at the boards, a hand on Kenta's ankle, as Megan slips through the connecting door to the kitchen and toilet.

Her pulse spikes and she stands in the dim corridor for a moment, gathering her wits. Her legs are lead.

Move, she thinks. Move your arse and grab that bloody mobile phone.

Then she's taking steps, surprised at herself, her body taking control. The fetid toilet is there, the coats hanging opposite.

Ridiculous. Now, of all times, she wants to pee.

Then her fingers are moving, the padding of the jacket closing over the pocket. She rummages. No sounds from beyond the door. Her fingers work along the strap and she pulls, feeling the weight of the phone. The phone catches on the lining. A muffled voice calls from behind the door. She swears. The mobile leaps from the pocket with a tug of fabric and clatters on the floor as she claws at air. Two voices, raised, come to her from the other side of the door. Megan drops to her haunches and scoops up the mobile, pressing the power button, willing the screen to kick in. She darts into the small kitchen, still holding the power button down and opens the cupboard with her left hand. She searches for a glass. The mobile screen is black. She runs water, then fiddles with the back of the phone and pries it away. No battery.

No fucking battery!

Her head drops.

Her eyes sting.

She stares at the water gushing from the tap as it turns from an earthy brown to crystal clear. With an effort of will she places the glass under the stream, presses the backing on the mobile and shoves it in her hip pocket. She hears the door at the end of the corridor open. Megan is wiping her eyes when Jun appears beside her.

'Okay?' he says.

'Yes.' Her voice cracks.

She nods and wipes her face, trailing hot tears across her cheeks. Silly cow, she thinks. What good is blubbing going to do? Where's the little girl who skinned her knees and fell off horses, only to pick herself up and get right back on? Daddy's little girl-soldier.

Is Emi a good little girl-soldier? she wonders. Megan hopes Inaba gets his shot at rebuilding his family. Every little girl needs her daddy. Every big girl, too. Add together all the days and weeks between visits, the months and years at university and in Japan, and she's lost so much time with her father. If they survive this she will do all she can to make up for some of those lost years. Yes, she hopes Inaba will get his chance. Maybe he secretly calls his daughter when he's out contacting the police. Not on his mobile, though, in case it would be traced.

His mobile.

Inaba will have a mobile on him. He'll have turned it off but he'll have one.

Get his phone. Call for help. We can still do this. We can still get out of here.

She picks the glass up two-handed, as if it contains the waters of life, and hands it to Jun. 'Your brother's drink,' she says, and walks back to the living room.

Jun feels a stab of regret for this girl, crying and alone back here. 'Thank you,' he calls.

Women. So weak, he thinks. So helpless.

#

Jackie had run with Himura like the devil himself was on their heels. The black vacuum of the forest had stripped the world of all sight and much sound. A snaking root and Himura's body on his shoulders had taken his legs and he'd tumbled into a thicket of bamboo grass, Himura pitching over his head to land hard a couple of feet in front. They had lain in the bamboo grass for an age, Jackie listening and sniffing the air. Then he had levered Himura onto his shoulders again and trudged on.

Jackie had stumbled upon an overhang, a ten-foot high shelf of earth churned from the ground like a solid earthen wave. He had left Himura in the mouth of the overhang, covered with his coat and that of the dead yakuza, and some bush ripped from the dirt. He needed to establish Harbour Base, a trianglular camp.

In the Rangers, three fire teams would cover approaches. In a perfect world, they would rotate to afford rest for each man. They would rig trip-flares, establish communications if required. In a perfect world, he wouldn't have moved Himura with a sucking chest wound without medical support, let alone lugged the man through the forest. But in a perfect world, he'd be in a restaurant with his friend and his friend's daughter, or on a sight-seeing tour, or catching a show in Sapporo.

Instead, Jackie sets to work. He pads toward the clearing, minimising noise, but stops well short of the treeline. He works by touch and finds the cufflinks he took from the dead yakuza back at the creek. The plastic tube separates in the centre and he tips the cufflinks out and checks the pistol. He releases the fifteen-round magazine. Five bullets left. With the tactical knife, he works at the bottom of one half of the cufflinks tube, carving a small hole, and straightens the clasp of a cufflink. He inserts it into the bottom of the tube. He takes a bullet and slots it down the tube, primer first so the bottom of the round rests on the point of the cufflink clasp. Repeating the process, he places the two makeshift cartridge charges on the ground. Next, the wallet. He takes a credit card and flexes the plastic between his fingers, then fashions a rough, angled tube from the card around another cartridge. Taking a couple of condoms, he ties them tightly around the makeshift tube to maintain its shape, then ties another, flat credit card across the bottom. He breaks the end off the necklace charm and drops it in the tube, followed by the bullet, primer-down. He ties flat cash cards to the bottom of the other two charges with condoms, then slots the magazine with the last two rounds home in the handgun grip and creeps into the trees.

He checks himself when he snaps some wood or rustles some grass, too eager to lay the charges. He stays in the shadows, avoiding moonlight but plotting courses, points of entry to the forest and hypothetical paths to their hiding place in the overhang. It's ridiculous, needle-in-a-haystack. Three cobbled-together cartridge charges to cover the entire camp perimeter and at least seven clear routes to the overhang. Never mind if Ishikawa feels ambitious and tries clambering over some of the sturdier undergrowth. Jackie shakes his head and plants the charges at intervals, pushing the card bases into patches of hard dirt with less give in the ground, and shoring the sides with small stones. With luck, a smaller animal won't set the charges off. With luck, Ishikawa and his man won't notice the charge in the ground if they come prowling. With luck, Ishikawa and his man won't come anywhere near Jackie and Himura at all.

Jackie threads his way back to the overhang, the pistol in a two-handed grip. Himura lies in the narrow crack in the centre. Jackie checks the sucking wound and throws the bloodied moss-packed condom to the side. He pulls the lining from the pockets of the dead yakuza's coat and sets them on the ground. Then Jackie unzips his jeans and pulls himself out into the cold night air.

Himura rasps, 'No!'

'I've got to try and control the air leak,' whispers Jackie, furious at the shock of Himura's voice. 'I need something wet to plug the wound. And shut up.'

He pisses, the patter of his water on the lining, grass and dirt below too loud for his liking.

Himura again says, 'No.' His protest is weaker.

Jackie says, 'You got a water bottle? I didn't think so.'

'Your piss is dirty.'

'The first problem is the wound and the air leak. If you survive tonight we'll worry about infection.'

Judging by the heat of the yakuza's face it may too late. Himura is burning up.

Finished, Jackie packs the wound with piss-soaked lining and grass. The ammonia smell of urine is a problem, so Jackie shifts the covering coat, smothering the odour as best he can, then rubs soil over his hands. The cold is seeping through his bones now, fatigue dragging his body down. He pulls a tangle of dried wood and bamboo grass with him and edges into the crevice. Jackie lies up close to Himura, shuffling until his back is pressing against the man's front, wrapping the man's arms around him. Then he pulls the grass and wood in front of him, as a makeshift camouflage. They spoon, Himura behind, Jackie facing out to the forest. The yakuza squirms.

'Body heat,' spits Jackie. 'Stop moving.'

They lie in silence. Himura's emerging fever warms Jackie through his layers and his eyelids flicker, losing focus as they stare at the black forest.

He drifts and dozes.

Somewhere deep, like under the sea, he swims with Fujiko Maki. They encircle one another. Their limbs brush, Jackie feeling the ripple of her legs pass an inch from his. Then their mouths join. Her tongue is in his mouth, his body enters her. He hears Fujiko call his name.

'Jackie San.'

The voice is a smooth hiss. Not Fujiko. A snake?

'Jackie.'

He swims up from the depths, the voice clear – Himura. He gives himself an inward bollocking for sleeping.

'Jackie.'

'Be quiet.'

'I lost my phone.'

'Shut the fuck up like a good wee boy and maybe Santa will bring you another.'

The mobile would have had its uses. It must have fallen out of Himura's pocket as he carried him through the forest, or dragged him along the dirt in the dark.

Himura says, 'The dead cop, Rei Miyamoto. The DNA. What does it mean: twenty-five percent match?'

'It means the killer is Miyamoto's half-sibling.'

'Half-what?'

'Half-brother-or-sister.'

The quiet grind of Himura's jaw working sets Jackie's teeth on edge. He's too tired to hush the man. They're so close to one another they're almost breathing their words.

Somewhere, a bird fusses in a tree.

Himura whispers, his voice thick, 'When Genda called, just before Ishikawa came ...'

'Just before you tried to kill me.'

'So, so.'

He waits for Himura to continue. Seconds pass and he thinks the man might be slipping away.

Then Himura gulps hard as if forcing something down his gullet and says, 'The file the OCB took in their raid on our office was about Miyamoto.' The yakuza oyabun sounds like every breath is a small victory. He takes a moment, then wheezes, 'Not Rei Miyamoto. His brother.'

'Yuji?'

'You know him?'

'Not really.'

'It seems we were blackmailing Yuji Miyamoto. He had gambling debts with us, then came to our fetish clubs. We began extorting money from him. Typical operation.'

'And Rei Miyamoto?'

'Inaba approached him.' Himura gasps, sighs. 'When the OCB

shithead realised we had our hooks in his brother, he had Goro bury the file – but Inaba kept a copy in a hidden safe in our office across the river.'

'And he didn't tell you.'

'Of course. He's a cock-sucking rat. Anyway ...' Himura, rustling up a measure of dignity, sniffs. 'I wouldn't know who the fuck Yuji Miyamoto is. Just another mark; I had bigger things to worry about.'

'So Rei Miyamoto was trying to break your gang and save his brother.'

'Save himself.'

Something moves in the black ahead, a twig cracking. Jackie hisses for Himura to shut up. He points the pistol at the darkness. Small feet scamper away. He waits for seconds, then relaxes.

'Save himself, you said?'

'Yes. You are right, Rei and Yuji Miyamoto had the same father. Different mothers. In the blackmail scam we had dug into Yuji's background. His mother had committed suicide. She was burakumin.'

Something small scurries nearby.

'Many Japanese think they're scum,' says Himura. 'Not human. The unclean people. Butchers, undertakers. The lowest class in Japan.'

'Sounds like a bullshit caste system to me.'

'Yakuza don't care. But the cops? Professional death for Rei Miyamoto. If the cop's superiors had discovered he shared blood with a buraku, he'd have been kicked out of the police. Career over.'

'And I thought we Irish loved our bigotry.'

Himura says, 'The brother, Yuji, had already been kicked out of Kamakura because of his blood.'

'Kamakura?'

Himura chokes and shoves his face in Jackie's back to muffle a cough. They both wait for a moment. Reassured by the silence, Himura says, 'A town near Tokyo, on the coast. It has many tem –'

'I know,' spits Jackie. He thinks of Yuji Miyamoto, the weight of the world on his shoulders, disillusioned by acts of violence in Kamakura while he trains for the priesthood. Or, Yuji Miyamoto, sociopath, indulging his predilection for violence while studying Shintoism. Kicked out of the religion upon the discovery of his ancestry, the shame of his tainted lineage. Was Yuji's story in the Suskino izakaya more than a confession of apostasy?

The shy, courteous, fine-boned young man who Jackie had sat and drunk, and eaten and chatted with: could he really have murdered two policemen?

Himura, voice slurring, says, 'The police in Sapporo are looking for you, too.'

Good luck to them, thinks Jackie, fat lot of good that does me now. They'll not find me out here.

He hisses, 'Where's Inaba keeping my friends?'

But Himura is still.

Jackie listens to the silence. A greater silence than before. A total absence of sound. The slivers of the trees, the clearing beyond, are darkening. An air of secrecy settles.

Then it snows.

Chapter 33

It's colder. Ian lifts a rough blanket draped over the back of the sofa and offers it to his daughter but Megan refuses with an irritated shrug. She's angry. A mobile phone with no battery, defeat snatched from the jaws of victory. She's never been much cop at concealing her feelings. How her very public temper went down with Yuji, Ian can't imagine.

At least, each time she whispers in English, he locks the three Japanese lads out of the mix and scores a small monolingual success. He could see Inaba looking at them as Megan told him about the batteryless phone. Had Ian spoken the language, there'd have been no pretext for their not speaking Japanese. He had felt a little less lost after the secret parlay. Paula, his ex, would have gloated. Typical Ian, making a virtue of his failings, a strength of his weaknesses.

Paula. Never cut out to be an army wife. Then again, Ian had never been cut out to be a soldier. Things had been okay between them until Megan came along. In the service, he had caught a glimpse of the violence man is capable of, so Ian had been too protective of Megan and neglected Paula. He'd driven a wedge into the marriage that ended with divorce. Paula's jealousy of Megan had angered him. He'd railed at her barbs that he'd left her for another woman – that that woman was his daughter. But she was right. He had given Megan so much of himself, there'd been nothing left for his wife.

Kenta still sits against the wall with the knife loose in his hand.

Jun paces again, smoking, worrying.

Jun has tried again and again to coax a phone number from Inaba and contact the cops himself. Inaba won't budge. Two hours

303

have passed. Two more until the police expect Inaba to call in. As it stands, Inaba can't drive to a pay phone in his condition. What should Jun do? He can't go with Inaba and leave Kenta with the foreigners. His brother is too unstable. Would they all have to go, the foreigners secured and blindfolded then led to the car? Too risky. Ian San and Megan Chan could try to run. They could cry out for help from the car.

Jun's head hurts. His chest feels thick and clogged. He's smoking too much. He wants someone else to take control, to make his choices for him. Like it's always been.

Megan watches him.

Frustration flushes her face. Her fear has boiled over into anger. She despises this filthy cabin with its oppressive walls, its stink of rot and damp, its dismal light. This bloody thug and his brother. Inaba, the wolf in sheep's clothing with his hard-man-with-a-soft-side bull-shit: a caring father who risks it all for his daughter, then beats his friend when his drug-addicted brother steps out of line. Nothing more than a cruel bully. His little girl is better off without him.

If she and her dad could get Inaba alone, away from Jun and Kenta, they could force him to hand over his phone, wherever it is. He is weak and Megan's blood is up. They could hurt him. She could use his wounds. She is sure, bitter and furious, she could summon the strength. If they could just get rid of the brothers. Her father touches her shoulder again and she jerks her body away with a loud tut. Inaba stares. A tut is a social taboo in Japan and a sign of great contempt. She knows the sanctimonious yakuza asshole is shocked at her disrespect toward her father.

'Love,' says Ian Sparrow, 'when I move, persuade that miserable bugger next to you to give you what you need.'

Her temper drains with the blood from her cheeks. 'Dad?' she says.

'Simple,' says her father. 'We need to distract the brothers grim. We know they won't kill us because they need us. I'll throw a fit, attack the blonde one and keep them both busy ...'

'No.'

'… while you persuade the leader to give us what's needed.'

'No, Dad. They're too unpredictable, especially the blonde. And what if this one plays up? We could both get hurt. Badly.'

'It's the only option, love. We don't have time. That chancer on the sofa can't guarantee the police will give him what he wants and blondie over there is getting more unstable by the minute.'

Kenta is staring at the floor. Jun, wrapped up in his own troubled thoughts. But Inaba is watching the father and daughter from the corner of his eye.

Megan whispers, 'These men could really hurt you, Dad. If you're out of it – or worse – do you really want me to be alone with them?'

'I've weighed it up. I'm no hero, Megan, but we need the phone. If he even has one. And the bandaged one likes me. I think he'll try to protect me if blondie goes mad.' He shifts forward a fraction on his arse. Inaba withdraws into the sofa an inch.

And there it is. Megan spots it.

They'd rolled Inaba's jacket up and placed it under his head for a makeshift pillow while Ian stitched him back up. Now the jacket is next to Inaba on the sofa. A clear imprint is visible under the fabric in the side pocket, stretched as Inaba shifted position. A small, flat tablet.

A mobile phone.

Megan's face turns scarlet again, burning now with a spike of excitement. She leans in to her father and whispers, 'It's in his jacket pocket, on the sofa.' Ian Sparrow, uncomprehending, shakes his head at her before she hisses, 'The mobile.' Her eyes flit from her father's face to the jacket. His eyes go wide with un-derstanding.

Then he frowns as his daughter scowls.

The phone is an arm's length away and yet completely out of reach. Megan's eyes well and she breathes deep to stem the tide. She sniffs. How much more can she take – the constant surge and shift of emotions – fear, anger, hope, dismay and then rage again?

The tumult inside rushes up her throat, demands release. She lets fly an explosive sob.

Jun stops pacing.

Megan is off the sofa before her father can raise a hand and she flies at Kenta, screaming, her head thrust forward like a battering ram. She throws her foot back and launches it into the Kenta's thigh as he cringes. She kicks him again, and again, tears blurring her vision, reason gone. Jun stares for a beat more then slaps her hard across the back of her head. She barely feels it, slings another kick at Kenta then turns on Jun. Jun flinches at the sight of her hot, tear streaked face, her searing eyes, her wrenched mouth. She shrieks in a language no one can understand and punches him in the face, her knuckle smashing off his cheek with a flat slap, his head snapping back on reflex.

Her slaps her hard across her face. Her head whips to the side.

Ian Sparrow roars, 'No!' as Jun raises his hand to strike her again. Megan steps closer, railing at him with spittle-flecked nonsense-screams. She punches him again, her fist glancing off his right ear. Jun hears Ian Sparrow's voice somewhere, dim, as his anger swells and he rises on the balls of his feet, knuckles white.

Shit! thinks Ian. *He'll kill her!*

He wants to pull Megan away, take the kicking himself, but his body rebels with a terrible inertia. He watches Kenta move as Jun squares up. Megan's wailing seems muted like Ian is underwater. His body is clay. He despises his fear.

Move, you useless bastard! Move, protect your daughter!

Kenta unfurls himself and begins levering himself up from the floor on the palms of his hands. He stands with his hands on his knees for a moment, catching his breath as Megan, her back to him, batters at his brother.

Ian sees Kenta cock his head to the side, observing this woman beat on Jun, and smile.

Please, thinks Ian. *Please don't hurt my little girl.*

Jun seems to shrink as his brother grows in strength and a terrible resolve. His arms drop to his sides. He knows the girl is done. His brother will beat her senseless. He lowers his head and takes her small fists on his head, his chest.

Ian roars, 'No!' and stands with a sudden fury – *No! Not my daughter! Not my Megan! Get away from her you fucking animals!* His face is terrible, adrenaline blitzing fear, banishing reason and the years.

Megan screams.

He hears it now. Not nonsense, not a mad shriek. A word – 'Phone!'

Then Goro Inaba grasps at Ian Sparrow's arm and hauls himself from the sofa, trailing the jacket, wedging it in the crack between the seat cushions. He throws himself at Megan as Kenta moves in. She slaps at his arms but Inaba puts himself between the girl and Kenta. He catches one of Megan's wrists as Kenta throws a right, slamming his fist into Inaba's ear, a dull slap of knuckle on cartilege.

Ian sits heavily on the sofa.

Kenta throws another punch, glancing off Inaba's shoulder. He sends a left into Inaba's back, Inaba spasming, grunting.

Megan screams again.

Jun throws out an arm to block his brother's next punch as Ian fumbles on the sofa. Ian's fingers seem thick and huge, his arm hollow with fear. One look, one glance as he rummages for the phone and he and Megan are sunk.

Megan's foot lashes out at Kenta, goading him, as Inaba slings his arms around her waist and Jun calls out, 'Oi! Oi! Oi!'

Then Ian feels the slim plastic surface of the mobile, snug between the seat cushions. The phone slipped from the jacket pocket as Inaba stood. He eases it from the cushions as Jun grabs at Kenta. Inaba is staring at Megan, a wildcat thrashing in his arms. The phone comes free. Ian slips it under his arse.

Inaba looks to him, imploring – *Do something with your fucking daughter!*

Megan sees, grabs at Inaba's tousled hair to distract him. He grits his teeth and clutches her wrist. Ian sits forward, keeps the mobile snug to his leg and slips it into his hip pocket. He stands again and pulls his shirt down to cover his arse.

Inaba says, 'Stop!'

Ian yells, 'Megan, I've got it!'

She still writhes in Inaba's grip.

'I've got it!' screams Ian, his voice cracking. He runs forward and grabs her shoulder. 'Megan!'

Inaba catches a slap from Megan across his face. He bellows a stream of furious Japanese, and raises his fist. Ian Sparrow punches him.

The blow was an instinct, the dull crack seeming to resonate around the room. Kenta and Jun stop. Inaba puts a hand to his reddened face. Megan freezes. Her eyes focus on her father, she feels his gentle strength as he takes hold of her wrist, catches his scent. The scent of bedtime stories, morning hugs. Her features, tight with rage, open.

'It's okay, Megan,' says Ian. 'I got it.'

Jun, uncomprehending, says, 'Listen to your father,' in Japanese.

Kenta licks his lips.

Inaba places a gentle hand on Ian's shoulder, then steps back and bows.

He says, 'Excuse me.'

Ian returns the bow. Megan throws her arms around her father and sobs. He soaks in her warmth, her strength and courage.

Kenta hawks up a gob of phlegm and spits it on the floor. He sits, his back against the wall.

Jun rubs his chin. Then his eyes. He shuffles to the connecting door. There should be blankets somewhere. Maybe an old oil heater.

It is colder still. Thin wisps of breath cloud faces for fleeting seconds.

There is a throb in Megan's head and a red welt on her cheek where Jun belted her. And Inaba's mobile phone lies snug in Ian Sparrow's pocket.

A short time later, she, her father and Inaba are asleep.

Chapter 34

Himura dies sometime in the coldest hour as dawn cracks the night sky.

Jackie had slept, exhaustion dragging him down into a deep and dreamless slumber. He had woken in the freezing darkness. Himura was taking watery, rattling breaths, each threatening to be his last. The darkness began to shift, objects close by taking firmer shape. Jackie rose slowly, his body aching, and went for a short scout. The snowfall had not been heavy, but enough to have thrown a film of delicate white over the open ground. When dawn broke, it would increase the risk of being spotted in their dark clothes.

As he squirmed back into the hide, the sky was casting off the night. Himura whispered, his voice clotted with mucus, 'My sister will be alone.'

Jackie settled back, his spine finding the man's belly.

'Do you hear me? I am going to die and Fujiko will be alone.'

Jackie said, 'We're all alone in the end.'

A wheezing laugh. 'You are a cynical bastard.'

'Where are my friends?'

Himura was quiet for a time.

Then, 'The cabin is near the spa town at Toya. Go to Mount Usu, to the northwest slope. You will see the Lake and the spa town below. Over half a kilometre or so above the town is a large hole in the earth on the slope, like a bowl. Full of water.'

'A crater.'

'Okay, a crater.' Himura's voice tightens in pain. 'The cabin is near the crater. There is an area surrounded by a fence. Volcano damage. The cabin is there.'

Jackie was quiet, giving the man time to get the information out.

Must be shite, he thought, breathing your last in another language to some gobshite screwed your sister.

Himura said in a laboured wheeze, 'Be careful. There is boiling steam on Usu. Poisonous.'

'Okay.'

Silence again. They lay together like lovers as the wan light clawed back the trees from the dark, the undergrowth revealing patches of dark dirt and bush where birch, pine or spruce had shielded the ground from the snow. Their breath seeped into the freezing air as the low sun blinded them, Jackie burrowing further back, pressing his body against Himura, desperate to withdraw from the light and steal the last heat from the man before they had to move again.

Funny, he thought. This felt more intimate than he had been with Fujiko, for all their grasping passion. He remembered the sleek, soft body, her wolfish grin as they fucked.

Himura never spoke again. The man passed with the last shadows of night.

Now, the sun still climbs the pallid sky.

Jackie strips Himura's body of its second coat. He looks at the death mask, the notched, black eyes two narrow schisms in the brutal face. A couple of crooked teeth have slipped from parted lips. For what it is worth, Jackie whispers the Lord's Prayer.

Himura had lived with death as an occupational hazard. He was a violent criminal, a manipulator, a predator and a parasite. No need to add that one to my ledger, thinks Jackie. But he can't shake a hollowness in his belly. Dawn blues, perhaps, but more likely, Himura was another exemplar of Jackie's great flaw. One day, maybe, a fatal flaw.

Christ, he thinks, I do love a lost cause.

The moment Jackie saw that sucking chest wound, it had become somehow crucial to keep the bastard alive.

A "cynical bastard", that was what Himura had called him. But Jackie was no cynic: he was a dreamer. The cynicism was an act, a front to offset his guilt at the violence of his life; the desperate pursuit of lost causes was a counterbalance to that violence.

Yet his words come back to him as the sun sears his eyes with cold autumn light. *We're all alone in the end.*

#

It disturbed Ishikawa, dozing in the dirt. While the forests of Japan's largest island, Honshu, were imbued with the very fabric of the nation's great religion, Shinto, the northern territories seemed a godless wilderness.

Dawn had revealed the huge, sweeping terrain of Hokkaido.

Ishikawa despised it. He despised it for its majesty, for its harsh beauty, its refusal to be tamed by the people of Japan.

He and his man had checked the weapons and eaten a protein bar each then the soldier had scouted forward, his sweater pulled over his nose to conceal his clouded breath.

Ishikawa sits awaiting the soldier's return.

He gazes at the high plateau of the clearing, sloping gently down, dusted white with snow. In the distance, the forest slings its arms wide around the azure water of Lake Toya, a hump-backed island squatting in its centre. To the south, on Ishikawa's left, sits the high, bald knuckle of Mount Usu, a sliver of steam seeping from its crater ten kilometres away.

Ishikawa shudders. The pain in his neck slashes his nerves, as though the gaijin where stabbing him over and over with needles of bamboo. But he is strong, his soldier fit. They are rested and well armed. They are ready.

A snap of dry wood and his soldier is there, crouching by his side.

'I found them. They're under some broken ground, over there.' He points to the trees around the curve of the clearing. 'About forty metres inside the trees. You can see a cloud of breath.'

'Jya,' grunts Ishikawa, 'let's go and finish them.'

#

Jackie screws his eyes shut then squints again at the treeline. He's sure he caught movement, a dark form flitting between the birch. It looked human, the size and shape all wrong for an animal. Now, as he tries to discriminate trunk and bush and branch from the tangle of forest debris and peppering of snow, he sees nothing.

Has the figure retreated or is it lying in wait out there?

Jackie's mother used to say, never kick 'til you're spurred. God love her, he doubts she would stand by that old Ulster proverb in the here and now. He reaches for the combat knife. Time for a little makeshift camouflage. Then he'll scout, taking a wide arc on the right to the treeline and work his way along back to the spot he's been staring at for a couple of minutes. He shuffles forward, Himura still lying in state in the crack of the overhang, until he can kneel with his hands on the dirt. He hauls Himura's coat over his own against the cold; then, feeling it constrict him, he drapes it over his shoulders and ties it around his neck with the drawstring in the collar.

The shot is like a handclap, followed by a panicked scream.

There are short shrieks and a rustle of fallen leaves and tangled grass. Jackie feels a small, warm surge of satisfaction. Thanks be to the good Lord above, he thinks, that one yakuza killer trod on one of the three cartridge charges Jackie had planted in the dark. That the gangster's foot fell solid on the bullet. That the tube casing held the bullet upright in the hard ground with its makeshift base, that the pressure of the yakuza's boot forced the bullet onto the metal at the charge's base igniting the primer, firing the charge into the bastard's foot.

The shrieking subsides to a whimper. Jackie catches vague movement. Then the shape of two men comes into focus. One is crouched. The other is standing rooted to the spot. The crouched figure begins moving. Forty yards or more away, but closing in. Then the other moves too. Lurching, awkward but moving.

Shite! Wounded but mobile. Shite!

Jackie's breath, fogging in front of his face, clouds the figures for a moment.

His breath, like a fucking signal fire leading them straight to his position.

Chapter 35

Idiot, thinks Ishikawa.

He and his soldier had covered a few yards when there had been the crack of a shot, a small spray of snow billowing like confetti, and the soldier began screaming.

Ishikawa creeps to him. The soldier is shot through the foot: a booby-trap. Shoe leather and woollen sock is shredded. Crimson blood splatters the snow.

'Shut up! I'll shoot you myself if you don't shut up!' Each word is like a skewer of pain in Ishikawa's neck, fuelling his anger. He raises the revolver.

The screaming shortens to high-pitched gasps. Then the man offers a shallow bow. 'I am sorry.'

'Can you move?'

'I think so.' The wounded man takes a faltering step. 'Slowly, but yes.'

The weak-willed little shit wipes a tear away. A fucking tear. The shame.

They move forward again. They see the fog of breath seeping from the dark overhang up ahead, like the steam of Mount Usu's crater. The soldier looks to his superior, Ishikawa in complete command now. He points ahead and they creep closer. Ishikawa dodges behind trees, catching glimpses of their target's breath. Fifteen metres from the overhang of earth, sunlight crawls into the crevice. They see a body. The fog of breath is thinning, a delicate ribbon now.

Perhaps Himura and the gaijin are breathing shallowly. Perhaps they are too cold and exhausted to move. Perhaps they are near death.

The soldier hunches over, gripping his pistol two-handed, slack-jawed.

Ishikawa gestures to him to approach the overhang.

Move in – kill them!

The soldier nods and takes a faltering step. Ishikawa brings the revolver level with his waist.

That's it, you imbecile. Draw them out. If you're good for nothing else, you'll do as bait.

Ishikawa takes aim at a point just beyond and to the right of his man.

His head goes berserk, flung forward with a sudden violence. All is white noise and flickering snatches of vision – the forest, the crying soldier, the dark overhang, the white speckled earth. A voice deep within him screams, bawling that something is wrong, that his neck feels torn and broken. He is on his knees – When? How? – and someone is next to him. Ishikawa sees boots caked with dirt. Ragged dark jeans, thick streaks of blood tinged with soil on the legs, the crotch. A filthy coat. A strong, callous face, fouled with earth, steam rising between drawn lips and clenched teeth. A demon. The large hands slathered in muck and blood, gripping a semi-automatic handgun, the pistol almost inconsequential in the terrible, controlled ferocity of the devil's stare. Jackie Shaw pulls the trigger a second time and shoots Ishikawa just above the right ear.

#

Jackie watches Ishikawa, transfixed, as the Tokyo yakuza slumps to his knees, head sagging on chest. After seconds that could be minutes he kicks the body onto the ground and scrambles for the man's gun. He drops his empty pistol and grabs the revolver. He drops to a kneeling position and aims at the wounded man still standing near the overhang.

He says, 'Gun!'

The man stares.

Gun, thinks Jackie, what's *gun* in Japanese?

But the man drops his empty pistol and covers his face with his hands. Jackie goes to him, revolver trained on the man's chest. When he reaches the yakuza he picks up the dropped pistol and shoves it in his waistband. He pats the man down and finds a wallet, compass and some small change. He can see Himura's body under the overhang, stomach slit where Jackie had sawed at the flesh, a probing slither of entrails spilling onto the dirt, the steam from the yakuza's insides now dissipated.

Lucky, he thinks. Lucky that the men who hunted him were up all night, tired and disorientated like Jackie. Lucky they were city boys. Lucky the cartridge shell went off, wounding one and distracting both. Lucky Himura had died only a short time ago. Lucky the tactical knife had been sharp enough to tear Himura's belly. Lucky the man had had an infection blazing through his body and his insides were still warm. Lucky the tangle of the forest broke up the plume of steam from Himura's exposed guts to give an illusion of breath and draw them in. Lucky they had been transfixed on the target, fatigue making them slow, allowing him the chance to scout to their left and come in behind them. Lucky that Ishikawa had sent the wounded man ahead, had left himself open and alone to the rear. Jackie had shot Ishikawa through the neck, then in the head. And Jackie's luck has held. The poor bastard in front of him has lost all fight and succumbed to fear, pain and exhaustion. The man's foot is a mess of flayed boot and sock and flesh. He stares at a point behind Jackie. His pupils are dilated and he is gasping for breath. His heart-rate must be up, too.

Jackie knows shock when he sees it. He shudders as the chill fingers of the morning breeze probe the forest.

He could shoot the miserable fucker, put him out of his misery. He just executed Ishikawa, may as well be hung for a sheep as a lamb. It would probably be a mercy, rather than leave the man to die a slow, lonely death out here in the forest. But even in the woods of southern Hokkaido, there could be a homestead or a farm or a road somewhere nearby. The lake is no more than ten miles away, with its spa town and villages. The poor bastard is no threat, wounded and frightened. If the man could ride the shock and keep warm he might make it.

Might not.

Jackie turns the compass in his fingers and shoves it in his pocket. He tosses the wallet and change at the wounded man's feet and steps back on the mulch of leaves, dirt, grass and snow, his gun trained on the yakuza.

The cold gnaws through Jackie's socks and boots. He will be lucky to get through this without frostbite. He thinks of Goro Inaba and the cabin on Usu and reckons he'll be lucky to get through the rest of the day. His boots shuffle as he backs away. His breath whispers in his ears and clouds his vision. Branches sigh in the cold breeze. Wood snaps. The forest settles.

No birds, he thinks. No morning song.

No life in this place now. Himura is dead. Ishikawa is dead. Even the still figure, rooted to the same spot in front of the overhang, seems a feature of the forest now, timeless.

At the edge of the clearing, keeping the revolver on the figure of the last yakuza, Jackie digs out the remaining cartridge traps, shaking the rounds from their tubes into his jacket pocket. When he is finished, the wounded man stands in the same spot. Jackie turns for a moment to see the view, Mount Usu smouldering in the distance. He takes a deep lungful of air, scoops some snow from the grass and eats, the powder freezing on his parched tongue. Then he walks backward down the shallow slope of the open clearing, gun still raised, watching as the scarecrow figure of the wounded man flickers between the trees before the forest consumes the lone, broken survivor of Ishikawa's yakuza hunting party.

Chapter 36

Typical, thinks Megan Sparrow. The moment Jun tires of pacing the room and sits his ass on a chair, her father starts wandering around. He looks at spots of mould on the wall, a grimy picture of an old tea advert hanging by the door and the scattered newspapers on the table.

Bloody men.

How can she concentrate? This is their window of opportunity with Kenta and Inaba gone to contact the police. If they can distract Jun, they might be able to make a call. She will phone Yuji. The police will take too long. They'll put her through various operators, ask too many questions. She and her father don't have time for that. But Yuji can go straight to his brother, if Rei has turned up. If not, Yuji can call the police himself and get things done faster. A native speaker – and native Japanese – will get a smoother ride when they dial 119.

But how to create the opportunity? They have been lucky so far, but Jun has brought a bucket into the cabin living room and left it in the corner. No more solo trips to the toilet.

They thought of overpowering him and making a run for it. Two against one but Jun is a gangster. Violence is a way of life for him and he would apply it with far more skill than either Megan or her dad.

Her father wanders back over to the sofa and sits next to her with a groan.

'What if I just belt him?' whispers Ian Sparrow.

'Then he smacks you back. It would be over in seconds, nowhere near enough time to make a call. And God forbid he takes the knife to you.'

'Thanks for the vote of confidence, love.'

Jun, used to the hushed gabble of English and bored with the broken, torturous attempts at communication with the gaijin father, ignores them. He reads another manga comic, this one about a champion angler.

Ian feels a flush of frustration. He and Megan have Inaba's phone, and yet are no closer to getting the hell out of here. Wherever here is. Ian makes to stand again.

'Daddy, please. Just sit down. I can't think with you pacing.'

Wounded pride is written across his face. Like father, like daughter: an open-bloody-book.

'Sorry, Dad.'

'That's alright, love.'

She nods at Jun, sitting at the table engrossed in his comic. 'Seen any good reading material over there on your travels?'

'It looks like demented hieroglyphics to me.'

She musters a smile.

'Two pages with some English on, though. Some kind of pull-out supplement. Teach yourself the language sort of thing.' He stares at Jun with a grim satisfaction. Now Jun is the outsider, engrossed in his comic and tuning out the foreigners' incomprehensible gabble.

Then Ian says, 'Jesus Christ!'

'Daddy?'

It's ropey, very risky, the idea cobbled together in his tired mind. It might, just, with a sprig of luck, work. They'll have to take five minutes to think things through but it's the best they can do in the time they have. It is a chance, and that's more than they had five minutes ago.

He talks it through with his daughter and something sad and warm settles inside him when he sees a glint in Megan's eyes from way back. When she was just a little girl. When he was the first and last man in her life.

Goro Inaba remembers a meet with Rei Miyamoto on a warm spring morning on the outskirts of the city. Miyamoto had been a quiet man, difficult to read.

The meet was at Makomanai Takino Cemetery and they strolled past the replica Easter Island statues, silhouetted against the white morning sun. Cop and criminal went through the usual order of business. Himura's activity, new Kanto Daichi-kai members, the syndicate's political manoeuvring and the proposed business with the Yamaguchi gumi. These were the early days of their relationship and they shared an acute mutual distrust.

'Do you have any family here?' said Miyamoto, gesturing to the regimented grave markers.

'No.'

'Me neither.'

They stopped while Inaba lit a smoke, his hand cupped around the flame.

'I don't have any family,' he said, 'except my daughter.'

Miyamoto said, 'Everything in Japan is family. Your gang is a family, the cops, every company. The whole damn country is a family.'

Inaba rustled up a snort of agreement.

'If that means we're brothers,' he said, 'I must have got the looks.'

Miyamoto, his mind somewhere else, said, 'But real family is blood.' He repeated the word, savouring the sound, the taste of it. 'Blood.'

As they approached the cemetery's large mock-up of Stonehenge he produced his mobile and introduced Goro Inaba to a snapshot of his brother, Yuji Miyamoto.

The photo was of a delicate-looking young man in jeans and a tight T-shirt standing on a hilltop wiping his glasses. His fine features were squinting against the wind. A whisper of a smile plucked at his mouth. It was a familiar face, like millions of other fragile-looking, shy young men in Japan. Handsome but hesitant with delphic eyes. None of the confident swagger of a rookie cop fresh from training or a young yakuza street thug. There was a lack of self-confidence. Or perhaps, something darker behind the lowered gaze.

Rei Miyamoto revealed that his brother, Yuji Miyamoto, like thousands of other shy young men in Japan, had his vices. Gambling, the wrong kind of women. And voyeurism.

'He's been going to one of your seedier hovels, The Invisible Man Club.' The cop's expression darkened and a sneer of contempt slunk across his face. 'Now he has a girlfriend. A foreigner. British. A pretty girl, smart. Well-mannered for a gaijin. And he is still slinking around Susukino sex clubs.' He shook his head.

Rei Miyamoto established the quid pro quo.

He was protecting Goro Inaba. The police was peppered with cops on the take, feeding information to the yakuza. That meant the criminal syndicates were consistently a step ahead in the game. Which meant that, aside from Rei, only a couple of his immediate superiors in the Organised Crime Bureau knew Goro Inaba was a police informant. Any hope Inaba might have of a new life was dependent upon Rei Miyamoto, his reports and lobbying for his yakuza informant. If Inaba could help Miyamoto to manage some murky, distasteful business regarding his brother, Rei would go to bat, ensuring Inaba San was taken care of and on the fast track to a new life when they had built a prosecutable case on Himura.

Inaba said, 'And you never thought to mention this before?'

'I didn't know you. I needed to get the measure of the man before I could entrust him with the wellbeing of my family. Just as you have, me.'

Inaba had flicked the cigarette at the fake Stonehenge surrounded by the contoured, landscaped grounds of the cemetery with its other replicas – the Easter Island statues and giant Kamakura Buddha – like a macabre themepark. The cop had tutted at the littering before cop and criminal had strolled on along the paths which scythed through the manicured grass and files of grave markers in rigid order.

The memory is wiped with the slash of a branch on the front passenger window. The car veers close to the siding, the wheels spitting gravel before swinging back onto the road proper.

'Fucks' sake!' says Inaba.

'It's under control,' says Kenta. 'Do I take this right?'

'Yeah.'

They are nearing the coast, winding down from the high ground. Jun, marginally in control, had decided to send Kenta with Inaba to check in with the cops. So, despite his detox, Kenta was driving to a small public phone on the coast near the town of Date, remote enough for two battered, seedy looking men to go unnoticed and call from one of the green pay phones next to the sea.

Two banks of thick vegetation crowd either side of the road, Uchiura Bay unseen somewhere below. Inaba catches a sign for a cemetery, Wakou, on the roadside. He wonders how Jun is handling the foreign father and daughter. Quite a pair, the two of them. If Emi grows into as strong and fine a young woman as Megan Sparrow, he will be a proud papa. The girl was brave, throwing herself at Kenta.

Like father, like daughter. He could see Ian Sparrow was an honourable man, straight as a die. Inaba had felt ashamed for the man when he had cowered on the sofa while his daughter brawled in the cabin – but the father showed his strength when he struck Inaba. Foreigners. He is fascinated by them, although he'll never understand them.

It has grown colder with an early snowfall. Inaba had shrugged on Jun's heavier coat, leaving his own jacket on the sofa as it was too light, forgetting his damn mobile was in the pocket. Not that he could have used it with Kenta on hand – but there were a couple of snaps of Emi on the memory card that he looked at in his weaker moments. Now he would make his call from the public phone on the coast and soon agreements would be signed, foreign father and daughter reclaimed by the cops. By this time tomorrow, they would be in the British Embassy in Tokyo. Jun and Kenta would be in custody. And Inaba would be breathing deep of the first day of the rest of his life.

A life with Emi? He could only hope.

He has lost so much time already. So many nights he could have kissed her smooth forehead before she slept. So many days he could have carried her, played with her, rubbed skinned knees. He wasn't there for the Setsubun festival, didn't teach her to use chopsticks or dance Bon Odori. She is only three – there is still plenty of time if he can pull this off. A lifetime.

#

'Macho Monkey?'

'It's just a pet name. His name means masculine in Japanese and he was born in the Year of the Monkey, okay?'

'And you're his Pooch Pearl.'

'Megan means pearl. I was born in the Year of the Dog.'

'As that abomination on your shoulder reminds me.'

'Now isn't the time for a discussion about my tattoo, Dad.'

Ian Sparrow smiles as he glances over to the table and the bored yakuza leafing through his comic. Jun is still zoned out, all the better considering what they are about to try.

The mobile is flat on the sofa seat cushion, screen up, behind Ian. Megan has kept up an inane conversation with her father while he keeps watch, slipping a hand behind her dad's rear end as she turned on the phone, then the location function, and keyed in Yuji's number on the screen. Now all she need do is hit call and start talking.

Not so easy-peasy-Japanesy, thinks Ian.

It was his idea to make the call like this, Megan slouched back on the sofa, speaking one way. It occurred to Ian that his ex-wife was right. Paula had always said he made a virtue of his failings.

He couldn't speak Japanese. But Jun couldn't speak English. So, why not make the call to Yuji, who was bilingual, while sitting in the room with the yakuza? Megan could give her boyfriend the information needed to contact Rei Miyamoto, if he had turned up, or the cop-shop in central Sapporo, if not. Help would come and this would all be over. With the location function on Inaba's mobile, the phone could be traced.

But, ignorant of English as Jun was, they couldn't risk using Yuji's name for danger of pricking the yakuza's interest, so Megan had decided on trying their pet names for one another, Macho Monkey and Pooch Pearl. Yuji should recognise the call was from her straight away. The only problem would be if Yuji spoke out of turn. Megan would have to blurt out the facts fast and shut him up from the off somehow. His voice, tiny as it would be, might be heard by Jun. Or Yuji might miss details as he spoke over Megan. But it was a necessary risk. This was their chance to take the initiative and actually do something about their imprisonment. It wasn't a matter of repercussions. They'd turned stir crazy just enough to throw caution to the wind and give it this one shot.

'And you think he'll be oblivious to what you say?' says Ian, nodding toward Jun.

'Yes. He might wonder why I'm gabbing on, but I'll keep it as short as I can. So long as he doesn't suspect there's something behind you on the sofa, I think we'll be okay.'

'Yeah.'

'And stop whispering, Dad. He will think something's up if I suddenly start talking in my normal voice after we've been mumbling to each other like a couple of kids in class.'

'Yes.'

'It'll be okay, Daddy.'

A bright summer's day flashes through his mind. A tumble. A skinned knee. Ian soothing, stroking hair. Reassuring. Megan is looking at him with a crystalline truth in her eyes – *I believe you, Daddy. I believe IN you, Daddy.*

He looks at her now, a strong, capable, willful young woman, and smiles.

'You're right: it will be okay,' he says. 'Do your thing, Pooch Pearl.'

Megan slouches on the sofa. They watch Jun as she reaches behind her father, touches the mobile screen to wake it up then taps the dial key. The tone is almost inaudible but Ian blethers something about the cold in the cabin anyway, covering as best he can. Jun turns the page, glancing at the sofa before pulling the comic close to his face and studying the panels.

Seconds pass. Jun licks his lips.

The dial tone is replaced by a tiny, twittering female voice.

Jun scratches his head.

Megan kills the voice message recording.

Jun coughs and looks to Ian and Megan.

'Everything okay?' he says.

'Fine,' says Megan.

He looks at her long and hard.

Megan feels her cheeks flush and her father fidget beside her.

Jun clicks his tongue and goes back to his comic. Terrible posture, he thinks, the girl slouching like that. Japanese women would never sit so slovenly.

Shit! thinks Megan. She didn't even consider that Yuji might not pick up. He wouldn't recognise the number they're calling from. He could be at work or at home with his family if Rei is still missing. He could be out searching for her if he went to her flat or tried calling her in the last day or two.

Jun takes a gulp of breath and drops the comic on the table as though about to speak.

Ian Sparrow clears his throat.

Then Jun yawns, long and loud, and rubs at his eyes. He takes a drink and leans back in his chair, staring at the ceiling.

'Are you hungry?' he says to Megan in Japanese.

'No,' says Megan.

'Thirsty?'

Ian and Megan gape.

'What?' says Jun, self-conscious. 'You want to piss?'

'Thanks, no,' says Megan. 'We're just tired. Sorry, didn't mean to stare.'

Jun stands and stretches. He bends backwards, his face looking at the ceiling.

The sense of anticipation is like a physical entity to Ian. 'Another crack?' he says.

Megan hits dial.

The barely audible chirrup of the dial tone kicks in again and Ian begins relating a football match from years ago, chattering to drown the sound.

Megan begins drawing her legs up on the sofa, tucking them under her. Jun sighs and tuts.

How can I concentrate on my reading with these two gabbing and fidgeting? thinks Jun. He puts the comic down as the dial tone ends.

Ian and Megan freeze. The message service recording will start. Jun will hear. The plan will be scuppered.

The sing-song female voice on the messaging service trills. Jun knocks his drink over and swears – 'Shit!' – drowning out the spiel. Megan kills the call.

Jun fishes in his pockets for tissues to mop up.

Megan says, 'Go and help him, Dad. I'll call again and leave a message. It's the best we can do. He's busy and I can say what needs to be said without interruption.'

'We don't know if your friend will hear the bloody phone message.'

'Like I said, it's the best we can do.'

Jun begins wiping the spilled drink with newspaper. Ian, heart beating a tattoo on his ribcage, stands as Megan taps dial. He takes a couple of steps before Jun turns on him.

The yakuza says, 'Sit down!' in Japanese.

Megan, feet on the sofa, lies on her right side, propping her head up with her right hand and shielding the mobile, now half an arm's length from her mouth, with her left arm.

'I can help,' says Ian.

Megan's finger hovers over the dial key.

'Megan Chan,' says Jun, bent over the table, glaring at her. 'I don't understand your father. Tell him to sit down.'

'He wants to help.'

'I'm fine. Tell him to sit down.'

Ian, standing in no man's land, takes another step. Jun straightens, his rangy body tensing. His fist closes tight around the sodden paper.

'Tell your father to sit down for his own good,' he says.

Megan shifts her finger a fraction and punches keys. The tone kicks in. She says, 'Sit down, Dad.'

Ian, confused by the exchange in Japanese, says, 'but, I – '

'Sit down, Dad. Please.'

Two rings.

Jun drops the towel on the tabletop.

'Daddy!'

Ian raises his hands, palms up, and retraces his steps.

The fourth ring. A click.

Jun stares at Megan. He shakes his head. The gaijin girl won't even move for her father to retake his seat. *A disgrace!* But it isn't his place to reprimand the girl. That would shame her father even more.

The chirping voice begins.

'Sit at the end of the sofa, by my head, Dad. Recite a poem, anything.'

Ian moves to the end of the sofa, stumbling through a limerick he half-remembers. Megan places her palm over the mobile, muffling the message.

Jun snatches the towel again.

The voice mail message ends.

Ian Sparrow collapses onto the sofa as the voice recording beep sounds.

Silence.

Megan stares at Jun. Ian stares at Jun.

Jun mutters as he wipes the newsprint over the table, boring a hole through the wood with furious eyes.

'Macho Monkey, this is Pooch Pearl – '

It takes Ian a moment to realise his own daughter is speaking. He hears the creak of the table, the sound of paper on wet pine as Jun works the towel. He watches the yakuza immersed in the task of cleaning his mess and remembers something Jackie said about the Japanese. How, when they set their minds to a task, they do it right. He listens to Megan, her tone conversational: 'This is Pooch Pearl ... location is on ... track this call ... held by three men ... hoodlums ...' – Jun shakes his head and pushes a stack of newspaper to the side – '...tell someone ... send help ... alone ... please ... need help ... Pooch Pearl ...'

Then silence.

How long has passed? Ten seconds? Less?

Megan sits up.

Jun strides across the room and throws the sodden paper in a bin by the door.

Ian grabs the mobile and shoves it in his hip pocket again. He looks at Megan. Megan turns to her father. They both manage a hushed laugh as Jun stares at them in bafflement, then lifts his comic again.

Chapter 37

A Smith and Wesson revolver, Combat Magnum. Six cylinders, only five of them snug with a .367 round. It could punch a big hole but you better make sure you hit your target, make it count, when you don't have a fast reload to hand. Jackie feels the weight of the gun as he clambers through forest, striking south for Mount Usu.

He has two more cartridges in his pocket, useless without a weapon to fire them.

The pistol he took from the last, shellshocked yakuza is a Glock. It has four rounds in the magazine and lies in his jacket pocket.

Nine shots and the tactical knife. Jackie reaches with his left hand and pulls the knife from his jeans pocket, unfolding it, checking it. He cleaned the blade but there are still a couple of flecks of Himura's dried blood on the steel.

The trees thin and a fluttering bird bothers the leaves overhead. He catches a glimpse of Mount Usu, miles away over bastard terrain, the swollen, rocky grey boil of its peak jutting through the forest-clad slope.

Mount Doom, thinks Jackie. Where's Ian McKellan when you need him? This is huge, sprawling land hammered by nature's brute enforcers, volcano and earthquake, scars hidden under a green fleece of forest. The dusting of snow is sparse on the lower ground around the lake, thickest on the upper slopes and non-existent around the scalded peak of Usu and its crater.

He checks the watch and tries to calculate the time back home.

He believes Ian and Megan are alive.

But if Jackie finds the cabin, what then?

He mulls over Himura's description of the place. If he's careful, he could be on top of them before they know it. Nine shots. Enough to put an end to this and stop the three rogue yakuza holding his friends. He doesn't want to pull the trigger but, God help him, he'll drop the bastards in a heartbeat if he has to.

Dead or alive, eh Jackie?

Dead: Rei Miyamoto.

Dead: Himura.

Jackie pinches the bridge of his nose. He had known the moment he saw the wound that Reizo Himura had next to no chance, but he'd had to try. Now Himura is dead and it stings.

He pulls the coat tighter and hears something rip. He rummages through pockets, tutting and fussing before his fingers grasp a slim manila envelope. Pulling it from the inner pocket of Himura's coat, he recognises the pale pastel colour, the size, the shape. He sees it again in Fujiko Maki's fingers and smells the heady scent of her skin. Hears the small, tight noises she made as they rocked on the sofa. He wonders where she is now. He wants to touch her. Against his better judgement, he could love her, given the chance. He's ready to love someone again.

But, Fujiko, your brother was an arsehole. Stubborn edjit had your sketch on him the whole time.

Jackie opens the envelope and takes a moment before pulling the paper from inside, like he's announcing the best actor category.

And the award for most deranged homicidal maniac goes to …

It's no surprise. The DNA result had already told the story. But he feels a jolt of something cold streak through his belly when he looks at the drawing of Yuji Miyamoto. To see the delicate young man on the page, like a police artist's impression, was a second's disconnect from reality. He studies the sketch. Vacant eyes stare back at Jackie. He remembers Yuji's deferential tone, his considered, impeccable manners. At the time it seemed charming, almost naive; now it looks like calculation. Jackie shakes his head at the thought of the young man butchering two police.

Fucking Himura, he thinks. If he'd shown me this picture back in Sapporo, things could have turned out different.

But now Himura is gone.

Fucking Himura.

And Jackie is, once again, alone. Out here in this huge, empty landscape. Not a soul to be seen for miles. It could be the end of the world. Or the beginning.

We're all alone in the end.

#

The car makes a winding descent to the coast. Inaba's mind makes connections like a spider slinging a web together.

Life; death.

Death; Rei Miyamoto.

Rei Miyamoto; burial.

After their meeting at the themepark-cemetery hybrid of Takino, he and the OCB cop had met in various spaces dotted around the extremities of Sapporo. Under the pyramid in Morenuma Park, they discussed Yuji Miyamoto's gambling debts and Inaba detailed the men who were tasked with extorting the money from him. In the parkland surrounding Sapporo Dome they covered Yuji's hostess bills and Inaba, as with the gambling debts, assured Rei that he would assume their responsibility, securing the file in his personal safe in one of the Kanto Daichi-kai offices across the Toyohira River. It wouldn't be too difficult to lose the goods on one faceless salaryman.

In the car park of Gateaux Kingdom water park – with Rei Miyamoto shifting from foot to foot, hands in pockets, eyes lowered – they had debated how to handle Yuji's visits to the Invisible Man Club.

The cop wore a long raincoat over a spotless suit, tie knotted high and tight. Inaba huddled in a leather jacket pulled tight over an Armani T-shirt, bulky jeans hanging loose on his bony hips.

It had been a Tuesday in early September and the complex was quiet, winding down for the winter season. The water slide, twisting like a blue-white snake in its death-throes, was scored and chipped. The car park, lawns and outdoor pool were deserted save for a stooped old man inspecting the grounds for non-existent litter. The Mankabetsu River drifted by at the edge of the car park. Inaba had finished recounting an extortion operation on a local recycling firm. A company director had entertained a client in a hostess club, stayed on after his companion retired for the night, and woken up in the morning in a love hotel room mocked up like a nursery, a bored-looking girl dozing in bed, the director naked save for a nappy, his head on her lap, a breast-pump clamped over each of his nipples.

'Fucking mama's boy,' said Inaba.

Rei Miyamoto said, 'What's your mother like?'

'You probably know. Isn't my family history on file at the OCB?'

'Yes.'

'Well, you can read.'

They walked down to the southern bank of the river in silence.

Miyamoto said, 'My mother is a good woman. A little much at times, a little domineering, but a good woman. My father hands over his salary each month and she runs the household. Clothes, feeds and cares for three grown men.'

Inaba thought of little Emi. Was that to be her future? The cookie-cutter fate of so many women in Japan.

'She cares for me most of all,' said the cop. 'It isn't fair, I realise. But you know mothers. A son always trumps a husband. And a blood son always trumps a stepson.'

And so Goro Inaba had listened as Rei Miyamoto confessed his family secret. Rei's father had had a passionate affair when a younger man. A folly, and more so because the girl had come from a lower class – the lowest class. The burakumin. A beautiful girl by all accounts but a bura nonetheless. The girl had had a son, Yuji, and lived with him and her violent, alcoholic husband until the husband died. The affair had continued until Rei's mother had discovered her husband's indiscretions. The bura girl had gone into the forest and committed suicide. Rei's father had insisted on raising the boy, Yuji. His wife, distraught, demanded they leave their home on the Izu Peninsula and her husband quit his job in Kamakura. So they had run, fleeing the shame and disgrace to Hokkaido and made a fresh start.

Inaba said, 'And you were part of that fresh start, eh?'

'I was born here in Sapporo.'

Time had passed, life had settled. Yuji, always wild, went on an ill-fated trip to Kamakura to pursue an honest life in the Shinto priesthood.

'An honest life,' Inaba muttered, shaking his head. Fucking priests. Shysters. Then he forced his face slack and bowed in contrition. 'So, what went wrong?'

Rei cleared his throat. 'The priesthood demands discipline, ritual and self-denial. Yuji is compulsive and decadent. He can be aggressive. A man of his passions was never going to be suited to life in a shrine. Then the priests discovered his heritage on his mother's side. He returned to Hokkaido under a cloud. But it was just as well. There was some trouble in Kamakura at the time. Violent crimes.'

Inaba caught a flicker in Rei Miyamoto's eyes. A turning inward for a moment, a reflection on something buried deep within.

He said, 'How's your brother's girlfriend?'

'The more I know her, the more I like her. I gave her a few things to show my appreciation of her spending time with my brother. A book, a bookmark. A pin-badge. Trinkets.'

'A pin-badge?' Inaba looks Miyomoto up and down. 'Who gives a pin-badge as a gift?'

'Think of it like a charm. Something to protect her and ward off evil.'

'Like an omamori?'

'Kind of. But Christian.'

'You're a Christian?'

Miyamoto met Inaba's eyes, a spark of defiance in his stare. 'Yes,' he said.

'It's all good. Like I give a fuck. So what's on this badge? A cross?'

'A fish.'

'What?'

'It's a symbol. Nothing more.'

They gazed at the river for a while, each in his own world. Inaba wondered if Miyamoto's Christian charm had been given as protection for his brother's girlfriend from Yuji himself. He wondered if Rei was looking for something to hold over his brother, perhaps to force Yuji to stop seeing the girl. Did he fear for her? Who knows, maybe it was sibling rivalry? Maybe Rei wanted to fuck the gaijin skirt himself?

After a time, Rei Miyamoto stood and said, 'Thank you for your continued help in this matter, Inaba San.'

'... *Inaba San.*'

A grating, metallic voice heavy with sarcasm pierces Inaba's day-dream memories.

Kenta says in a mock-deferential whine, 'We're almost there, Inaba *San.*'

Inaba stares out at the choppy water of Uchira Bay, the colour of spoiled pork. They are on a small road, train tracks on their left. Inaba grunts, his eyes on the sea, his thoughts drifting with the heaving waves. He remembers the pin-badge.

A fish.

Himura had told him the killer tapped the glass at the Invisible Man Club with a small pin-badge.

Could the killer have been Yuji Miyamoto?

Rei had told him that the girlfriend, Megan, studied at Hokkaido University – so he had leaned on a contact in admissions for Megan's address and checked her out. He had become fascinated by her, watching her from his car, from a café across the stereet, on the opposite platform of her subway station. He didn't desire her. Her life was mundane. But she was a portal to the future: someone's daughter, studying at a prestigious university, thriving, independent. She could be Emi in twenty years.

Then Megan's father and the other, big foreigner had turned up.

Inaba had watched them as they sat near the Old Government Building, sipping drinks and laughing in the pedestrian plaza. Events had taken over, the idiot Fox had interfered and Inaba's hand had been forced.

Reality rises and crests – he feels a mad surge of vertigo – and then eddies. Memory washes over him again.

He had looked to the river on that September day, the deserted monolith of the hotel behind, as Rei Miyamoto had unburdened himself. It had been easier for Inaba to stare at his surroundings than look the cop in the eye.

Miyamoto had said, 'If you don't mind, I'll have one of those cigarettes.'

Inaba had shrugged, taken the crumpled pack of Kents from his pocket and handed it over.

Rei Miyamoto coughed. 'I want you to use whatever contacts, whatever leverage you have to investigate my stepbrother. I want every morsel of his burakumin background. My parents shouldn't have any nasty surprises as they approach their later years.'

Inaba knew, the cop's career could do without any unsavoury revelations, too.

'Use a PI, use a contact at the Ward Office, City Hall, connections down south,' said Miyamoto through a billowing cloud of tobacco smoke. 'Then bury it. I want every shred of my brother's mongrel blood wiped from the record. Nothing on the family registry. No trace, anywhere.'

'And how the fuck am I supposed to do that?'

'You're a gangster, aren't you? Bribe, blackmail, intimidate. Family records are maintained by civil servants. Civil servants are sheep, yakuza are wolves. Do what comes naturally.'

'And you're the fucking sheepdog.'

Miyamoto ground the cigarette out on the ground, wiped the ash from its dead tip in the grass and looked around for a rubbish bin. Finding none, he pocketed the butt. His eyes turned to Inaba, as flat and glassy as the river slipping by.

'You do this for me, you'll be out of the gangster life in six months.'

'Okay.'

They turned and begun climbing the shallow bank, back to the empty resort grounds. Miyamoto stopped at the top of the bank. He said, 'One more thing. I want you to set up a meet between Yuji and I, in the Invisible Man Club. I'll tell you the date and time, you ensure there's access for me to get in and out, unseen.'

'What're you going to do?'

'Family business. I want Yuji to know that I am aware of his dirty little secrets. I want to confront him in that place. I want to say some things to him in the sordid little hovel of the club. Things between him and me.'

Inaba had shrugged and said, 'Sure. You know, some of my friends – a lot of the men in the Kanto Daichi-kai – are burakumin. They're good guys. No different from us.'

Rei Miyamoto had shaken his head, stood tall and adjusted the knot of his tie.

'*You*' he had said, 'no different from *you*. Don't count an officer of the Hokkaido District Police among your degraded little cabal.'

Degraded little cabal.

Is that what Inaba, Jun and Kenta – the burakumin brothers – are? A degraded little cabal?

Inaba has still not told Megan that her boyfriend's brother – step-brother – is dead. Has not told her about Yuji Miyamoto's dirty little habits.

The car comes to a shuddering halt.

'We're here,' says Kenta.

Here, is a narrow potholed road, devoid of markings with a dusty siding. The sea is metres away. Two green public phones sit by the roadside. Inaba opens the car door and eases his legs out, one hand on the dressing over his gut, the other gripping the door as he hauls his body up. He smells the salt-tinged air like a con just released from prison and hobbles to the phones, an old man before his time.

Chapter 38

A boxy Nissan passes an advertising hoarding, three-storeys high, standing proud between a gravel car park and a schoolchildren's crossing sign. The last outpost of Jozankei Hot Spring resort before the high country and the vast open spaces of Shikotsu-Toya national park. The man behind the wheel watches the concrete bric-a-brac cluttering the slopes of the Jozankei valley. On the passenger seat sits a lobster-red mask with vacant eyes.

Yuji Miyamoto laughs.

Hot springs. Boiling waters from the asshole of the earth, filtered, tempered. Sanitised. Like everything else in this pampered society.

I'll give the gaijin a real Japanese demon. One they can write about in their English newspapers after I slaughter and gut the whore bitch Englishwoman and her devoted daddy.

He glances in the rearview mirror and looks back to the road.

My eyes are my best feature. They are hypnotic. Beautiful, dark, captivating. Women look away from them because of it. Because they'll never want another man if they don't. It happened to the English bitch. So much that she risks her thick Western neck to contact me, not the useless, pathetic cops. She even gave me the chance to trace her call. And now I have a date with the devoted Miss Sparrow. The anti-Mother. The greatest sacrifice.

He glances at the sprawl of trees to the left as the car climbs toward the summit of Nakayamatoge.

Hokkaido. The mountains untamed, wild things roaming the forests. The Ainu, almost as wild as the forest creatures to many Japanese. They don't conform to the modern ideal of Japan either.

We have fleeced them, subjugated them, swallowed them

337

whole until they are a tourist attraction. Tourists go to their vil-lages and take their photos and buy their wood crafts. They consume the Ainu, like they consume their foreign brands and their electronics and their whining J-Pop and their squealing pornography.

Like I will consume the souls of the gaijin. A thought strikes him. *Perhaps even the flesh of the girl. Bitch burger.*

He feels himself harden.

Frigid cunt. Fuck it, if I can't have her body one way I'll have it another.

He pats the phallic nose of the mask.

Six months! Six months of talk, talk, talk. Picnics by the river, endless stories about England, her family: fucking football! I'll never watch Chelsea again. Holding each other in her apartment, cuddling with our clothes on. Lying in our underwear and ...fuck all else! Soiled mail order panties and warm liver in a jar can only get you so far.

"Not yet, Yuji. I'm not ready, Yuji. I'm not sure, Yuji. *I'm teasing the shit out of your cock for fun, Yuji." Who does she think she is? Princess fucking Diana? Hollywood movies are full of shit! All those botoxed Americans jumping in and out of bed with each other on a whim. I thought it'd be back to her place for blow jobs and a bed-in after a cup of tea. My first taste of gaijin.*

And then the shameless barbarian strumpet wants to hold hands in the street! On the subway! In public! Even kiss in the fucking park!

I tell you, we are living in changed times. More young Japanese are following this brazen Western penchant for public displays of affection.

Yuji Miyamoto feels the erection grow. His eyes roll back to the rearview mirror as the car crests the peak and begins its descent to the open land below. He knows his attention is drifting from the road. To dispel his growing excitement, his thoughts turn to his half brother. He sees him in his mind's eye, addresses him.

You asked for the meet in Invisible Man. Knew I went there. I couldn't give a shit.

And you always were a violent little asshole, Rei, despite your holier-than-thou Christian bullshit. My little brother but physically bigger. I came prepared. A knife I bought in a hobby shop. Good size, jagged edge to the blade. And the mask. It was part of the fantasy, see? I wore it when I watched them: the girls in the Invisible Man. No one saw it in the dark, or in my bag as I entered. It heightened my anonymity, gave me power. It made me less than human yet more than a man so that, as I grew hard and my own hot breath warmed my cheeks and the girls sat or walked or read, I became a creature they could never comprehend. Then, close to the end, I'd wank and finish and put my dick, and the mask, away.

The knife and my mask were in my bag when I met you.

I came into the box and she was there: the Mother. I bowed to her in the dark and almost fell over you, brother, as I stepped forward. Arrogant prick, you were sitting in the seat watching her. It was so dark in that box; but I could see enough that I knew you never turned around. Couldn't even look at me as you warned me off. Told me I had to control my impulses, stop the gambling, the clubs. I was a liability, a shame to the good name of our parents.

'Parent,' I said.

'Yuji,' you said, 'you need to understand: I am a policeman in the Organised Crime Bureau. Like your yakuza friends here, I have powers beyond the confines of regular society.'

You told me you'd wiped all trace of my "lineage" from the family registry, that this stain on my blood no longer existed.

That my mother – my beautiful, loving, damaged, devoted blood mother – had been wiped from my past, my life.

YOU ERASED HALF OF WHO I AM.

That was the beginning of the end for Yuji Miyamoto.

Then you, sanctimonious asshole that you are, told me you were doing this for my own good and quoted from your blasphemous

Christian scriptures. Leviticus 19:17, "Thou shalt not hate thy brother in thine heart."

I put the mask on and killed you.

When I'd finished, I tapped the glass with the Christian badge you'd given my English whore in tribute to the Mother, Amaterasu. It was then that I knew Megan Sparrow would die, that she would be sacrificed to the Mother, and I would be reborn.

The pin-badge. He remembers pocketing it from the Megan Sparrow's apartment when she had gone to the toilet. He checks the road, the grey asphalt stretching ahead.

Later, our "family" called my phone. In the background, my bitch step-mother sobbing and a Buddhist priest droning his incantations on and on. You were a Christian but we had a Buddhist ceremony. Why? For her. Because, even with her true son who she worshipped with her every breath, in the end it was all about her. My father too weak to refuse, to stand up to her. Castrated by years of marriage.

They asked where I had been, why I hadn't been there for them. Our father said he'd already lost one son. I made my excuses. I said I had had a sudden business trip, bullshit that no one believed. And you, Rei? Your restless kami, your spirit, is flitting around Sapporo like a lost child searching for its mother. Poor little Rei, forever alone, desolate in the endless black.

Patronising, self-serving bastard.

I can imagine it, my parents weeping as your body went into the oven.

Then sorting through the ash with their chopsticks, picking out the bones. Placing them in the urn to be brought home and prayed to, appeased with gifts and snacks at the household altar. And our father: what about his duty to me, his son; or my mother, his true love? Never mind his duty and honour – where's his love for me? Where has it been for over two damn decades?

It took the death of my blood mother, the woman he loved, to move his weak ass and take responsibility to raise me. Then that bitch wife, my stepmother, ignoring me, shunning me. Forcing us to move far from our home. Sniping at me, bullying him, crying with frustration and hatred when she saw me. Crying with joy when you, my fucking brother, was born. All those years my father failed to fight my corner, failed to defend me against her.

My father is just like the rest. All about their wa, the harmony of the collective. Unless they're refusing burakumin jobs, blocking marriages and calling us inhuman. Calling my mother an animal.

Well, I'll give them a fucking animal.

I'll give them a feral fucking beast from their worst nightmares. I'll leave such carnage at Toya, they'll be locking their doors and praying to the Shinto gods for mercy. The gaijin too: they'll see their people torn to shreds. They will know the terrible darkness at work in Japan, our purity, our superiority: the malice we can visit upon outsiders.

Shit, I'm starving. I'd kill for a McDonald's.

He passes the huge cone of Mount Yotei and shifts position in the seat. Soon he will reach the amusement park and resort hotel of Rusutsu, with its convenience stores. He can grab a snack there and have a piss. Then it is another half hour or so to Toya.

Yuji Miyamoto opens the glove compartment and feels around. His fingers brush the metal cans of bear pepper spray bought from an outdoor pursuits shop. The hard plastic of the two tasers, picked up from a far-right-leaning shop owner in Sapporo, offers reassurance. He closes the compartment and pats the mask again.

The second cop was nothing. Just practice.

But in the moment, by the river in the dark, it was everything. I was hunting; he was prey. He stumbled across my path. Every fibre of my being screamed out to slaughter that man. I was enveloped in the act. For that moment, I was Tengu.

The British girl, Sparrow, is my ascension. She will be my climax: the last shred of Yuji Miyamoto will be gone and I will become the Tengu in entirety.

He remembers the foreigner he passed in Susukino, the voluptuous ass swinging along the street. He grows harder and almost veers off the road.

I want that bitch bad!

Shit! Better think about fucking baseball.

Chapter 39

Had the cops screwed Goro Inaba? They wouldn't dare.

He was gold dust wasn't he? First lieutenant of the largest yakuza syndicate in Hokkaido turned rat. A direct source of information and their best chance to bust Reizo Himura and put the Kanto Daichi-kai out of business.

And yet Inaba is a liability. An OCB detective dead, murdered in a squalid Susukino fetish club, wasn't the kind of headline the police welcomed. There had been enough scandals of brutality, ineptitude and corruption through the years. At present, the story of a hero cop's disappearance and the subsequent discovery of his remains in the mountains surrounding Sapporo would be a tragedy. Mention of the Invisible Man Club would create a farce. The burakumin connection would make it worse.

Still, he has the two gaijin.

Inaba hears the supercilious voice on the other end of the line in his head again – '... require authorisation from the Criminal Affairs Bureau and Security Bureau at the secretariat level. Two representatives are in-flight from Tokyo as we speak. When they arrive in Sapporo, they will review the documents and, once satisfied, stamp them with their personal hanko. The documents will then be dispatched to southern Hokkaido, at a location of your choosing, by police motorcycle.'

Bullshit. Inaba has learned enough about the NPA thanks to Rei Miyamoto – and his life as a yakuza – to know this is pure flam. Something's wrong. Someone is blocking the deal. Stalling. Does Himura know of Inaba's betrayal? Has he put a tame cop into play? Have they found a lead on the foreigners somehow? One of the problems with hiding out and cutting communications with the outside world is you have no idea who might be fucking with you.

Maybe it's time to fuck with the foreigners. Cut a piece of flesh off, send it to the suits at the NPA. Show you're serious.

He stares out the car window as the countryside slides by.

You're paranoid. This is Japan: slow is how bureaucracy works here. How the bitch cops work. That's the reality.

And the big gaijin, Jackie Shaw. What happened to him? The police have not mentioned him during any of their calls. Inaba spared him when he could have cut his throat – that should go in his favour if the Irishman went to the cops. But what if Himura had gotten to the foreigner? If the cops find the big gaijin floating in the river or dead in a park, will that go against Inaba?

Kenta says, 'You still trust the cops?' His tone is too light, forced. He concentrates on the road as he drives but cogs are turning behind his eyes.

He suspects something is up. Of course he fucking does.

Inaba says, 'I have no reason not to. You know this country. The cops are civil servants. The civil service won't draw up one document when a fucking book of them will do. Then some guy has to pass it to his boss, who delivers it to his, who probably has his wife read it and on and fucking on.'

'Yeah. Slower than a stream of old man's piss.'

Inaba laughs, too hard. The frail bond that has kept the brothers onside is almost at breaking point. 'We have to call back in four hours, right? Let's bring one of the gaijin with us next time. The girl. The voice of a Western woman should move things along.'

'It's risky. What if she tells them something? She speaks our language.'

'Okay, the man. A father blabbering away in English will scare the shit out of some little bureaucrat more than any fucking yakuza could.'

Now Kenta laughs. He has come through a trough and is riding the withdrawal rollercoaster to a crest. He looks strong, alert, buzzing with nervous energy. Inaba likes him better in the depths, morose, weak, without fight, even if he is trying to kill them with his driving.

Inaba checks his watch. They will be back at the cabin in twenty minutes. They will break the news to Jun. By that time, there will be another three and a half hours before the next call to the cops. Inaba might find an excuse to go out, sneak his mobile from his coat on the sofa, call Aina. He wants to know how Emi is, maybe hear her small voice. He needs to remind himself of why he is here in the first place.

Yeah, that would be good.

That's what he needs. When Kenta crashes again and Jun is busy with his junkie brother, Inaba will slip out and make the call. He hopes Aina will let him speak to his little princess. His Emi.

And if the NPA stall again: Fuck it, he'll go to the press. The liberals at the Asahi. They'll jump at the chance to put some hurt on the cops. Maybe they'll make him a hero.

#

The warmth is heaven. Up here on the higher reaches of Usu, Jackie threads his way down through cracks and lava gullys in the rock. He feels the heat, the immense power, radiate through the stony ground. The upper reaches of the volcano are a moonscape surrounded by snow-draped forest, the lake below like a sheet of iron forged by the maker himself. Jackie's hand and face throb as he passes steam vents in the rock. He feels a stab of pain in his thigh, a dull ache in his flank.

Up here, within sight of the summit, is a land of poisonous gasses, boiling pools of volcanic water. His friends must be so close now. He sees the rough grass a short way below. He stumbles and slides down the last stretch of rock before landing on his arse in the grass. He crouches and scans the terrain. No snow here, with the heat of the volcano's furnace below the thin crust of earth. Jackie spots Himura's bowl full of water, the crater near the cabin where he should find Ian and Megan, down the slope to his left. Smaller craters pock the surrounding area. He feels a new surge of cold elation. So close now.

He sees the first signs of damage. The ground is savagely warped where the volcano wreaked havoc back in 2000. He should find his friends in just such a warped patch of land.

Jackie checks the pistol again. Still three rounds in the magazine, one in the chamber. He slides the magazine home in the grip. He takes the tactical knife from his left coat pocket. He lays the weapons on the grass, then eases Reizo Himura's coat from around his shoulders. He rolls it roughly and places it on the ground, then shoves the Glock in his own right jacket pocket, the knife back in the left. He knows he is fussing over the tools: exhaustion making him anxious.

The wild grass is hard going, hiding sudden ridges in the earth hammered up by the eruption and troughs where he almost goes over and snaps his ankle. He can still feel the heat, whether in his head or below ground he isn't sure. He feels insignificant in the presence of the volcano and its terrible power. Long after Jackie Shaw has breathed his last – today or years down the line – the mountain will still stand.

Calm down, Jackie Boy. You'll be walking the streets with a sandwich board hollering shite about end of the world next.

It's just three men and me.

Just them and me.

Jackie reaches the water-filled crater and skirts the rim. Twenty yards ahead is a fence with a sign, a simple graphic of an erupting volcano, a scrawl of Japanese characters and, in English, a message for the tourists – *Danger! Volcano Damage!* Beyond the chain-link, Jackie sees a road swallowed by the earth. It remerges from the churned landscape twenty metres on, littered with broken telegraph poles. The ground has risen to consume a house, only the ridge at the centre of the roof and a metal chimney pipe from a wood stove visible above ground. Nearby, the earth has ruptured, forming huge, rough steps in the slope where the mountain has buckled, splitting a school playground.

The fence encircles a large area. Further below is the wooden thread of a boardwalk leading down to the town. Jackie glimpses the highest floors of some of the huge lakeside hotels that comprise the spa resort of Toya Onsen, then the lake with its humpbacked island in the centre.

He crouches when he reaches the fence. Somewhere in the zone of destruction is a cabin, sunk in the earth. Its doorway is accessible from a breach in a trench in front, the earth having risen at the rear to enclose the back of the wooden structure. The tarred roof is open to the elements, at the same level of the ruptured land that encircles the cabin. One way in – one way out. Inside should be his friend, Ian, Megan Sparrow, and three yakuza.

The fence is flimsy. Who in Japan would dream of breaking rules and slipping inside the prohibited area? Who would want to anyway? He crawls under the chain-link and into terrain pulverised by the violence of nature.

Then Jackie Shaw eases the handgun from his pocket and moves off, ready to visit some violence of his own.

Chapter 40

'I just don't understand,' says Jun, his eyes screwed shut. 'You said you just needed to check in with the cops. You said they'd be ready with the deal. You said you'd be back with details.'

Ian Sparrow sees the concerned look on his daughter's face and hears the tight, fragile tone in Jun's voice. This has been going on for well over an hour, periods of brooding silence broken by an exasperated outburst from Jun. Kenta is wallowing in his withdrawal hell again, slouched in a chair at the table, playing with something in his pocket. Ian wishes he had a watch. He has no idea of the time, no idea how long has passed since Megan called Yuji. Had the young man heard? Was the message still on his phone, ignored? Had Yuji called the police? The uncertainty is torture.

In the centre of the room, Goro Inaba says, 'This could be a good thing, Jun. They said there are two men flying up from Tokyo to stamp this thing. Fucking Tokyo. They're taking this deal seriously.'

'Or they're taking us for fools.'

'And them?' says Inaba, gesturing to Ian and Megan. 'You think they're dispensable? You think the bitch cops are going to abandon a couple of Western gaijin?'

'I think some asshole in the NPA might think he has a better way. I think they can record all the places you've made calls from and try to get a fix on where we might be. The more calls you make the more data they've got. Then some Counter Terrorism Unit, armed to the teeth, starts crawling around with their dogs and their special cameras – and next thing you know they're battering the door down and we're all dead.'

Inaba shakes his head. 'No, no, no,' he says, like he's convincing himself. 'Too risky. And how are they going to pin down a location?

I've called from east, west, north and south of Toya. The lake is thirty miles around, forest and mountains everywhere.'

'We're going to bring one of the gaijin next time,' says Kenta. 'And this.' He produces Inaba's knife from his pocket and impales the blade on the wooden tabletop. Megan jumps. Ian starts with her then puts a hand on her leg and stares at the blade embedded in the table.

'There's no need for that,' says Inaba, touching his stomach. 'The cops hear a frightened foreigner blabbering in English, it'll be more than enough to put the shits up them and speed things along. Hell, we can call the British Embassy in Tokyo, too, bring some more pressure down.'

Kenta says, 'Or mail them a finger.'

'No,' says Inaba. He points to Ian and Megan. 'Like it or not, they are the key to us pulling this thing off. We keep them in one piece, the bitch cops will play by our rules to get them back.'

'Or keep stalling until they can think up an alternative.'

'Like what? Who the fuck can find us here?'

Jun looks at the father and daughter on the sofa. 'What about Himura?' he says, 'He might remember this place.'

Inaba hesitates for a beat.

'Himura's got enough on his hands,' he says. 'He'll be busy keeping Ishikawa sweet and dealing with the fall-out of a cop's murder in his own home.'

Jun massages his bandaged hand, his once open features now unreadable. Inaba's shoulders hunch as he ignores Kenta and addresses – appeals to – him.

'Listen, Himura doesn't know about these two.' He nods to Ian and Megan. 'He doesn't know why I would run. The Organised Crime Bureau is tight, they wouldn't give out information to rank and file cops. If Himura thinks it's suspicious that I'm not around, that I've done something to hurt the Kanto Daichi-kai, he'll also think I'm trying to get out of Hokkaido. Out of Japan. Why would he suspect I'd be sitting here on my ass, waiting for him to remember the cabin and turn up for a reunion? This place is supposed to be out of commission, anyway. All he knows is someone cut up a cop in the Invisible Man Club, that the cop was my tame bitch, and that I've disappeared and you guys aren't around. He probably thinks we did it and are on a boat to Honshu, or Korea, or fucking Vladivostok by now.'

Jun shrugs and looks at his brother. 'Makes sense.'

'Where I sit,' slurs Kenta, 'nothing makes any fucking sense.' He closes his eyes and his chin drops to his chest.

Jun swallows and turns to Inaba.

'Okay.' A pause. 'Okay.'

Inaba's desperate grin shatters any last vestige of normality in the scene.

Normality, thinks Megan. She's lost sight of whatever that is.

She almost wishes she didn't understand so much of the conversation, almost envies her father in his ignorance. Except she can hear in the soft whistle of breath through her dad's nostrils; her father can feel the thick, volatile atmosphere in the cabin.

Inaba needs Emi. He needs to hear her voice or, at least, look at her picture. Alone.

He pats down his pockets and says 'Looking for my cigarettes.' Idiot, he thinks – no need for a running commentary. He looks over to his jacket that contains his mobile, lying on the sofa. He walks to the sofa and gives Ian and Megan a reassuring smile, then lifts the jacket and slings it on his wiry frame.

'I left them in the car,' he says. 'I'll just grab them and come right back.'

The car is parked down at the start of the Usu tourist trail boardwalk, a thirty-minute walk there and back. Enough time for Inaba to call Aina with his mobile and, if he's lucky, hear Emi's voice. Screw the cops, or traces, or any of that shit. He'll keep the call short and ditch the mobile after. Anyway, this is the endgame; his future is guaranteed. Jun and Kenta? Too bad for Jun but sacrifices had to be made if Inaba was to have a chance at a new life. And fuck Kenta.

Inaba rubs his throat. It's becoming difficult to breathe in the stifling confines of the cabin.

'Have one of my smokes,' says Jun.

'Bit harsh for me. I'll only be thirty minutes.'

'Thirty fucking minutes? You can barely walk.'

'We have plenty of time until the next call.'

'Why bother if it's just one cigarette?'

'I haven't had many in the last few hours. I want to enjoy this one. I'll stick to my own brand and smoke it on the walk back.'

'I'll come with you,' says Jun, 'you're weak.'

'No,' says Inaba glancing at Kenta. Sullen, unpredictable, violent Kenta. Kenta catches the look. He pulls the knife from the table and raises an eyebrow.

Jun says, 'But – '

'Let him go,' says Kenta. He closes his eyes again.

Jun opens his mouth to protest then slouches, defeated.

Inaba nods, walks to the door and slips outside.

Jun, Kenta, Ian and Megan sit in silence for seconds that stretch to an eternity.

Ian feels a prickle of fear under his skin. If Inaba discovers his mobile is missing from the jacket, will he suspect he and Megan of taking it or think it's lying somewhere in the cabin? And what happens now? Is Inaba going to run? Can Jun control Kenta's murderous urges? More bloody uncertainty.

Megan waits for an opportunity to whisper to her father, tell him to shove Inaba's mobile into the crack between the sofa seat cushions again. They might get away with Inaba thinking it slipped out as the jacket lay on the sofa.

Jun paces the floor, worrying, doubting, sensing an end in sight, no idea if it will be happy or tragic.

And Kenta opens his eyes and runs a finger down the cutting edge of the knife, then puts the finger to his lips and slips out the cabin door in pursuit of Goro Inaba.

Chapter 41

Jackie is almost on top of the cabin before he spots it. He is on his belly, crawling through the snow-spattered grass, when the ground falls away in a smooth, seventy-degree incline to reveal the tar-coated cabin roof. The roof is sloped gently upward to its centre. Around the cabin, the ground has risen like uneven bread. Windows, below ground level, are hard against the earth.

He crawls around the high ground on the left side of the cabin clutching the Glock. Nearing the front of the shack, Jackie takes in the shallow trench in front and the breach cut into the natural revetment in front of the door. Thirty yards beyond lies a ridge.

Climb on the roof, he thinks, as quiet as possible and try to find a point of entry. Or create a distraction. Something to bring the yakuza out into the open. Hit them at the front door where they're constrained by the trench, with Ian and Megan still inside.

The grass is cold and damp. The chill seeps into his bones. Yes, he thinks, he can climb from the lip of the raised earth, ease himself on to the top of the shack and, once perched on the roof, plan his attack.

Jackie crawls to where the ground and the sunken cabin meet, the roof almost level with the ground on which he lies. He eases the pistol into his pocket and reaches out, placing his palms on the tar and taking his weight on his arms. He swings one leg over and onto the rough surface, then the other. The smell of wood and tar carries on the autumn breeze. He spits a curse as his boot scrapes on the surface, then moves slow on hands and knees. He crawls to the wooden ridge at the centre of the sloped roof then slides along the thick horizontal beam to the front of the cabin.

The door opens. He flattens himself, arms splayed on the tar at his sides, body on the central ridge. His hand slides along the rough surface to his coat pocket and finds the Glock. His breathing sounds like waves pounding in his head, his body wired again. He chances a glance over the edge of the roof and sees a lean figure emerge from the cabin with a posture telegraphing exhaustion. The figure turns back to the cabin door and Jackie ducks back from the rim of the roof. He counts ten seconds in his head and peers over the edge once more. He sees the sharp jaw and strong features knit in confusion or indecision, focused on the cabin door, of the scrawny thug who wrestled with him back at the old Olympic village as the frightened girl, Aina, looked on. The gangster who got a knife slash on the chest. Goro Inaba.

Jackie sees the plaza downtown in his mind, Ian and Megan and Jackie drinking coffee, joking around; the wiry man watching from across the open concrete, mobile phone in hand. The same man. Same lean frame. Same fucking jacket.

Inaba searches his pockets a couple of feet away, rummaging in each two or three times. Then he walks off, laborious, like he is hurting bad.

Inaba – so Ian and Megan must be here. Himura, you mad bastard! You were right.

Jackie coils his finger around the trigger of the pistol.

It would be so easy. Aim, squeeze. The Glock could do some damage at this range. One down.

No.

There are two more. Inside with Ian and Megan. The other yakuza will panic with the shot. God knows what they might do to his friends.

Jackie hears a tortured squeal. He sights on Inaba, applies pressure on the trigger, centres on the target's back. A second yakuza appears in his sightline. The squeal, the cabin door creaking open again. This man is on edge, walking like a marionette as though his body can't contain his nervous energy. He stops dead in his tracks at the sight of his scrawny partner standing a few yards away.

Inaba turns to face the man. They stand like two stags sizing each other up. Neither wants to make an approach, neither wants to concede ground. Neither says a word.

Jackie scolds himself. The gun is too easy, a comfort blanket. It won't sort every problem, will create a lot more. Fact is, at this range he doesn't know if he'd drop them. But if these two specimens don't notice him sprawled on the roof, if they fuck off somewhere to settle whatever differences they might have, it's all good. One yakuza left inside with Ian and Megan.

And please, God, let my friend and his daughter be in one piece.

He wills the two gangsters to move off, to go at each other, to do something.

As though on cue, the second thug makes for Inaba. His hands are tight by his sides. Inaba takes a step back and Jackie catches a flash of light on metal. A knife in the jerky thug's hand as he closes the distance on Inaba. Jackie realises the knife man is Tweedledee, one of the thugs with Fox who beat Jackie senseless in Susukino.

Jackie swallows down something sharp in his throat.

I'm about to watch a murder and do nothing.

Inaba spared him back at the apartment. A cold spike of guilt drives through Jackie's gut. He should cry out, fire the Glock in a warning shot. But he won't. Simple mathematics. A fight will leave one – or maybe both – men on the ground and out of the game. It could draw the last yakuza out in the open. That gives Jackie better odds on sorting the opposition and getting his friends out in one piece.

Tweedledee closes on Inaba, his blade still clutched tight to his thigh. His shoulders are set back, his chest jutting forward. The wiry Inaba looks beaten, haunted. He slumps and he wipes his hand across his face. Then he drops his arms as though he's decided to embrace his fate and welcome the knife.

Jackie mutters, 'Shit.'

He braces as Inaba's body goes slack, as Tweedledee cocks the elbow of his knife arm back and tilts the right side of his body to gain traction as he comes in with the blade. The knife thug closes, gaining momentum as he jacks himself up to fillet his fellow yakuza. They haven't said a word, faces blank.

They are less than ten feet from one another.

Five.

Inaba's eyes close and he shouts a word Jackie doesn't understand.

'Emi!'

Then his broad lips strain showing large white teeth and his face contorts in sudden, searing pain. He drops.

That short, that simple, thinks Jackie.

But there's still a couple of feet between Inaba and the knife man, Tweedledee.

The knife man steps back. As he does so, Jackie has a fleeting glimpse of a creature at the ridge beyond. A creature from a child's night terrors with huge, furious eyes, a hell-red, scowling face and obscene nose. Something frigid scuttles through Jackie's groin. Tweedledee drops the knife and goes to his knees.

The Tengu has come.

Inaba is on the ground, body twitching in small movements like a flickering image on a screen. The Tengu crouches over him. It sits on its long, thin haunches, squatting like some giant misshapen spider, hellish face intent on the knife thug still kneeling before it as if in worship. The demon's legs and arms are in black jeans and hooded top. Two sets of double black wires are embedded in Inaba and Tweedledee. Jackie sees a black object trimmed with yellow clutched in each of the demon's gloved hands. Tasers.

Inaba stops moving on the ground. Tweedledee is still on his knees, his head shaking as though he's wrapped in some terrible argument, refusing to drop.

God knows how many volts and he still isn't down.

The Tengu looks down on Inaba. The phallic nose jerks as though the demon is sniffing its next meal. It drops the taser from its right hand, yanks the small probes from Inaba's body and reaches behind its back. As the arm comes back into view, Jackie curses under his breath. The Tengu holds a glinting blade, the length of a machete but slim with an elegant curve.

Jackie eases the Glock into a firing position.

Thoughts ricochet through his mind as he takes aim. How did the monster find this place? Who has he come for? Megan? Inaba? Was Yuji Miyamoto really behind the mask or another interloper like Ishikawa? Whatever the answers, the killer must be headed to the cabin, not away.

The ramped front sight sits snug between the rear notches of the Glock. Jackie breathes out, the gun centred on the Tengu's chest. It drops the second taser and places its left hand on Inaba's chest, raising the blade. Jackie holds back on applying pressure on the trigger. His friends are still inside with a violent, probably antsy yakuza. The shot could send the situation spiralling out of control.

And you're in control now?

The Tengu brings its long knife down. It rests the tip of the blade on Inaba's belly. With a small thrust it'll pop the skin and slide through gristle and meat. If the killer takes care of these two, it evens the odds a little in Jackie's favour.

And then? I'll still have to deal with the psycho-killer. The masked headcase has to be put down – but Inaba held back when we fought in his flat: there's a chance I might be able to reason with him. Lesser of two evils.

Tweedledee is on his hands and knees in the grass, convulsing. He retches, then vomits up a yellow stream.

Who're you kidding, Jackie boy? Let this maniac do you a favour then pick off the survivors.

The Tengu rests the tip of his blade on Inaba's stomach and brings his left hand up and flat on the hilt, the right on top, ready for the thrust.

So much death. I've killed men before. What's watching another life snuffed out?

But the others were fighting; not helpless, wretching their guts onto the ground at the killing stroke. This won't do.

Jackie feels his finger snug around the trigger and applies pressure as he sights on centre mass of the monstrous figure crouched over Inaba. He's ready for the clipped roar of the shot, the recoil, ready to acquire the target again, fire a second round if the first doesn't do its lethal work.

One shot.

Centre mass.

Breathe. Apply pressure.

One shot.

A blur of matted blonde hair.

What the fuck?

Tweedledee. Roaring, hurling himself at the Tengu.

Jackie's heart races as he sees the blonde yakuza's back, sees him thrust forward with the knife. He wills him on. The Tengu and knife man meet. The struggle is slow and quiet from Jackie's perch on the roof. He can't hear the desperate grunts, the slapping of fists on skin. The frantic sighs as two men fight to survive. In combat, man as feral animal, red in tooth and claw.

He sees Tweedledee lunge and feels a spike of adrenaline, a surge of hope that the monstrous killer who slaughtered his own brother will be put down.

The blonde yakuza swings to his left, the Tengu gripping his collar, and falls. He lands on his back and screeches, his legs and arms flailing like an insect upended on its shell. The Tengu's blade is already tainted with blood and drives into his victim twice more. A fourth stroke and the blade stays in, buried deep in the yakuza's gut. The Tengu changes grip and begins sawing.

Tweedledee howls.

Jackie fires.

A clumsy shot, the report cracking the chill air and tumbling down the mountainside. The Tengu melts from view, slunk into the crazy-maze of depressions in the hammered slope. The two yakuza lie in the tangled grass, one rolling from side to side, life billowing into the cold autumn daylight with the steam from his insides. Jackie jumps to the ground at the front of the cabin, landing hard, and clambers to his feet. He runs at a crouch to the men, scanning the slope for the Tengu. He drops to his knees beside Inaba. The man is alive and breathes in short, shallow sighs. Tweedledee lies a couple of feet away, his insides out. The smell is overpowering.

One round would put him out of his misery. Just shoot the poor bastard and be done.

A slap of boot on wood. Jackie's head snaps up. The cabin door bursts open and another man runs out through the breach in the trench. The man has a bandaged hand, unkempt hair and a spray of black stubble on a long face crowded with large, brutal features. A face collapsed in rage and anguish at the sight of the dying man, now still but for one arm drawing lazy circles in the air. The bandaged man runs forward through the opening in the trench and stops ten yards away at the sight of Jackie. His eyes go from the dying man to the pistol in Jackie's hand and back to the prone figure. The bandaged man wipes a sleeve across his eyes. He sniffs and his face crumples. Hot tears clear tracks through a coating of dirt on his cheeks. The man looks to Jackie like a frightened, lost wee boy. He says something in Japanese and bows.

Jackie, stupid with confusion, bobs his head in response. He isn't sure if the bandaged man is bowing at him or the dying man on the ground.

Then the weeping yakuza turns and runs back to the cabin. The door flaps against the frame. Voices drift from within. Jackie hears a woman's voice, high and frantic.

Megan.

Another, deep, male. English.

Ian.

The ground seems to surge upward. Jackie's found them. He snaps to his feet and takes an anxious step toward the cabin.

The bandaged yakuza, wide nose dangling snot, strides into the open ground with a gun in his hand. His eyes narrow, red-raw, and he raises the revolver as Megan Sparrow screams, almost drowning the crack of the Glock as Jackie fires two shots in quick succession. The pistol shudders in his hand, the cold air flattening the angry snap of the report. The bullets punch into the bandaged man and his chest twitches. His eyes go huge as though he's seen some terrible truth.

Megan stands in the cabin doorway, an arm snaking around her waist from the dark within. She blinks and takes a step forward, dragging her father into the light. Jackie lowers the pistol as the downed man's bandaged hand reaches up to the grey sky.

Megan screams, 'You bastard! You killed him!'

Ian says, 'Love – ' and leaves the word hanging in the pale glare of the watery sunlight.

The girl heaves as though something is stuck in her throat. She stares at the bandaged man on the ground, his knee cocked, then straightening. Her hands are at her chest as she gulps and bawls. Grief in all its ugly glory, thinks Jackie.

It had to be done. A man comes at you with a gun, you put him down.

Jackie and the three yakuza are silent, Megan sobbing, Ian whispering to his daughter. Inaba lies unconscious taking shallow breaths. The blonde, butchered man, Tweedledee, is dead. Jackie counts three gusts of wind scour the slope before the bandaged man dies, still reaching for the heavens.

Jackie drops his head and kneads the back of his neck with his left hand, the right still holding the handgun, one round left. He thinks of the troubled road that has brought them here – he, Ian and Megan – thousands of miles from their homes on the other side of the world.

A bad business, altogether. Lord save us, let's hope it's the last of it.

But, of course, it isn't.

The Tengu.

Behind Jackie, Inaba finds his voice and bellows, his cry cracked and distraught.

Chapter 42

'Run!'

The Tengu stands, the wiry body clothed in a short black coat, black jeans and boots, behind Ian and Megan on the ground above the cabin. Father and daughter stare at Jackie, confused by the carnage and Inaba's frantic scream in Japanese. The Tengu closes in with a terrible grace, the blade glinting in the sunlight where the demon has wiped it clean.

Jackie echoes Inaba in English, 'Run!'

He plants his right foot back, blades his body, and fires the Glock. The round misses, nipping at the dirt next to the roof but, like a slap across the cheek, shocks Ian and Megan into action. They run. The Tengu jumps the last couple of feet from its perch, stumbles on landing and drops the knife. The red, hellish face turns to Jackie.

Jackie runs at the demon. He roars, ejects the magazine and slots it home again, bluffing he has more shots. The Tengu stares at him. Into him. The vacuum of the black eyes seem to draw him on. The eternal scowl on the furious mask tilts to the right to watch Ian and Megan running down the slope. Then the demon bolts, scuttling across the broken ground after its prey. Ian and Megan disappear over a crest notched with ragged mounds of earth. The blade lies where it fell.

Jackie feels a swell of panic as his friends, then the killer, drop from sight. He scrambles to his feet and makes for the crest. He, Ian and Megan lurch and stagger, a ragged chain of desperate souls scrambling across the flank of the volcano; only the Tengu moves with a fluid agility, closing on Ian with easy strides, hurdling knots of tall, rough grass. The terrain is a nightmare, buckled and gouged. Jackie expects to go down with every step, to snap an ankle. The killer is fifty yards in front of him, almost within touching distance of Ian, as Megan begins running up a ridge, steam seeping from an unseen vent somewhere below. She falls. Her scream, smothered by the dull thunder in Jackie's ears, twists her face in pure terror.

Jackie shouts, 'No!'

Megan clambers to her feet and limps up the ridge.

The Tengu reaches into a coat pocket. Jackie's foot goes down a pitted trench in the grass and he flails for balance as the empty pistol sails into the air and lands somewhere to his right.

Ian Sparrow clenches his fists, ready for the Tengu, adrenaline fuelling his rage at this bastard who means his little girl harm. He will grapple and batter and bite and claw at this fucker – this thing – and keep it from Megan. He will buy her time to get away, find help, reach safety.

Jackie sees the small canister in the demon's hand and yells a warning. He watches as the Tengu aims the can. Ian thrashes at air, grasping at his attacker even as he topples, as he knocks the spray from the Tengu's hand. Then he folds like a broken tent.

The killer stomps once on Ian Sparrow's head and takes off after Megan.

Jackie yells, 'Bastard!' and runs to his friend, sees the Tengu crest the ridge then disappear over the other side. The canister lies a couple of feet away. Jackie grabs it. Bear spray.

Ian is fetal in the grass, an ugly gash above his right eye. Jackie imagines the sudden, blinding pain in Ian Sparrow's eyes as the spray bit, the thickening snot filling his friend's sinuses, streaming from his nose. The burning skin, like a swarm of bees stinging. Ian can't speak, busy keeping his lungs from making a break for it up his throat, wracked with vicious coughs. Spittle and vomit already fleck his chin. He's going through hell. But he'll live.

Jackie bends low to Ian's ear and says, 'I'll get Megan.'

As Jackie climbs the ridge, it looks as though he'll drop off the edge of the world, the horizon gone as the land rises leaving only the drained sky. He hears a scream as he reaches the crest and finds a natural bowl below, peppered with patchy grass in its upper reaches. At the foot of the crater a trail of steam seeps from a crack in the scarred ground. Two figures are locked together. Jackie can't hear the slaps but he winces as each blow lands, the screams rising in pitch and intensity as the girl takes a beating. The grass tugs at his feet as he pitches down the slope, almost wrong-footing him once, twice, then catching the bridge of his boot and sending him hurtling down to the scree and dirt of the lower reaches. His arms windmill as wall of heat rushes up to meet him and then he's gone, his body over-balanced, feet kicking up dirt as he plummets forward. His hands hit the ground, stones shredding his palms. He pivots his body to land on his shoulder and rolls.

Jackie realises Megan is shrieking his name. He grinds to a stop in a cloud of dust.

The Tengu reaches for Megan's neck.

Jackie calls out, 'Yuji! No!'

Megan thrashes her arms and scratches, savage, at the killer's neck. Jackie scrambles to his feet. The Tengu delivers a brutal slap; Megan's head snaps to the side. For a mad second the struggling couple freeze, she with her hand to her face, bloodied mouth open below wounded eyes, the killer with a fistful of Megan's hair in his left hand.

Jackie takes a step forward – *Ten yards to the bastard.*

The Tengu drops its right hand. The hellish face bores into the red-raw eyes of its victim. Its hand slips inside the black coat and emerges with a second, small, gleaming blade. A fighting knife, the killing edge not much longer than a man's palm. Megan stares at the killer as though uncomprehending.

Jackie feels a cold spike in his chest.

I'll never reach them before that fucker takes the knife to her throat.

Still yards away, desperate, he hurls the can of spray he grabbed next to Ian. It sails over and past the Tengu and disappears in the steam.

Megan's mind is sharp and racing, yet disconnected. It has sought safety somewhere deep inside.

Megan Sparrow of Churchdown, Gloucestershire, daughter of Ian Sparrow and Paula Cunningham, star pupil at Pate's school, Gold badge holder in swimming proficiency at the council pool, can't believe – won't believe – this is happening to her. The blood-red, wrathful demon face in this hot, steaming crater is dreamlike, disconnected from this world.

And yet.

Yuji.

She heard Jackie Shaw call out the name, Yuji.

Her Yuji?

Something clouts her hard across the face. The violence shocks her, its power frightening. She tastes a thick, viscous copper in her mouth and has a vague conception of biting her tongue. She imagines herself drowning in blood, her nose clogged, ears flooded. What shame. A gold badge swimmer, going down so easy.

No!

She will strike for the surface. Power upwards.

She glides through the blood, light growing above as she nears salvation. A truth above the calm waters, realisation growing with each stroke.

Her mind breaks the surface.

#

She throws her entire frame behind the punch, one foot flying backward like a baseball pitcher as her fist connects with the Tengu's leering face. Jackie hears a snapping sound and the mask splits to reveal the fine, boyish features of Yuji Miyamoto. Megan takes a step back, her hand covering her mouth like she's about to be sick.

Jackie takes a step forward. Yuji's twitching knife arm stops him. He has the mad thought that he's intruding.

Megan takes her hand from her mouth.

She says, 'Yuji.'

The young man looks at her, impassive. She balls her hand in a fist and punches him a second time, a clumsy effort, knuckles cracking off his ear. She pounds at him, stabs at him with her hands as though she's gripping a knife. As though she's the killer. She makes small, tight sounds with each slap and punch, her cheeks crimson.

Yuji blinks. His eyes widen.

He takes it for a few more seconds, rocking back on his heels with each blow. Then his features set in another mask – this time of skin and bone. Colour drains, his face a papery grey like a chain smoker, and he grabs Megan's right wrist. His nails dig in, like a child in a tantrum trying to hurt a grown-up. Megan's brows knit, pain and fear battling her rage for supremacy. She tries to cover her face. Yuji Miyamoto raises his small knife to her throat as Jackie scrambles across the scree, arms outsretched.

A bang like a firecracker.

Yuji ducks as the can of pepper spray explodes in the heat behind him. He releases Megan's hand, releases the knife and drops to his knees, clutching at the back of his neck. He tears at his cheeks, the spray scorching his skin. Megan screams with her head tucked under her arm. Jackie, out of range of the blast, stops dead as though any movement might upset the delicate balance of the scene.

Megan's face emerges from the crook of her arm, eyes streaming, face now scarlet but focused, set in anger. She balls her fists and hammers at Yuji's skull with wild haymaker blows.

She screams, 'Bastard!'

She bends to the ground and Jackie sees her face has been spared, although her arm must be on fire. He thinks she will go to her knees like Yuji – but she lifts a rock, her shoulders straining with the weight, and stands over the young man, framed by the rising clouds of steam a few feet away.

Jackie recognises something in her eyes, something he's seen in the mirror on his worst nights. He runs, skin prickling as the heat envelopes him, billowing from the steam and radiating from the earth below his boots. He smells the hot pepper spray. Everything slows as though he is battling through water.

Megan shrieks again, 'Bastard!'

Jackie calls to her but she's too far gone. Her own scream drowns his shout.

'Bastard!'

He sees Yuji, head bent as though in prayer, sees the wild fury in Megan's eyes. Imagines her bringing the rock down on the delicate skull, the crack of bone, blunt force impact on the young man's brain. The jolt as Yuji Miyamoto ends: an empty shell breathing and shitting for however long his heart goes on, or dead. Megan's future of hollow mornings and barren nights, alone in her guilt. Yet never truly alone, the soul she's stolen forever there, tied to her until death brings her own, tortured release.

'Bastard!'

Jackie barrels into the girl, taking her on the arm. The rock hits the ground with a dull thud. Megan, arms out as though grabbing for a ledge, lands hard on the scree, her bloody mouth crooked with pain then fury. Her hard eyes flare. She spits a gob of crimson and hisses at Jackie.

'Bastard!'

Yuji, on his knees, stares at Jackie with raw eyes. He babbles in Japanese.

Jackie says, 'You're done. Stand up.'

Yuji struggles to his full height, his delicate mouth tight. His face is Tengu-red, the spray eating into his skin. His eyes and nose stream. Looking at him, naked without his mask, it is difficult to believe the willowy young man could have slaughtered two policemen with nothing more than a knife and his own bare hands.

The strength of a madman, thinks Jackie.

Yuji tilts his head back and, as though in answer, speaks in English.

'You are in the presence of a god.'

'If you're a god,' says Jackie, 'you're in the wrong place today.'

Yuji Miyamoto offers a small bow and runs into the scalding steam. His slight frame is consumed by the white-grey vapour, his jagged, agonised shriek swallowed by the cry of his former lover as Megan Sparrow opens her lungs. Jackie stands transfixed, staring into the steam as though the young man will reappear and step out again untouched. The screams reach a crescendo with a flat crack as a second can of bear spray in Yuji's pocket explodes somewhere farther off in the scalding heat. Jackie and Megan flinch but no spray spatters them.

Jackie turns to Megan and offers a hand. She wipes at her eyes, pulls matted hair from her face and stares at him. Then she scrabbles to her feet, clutching her arm, and runs for the slope leading to her father.

Jackie wanders to edge of the crater bed. He places a hand on the dirt to steady himself and sits down.

He waits. He waits for his heart to slow. He waits for someone to join him. Ian Sparrow, even Inaba. He waits for the police. His body soaks in the heat of the crater. He feels his cheek burn, his leg and sides throb. His jeans are wet, the sword wound from the love hotel opened. His mind drifts to Fujiko Maki, her beauty, her body on his. Then Ishikawa, the Tengu imposter, slicing her back. Another damaged woman in his past. New unwanted memories for the collection.

As Jackie Shaw waits, he thinks.

We're all alone in the end.

Chapter 43

Jackie lies back and gazes at the slate sky above. He remembers lying on a grass bank in Castlereagh, East Belfast under a pastel sky, life rolling by at a mellow pace. He had been a kid and it was the first time he had a real drink, a can of lager smuggled from his friend's house. He and his mate, Garty, both spewed at first, then hit on the idea of holding their noses while they chugged the beer. Time had slowed that afternoon, a couple of hours stretched into a full day, before they'd eaten a couple of bags of Tayto cheese and onion, believing that would mask the booze smell.

Garty died three years later. Hit by a getaway car at Bridge End on his way home from school after a couple of gunmen had shot a van driver on Ann Street.

#

He listens to the soft hiss of the breeze as it passes overhead, scouting the upper rim of the crater. The muzzle-flash burn on his face is throbbing in time with his heart, slow and steady. He thinks of the bandaged yakuza striding from the cabin, gun in hand, eyes mad with anger or grief or both. Jackie had to put him down, had no choice. It was ingrained. Survival. If Jackie survived, his friends had a shot of making it, too. And they had. Ian and Megan Sparrow, battered but in one piece. Megan would never forget today, but at least she didn't have Yuji's blood on her hands, and she is strong like her father. What was it Jackie's ma always said? Time's a great healer.

He is too tired to move and finally, thank God, to think. Despite the pain, the bad dreams to come, the scalded body lying somewhere in the plume of steam in the centre of the crater, Jackie Shaw feels a measure of peace.

Time passes.

Something small and insistent taps the crown of his head, bothering him awake. He hadn't realised he was asleep.

He digs his elbows into the dirt at his back and struggles to a sitting position. He cranes his neck and sees the scree tumble down the side of the crater, Ian Sparrow struggling down the slope.

Jackie hears the warm West Country accent.

'Up, you lazy git. The cavalry's arrived. Time to go.'

His friend.

British Embassy,
Tokyo,
Japan

英国大使館
東京
日本

Jackie takes a sip of the cheap, tepid coffee.

The room is like dozens he has sat in through the years, plain and tired with pock-marked walls and a cynical paint-job. He sits behind a school-desk-like table.

UK soil in the heart of Tokyo. The British Embassy, a grand façade built in 1929 after the Great Kanto earthquake had put paid to its predecessor, all pilasters and crests and cornices topped by a wide pediment. Dominion of the Ambassador, Deputy Head of Mission, of the great and the good. The venue for receptions, dinners, New Year parties and balls. But Jackie sits in a different structure set in the Embassy grounds. A seedy complex of portacabins, preserve of the plebs: the low-ranking civil servants who stamp and process and advise and despair, and the British and Japanese citizens who come calling for help, or a visa, or in demand of answers.

He hasn't seen Ian or Megan since their flight from Sapporo touched down at Haneda airport. Megan had greeted him with sullen silence as Ian led Jackie to the police and the dead and injured yakuza in front of the cabin. He'd seen her on a couple of occasions since, her appalled stare maturing to one of distrust, then caution, then an acceptance of sorts. She had almost offered a smile as they disembarked at Haneda. They had been received by a welcoming committee of Japanese cops and two officious-looking Caucasian men in ill-fitting suits who channelled the father and daughter through a doorway in the terminal. Ian stretched out an arm, called to his friend, and was gone.

Jackie swallows the last of his coffee, the grit catching his throat on the way down. He wonders what happened to the surviving yakuza, Goro Inaba. Was he being interrogated in some hospital room? Would he find the new life he craved? Or end up with a shank in his back in a Hokkaido prison?

Did Fujiko Maki know about her brother's death? Did she blame Jackie? He had been callous with Reizo at the last. Perhaps he had owed the man more than that. Himura could have killed him for what he'd done with Fujiko.

Jackie didn't love easy. He had had a passionate affair with a woman in Belfast many years ago. The wrong woman. That woman was strong, and very powerful now. But alone.

Here, decades later on the other side of the world, Jackie had been with the wrong woman again. And he has left Fujiko Maki alone.

The door opens.

A heavy-set man with a wiry brush of mousey brown hair and a grey, office-bound pallor eases into the room. He has a narrow nose and a tight mouth with thin lips; they purse as he hefts a stack of papers and files onto the tabletop. He nods, sits opposite Jackie, and gazes across the table. The small, deep-set eyes of the man whisper of supercilious pretension. Seemingly satisfied with what he sees, he smooths his grey tie, draped over a burgeoning beer gut.

'A pleasure, Mr. Shaw. My name is Donald McPherson. I hope you've been made comfortable.'

A Scot. Perhaps chosen to parlay in the vague hope that his Celtic blood will inspire a sense of kinship in Jackie – Gaelic brothers, united against the English with a wink and a dram. But the flat vowels and hammered down rhoticity speaks of privilege.

McPherson clears his throat and adopts a stern frown, steepling his fingers.

'Yes,' he says, agreeing with no one, 'you've been through the mill, and no mistake. Two British subjects abducted and you missing, roaming the forests, only to be found with a couple of dead gangsters and a young man, a Yu-ji Mi-ya-mo-to, scalded to death on the slopes of a volcano.' He butchers the Japanese name. 'Well, you're safe now.'

'Am I?' says Jackie.

A pause.

The man clears his throat.

'Of course. We are on British territory.'

Silence.

McPherson's frown is followed by a disappointed, almost

wounded shake of the head. The small, mean stones of his eyes sink deeper into a maze of wrinkles. He might be in his fifties but looks older, the threaded veins of a drinker mapping the countours of his nose.

Jackie says, 'I want to go home.'

'No doubt. See your sister,' – he opens a file – 'Sarah. Brother-in-law, Thomas. Their kids, Daniel and Margaret. You don't have children, do you? Never married?'

'Close a couple of times. Hit the bar once.' Jackie leans forward, reaches across the table and closes the file.

McPherson swallows.

Jackie says, 'I want to go home.'

'Mr. Shaw – '

'I want to go home. If you don't sort it, a friend will release some information regarding a Stuart William Hartley to the media. A Scotsman, like you. Very like you. He employed me to carry out some work for the Security Service. On the side. Hartley knows what I've got on him and he will not, under any circumstances, allow that information to come to light. So whatever smokescreen you're chancing your arm with here, whatever bother you're having with the Japanese authorities, call Hartley in London at Thames House. He'll sort it faster than you can suck your line manager's dick.'

McPherson's face flushes. He looks like he could do with a drink.

'Mr. Hartley is no longer with us,' he says.

'A great loss. Call whichever spook got his desk with the view over Lambeth Bridge and have Five do what they do best: go running to Six for help and let the big boys sort this out with the Yanks. No doubt the Empire doesn't have the necessary clout in this corner of the world to handle things on its own.'

McPherson purses his lips again.

'Mr. Shaw, you have been through a great deal. I understand that. And I want you to know, I am not your enemy here, despite whatever assumptions you may have made. But the people you refer to – '

'MI5.'

'The people you refer to ...' McPherson peers out from furrowed brows. 'Let me be clear, Mr. Shaw. Stuart William Hartley resigned from the Security Service six months ago. It wouldn't be uncharitable to say he was encouraged to leave. Wherever he is, and whatever he is doing now, is of no relevance. He is no longer an officer and, under the Official Secrets Act, his record is sealed. Any leverage you may have had on the agency for which he worked is gone. A deplorable contravention of agency policies and practices, even if investigated fully in a post-mortem enquiry, his record expunged and rank stripped, is utterly meaningless.'

McPherson smooths his tie again, his fingers fluttering over the weave. 'You are embroiled in a serious criminal conspiracy involving kidnapping, murder and organised crime. No one in this embassy is implying for a moment that you are the aggressor or anything less than a victim. But the Japanese police and justice system is a strange beast and less than balanced in their treatment of non-Japanese. There are people in London who could exploit this, make things difficult for you. I am not saying you are in danger of imprisonment.' He breathes deep.

'I am not saying you aren't.'

His eyebrows crawl higher on his weathered forehead. Jackie notices McPherson's skin is flaking – almost crumbling – from his face.

The man says, 'It is your misfortune – or not – that you have come to the attention of these people. I am aware of incidents in Belfast and London over the last few years, very violent incidents where you – for want of a better expression – thrived. I know your record in the army and RUC, and Royal Hong Kong Police Force. It appears you have talents that are greatly appreciated by certain parties in the agency of which we speak. Were you to consider lending those talents to the relevant departments in the future, should they be required, I would imagine it would facilitate your expedient repatriation to the United Kingdom.'

Jackie smiles.

McPherson flinches.

'You aren't one of *them*,' says Jackie. 'They are here, in this embassy, in some form or another. But they wouldn't be the ones to step into the cage with the whip and the chair, because they know what I'd fucking do to them.'

He sees what little colour is left drain from the pulpous face. McPherson's fingers grip the edge of the desk. His mouth is open, nostrils flared.

Jackie recalls faces from his past, all gone: among them, Irish paramilitaries, terrorists, Albanian gangters, Chinese Triads, Japanese yakuza. A mental litany of violence. Tired of hurting he leans back in his chair, studies a crack in the ceiling, empties his mind and finds the abyss staring back. He gets acquainted.

McPherson breathes in a soft whistle.

Jackie covers his face with his hands. He's done bad things. People have died. Have others lived? Has he spared innocents by wading through shit and blood?

He must have.

Surely.

People died for all the right reasons. Bad people, by any reckoning. Killing was hard but you developed callouses to live with it. And something out there in the abyss is whispering a truth – out in the forest near Toya, on the slopes of Usu, even in the bathhouse with Himura and his men, he was truly *alive*.

God, I'm tired. Give my head peace.

He drags his fingers down his face and lays them on the table, then offers the civil servant a thin smile.

'I want to see my friend, Ian Sparrow. And I'll have a decent cup of tea while you're at it. When you bring Ian in here, go back and tell whoever sent you that you've made your proposal.'

McPherson nods and stands. Jackie pushes his chair back from the table and hikes his right ankle up on his left knee.

'Tell them I want to go home,' he says.

God help him, he was never more alive than in that fucking forest with the yakuza after him.

Something gives in his frown and his shoulders relax.

'Now, away and wet the tea,' says Jackie, 'and tell them, when I go to Belfast and see my family, then, and only then, I'll think about their proposition.'

He nods at the door and says, 'Tell them. Tell them I want to go home.'

Acknowledgements

Despite having lived in Japan for over thirteen years, *Dry River* was a challenging book to write and I received a great deal of help and guidance from Chris Zuk. He provided invaluable insight and has always been, and continues to be, a very real and trusted friend in Sapporo. My thanks also go to Micci, who offered fantastic background atmosphere and some top notch whiskey. As always, I am extremely grateful to my editor, Robert Dinsdale, who never fails to polish my work, and to Humfrey Hunter at Silvertail Books. I only hope *Dry River* repays his continued encouragement and undying faith in my work. Finally, of course, while *Dry River*, like any crime thriller, highlights much of the worst in a society, I am forever thankful to my wife and daughter, Tomoe and Hana, who embody the very best of Japan and continue to inspire and support me.

Author's note

For those who are interested, The Invisible Man Club was a real venue in the Susukino area of Sapporo. The volcano damage on the slopes of Mount Usu at Lake Toya is also authentic.

Lightning Source UK Ltd.
Milton Keynes UK
UKHW040705120619
344229UK00001B/91/P